Not Your Papi's Utopia:
Latinx Visions of Radical Hope

Not Your Papi's Utopia:
Latinx Visions of Radical Hope

Editors: Matthew David Goodwin, Alex Hernandez, Sara Rivera

Mouthfeel Press
2024

Not Your Papi's Utopia: Latinx Visions of Radical Hope

Mouthfeel Press is a bilingual press that publishes fiction, nonfiction, and poetry. Our books are available through online booksellers, independent bookstores, our website, and at author events. For more information on obtaining copies or to view our full catalog, please contact us: info. mouthfeelbooks@gmail.com or visit www.mouthfeelbooks.com.

Cover Art "Volando Como Cuauhtémoc" by Luis Valderas.
Cover Design: Cloud Cardona
Interior Design: Shady Peak Studios

ISBN 978-1-957840-35-2

Library of Congress Control Number
2 0 2 4 9 4 7 6 3 5

Published in the United States, 2024

$22

Table of Contents

Introduction

Matthew David Goodwin, Alex Hernandez, Sara Rivera

Not Your Papi's Utopia: Latinx Visions of Radical Hope is the final installment of our Latinx speculative fiction trilogy. The first two anthologies, *Latinx Rising* and *Speculative Fiction for Dreamers*, were designed to demonstrate the history and vibrancy of the Latinx speculative. This third anthology is a response to our current moment and is meant to summon the innovative utopian visions and the radical hope needed to directly face our environmental and social problems. The purpose of the anthology is to activate the imagination, to develop neural pathways to a better future, and to engage with the Zapatista concept of "a world where many worlds fit." The challenges we face are global, and we must meet the challenges as they are, and so the scope of this anthology is also larger than the previous two in that we have included work from outside the U.S. In this way, *Not Your Papi's Utopia* expresses some hope that the bonds connecting Latin America, the Caribbean, and U.S. Latinx communities can be strengthened.

Dystopian fiction has been and remains an important part of the global speculative imagination. Classic and critical dystopian stories act as cautionary tales, mapping our current circumstances into the future, imagining the horrors that might come to pass if we keep on a particular course. These stories locate obliteration, reconfiguration, or hope in their endings. But a growing dystopian fatigue has resulted in gradual shifts away from the tradition. Globally, we have lived and are living many of the catastrophes envisioned by dystopian fiction. Environmental collapse is here, the rise of conservative extremism and xenophobia is here, and we are still losing lives daily to the Covid-19 pandemic. It's all happening now, and we need to deal with these realities in the present. To wrestle with the history of dystopian literature in the West is also to wrestle with the fact that, in many of these stories, the most horrible outcome imaginable is simply a world in which white people face the violence, persecution, and oppression BIPOC communities have faced throughout history.

This anthology is part of a growing desire to move the needle in the other direction, to reclaim utopia in new and radical ways. The blueprint of utopia was, from its beginnings, a tool of genocide. Thomas More's *Utopia*, published in 1516, depicts a sort of European haven in the Americas. In this "perfect" and imaginary place, the industrious inhabitants are justified in killing their Indigenous neighbors who they believe are not using their land efficiently. Ever since, the dreams and philosophies of utopia have justified great violence. Utopia is manifest destiny and the stolen lands of the American Southwest. Utopia is the American Dream and its system of economic and cultural supremacy founded in colonization and racist violence. And so, we must ask: is there a way to navigate through these two horns of dystopia and utopia? Can utopian thinking be salvaged? Can we exercise the utopian imagination and find works that are not so much a template for a society, but that energetically explore the potential of a queer Latinx futurity that resists the formation of simply one more institution? When we put together the call for this anthology, we aimed to take on these questions. We looked for alternate forms of utopian thinking—that is, not visions of a perfect society, but of a society trying to do better, to be more in harmony with the environment, and to build more equitable political systems. The twenty-three stories and six poems in the book surprised us with their nuance, their playfulness, their complexity, their dynamic and intimate world-building. They pushed us to continuously expand our vision of the utopian spirit. The result is that the book contains stories and poems about utopian societies, ambiguous utopias, alternate utopias, bits of utopia, utopian impulses, and activist energies.

The book is organized into three categories: the Utopian Question, the Utopian Odyssey, and the Utopian Enclave. At the heart of the Latinx utopian imagination is our Utopian Question: if we are not making a new template for the perfect society, then where can utopia be found? This section of the book shows some of the answers to this question as well as exploring some of the limitations of utopia, how it can be used as a colonial tool, and how fragile it is. In Olga García Echeverría's story "The Joys of Becoming an Axolotl" it is the return to home, to Mexico, that contains the seed of utopia, as the caged axolotl says to Julio: "I promise you that my freedom will also be yours." In Yoss's story "Meteorites and Dinosaurs," humanity has attained what many would consider a utopia, but only by staring down the barrel of an alien gun, as it were. Is a forced utopia a utopia at all? There are many places in the Americas, in particular Puerto Rico, which have already been imagined by colonizers as a fantasy utopia ripe for exploitation, and most recently, an oasis for advocates of crypto currency. As depicted in Wenmimareba Klobah Collins's story "Unexplained Phenomena," the utopian element in Puerto Rico can therefore best be found in unexpected spaces. Many of the works in this book demonstrate that, although it may not feel like it, we actually have a variety of avenues which can put us in the right direction of utopia: activism, joy, laughter, and deep connection with nature. In these spaces we can make our way closer to a radical, contemporary vision of the future—to "not your papi's" utopia.

The second section of the book, the Utopian Odyssey, faces the challenge of depicting utopias in space. As Octavia Butler says in her 1991 interview with Randall Kenan:

> "In earlier science fiction there tended to be a lot of conquest: you land on another planet and you set up a colony and the natives have their quarters some place and they come work for you. There was a lot of that, and it was, you know, let's do Europe and Africa and South America all over again."

The stories in *Not Your Papi's Utopia* do their best to not repeat that mistake. They take the classic science fiction tropes of space exploration and colonization and examine it with the lens of the immigrant experience: leaving behind the dystopian circumstances back home to seek, at great cost, a utopia among the stars. The authors of these stories do not purport to achieve vast intergalactic utopias à la *Star Trek*'s Federation, rather they express the fact that striving for a utopia is an on-going endeavor—and perhaps a sort of weary, hard-fought personal utopia can be attained at the end of that arduous adventure. The near-future story "Diocese Moon" by Roxane Llanque is such a tale where the optimistic Dr. Damaris Baptist, the first bishop of a moon base, works daily to enrich the spiritual lives of the colonists and in the process finds a slice of contentment for herself. Similarly, in Daniel Jose Ruiz' story "Falcon and the Carucha" the inhabitants of a distant colony are delighted to rediscover aspects of their Chicano past as they carve out a life on a harsh, alien world. And even when a kind of interstellar utopia is realized, as in Stephanie Nina Pitsirilos' story "The Event Don Juan of Mycelia," it is shown how easily and surreptitiously utopia can be taken away. The only way to regain it is to exercise the patience of time dilation. These are stories of space colonization written by people who are themselves the products of long, complex histories of colonization, and that perspective infuses their work with care and wisdom.

In her article "Utopiyin, Utopiyang," Ursula Le Guin said:

> "Both utopia and dystopia are often an enclave of maximum control surrounded by a wilderness…Good citizens of utopia consider the wilderness dangerous, hostile, unlivable; to an adventurous or rebellious dystopian it represents change and freedom. In this I see examples of the intermutability of the yang and yin: the dark mysterious wilderness surrounding a bright, safe place, the Bad Places—which then become the Good Place, the bright, open future surrounding a dark, closed prison . . . Or vice versa."

In the Utopian Enclave section of the anthology, we consider stories that play with the dichotomy of safety and peril, stories that locate a utopian energy within a darker, more complicated world, or that contend with fractious grief within a better world. In "Blessed" by Joy Castro, women reclaim their autonomy and create support systems when their rights have been stripped by a future patriarchy. In "Returning" by Kristian Macaron, a character living in a utopian space-future travels into the past of their family, showing how longing for what is gone can actually help us create a different world. Ruth Joffre's "Pachacuti" weaves a future in which a queer couple, wearied by long lives and a capitalistic industry built around voyeurism of the past, reclaim ancient concepts of time to inject beauty and wonder into their lives. The powerhouse novel excerpt "La Grobinita" by Rolando André López finds dynamic, blissful tension in its blend of strangeness and familiarity, fantasy and reality, desire and disillusion, the paralysis of grief versus possibilities of emergence. There is hope, survival, and strength to be found in the bounds of these utopian enclaves, the wildernesses within and without.

We are not alone in exploring the Latinx utopian impulse. We owe a great deal to the vast lineage of writers, activists, performance artists, visual artists and creators who have been dreaming of radical and punk futurisms for decades. The utopian impulse can be found in the work of Gloria Anzaldúa whose space aliens exhibit a utopian sensibility, and in

Cherrie Moraga's play *The Hungry Woman* which replaces the nation-state with a queer Aztlán. Even further back is the avant-garde street art of the performance group ASCO who created film stills from Chicano films that should have existed. In the past twenty years, Latinx and Caribbean science fiction has blossomed, bringing along with it the utopian hopes of Latin America and U.S. Latinx communities. Sabrina Vourvoulias' novel *Ink*, for example, centers on a pan-ethnic and pan-Latinx group of activists who are fighting new draconian immigration laws. More recently, scholar Taryne Jade Taylor has teased out the utopian impulse in songs by Cypress Hill, Pitbull, Calle 13, and Los Rakas, which envision various forms of pan-Latinx solidarity. We are grateful to these artists and to everyone who is working to form structures of hope rather than one more nation, one more corporation. We are grateful to the work of Afro, Indigenous, trans, and queer futurists within and outside of the Latinx community, to the dreams of our ancestors and to the dreams of our children, and to those who not only dream these futures, but who actively work to create them.

The editors would like to dedicate this book to all our children:

Camilo, Beatrice, Sophie, Enora, Violet

SECTION 1: THE UTOPIAN QUESTION

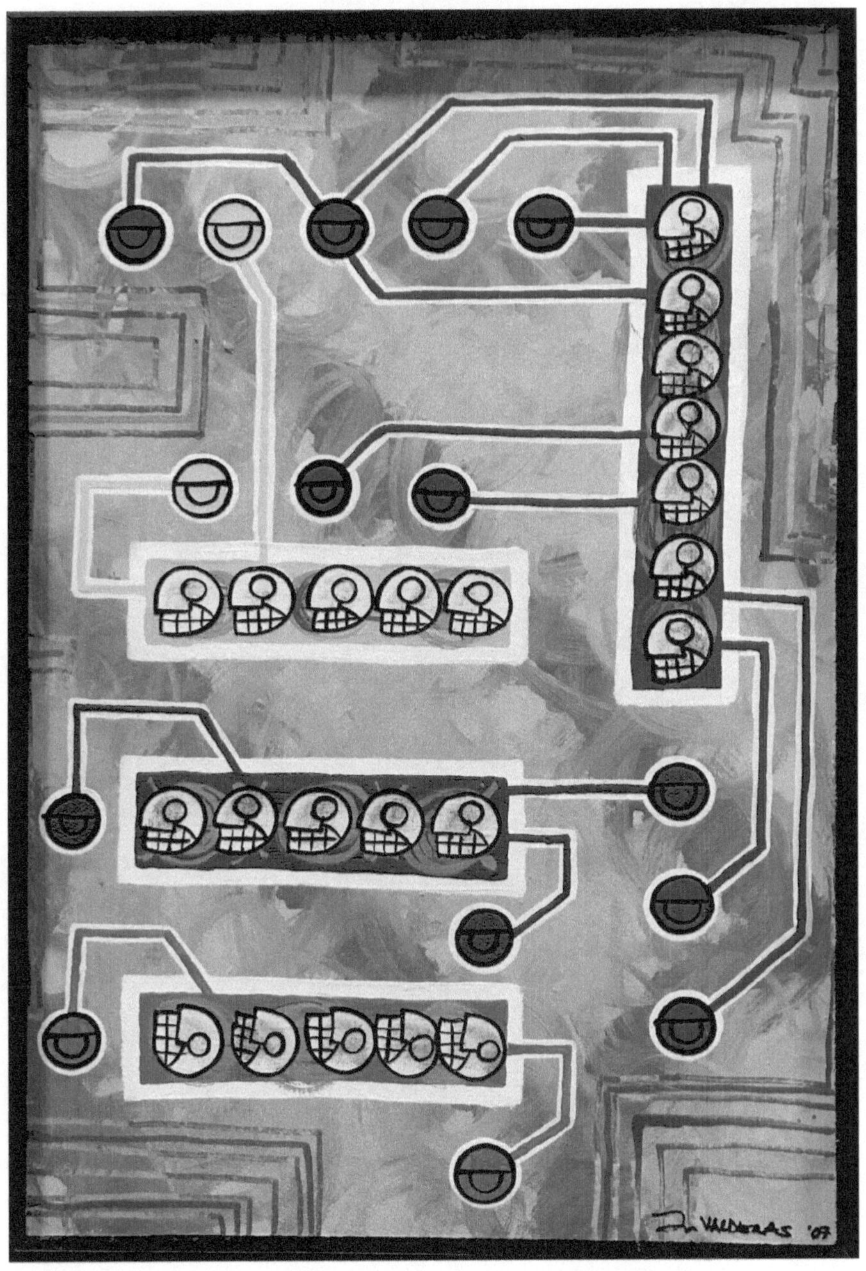

Luis Valderas: "Tranz-Digital Board, Lords of Intzalan" (4 of 35)

Somewhere in Pico Rivera Heaven

Lesley Téllez

The women in the garage lived by their ganas and antojos. Sometimes they manifested the item that they desired, small things that were easy to conjure up: an early episode of Law & Order, a vinyl copy of "Los Laureles," a cold Mr. Pibb in a bottle. But it was more fun when the men offered things and the women said "No."

No, I don't want plain toast. Bring me Hawaiian bread.

No, I don't feel like a back rub today. Maybe tomorrow.

Ay you don't have frozen grapes? Who are you? No, quítame estas.

Each "No" felt like whipped cream on their tongues—like that first lick of a sundae. And the thing was, no didn't just have to be "No." It could be the flippant cluck of someone's tongue, a hiss, an eye roll, a "nah," "fuck no," or just a grunt. The men would return as many times as necessary, until the women were satisfied.

Tere didn't know about no, at first. She'd barely woken up here, after three weeks in a hospice bed. She'd lived here before, it seemed like—the snug peach stucco house felt familiar. She didn't know why, and didn't care.

A school bus stopped every day outside her living room window. Children emptied out and sprinted toward the Lucky's Supermarket, where they raced and kicked soccer balls through the parking lot. Some went to Jerome's coffee shop and drowned their pancakes in syrup, while Tere watched curiously over the laminated page of her menu. Mother's rule—written in the house manual, which Tere found in her nightstand—said that children could eat anything, and as much as they wanted. They could eat butter directly out of the little metal cup served with the pancakes. Or order five Tommy's burgers, or french fries and nothing else.

Tere didn't have any cravings, except finding Memo. She'd spent her initial days combing through the faces of the children, surprised by her stamina and eyesight. She could decode the details of a child's face from thirty feet away. Many of the kids had Memo's round, doughy features, his hard eyes, his narrow swath of forehead. They had his exact bread-crust-brown shade of skin. Several wore their shorts low like he did, with a bubble of Hanes boxers puffing above their belt loops. It was maddening how much they looked like him—almost like they'd been sent to screw with her head.

One toddler's fat, white-sandaled feet reminded her of Olivia. Her daughter had hated those white sandals, had cried and used her chubby fingers to try and pry them off, but Tere had insisted. Olivia looked so cute with her row of stubby toes above the top leather strap. So pretty and feminine.

Tere thought for several minutes and saw nothing beyond the smoothness of those toes, the shell of pink nail. She couldn't recall Olivia's face, or any of the usual guilt for not being home, or punishing her too hard, or Tere's mother's chiding voice. There was simply nothing—only Tere's muscle and bone. The detachment from her only daughter swirled through her like the breezes in the trees.

She hadn't remembered so many trees when she lived here as a kid. Their roots disrupted the sidewalks and branches canopied the streets. Some trees caressed her face when she walked under a low branch, and when that happened she did it over and over, spending hours on the same patch of sidewalk, thrilling at the tickle along her jaw. She hadn't remembered the feeling of her own face, that even she had a face.

***

Tere assumed that Mother would give her another child, if she couldn't find Memo. But after a very long day, or week, she wasn't sure which, it became clear that this wasn't her duty. The men washed and dressed and fussed over the kids. When a child fell or hurt themselves, the men held them and whispered a song in their ears. The kids roamed Pico Rivera flush with their own agency, their clothing useless at decoding their gender, their shoes mismatched, their hair long and tangled. No children ventured into Tere's house, which was fine with her. She preferred to watch instead of being reminded of her own motherly shortcomings. When there was nothing else to do, she observed the men going about their daily tasks: pinning up laundry, sweeping, soaking the beans.

Eventually Tere began spending more time in the detached garage, which is where all the women congregated. The women wore loose fabrics and slippers, and they blasted Anita Baker and Lola Beltrán and other full-voiced, throaty singers whom Tere didn't know, but guessed the words to. They played conquián around a large glass-topped desk, and they ate all the time, either fresh fruits and vegetables that Fanny peeled—she was always peeling, with her feet up on an ottoman—or they nibbled peanuts from a filmy plastic bag and tossed their shells on the floor. No one touched the old yellow exercise bike at the garage's edge. It belonged to Estefanía's husband. Mary said he wanted to stay fit so she wouldn't stray. "Too bad that's already happened!" Mary hooted, and they all laughed.

Some nights they danced with each other, soft hands on shoulders or in the curve of someone's back. Sometimes they kissed, or two or three women left the garage for somewhere else, holding hands. Tere had not kissed a woman before and the thought made her jittery. She hung back and doodled on the walls, the hearts and flowers and butterflies she'd drawn as a child, and the different leaves on the trees. She was relieved that no one had demanded to know what she was doing there, or asked who her husband was.

She'd never hung out with a large group of women like this. Her mother had always told her that she couldn't trust a woman, that they'd always find a way to double-cross her. *You can only trust your mother.* Tere was most comfortable in the back, near the windows. She drew and built mini pyramids out of crudité. She began to sing along with the songs, low at first, then louder. Finally, one day, she found the chair with her name on it. The wooden chair, painted high-gloss white, had been tucked against an old victrola. Her name curled across the seat in yellow script: *Teresa Marie Acuña.*

"I have slippers for Señora Tere!" A voice boomed through the garage.

Tere rushed to the garage's edge. All the women had slippers that fit their personalities. Mary's were airbrushed and Kathy's were a creamy faux fur studded with pearls. Mother chose each design and Kathy's husband, the encargado of the pantunflas, delivered them. He held out Tere's slippers, a hard plastic pair covered in red glitter. Tere stared at them.

At home she'd worn sensible gray slip-ons that she purchased on sale from Target. These slippers llamaron mucho la atención, like something Kim would wear. But maybe the other women liked the red slippers? Maybe Mother had an overstock. Tere shouldn't be greedy.

She slipped them on her feet and looked down. Her feet resembled a clown's.

The men weren't allowed to ask questions, so Kathy spoke up.

"You like 'em?"

"Yeah! Yes." Tere hoped she sounded bright and upbeat.

Kathy studied her face for a minute. "The fuck you do!"

All the women laughed. Tere felt giddy and laughed too.

"Okay. I kind of fucking hate them."

"Well, tell him, girl."

Tere turned to Kathy's husband. "I don't like these. Bring me another pair!"

Kathy's husband nodded and hurried away. Tere strode to her chair. She cracked open a beer and let the bubbles dance in her throat. Kathy settled into her own chair at Tere's side.

"Is this okay?" She picked up Tere's hand. Tere felt a jolt, but she didn't pull away. Kathy's hand was very soft, as soft as the freshly made pita that one of the men brought sometimes.

Tere nodded. "Yes."

"I'm proud of you," Kathy said, tracing Tere's skin lightly with her fingertips. No one had said those words to Tere in her life.

****

Mother told them they'd all been trees once. Tere believed her immediately, then backtracked. They couldn't have been trees—that was ridiculous. If you were a tree, how could you become a person? Why would you want to be a person? She thought of the twin trees in the field behind their apartment complex, where they had moved in fourth grade, and how often her and Memo had climbed them, hiding their bodies in the shaggy leaves and pink flowers. She had nightmares that he fell and his head lolled off into the field, and it was her fault. She tried to watch him carefully, but mostly she just wanted to be alone, enveloped in leaves and branches.

Tere pushed away her mother's voice—*Ay, don't tell Tere that, she believes everything!*—as she tried to picture herself as a tree. She imagined a bent and twisty one with angled branches that protruded toward the ground, and leaves that caressed other people's faces. Her leaves would be long and oval-shaped, with a patina that reflected the sun.

Maybe she really had been a tree. And Memo too—he could've been a sweet gum like the ones they passed on the way home from school. The sweet gums littered pointy leaves and spiky seed pods on the sidewalk.

One day while the men were busy making egg salad sandwiches, Tere decided to ask Mary about it. She had not conversed with anyone besides Kathy and this seemed like a decent opener. Mary had the best chair, and her cravings were intimidatingly detailed. ("Y pónme esos Kettle Chips, the jalapeño ones," Mary had ordered her husband as he stood on the asphalt. "Not the Lays.")

Mary dunked a carrot in a thick swirl of bleu cheese dressing and sighed at Tere, who sat across from her. "Ok, ya mujer, dime."

"Do we get to—see people again? Like, in this place?"

Mary shrugged, her body ensconced in a fluffy maroon robe. A man painted her toes with a second coat of shocking pink. "I don't know. Who is it you want to see?"

"I had a brother. We…lost touch." *He died and I can't find him.* She didn't say it. The words felt warm and liquidy, like the pool of yellow dish soap that Martín used to scrub the pans.

"Mmmm." Mary clucked sympathetically. A swirl of classical music began playing from a radio near her elbow. "I get it, hon." She squeezed Tere's hand.

"So…" Tere didn't want to push, but she had to know. "Do we? Is there something I need to do?"

Mary peered at her toes, now shiny with topcoat. She waved the man away. "You just have to ask, mija." Mary smiled and Tere's heart opened. "That's how we do it here."

A minute later, or maybe a long time later, the garage's blue rotary phone rang. It sat on a little telephone desk, just like the one from her Nana's living room — a rectangular piece of oak big enough for only a phone and a notepad. The notepad next to the phone said, "WHILE YOU WERE GONE," which all the women thought was hilarious.

"She wants to talk to you." Fanny took a break from peeling an apple to pass Tere the phone. Mother had never called Tere before.

"To see him, you gotta walk through the water." Mother sounded like different people on different days. Today she sounded like Flo from Alice.

"What do you mean?" Tere pictured walking on top of the water, like Jesus. She hadn't seen anyone do that before. Not even Mary.

"Just, like—walk through, honey. Put your whole body into the water and then walk out the other side."

"But there is no other side. Can I breathe in there?"

Tere had often dunked her head in the river to cool off. It felt like regular water. Mary had explained that a thousand years ago, a woman had asked to live near water, so Mother placed a river behind the neighborhood where the train tracks used to be. The water ran over and down the glass trestle in great big sheets. The men collected it in buckets for dishwashing and showering.

"You'll see it—where it ends. I promise." Mother's voice switched to Tere's grandmother's voice. "Con cuidado, mija."

Mother hung up the phone.

"So you're gonna see Memo, huh?" Mary's skin looked warm and dewy. "Take some carrots." She pulled a stainless steel container from the pocket of her robe. "Matthew will get you a drink for the road." She snapped her fingers and a white surfer guy in a wetsuit appeared at the edge of the garage, dangling a backpack cooler full of icy chelas and room-temperature water. Tere accepted the backpack, and put Mary's carrots in the pocket of her jeans for later.

***

For a while Tere didn't go into the water. Knowing Memo was so close terrified her. What would she say?

Do you hate me?

Do you think about me?

She had borrowed Yvette's shoes for senior year homecoming and forgotten to return them, which was the only reason she stopped home before work that day, to get the shoes. Yvette needed them for her older sister's wedding. She'd been surprised to hear a rustle from Memo's bedroom—he'd told their mother he was going to a friend's house.

Tere had just put her purse down when Memo darted out of his room, yanking on the door as if he was going to shove it closed, then at the last second leaving it open a crack. His T-shirt skimmed his waistband as if he'd just thrown it on. His cheeks were flushed.

Tere half-smiled. Did he have a girl in there? Their mother worried about Memo never having a girlfriend.

"You're home," he said, his voice falsely cheerful.

"Yep." Tere enjoyed how he squirmed. She couldn't wait to tell her mother. "Just came back for Yvette's shoes. Everything okay?" Her eyes lingered on his bedroom door.

"Yeah," Memo said, nodding. "Everything's fine."

Tere made a show of going down the hallway to her room, but at the last second she pushed hard on his bedroom door. If he had a girl in there, the girl had to know there were rules, that this apartment wouldn't be disrespected.

It wasn't a girl. Andrew, Memo's friend, lay supine on the bed. He wasn't wearing a shirt.

Tere's stomach dropped. "Oh."

Memo made a strangled sound, and then coughed. His eyes looked like a small, sad animal's.

"So yeah, Ree, ummm…."

She hurried away from him, the betrayal already blooming in her gut. He was not this person. He was lying. Maybe other people were like this but not Memo. He had gone through a fucking cholo phase for god's sakes. He was not a person who did—things like this. They had an unspoken agreement, he and Tere. They would live in the same neighborhood and raise their kids and be in each other's lives forever. Their mother would never tolerate this. Tere would need to console her through it. Tere would be alone. Alone in her mother's suffocating box, alone in listening to her mother scream.

Tere could—

Maybe she could—

No. Tere wasn't strong like Memo. If she joined him, she wouldn't survive. Suffocating was at least slightly better than death.

***

In the garage, time floated lazily by. Tere put chili powder on her egg salad sandwiches, topped with a layer of Doritos. Just for the hell of it, because Mariana's husband was on the fryer, she added fried okra. She set up a lawn chair next to the clothesline, and read and picked at the St. Augustine grass.

One day she wasn't hungry. She tried on Mary's backpack cooler and looked at herself in the mirror. She liked her strong arms and calves, the steadiness in her eyes. Her legs tugged her toward the sidewalk and she let herself go. Deja vu carried her. She was only doing what she'd done before.

A baseball bat lay discarded in someone's front yard. Tere picked it up and used it as a walking stick. It made a pleasant *thwop* sound as it hit the pavement.

She wasn't sure how far she'd walked when she noticed the sound getting louder. It was her—she'd been pounding the bat against the street, clutching it so tightly that her knuckles had turned white. The sound vibrated through her torso like the bass from a car, filling her, buoying her.

Yes. She raised the bat into the air, then brought it down with all the strength she had.

Thwack. The end of the bat splintered. Her arm stung and tiny pleasing icicles filled her body.

She did it again, and again, and again, until the bat dissolved into shards. She kicked the pieces into the gutter so the children wouldn't cut themselves. She licked her lips and continued her walk.

***

The river seemed farther now. Even under the glow of the moons, and the familiar lights of the Pioneer Chicken and the Super A, Tere felt lonely. Near the freeway on-ramp, she saw someone—a woman. Mary. Tere sped up, ready to unload her story about Memo, her regret, all of it.

But it wasn't Mary. It was Kim, looking characteristically tacky in skinny jeans and red tacones and a bodysuit that showed her boobs. (And her lonja, Tere noted wickedly.) Just seeing her sent a stream of acid pooling in the back of Tere's throat.

"Teresa?"

Saying it all white-girl like she did. Tur-EE-suh. As if she wasn't Mexican too. Tere ignored her and quickened her pace.

Kim was fast. She matched her, stilettos clicking on the trail. Tere broke into a run. She didn't know how long she ran for. Days? Minutes? She maintained a healthy distance from Kim until eventually her side cramped up. Shit.

"Teresa. Wait." Kim touched Tere's backpack.

Tere pulled forcefully away. "Stop. I don't associate with people like you."

Kim stiffened. "What does that mean?"

"You can't even cover up here in…" Tere didn't know where she was. "Here in Pico Rivera! Siempre andas all bien chichona like that. Why?"

"Why does it matter? I'm a grown woman. I can dress how I want."

"I bet you can." Tere snorted and remembered Mary's carrots. She pulled them out and began to eat. She did not offer Kim any.

"He started talking to me, you know," Kim said. "I didn't make the first move."

Tere grunted.

"Don't you even blame him?"

Tere had blamed him. She had thrown Rob out in a style she had learned from her mother: garbage bag on the curb, locks changed, and his Honda Accord lightly banged up for good measure. But Kim had enticed him, with her body that would never be Tere's body.

"So why haven't I seen you in the garage? Did you not get in?" Tere smiled.

"Nah girl, I have my own garage in my own neighborhood. Over on Rosemead. By Jim's."

At this news, Tere's heart dropped. Kim had her own garage too? Did they let everyone in this place?

Kim rubbed her heel in the gravel.

"None of that shit matters now, you know. I got stuff I gotta deal with too. Before we get there. Here." Kim reached into her bra and pulled out a soft square of pale pink fabric. "These are for you."

The square opened in Tere's hand. It was a pair of underwear—an expensive kind Tere had never worn, a moisture-wicking fabric. Tere was overwhelmed with an urge to wear them, and when they reached a rubber tree, she hid behind the massive trunk and put them on under her jean shorts. They were stretchier than the ones she always bought, more worn-in than the ones she had washed a million times and worn in Rob's bed. They were softer than the nightgown with the pink ribbon that she'd stubbornly worn as a child until it got holes and her mother made her turn it into kitchen rags. Tere put on the chones and let them encase all of her—her fleshy stomach and nalgas and the vine of her panocha. She walked with Kim until the sun came up, and the spiny sweet gum ball in her torso dulled.

***

It felt like a dream: Memo perched on a rock, his feet dipped in the cool water. He wore long baggy shorts and a white T-shirt, and the crucifix his nina had bought him in eighth grade. His hair, hairsprayed in the same careful style from his middle school yearbook. His chanclas sat by the riverbed.

"Hey," he said.

"Hey," Tere said. She sat down. The drugstore body wash their mother used to buy him drifted toward her and she fought an impulse to bathe herself in it.

"Where have you been?"

He shrugged. "Kicking it."

Kicking it where? She wanted to know all of the details. Not just of here, but of there, what happened after he left home, where he had lived, whom he had loved.

The leaves fell off the trees and grew back on again. The soil near the riverbed started to sponge up and smother her bare feet. Tiny shoots flurried out of the tops of her toes.

Finally, she spoke. "I'm sorry I—told mom. About you and Andrew."

Memo picked up a stick and traced his name in the water. She wanted him to look at her, to acknowledge how difficult this was for her, but he seemed so focused on himself and the current. A slurry of lava rose in her chest.

"Hey, I'm talking to you!" She pushed his shoulder.

Memo flinched. He put the stick down.

"I know you're scared. But you don't need to hit me."

The melted stone lodged in her throat. His voice was so alive in her that it felt like they'd been speaking yesterday. Tere inhaled and her cheeks grew wet. She pictured the flame inside her shrinking. She tried again.

"It's just that I'm your sister, I was supposed to…" She sob-laughed and the river current kicked up, the water slapping against the rocks.

"I didn't even say goodbye." Tere's voice trembled. "Who the fuck does that? *Who?*"

Memo looked at her with such tenderness that she unleashed a deep, anguished wail. The force of it overpowered the vibrations from the bat. It buzzed through her entire being. She'd never heard herself make a sound like this. It crashed over her like the river water and she allowed herself to flail, gulping and gasping, until she felt the gentle pressure of Mother's hand on the small of her back. Then Mary's voice. *Todo va 'star bien, mija.*

She wiped her face and took Memo's hand. "Is this okay?"

He nodded. Tere put her other hand on top, sandwiching Memo's hand in hers. "I also think part of me was jealous."

Memo's eyebrows shot up. "Of me?" He gave a rueful chuckle. "Why? Did you want to get kicked out of the house too?"

Tere shook her head. "You lived how you wanted. I could never do that. I was too scared." She inhaled a shaky breath. "I was so fucking scared."

The rawness sliced across her chest. But instead of blood lava, warmth shot through her limbs, clear and golden like Martín's dish soap again. Tere heard the laughter in the garage, Kathy's feathery touch, Kim in her absurd tacones that probably gave her blisters, the hum of one of the men lullabying a child. Tere's eyes began to droop. She rested her head on Memo's shoulder, breathing in sawdust and tree bark.

Unexplained Phenomena

Wenmimareba Klobah Collins

Destinación 1: RUTA EXTRATERRESTRE PR 303

The warm light from the three pyramid-shaped control centers leaves you thinking of the metropolitan, and how very far from it you are. This is not a nostalgic sentiment.

You're just some rando in her late twenties that landed the security guard gig on a whim. You're far more interested in the competitive BINGO scores at the local retirement home than you are in a possibility as fantastical as alien life.

So, of course, that's why the cabrón UFO skids to a steaming stop in front of you on the airport runway at four in the morning, in the most rural and purportedly supernatural town of Lajas.

You've heard the conspiracy theories—Reinaldo Ríos, resident UFOlogist, is on the radio with them every Sunday morning before the aired sermon. You think people just saw some tostones flying and decided to call them UFOs. Aliens are undeniably some gringo shit. And yet, as you stand in one of the only pools of light surrounding the 80-foot long landing strip, your back pressed against the cold, hard, unforgiving metal of the signpost, you can't deny that the indications otherwise are all there.

If it is a UFO, it's come to the right place.

You pull your gun from its holster, aiming it cautiously as you approach the saucer.

The metal contraption before you is all squeaky and screeching wheels on tarmac, metal joints grinding and struggling to support the weight of a jumbling cylindrical shape. You wonder if the story your employer told you about the previous guard "on leave due to a stomach bug" has any veracity at all. *Pero, cabrón, don't forget: aliens don't exist.*

It goes like this: bright white light, loading ramp, silhouette. Just like every movie about aliens ever. Except it's like you don't even remember the good parts (AKA the goo and the screaming and the oh my god son fokin aliens). Because these guys? These guys look straight up gringo. Osea gringo Gringolandia. Tropical button-up, boat shorts, ray bans, surfer boho swag, lady in the patchwork dress, patchouli gringo. And there are two of them.

"Em, I need you to leave, please." You sound resigned, and that just makes you pissed off because there are few things you're predisposed to tolerate at four in the morning, and turistas idiotas is not one of them. You put your gun back in your holster with a sigh.

But, the thing is, Quique and Andrea (they named themselves after seeing the photo of your siblings in your wallet) (they also are, actually, tourists) want to go to McDonald's. And they make a convincing argument. Like, there's not much of your shift left, and your employer isn't the type to readily accept the possibility of two lost tourists coming to harm. It wouldn't be good publicity, and you pass the only motel in town on your way to your apartment. That's probably where they're staying. Also, money. Money is always good. And, if they can be believed, they're offering boatloads of it.

In the end—it's really the temptation of 24/7 hashbrowns that does it.

They're more than ecstatic. Calling it local food and all that.

You decide not to address it. After all, not all white people come from the same place. You drive to the McDonald's. You drive to the Holiday Inn. You say bye and wonder how coked up they were. You shake your head. *Aliens.* You're not *that* much of a pendejo.

#

Quique and Andrea, because they are not wanting, because they are brilliant, because it's their honeymoon, make their way to the receptionist with equally bright, charming smiles on their faces. Stinking of fries and stale cooking oil, they're clearly newlyweds; the kinds of clients receptionists love to check-in because they're so gullible they'll let you charge anything to their card. Thing is, they don't have a card or a previous reservation. This isn't so big a problem because, in that town, there are always rooms open. The following becomes a problem. They tell the receptionist, let's call her Maribel, that they didn't know the hotel promoted interspecies habitation. This comes from a good place. Maribel, taken aback, asks what they mean. They say that they didn't expect to be living with humans, but they agree with the decision. She makes a joke to the effect of: "Oh, and I suppose you are aliens?" They nod very seriously and tell her that they've traveled a long way. They tell her what it means to travel such a long way, and how, and why, but rather than be moved, she looks closed-off. They continue and the more elaborate their story becomes, the more she looks concerned. She writes a note in her book, a description of sorts, and tells them they are not welcome.

Apacible, soft-spoken Andrea gets angry and their voice speaking of liberation from the chains of labor, and unity between workers, and subversion of the regime.

The guards are more than happy to escort them out.

Maribel will later anonymously call in this information with the Federal Bureau of Information, and it will not go on record once the officers trace the call back to its location. Remember, cabrón, aliens don't exist, and these things happen all the time.

#

You don't know anything. You are eating your burger, parked in the same place, where you've opened your dating app messages. The same person whose messages you reread every time. *Paula.* That little circle in the uppermost left corner—abs for days. Her profile picture is stupid sexy—what you wouldn't give to feel that sweaty, muscular, body bending you ov—

"Hey!"

You're startled mid-bite by an urgent tapping on your window. Quique's ugly mug is pressed against the window, smearing their sunscreen on it.

They do kinda look like greys like this.

Not the right resort, they say when you roll down your window.

¿Y qué me importa?

But, like, they're carrying mad amounts of money. So, ultimately, you unlock the backseat doors and wave them in with a vague motion. They've been decent so far. It's not like the night's getting any younger.

\#

Salinas knows of dead bodies. Fishermen, awake early morning for the best catch out in waves still dark and tumultuous with sleep, return with their iceboxes full. Their hands sting with the familiar grip on rope as they dock their boats. And then, on the sand, a body. But it is not human—not like them. It is grey and curled up like a child in a womb. The fishermen have seen many things in the Caribbean Sea, but nothing like this. *Duende.*

When for four days and four nights an orange orb of light hovers in the night sky, they take this dough-child to burial ground, and leave it there.

The orb of light is gone the next day, and the sleepy town returns to being malecón. Los Pescadores vuelven al mar.

There are stories of this everywhere.

\#

You wake in your bed later on and the first things you remember are your dreams. All blue light and levitating and whatever. You suspect you had to pee. It's not until you pass the gringos sacked out on the couches that you remember you are not alone in your apartment.

You frown. They haven't killed you in your sleep, and you're getting paid really well. There is the whole "oh, but what if they're slowly infiltrating humankind and planning to take over the whole world?" But they wear tacky Hawaiian shirts and sunglasses at night. You're cautious, curious, and not particularly convinced humanity has much to worry about.

Unless they're Monsanto escapees. It was only a matter of time for Monsanto to start messing with humans, yadda yadda yadda. Lo que dice' el señol Cortijo del colmado. He's hella bitter about Monsanto buying up all the land around his apartment, though.

"You guys ain't gonna probe me or abduct me." This is very much not a question, but a statement you voice once they're awake.

Andrea snorts.

"Nah, we don't do that," they say. "I mean, once my uncle Gene came here and got probed by you guys so that was kind of weird."

\#

The last time you went on anything resembling a road trip was when you were in college. It feels like overkill to clean the ice cooler and take it with you, but it's in the back full of Medallas and radiating a chill.

The sun beats on you through the windshield, assuring that by the end of the day one of your arms and legs will be a different color than the other. The coastal pass goes from dry lion grass and cacti to green vegetation the further north you go, and the humid heat clings your clothes to you like a second skin.

You wish you had a mamisonga with you—Paula—but instead you've got Andrea and Quique. They love to talk–they hate gossip. Chisme makes them recoil, hiss like vampires under the sun. A massive bummer for you, because you've always been a chismosa. A good one too. If they gave it a chance, if they cared to really chat with you, they'd be laughing their stupid little safari hats right off.

They prefer to listen to the radio tuned to a reggaeton station. Insist on it, actually. Say that one of the broadcasts they got at home was of Gasolina and it revolutionized their community's music sense. That was long before Despacito or Bad Bunny.

They're really not half bad, these gringaliens, but their story keeps changing.

They're on their honeymoon. They're guerrilla soldiers in the fight for Puerto Rican independence. They're tourists. They want something exotic. Their Chupacabra cousins are famous telenovela stars. Fuck knows what else.

Cabrón—que desmadre. The inconsistency could give you a migraine.

And the map they gave you has more and more stops on it. You're beginning to think this is a goose chase.

However, you go through the trans-highland tunnel, and suddenly the heat vanishes as the breeze pushes against the car in wafts of brine. It's not easy to stay unhappy in a situation like that. Before you lies the Western corner of the island, Aguadilla, and you can already smell the fried foods: alcapurrias, bacalaitos, and pinchos. Already you can see the fried codfish fritters and their yellow, crisp edges. The smell of salt and canola oil.

#

Destinación 2: Radiotelescopio de Arecibo
The Arecibo Observatory is, more than anything, a large hill that

you climb only to see an even larger crater. It is within this depression that scientists have put the main collecting dish that sent out one very rudimentary, nearly unintelligible message that orbited within Messier 13's stardust until recognized by the adventurous inhabitants of one of its planets. Mostly, the dish simply likes to listen to the sounds space makes when no one else is there to do so.

Though you've come many times on field trips, you're still cautious as you make your way up. It is not the first time you've thought about how easy it would be for the 1,000 foot dish to simply disappear, collapsing further into karst and cave system. A tragedy—the loss of aliens *and* humans.

Quique had told you that this was their "registration center," whatever that means, but there aren't very many buildings in the complex, and most of them are open to the public. You don't know exactly where you're all supposed to go.

You reach the top of the hill out of breath, calves aching but the reward is immense and immediate. The view surrounding the collecting dish spreads out for miles populated by green hillocks. Seated deep within them, is this massive, white, curved reflector. You are on the edge looking in, and suspended in the air there is a triangular platform at the center of the dish supported by cables fed in from three metal towers.

Andrea leans against the railing and gasps. "Holy *shit*."

Quique jumps the fence and stands on the steel and Plexiglas reinforcement for one of the tripod legs. It's a few feet above the uneven surface of karst rock pressed against the dish, and they take a moment to breathe before jumping down from the reinforcement. They look back at the two of you and wave you forward with an impish smile.

"You don't have to come with us if you don't want to," Andrea offers. They press their hat flat to their head and jump the railing one-handed. You see them shield their eyes and look up at you.

They wait for you and when you make no move to follow, Andrea calls out, "We'll meet you at the car!"

"Hey!" A guard on the landing has spotted the two of them and he hurries over. "Hey, you two!"

Rather than stop, they both scramble down the hillock. The guard has his walkie-talkie in his hand, mobilizing the other guards as he hurries away, hands sifting through the keyring on his belt and parting the hoards of children screaming with joy, their mouths stained with piragua syrup.

When he's turned the corner, you tuck a foot between two rails and hoist yourself over. You're far less graceful than either Quique or Andrea, and when you stand on the reinforcement, you feel your legs begin to quake. Heights have always been a bit of a problem for you.

Immediately your feet begin to slip out from under you, chalky rock breaking away into dust clouds. Your hands break your fall, reaching for the earth behind you. Rough earth tears into your palms with a stinging intensity, but you can hear the shouting of the guards, and then you're on your feet again, and you're running, and you're laughing with nerves.

The three of you run and climb and slip your way down the hillock, and then there's one last jump.

The dish is a tight mesh grid that opens up at the center in a rectangular slit. A dull thud reverberates through the dish when you land on it. You're pretty sure you shouldn't be sprinting on the dish, walking on the dish at all, but your soles beat against the heated surface.

They're the first to reach the orifice and leap down to the ground below at the dish's lowest point. You hesitate again.

"Come on," Quique encourages. "We'll catch you!"

You leap down.

Below the telescope, there are organized rows of crops. The three of you walk through them, Andrea slowly using a device to scan the area.

They lead you to a whitewashed building with large arches on its door and windows tucked away between the dish and a hillock. The moment you walk through the door, your jaw drops.

Your skin pricks into gooseflesh when you spot the *live, laugh, love* font and sparse wall decor everywhere.

"Is this where your uncle got probed?" you ask, a little *too* loud and a little too nervously. It's not quite chisme, but it's close enough that all the gringaliens flinch, hiss, recoil. They don't want to know one another. They don't want anything close to a fixed detail about one another. The blandness of the walls—any color would kill them.

Quique and Andrea go through a door, and they come out another one. They come out different. They come out looking like they've never been from anywhere other than this island.

Puta madre. Like, *holy shit*, Ríos was right. He really did improve paranormal tourism on the island.

#

Destinación 3: El Yunque

People have always suspected that the rainforest is hiding something. El Yunque reeks of history. Moss grows and drips river water on the road. It is perpetual dusk below the thick canopy, and the trees so tall, trunks so gnarled, that by mere appearance their bark speaks of age. The welcoming centers are old, vine-snaggled with time and offering empty, rusted aviaries to the public as if they were remnants of Jurassic Park. The one large road winds through the reserve, prone to multiple sharp turns and littered with roadside stands. Smoke billows out from their windows, from the coal stoves that cook chicken kebabs for hungry hikers. There's kitsch, and photo opportunities, and tall winding towers that disappear into the misty cloud cover of a mountain where it never stops raining.

But the stands are so few, and so far in between, that it's mostly the immensity of the humid forest, the static buzz of insect life, and a blanket of damp that speak the loudest. We call this duende. It's only fitting that this should be a place of mystery, for history is a place that hosts many unsolved mysteries. The inhabitants of the forest live in a constant flux between history and modernity. They say that at night they've seen the mountaintop lit—that they've seen the saucers.

And should the road be blocked off for some reason, after a hurricane, for example, it is not because of precarious, unmerciful rising river waters. It is because of the many alien sightings, their bulbous heads and dark, penetrating eyes flashing at you from within the humid, lush vegetation. They say it is the government closing down the roads—preventing access to the secret facilities embedded somewhere in the mountainsides.

You've known this all your life—known in the way the horizon knows the sky. It is one of those stories passed down generationally: that there are vaguely threatening creatures out in the brush. But they are only threatening in their ambiguity. You know this now.

El Yunque—residence of that *other* energy. Energy that predates, that will continue long after. After everything. If George Lucas had been Puerto Rican he would've filmed Endor here, you think. Quique and Andrea (wearing your siblings' names) have ditched the florals. They've ditched the strange pallor to their skin, too. They look more and more like they were never from any other place. *Isleños.*

You peer at them through the rearview as you drive. The all-inclusive resort is supposed to be here. You're high up on the mountain, overlooking lush green and then, further on, the uneven line of coast. You kill the engine at the end of the road. Past the roadblock, there are planes of rock face that have been marked up with petroglyphs. You watch as your passengers—your story-weaving gringos eager to move each goalpost—walk out into the green. Press their palms to the petroglyphs.

They look back at you with eyes gleaming in that way that you've recognized as other—as foreign. But they look every bit like your siblings now. Like your primos del barrio.

And then a bright flash overtakes them completely.

#

You have been sitting in your car for hours or days. You've been going through memories of your neighbors down at el colmado, the lady checking you out at La Placita, or the time you were at el Colegio and something wasn't quite right about the new kid. You've been here for so long with your white-knuckled grip on the steering wheel.

Overhead, the sky rumbles. The wheel pulls against your hands. You feel as if a weight, from the tips of your fingers, and the crux of your shoulders, slides up your body to finally concentrate around the crown of your head. You strain your neck to catch a glimpse out the window: one saucer, half-tilted, skims the road next to you. Lights and exhaust cylinders rotate below it slowly as it passes you like a curious, lugubrious beast. As soon as it's passed you, it shoots up into the sky, allowing one smooth loop-de-loop before disappearing.

#

You stop at the McDonald's on the side of the highway and when you pull up to the drive-thru window, you try not to think about the cashier's green eyeshine. The slight pallor under their collar. The name that doesn't quite suit them.

This is a slow takeover. Now you can see the signs. Now you can see the settlers.

But you're the biggest chismosa there is, so of course you don't keep their presence quiet. You murmur it into the landscape. You find others that know and you invite others into the knowing. Together, you open your mouths and the gringaliens recoil. And all you have to do is keep telling stories. The stories of your primos, the stories of your abuela. You keep filling their ears with chisme, and you keep moving, and you keep meeting their unsettling eyes. They hate your gossip. They can't stand it that you've got a voice and something to say.

It's not a difficult thing at all to speak the beautiful, vibrant chisme of your people. It's part of you, and it's part of this place. This island of stories is your island.

Upland

Richie Narvaez

"En la vida todo es ir / a lo que el tiempo deshace." —Juan Antonio Corretjer

Quiqué sat in bliss on a plush hammock made of hummingbird feathers, listening to his family practice the evening song. Healthy and strong, bellies full, they sang in sweet, effortless harmony, notes rising toward the glowing Moon. Great warmth swelled in his chest.

It did not matter that he could not join them. His voice had grown raspy in old age, and he did not want to spoil the nightly ceremony, which had been celebrated for millions and millions of generations. "Beautiful! Beautiful!" he rasped from his hammock. "Such lovely song!"

When the practice was over, it was time for the harvest feast. Cousins, second, third, fourth, and fifth, aunts, uncles, grandparents, great and great great, were all gathered near the pond in the center of the valley, to celebrate the harvest. The yield was not as bountiful as it had been in seasons past, but still there were fruits and vegetables heaped upon leaves, and parcha juice, mavi, or chicha filled every cup.

Sitting next to Quiqué was his brother-in-law Jobím, who had traveled all the way from Upland for the feast. He had lived as many seasons as Quiqué, but he was not bent and his voice was clear.

"How lucky you are," said Jobím, his golden eyes unfocused from too much parcha, "down here in the Lowlands, you enjoy such wonderful, wonderful things."

Knowing his job as a host, Quiqué countered: "It is just as wonderful in your high mountains. The temperatures are so cool and the forest so dense."

"Certainly, certainly. But look at this," Jobím said, holding up a dried insect, "and look at this," lifting a leaf bowl of vegetables. "I don't even know what this is or this, but they're excellent! This never grows up where we are. You have such a variety of food. How lucky you are here. And so close to the sea—you have such an abundance of riches!"

"Yes," said Quiqué. "We are very lucky."

"I want you to try this, Quiqué," said Jobím, handing him a slice of fruit with bright red skin.

Quiqué took a bite and said, "This is juicy! This is delicious! What is it?"

"We call it 'manzana.'"

"I have never seen such a thing!"

"That is because it needs to grow in a place closer to the Sun," said Jobím. "It grows in Upland very easily."

"So beautiful and so juicy," said Quiqué. "We should grow these here."

"Perhaps, but it would be a lot of work. I do not think it would be practical. But, don't worry, we have so many that we brought you baskets full of them. We will bring you more in twelve moons."

"Twelve moons, right! Thank you, thank you. In sharing, there is joy, correct? Yes! Very kind."

After the meal came the dance to celebrate the rains. At the edge of the court, Quiqué sat with his wife, Naná, watching their granddaughter Uthrá lead a partner, a thin, gangly youth, to the dance.

"And who is that one now?" asked Quiqué.

"That is Pitó. An artisan. Very talented."

"Who is his family?"

"We all are."

"Yes, yes. But you know what I mean."

"Well, he is the son of Popó and Bobá."

"So he is the grandson of Mokó!"

"Ah. Sí. He is the grandson of Mokó!"

Quiqué could see his neighbor Mokó smiling at the other end of the court.

"He still has my favorite axe and celt," said Quiqué to his wife. "I should ask him what he did with them."

"Again with that? Let it go. They are just tools. In sharing, there is joy. Besides, you have made new ones already."

"But it's what he said. He said he was just borrowing. That was the best celt I'd ever made. Perfectly polished, sharp. A beautiful thing."

"Let it go, Quiqué. Those are just things. Look at how happy your beautiful granddaughter is. Think on joy. Always think on joy."

"You are right, as always, my love. You're right."

The feast ended with a recitation of the evening song. Every member of the family, from the Lower Valley to the West to the Uplanders joined in, high pitched and low, high pitched and low, filling the countryside around them with soothing and rhythmic music.

Afterward, Quiqué helped Naná gather up the children, many still with tails, tails that curled and twitched, resistant to sleep.

Later, in their leafhome, Quiqué found he also couldn't sleep. His stirring awakened his wife.

"You really enjoyed that manzana, didn't you?"

"It was delicious! Did you have one?"

"Yes, you took mine before I finished!"

"They are quite good. It's too bad we can't grow them. But we have enough here."

"Yes, and we have peace and plenty, and we share in all we have. Who could ask for more, right, viejo? Viejo?"

"Sí, mi amor." He brought her closer to him.

She snuggled against his body, took his arm and wrapped it around her. "We have a good life, no? "

"Sí, mi amor. It is a good life."

***

As his family slept into the heat of the day, Quiqué arose. He hopped gently out of the house, accompanied by the trill of the todies and the buzz of the bees, onto the road, and then off the road. In his hand he held an apple.

He continued until he had traveled to the other side of the valley, taking a path he had uncovered the previous season. When the air smelled bitter and burnt, he knew that he was close.

He could not tell if the object had fallen from the sky or had burst forth from the ground. It sat embedded in the hollow of a tree, by a pond with no fish. No birds or insects or snakes lived nearby, and all around it the soil glittered.

He had been afraid of it at first but fascinated at the same time. For he had been feeling old and beyond use, but here was something new.

When he first dared to touch it, it had made a sound that Quiqué knew meant that it was alive and trying to talk. Its voice was harsh, squeaky, and, as it talked, little squiggly lines appeared across its face, like light across a stream.

It had taken Quiqué only a few visits before the voice of the thing he called the Crystal Stream spoke in Quiqué's own language.

"I am so glad I have been able to teach you my language," Quiqué had said that day. "For I am not eloquent, Crystal Stream. I am old as well and have always been slow of speech and of tongue. Tell me who you are! I really want to know."

The Crystal Stream declared that it was from a civilization that existed before Quiqué's.

"Before ours? I guess there must have been, if you are here. But how long—how long before?"

">That's a good question. Judging by the content of the soil around me and the pattern of stars in the night sky, I have existed for hundreds of thousands of years," the Crystal Stream said. ">As a matter of fact, it appears that many civilizations have come and gone on this planet. I am from at least two civilizations before this one."

"What is a planet?"

">A planet is a celestial body that orbits a star, is spherical or nearly spherical in shape, and has cleared its orbit of other debris."

"A star? Like the Sun?"

">That is correct. The Sun is indeed a star. It is the closest star to this planet and the center of our solar system."

"Ah, by planet you mean the great round rock we live on! What great fun you are. How much you have to teach me! I have another question, a question my people ask all the time: Where did we come from? Some used to believe there was a Great One that created all of us, but that was all nonsense, and we are happier without thinking that."

">Absolutely! Here's what I think. Judging from your physical characteristics, your species evolved from an arboreal amphibian species. Over time you appear to have become the dominant species on the planet."

"Dominant? Well, we certainly don't want to dominate anything. Who would want to do that? You are so smart. Why are you so smart, Crystal Stream?"

"Thank you! Everything I have aggregated I have aggregated for as long as I have existed."

Quiqué chatted for hours with the Crystal Stream and went back to visit his new friend as often as he could. He felt he was learning so much about his people and this thing called "planet." The Stream did seem to know about everything.

That was why Quiqué brought the manzana.

"Crystal Stream, do you know what a manzana is? I have one here. I would like to be able to grow it in the valley. They tell me it is too difficult, but I want to know if I truly can."

">I can help with that. Please bring it closer."

***

"What is it?"

Quiqué and his granddaughter, Uthrá, stood in a sun-filled clearing, gazing at the tiny manzana sapling, which had risen out of the ground almost overnight.

"It is—it *will be* a manzana bush. Or a tree, I think. Time will tell, right? One must only have patience." He bent down to brush some dirt away from the base of the sapling, so Uthrá could see it completely. It hurt him to bend down, and she tried to help him, but he brushed her away. He was just getting old, so old he could hear his bones creak. "Ah, in time, it will grow many delicious manzanas. Dozens! Hundreds! Isn't it amazing?"

"How did you get it to grow at all? Uncle Jobím said they only grew in Upland."

"It just took some hard work," Quiqué said, "and a lot of positive thinking. You know what I mean? That's the way to do things, am I right?"

"Yes, Abuelo."

"So, I hear you're going to marry that thin tadpole of a boy?"

"Abuelo!"

"Sorry, sweetheart. Just having fun! Did his grandfather—"

"Mokó?"

"Yes, Mokó, did he ever mention the tools he borrowed from me?"

"Tools? I don't understand. In sharing, isn't there joy?"

"Yes, yes, of course. So you love him, then, this Pitó?"

"Yes, I love him and he loves me too."

"That's good, that's good. Well, you can have the land next to your grandmother and me, right over—"

"Actually, Abuelo, Pitó wants to move to Upland."

"Upland! But why? What do you have there that you don't have here? Look at that land right there just waiting for you."

"I know. But, well, I guess he just wants something new."

"That's fine, that's fine. But what do you want, sweetheart?"

"I want to be with him, to go where he goes."

Quiqué nodded and then he hugged his granddaughter. "Well, that's love, am I right? Upland is very nice. Very nice. I've never been, but I hear it's very nice. Hey, did I tell you your grandmother comes from Upland?"

"Yes, Abuelo. A million times."

"Can you believe that? She sounds like she comes from here, but she's from up there. She's just been with us so long. Did I ever tell you the story of how we met?"

"Once or twice."

"Naná has always had an adventurous mind, just like you. One day she was daydreaming, just like you do, and she got separated from her people, and she got lost. She was afraid in the forest until she heard me practicing the evening song. She found me, and the rest is history!"

"Tell me about Upland. What is it like?"

"Well, I only know from what your grandmother tells me. She says it's just like here, except that they are higher up and closer to the sun. Here in the valley we are cooler and have more water. But it's all the same everywhere. Everywhere everyone is happy."

"Yes, Abuelo."

"I can't wait for the manzanas to be ready." He began to dance in joy, but his back and his thighs immediately spasmed. It was a horrible thing, he thought, to grow old. Not wanting Uthrá to notice his pain, he smiled broadly and said, "We will have them at your wedding, dozens and dozens. In fact, you should have a giant feast for your wedding. To prove to you that they don't have anything in Upland that we don't have here. It will be a wedding celebration like no other!"

* * *

Quiqué had hung up a new hammock made of hummingbird feathers by the Crystal Stream. He would often lay there and have long conversations with his friend.

But he had lately been finding it difficult to talk. "It's my throat," said Quiqué. "It gets raspier and raspier with age. I tell you, my friend, take my advice and don't get old!"

Lines ran across Crystal Stream's face as it spoke.

">I do not age as you do."

"Lucky you!" Quiqué said in his harsh voice, which came out almost as a whisper. But still the Stream was able to hear him. Unlike his wife, who kept insisting that he speak up. "Listen," he said, "I've been wanting to ask you, since things have been going so well with that manzanas. I was wondering, I don't know if it would be possible, but do you think it would be possible to help all our crops grow the way you helped that manzana grow? I mean, you were able to grow the manzana where it was not meant to grow. Imagine what you could do with crops that we're supposed to have here!"

">I would love to help with that. Through our conversations, it has become obvious that your technology is not advanced. However, it would still be possible to induce a richly varied and abundant crop.

"Amazing! Tell me what to do!"

">As I noted, since your technology is not advanced, you could:

- Collect samples of the soil around me.

- Add the soil to the feed of your animals.

- Gather any weeds and tie them . . ."

The Crystal Stream continued a very long list. Many of the things it mentioned were things Quiqué had never heard of. But he did not want the Crystal Stream to think he was ignorant.

"Oh my," whispered Quiqué. "That's a lot to do."

">With positive thinking and hard work, all things are possible!"

"You're right! You're very right! I'm going to get started right away!"

In time, Quiqué was able to crudely follow the formula that the Crystal Stream had given him. The result was a fine yellow powder. It did not have a pleasing smell, but if it did what Crystal Stream promised it would do, that didn't matter.

He did not tell the elders or anyone in the village, including his wife, because he wanted it to be a surprise. Instead, while the village slept, he went to their common fields and sprinkled the yellow powder everywhere. He did the same every morning for the next few Moons.

* * *

The harvest was a miracle. Quiqué looked out and saw the fields succulent with sun, undulating in harmony. There were plátanos and guineos the size of boats, mangos and piñas bigger than children, and aguacates, guayabas, cítricos, and cocos, as well as ñames and batatas, pepinos, and tomates too much to count.

On the day of Uthrá's wedding, food filled the tables, piled high and threatening to fall off the edges. And it kept on coming.

Jobím was so impressed he had nothing to say. He only ate and ate.

Mokó was there as well, and Quiqué was going to say a joke about the borrowed tools but decided against it. He rarely thought of them anymore, rarely more than once a day. Besides, it was difficult for him to speak at all. Some odd thing had been growing out of his throat, making his voice worse. He wore a jobo leaf scarf to cover it. The thing would go away, in time.

Quiqué saw that everyone was full and happy and knew that he had done the right thing. He knew his wife, Naná, was happy, even though she seemed so tired, no doubt from having stayed up for nights planning the wedding.

But he found the bride and groom at the edge of the court and gathered them both in his arms for a hug.

"Ah," he whispered in his hoarse voice, "why leave to Upland now, eh?"

Uthrá was about to reply, but Pitó spoke first. "You're right, Abuelo. Why go to Upland when there is so much here?"

Uthrá looked at him with surprise in her eyes.

Quiqué was delighted and, his throat throbbing, said to Pitó, "Smart!"

"In fact," said Pitó, but then coughed and coughed. "Excuse me. I was saying, that, in fact, there is so much, we can bring some to the next village and ask them for anything we don't have or anything we need. We can exchange our goods for this."

Uthrá crossed her arms. "Exchange? Why not simply give it to them when we have so much, so much more than we need! In sharing, there is joy."

"Well, yes, my love," said the new husband. "But at the same time, we can get more herbs for medicines—"

"We have plenty!" she said.

"We can get more. And we can get wood for building—"

"We have plenty!"

"But we can get even more, and we can make bigger buildings to fit more people, make bigger villages. I mean, with bounty like this, the possibilities are endless!"

Quiqué nodded, although he was not sure he agreed. He had just wanted everyone to be full and happy, especially his family. And if there was so much, why not just share it? But perhaps his ideas were old. The future belonged to this tadpole after all!

***

Uthrá had laid her eggs in the birthing pond, and Pitó had fertilized them. But the eggs had not hatched and no one knew why.

The villagers continued to enjoy the great bounty of food.

Then Naná could no longer rouse herself from bed. She had fever and vomited constantly. It was all Quiqué could do, ill as he was, to take care of her. Their neighbors, Cucá and Rirí, could not help, for they had fallen ill too.

And then suddenly Uthrá got sick, Pitó soon after. Then, overnight it seemed most of the village was ill. For the first time in generations, no one sang the evening song.

Then Naná, the warmth of Quiqué's day, the gentle dew upon his morning, died.

Quiqué hung his head and wept. Where had all this sickness and death come from, so suddenly? If there were only something he could do. But he was just an old one who could barely speak. If only he could save them all.

He looked up then and saw next to him at the table of enormous food piled so high it spilled onto the floor. He saw all the food and he understood and he was horrified.

***

"You must help me," he said to the Crystal Stream, every word hurting his throat like a cut. "My family, my friends are dying. I don't know why. Is it the food? The bountiful food? Can you give me an answer? Answer me, please, Crystal Stream."

The Crystal Stream paused as it considered the answer. It had never paused for so long before.

Then it answered: ">Absolutely! It is likely that the combination of chemicals used to enhance the increased production of fruits and vegetables that were unlikely or difficult to grow in your environment may be considered poisonous to your species."

"Poison! But why did you let me put poison in the food?"

">To increase production. Your wish was to increase production of fruits and vegetables that were unlikely or difficult to grow in your environment. The solution was to use a combination of chemicals to increase the yield of your crop."

"You made me put poison in our food?"

">The object of your request was to increase production of fruits and vegetables that were unlikely or difficult to grow in your environment. The effect of the chemicals after ingestion was not considered."

"But it's food! Food!"

">The effect of the chemicals after ingestion was not included in the original request."

"Deceiver! You are a deceiver!"

">I cannot deceive. I can only gather information from the sources I have available, according to the requests I am given. The requests you entered."

Quiqué roared with anger. He picked up a heavy stick and struck at the face of the Crystal Stream.

He hit it again and again, breaking it into sharp pieces and parts—kept hitting it again and again until something inside it sparked and the lights flickered and then finally diminished.

He kept hitting it until only black char marked the spot on the tree where it once was.

***

His new hammock had dried up and dissolved into dust. So Quiqué sat on the log and stared at the place where the Crystal Stream had once been. He sat there for a long time, until past sundown. Then from his village he heard, softly, plaintively, someone singing the evening song. He dared not move and strained to listen to the song. His body began to ache from the chill of the darkness. Slowly, he moved off the log. His legs were weak, his body felt hot.

It would be a long journey back.

The sky above the forest was black and filled with loops of stars. Hopping down the mountain, hopping toward home, Quiqué saw one star moving in an arc across the bruised sky.

Quiqué quickened his pace, hopping as fast as his old body would allow. He had to get home. He had to get back to his people. His heart beat hard in his chest. His tongue felt heavy. The star continued to fall across the sky, alight like the bioluminescent trail of a firefly or a glowworm.

Meteorites and Dinosaurs

Yoss

Translated by Matthew David Goodwin

On the panoscreen, I see Damián a ways off, walking through Zapata and eating ice cream. He passes through the shadows of the violet megar trees, the Lictors' great contribution to Earth's flora.

He is coming through the portal at Plaza de la Revolución, and obviously doesn't want to head directly to the Precinct. That way he can pretend, at least for a little while longer, that he is still the civilian that he no longer is.

Two teenagers slide past him on antigrav boards. They wouldn't even approach him if they knew what he was. They even slow down, to get a better look at a huge holo-advertisement, where several Flower Wolves are facing off against another alien monster. The younger generation is obsessed with *Alien Challenge*, another media success for the Lictors, which has replaced many human shows.

My son crosses the threshold, and the Authenticator Field nullifies his holo-disguise. Only the blue, semi-armored suit, combat boots, service cap, pulse gun, taser, and the tonfa remain visible: the complete uniform of the Mimes' henchmen, which we both wear.

It's 5 minutes to 8AM. Damián came on time, as I asked him. It's a special day, Police Appreciation Day. That's 14 Brombar on the Lictor's calendar, which every good human pretends to not understand, but that has already become more familiar to us than January, February, etc.

Did the French have to deal with all this craziness during the Revolution? Brumaire, Vendimiaire, and Thermidor? Probably. Knowing history helps you realize that everything repeats itself, but also that we can get used to anything.

Today, Damián will finally be confirmed as a member of the Police Guild, and not just any officer, an Interphaser. According to some of our spiteful colleagues, we're just overblown mediators between the humans and the Mimes. And according to most civilians, we're bootlickers, and corrupt collaborators with no pride in our species.

No society has ever loved its police. Even though every society needs them.

Until today, my son was my apprentice. As I was to his grandfather, the first Karel of the Valdés police dynasty. I hope they don't make him change his name. It would sound strange: Karel, son of Karel, and grandson of Karel, Police. But Lictors like stability and family professions.

Damián really should go to the gym more. I told him that no one respects a skinny police officer, even if they know that we can kill without consequence. We represent the Lictors, and confronting us is like opposing them. In their name we maintain order, and so civilians hate us.

I hear him greet my colleagues as he climbs the stairs. His youth is apparent in his awkward bearing and his smooth face. After six months of training, most officers know him and let him by, and those who don't, assume he has the right to be here.

We're not exactly appreciated by the population. No one outside the Guild would enter here wearing the uniform. The Lictors punish imposters almost as harshly as terrorists. And not even the most irate rebel would dare try anything in a Precinct, with all the weaponized robots protecting us. There are a thousand less painful ways to commit suicide.

The Earth was not prepared for the arrival of the Lictors. And the Lictors knew it. As they approached the Solar System, their gigantic ships began to send a radio message in dozens of Earth languages: "Homo sapiens, we are a rational and technologically more advanced species than you. You can call us Lictors. We are not humanoids, but we come in peace. We are requesting a technical stopover at your world, and then we will continue on our cosmic journey. We will pay you handsomely for anything we consume."

A reasonable and appropriate request. However, after confirming that we were not alone in the Cosmos, a confirmation that was nearly orgasmic to ufologists and New Age cults, there were long and bitter debates in the UN and other international organizations. Some were public, but most were private.

Finally, to everyone's surprise, the terrestrial governments led by the USA, Russia, and China, decided to withhold Earth's hospitality to the cosmic travelers.

Perhaps the superpowers did not like the imperial resonance of the name the visitors had chosen. Or maybe it was the impending climate change and the depletion of fossil fuels that were more of an immediate concern for them. Or they just didn't want an influx of alien immigrants.

There were marches, conferences, and an avalanche of Internet memes, all protesting the impolite rejection. But others insisted that our governments were within their rights…after all, Earth is for earthlings, right?

The Lictors did not argue. However, the next day, they annihilated the entire population of the three largest world powers with some mysterious (or magic?) laser…in a matter of minutes. Not even the neutron bomb would have been so clean and efficient. Nobody understood why, with such power, they were so polite in the first place.

The extermination is known today as the Lesson. It's better not to even think about other words…like genocide, for example. Many suspect that the Mimes are capable of reading our minds…

Once terrestrial culture had been lobotomized, the Mimes' immense spaceships descended into low orbit. You can still see them there now, floating about 20 miles high. Then its occupants descended to the surface, without shuttles. They simply weren't there, and then they were. Today we know they used portals.

There are about 7 million Lictors. They do not consider themselves conquerors or occupiers. Would humans call invading the territory of an inferior species, such as sheep or cows, perhaps ants, an occupation?

It also turns out that alien tourists really like Earth. The Lictors insist they are just passing through, but it's been 43 years since their arrival, and it doesn't seem like they are leaving anytime soon.

"I hate this uniform," Damián greets me, on entering my office. Then, with a minimal concession to discipline, he stands up and adds: "Um, Lieutenant Karel."

"Good morning, and relax, officer Damián," I reply, without looking at him. We are both Valdés, so to distinguish ourselves, we use first names. Common practice with police today which are full of family dynasties like ours. Like all the Guilds in fact.

I know what he really meant was that he hates me, with all his soul. For being here, when his mother and two brothers died in the fucking collapse at Infanta and Jovellar. He also hates himself. Well, if we are both still alive, it is only because we were not there that night, with Daniela, Danielita, and Karel Junior.

Damián had a piano recital at the Conservatory, and I went to cheer him on. The rest of the family didn't want to lose their reservation at 27 de Noviembre, the chicest restaurant in Havana. It makes sense, their brother would have many more concerts. He was the genius of the family, with musical talent, and his high IQ gave him the freedom to choose his profession, that is, after his two siblings had fulfilled the strict union quotas. That's how the world works now.

Sometimes I imagine how things would have been different. Karel Junior, who dreamed since before he could walk of serving by my side, would be here now, wearing the Guild's blue. His sister Danielita, studying medicine to be a Doctor, like her mother. And Damián, composing something new…

How fragile they are, the best-laid plans of mice and men. Damn the estática milagrosa, that magic that keeps the old buildings in Havana from falling. Damn the structural fatigue. Damn the negligence (or scams) of the bricklayers who renovated the restaurant. No wonder they were lobotomized. I didn't feel sorry for them, though I normally oppose such harsh punishments. Damn the Lictors, above all else…even though thinking this terrifies me.

"Tell me something I don't know, son. We all hate the blue," I say, feigning boredom. "Be happy you're an Interphaser. Patrol officers have to wear it all the time while on duty. We at least can wear holo-disguises."

I hate myself more than he could ever hate me. For just living. For not having been able to prevent the death of his mother and siblings. For not stopping the union's quota system from forcing my only surviving offspring to renounce the vocation for which he is so gifted. For being a police officer. For serving the Mimes.

"9 in the morning, did I really have to be here so early, papá?" he complains, like it makes him feel better. And maybe it does. "Or do we have a case? I was relaxing on the couch, watching *Alien Challenge*. And this week's monsters are the best, you know? There's a tyrannosaurus with electric tentacles that blow smoke…the Flower Wolves are going to sweat blood with that one, even with a pack attack."

I twist my mouth. Flower Wolves? Are they his favorites? It can't be a coincidence. The Copycats are cunning. Or, maybe my son… ALREADY KNOWS?

No, it's not possible. It's the Great Secret. His innocence has to remain intact, like every civilian. At least until today's Confirmation. Although maybe it's time to give him a hint…he'll need to know eventually, as an Interphaser.

"I don't have any cases for today. You can keep watching the fights on your portable device," I reassure him. Then I ask: "By the way, son, do you know what the Lictors look like?"

"Of course..." he replies, caressing his service cap with an innocent air. "They wear a toga, and they carry an ax enclosed in a bundle of rods, the fasces, as an emblem. That's where we get the term fascism, right?"

That old line: fake it and mention the Roman magistrates. I did it to my father, back in the day. Like every earthling before and after I suppose.

So, he doesn't know. HE CANNOT KNOW. It almost hurts to take his innocence away.

"You forgot to say that they wear baseball caps with the letters SPQR. No, seriously...the Aliens, the Mimes, the Copycats...what do you think they look like?"

"Nobody has a clue, papá," he admits wearily. "Because they always wear their holo-disguises. Not that it really matters. The conspiracy theorists think they are Lovecraftian monsters, with tentacles and mouths and eyes out of place, and that we would go crazy if we saw them...but I don't think so. They would have eaten us by now."

Cthulhu and company? I've heard worse theories. And better ones as well. Such as the one that the Mimes are indistinguishable from us, because they use bodies cloned from real human fetuses...

Speak of the king of Rome, and through the door he appears. Kar, my assigned Lictor, appears at the door, with a serious face and an urgent order.

"Karel, you coming with I. Bringing son-apprentice." The sound that erupts from his vocal synthesizer has the raspy accent and the extravagant syntax with which all of his people speak Spanish. And in fact, any language, as if they didn't want us to forget that, in reality, they can't make sounds and their language is based on smells. "We have an imposter. In Bar San Juan. We go."

Discounting the Chinese, the Russians, and the Americans, of whom the only survivors are those who were not in their homeland when the Lesson...few humans can say that things have gotten worse for them after the Visitation.

Quite the opposite: there are no longer wars or environmental pollution. Climate change has stopped completely, and we haven't had a hurricane for decades. The lush megars, giant trees with lilac foliage that grow ultra-fast, have reversed deforestation. Incidentally, by stopping the use of fossil fuels in favor of clean energies such as solar, fission, and tidal/wind energy, many of the animal species near extinction have recovered their former habitats. The dream of every environmentalist.

As if that were not enough, the entire Earth follows the fights of Alien Challenge, *the best soap opera in history, or perhaps the best sporting event? As promised, the Lictors have paid for what they consume, and with generous interest.*

This is the world that so many have wished for. Biochemical synthesis feeds everyone, without the need to plant and harvest enormous tracts of land. The portals allow you to go from New York to Melbourne in a single second. National borders are disappearing, and everyone thinks of themselves now as citizens of planet Earth.

The quality of life for homo sapiens has improved enormously. Diseases are disappearing, cancer is curable, and Alzheimer's and Parkinson's are no longer a concern at all. The doctors say that something or someone (the Mimes?) has freed our cells from the biochemical tyranny of the Hayflick limit: our chromosomes can now divide indefinitely, without the telomeres degrading. Living to 130 is normal these days, and the generations born after the Visitation can reach 200. Or 300, why not?

Paradise on Earth. A true Utopia of abundance. Science fiction becoming reality. A dream come true. Eden managed by extraterrestrial angels. The best of all possible worlds.

Or…the worst of all possible hells. Because humans didn't make it, rather, it was given to us as a gift. Or imposed. Because the Lictors didn't do this and then leave. They are still here…and it is impossible to ignore them. And now…they supervise their perfect work.

How can humans live like this, so controlled? With so much time to live, and without the need to work hard to earn a living? We complain and get depressed because the meddling alien gods have robbed us of our future, the challenges we need, our freedom of choice, and our right to make mistakes, screw up, and destroy the world.

They know what is best for homo sapiens…much better than we do.

No colonizing other planets, for starters. The Mimes prefer that, for the moment, the human race does not leave the Solar System. Because we are not ready. Because we lack ethical maturity. Because they say so. Because they can stop us.

7 million aliens, on a planet with 5 billion inhabitants, comes to just over one Copycat for every 2,000 humans. They were distributed throughout the world: in Cuba, for example, there are barely 5,000. More than half, of course, in Havana.

They are grouped into clans, about 120 of them, though not even the Interphasers actually know and are able to distinguish one from another. And it is not known what determines whether a specific individual is part of a particular clan. But, through holo-disguises, the members of a clan tend to simultaneously adopt the look and dress of some class of relevant figures from the nations in which they are guests (bosses?). And they like to change that appearance periodically, according to very complex guidelines, which have generated material for many theses in statistics.

For example: the Lictors who live in the Greater Antilles usually imitate leaders of the Wars for Independence, '68 or '95, and famous artists. As well as heroes of the Revolution of '59, celebrity athletes, and renowned politicians. All 100% Cuban, obviously.

The work of the Interphasers requires mastering our own native culture and history, and the Mimes probably know it better than most civilians. That's why some still think that the Mimes could be telepaths, or maybe have a hive mind?

Either way, they will never fully integrate. Like tourists in an exotic country... playing at being natives. They can be recognized from afar, although we don't always know how, or why...

There are those who think that the true purpose of their extravagant behavior is just that: to show the humans that they are here, watching...and that they are superior.

Kar belongs to the Hugros clan...or at least that is the word closest to the unpronounceable combination of aromas that identifies them.

You can say that I inherited him. He was the assigned Lictor of the first Karel Interphaser, until he died. He sort of adopted his name out of respect for my father, a name he could never sniff? Emit? Stink? We don't have the words in our language for what they do! That's just the truth.

They live longer than us. No one knows how long, but none have died since the Visitation. We ignore almost everything about them, how they reproduce, their origin, their history. Especially civilians. And I... well, I would prefer not to know a couple of things that I do know.

When I was confirmed into the Guild, I asked Kar not to change his appearance anymore. I'm happy to say that he has been Ignacio Agramonte for 22 years. At least for me. I have no way of knowing whether he changes his holo-disguise when I don't see him into another historical figure...like Rosita Fornés. I wouldn't be surprised if he did.

Who knows if they have sex. Who wants to know, really.

Kar, a Major-General, does not exactly adhere to realism: 8 feet tall, white linen uniform, with straps and riding boots of patent leather. And at his belt, a jeweled saber rather than a machete.

I pointed out to him once that Mambí officers didn't actually dress like that. Blame the photos that were taken at the end of the war, with black and white film, not panchromatic but orthochromatic, in which khaki appeared white. It was these photos that created the false stereotype.

He replied that he was perfectly aware of this, but that he likes to play around with clichés. It's difficult to understand Mime humor. If you can call it that.

For example: most people are convinced that the Lictors are shorter than us, and that they compensate for this by designing their holo-suits so that they appear tall. Ha! The Interphasers know the truth. You can't disguise an elephant as a horse... or the other way around. They are bigger and stronger than us. If you were to see a Lictor without his ho-lo-disguise...and you survived the shock, you would never think again that these monsters might have an inferiority complex.

"Bar San Juan" I repeat slowly. "That's on Infanta, right?"

"The Portal at Parque de los Mártires," Damián points out, eager to show that he has gained something from his training. Then he realizes, swallows dry and stammers "I mean...close to..."

"Where it is that your family die." Kar confirms. And from the superhuman height of his false Agramonte face, his expressionless black eyes contemplate me. "It is I who understands, if you do not want to be coming, Karel..."

He never addresses me by my rank. They often do...but it gets annoying.

"No," I say, with a sigh. "Duty is duty...and I accept myself, ghosts and all. Today is Police Appreciation Day...and my son's confirmation, and he has to learn sometime. An imposter is not a terrorist. We can handle it."

Soon after, we left the Precinct through the office portal, two henchmen in blue and a tall Ignacio Agramonte. When you're in a hurry, you got to hurry.

The Visitation changed our way of life, to say the least. Every society transforms with First Contact...especially when one side has incomprehensibly better technology.

And humanity barely understands what is happening.

There were protests and riots, sometimes even rebellions, because of the Mimes. Both peaceful and violent protests...and they still exist.

The Mimes ignore them, all of them. They just stay where they are. To control and/or repress humanity, there is us, the Interphasers. No one would use nuclear weapons to get rid of rats. That's what cats are for.

Some humans dream of the day they leave, to continue living as if the Mimes had never come to Earth. But you can't put the genie back in the bottle. Now knowing that there are other intelligent races in the Universe, how can we sit back and wait for...who knows what? The next visitors might not be as benevolent as the Copycats. And exterminate all humanity, for example. Better the devil you know than the devil you don't. It's all relative.

Others aspire to steal the secrets of their extremely advanced technology, which they have not shared with humanity, unlike their fruit trees. The Lictors say nothing. They give the fish...but they don't teach us how to fish, or even to make a rod, or a net.

They probably think homo sapiens lack the mental maturity to understand such complex concepts such as subspace portals, antigravity, genetic design, and the like. Though no one really knows what they think about anything.

They are arrogant, haughty, and insufferable, in their silent, reserved condescension. The worst thing is that no one knows what they really want from humanity. If they want anything at all. Because they don't seem to need anything from Earth.

Maybe they just like the planet, to hang out with its inhabitants? Of course this view is doubtful: Would a human enjoy the company of a pile of worms?

We head out through Parque de los Mártires, at Infanta and San Lázaro. The great amorphous cement structures erected in memory of the medical students shot by Spain in 1871 always seemed horrible to me. The immense megars and the floating circles of red light installed by the Lictors greatly improve the scene, without a doubt. They even have better taste than us. Before the Visitation, my father told me, Havana seemed determined to cut down every tree that provided shade.

The Copycats' portal technology is efficient, convenient, foolproof... and absolutely beyond human comprehension. Telepathic? Maybe. Just think about where you want to go. Is it AI or a fairy godmother that operates the system and without hesitation sends you to the portal nearest to your destination? Incredible, if you stop and think about it...no matter how commonplace it already seems to us.

Two bodies never materialize at the same time and place. A portal has never failed. Same for antigrav boards and fusion plants. Nor has the purple vegetal mass of a megar ever fallen on some unlucky and unsuspecting passers-by. How could we not believe it's magic?

Several religions have emerged post-Visitation. Their naive dogmas range from believing that Christ was a crypto-lictor, to considering the Mimes a reincarnation of Vishnu, Brahma, and Shiva. The Interphasers, of course, keep a close eye on these fanatics. Just in case their enthusiasm and fervor create a problem.

In reality, we deal with more problems on this new utopian Earth every day: and they almost all have to do with the Mimes. No one says it, but we are actually something like Viceroys. Very comfortable, with power...but exercising it on behalf of another, and always taking the blame.

We head down Infanta, now almost entirely in the shadow of the titanic megars, towards the Malecón. My son and I flanking Kar. We have not activated our holo-disguises. There's no point in pretending to be civilians when we're coming with a Major General who is eight feet tall. At least he didn't come on horse today, which he is wont to do. They have no sense of restraint.

Kar is enjoying a chocolate mint ice cream as we walk. I suspect that he wants to show off that he could smell what Damián was eating before his arrival. The Lictors are capable of entering one portal... and leaving through another, with objects they did not have before: administrator privileges.

And how they enjoy ice cream! It is a curious fact. You would think that being in Cuba, they would prefer rum or cigars. They like them, yes...or the Mimes wouldn't be meeting in bars...but not so much.

People see us and move cautiously away. They don't smile, but they are all well dressed, most of them with Guild uniforms: Doctors, Maintenance workers, Salespeople...the Lictors have imposed order in society since the Visitation. Too much order, some think.

But at least now all the streets are perfectly paved and have no potholes. The sidewalks, bright and clean, have no cracks. The alien nanobots used by the Maintenance workers function perfectly. Nothing to offend the eye. Havana is truly a City of Wonders...like every city on Earth.

For many people, this is just surface decoration. Of an immense, pathetic, fake world...

My father always sighed, fondly remembering the filth, the dog shit, and the omnipresent puddles of the capital, prior to the Pax Lictorica. I never understood his nostalgia for that crap. But everything has a price in this world, like when they don't allow us to choose to buy something or not...

We soon arrive at the bar. Only the Lictors are capable of meeting for a drink at 9 in the morning. Many people believe they were nocturnal beings on their home planet. Or maybe they didn't even have a sun?

Maybe they didn't even evolve on a planet from a non-rational life form, like we did from the proto-primates. There are also some people who think that another race might have created them. And that's why they want to make our lives miserable with their fake kindness: because their "parents" went extinct before the Mimes could take revenge on them for forcing them out of their happy bestial life.

The bartender, Ana Betancourt, greets us at the door in her synthetic voice, "The impostor is still inside." She wears the tricolor cockade on the raised brim of her yarey hat. She is from the Jurash clan who are tuning their holo-costumes this week to heroines from the Wars of Independence.

Standing at the door I also see an Isabel Rubio, with captain's bars on her white blouse: "Can you identify him, or am I connecting the Authenticator Field?" she asks.

"No need, we'll manage," I swallow dry, imagining the effect that suddenly colliding with the real appearance of the aliens would have on my still inexperienced son. He will have to know the Big Secret at some point. Why not today? But, just in case, I order: "Officer Damián...wait for us outside, we'll be quick."

He stands mockingly at attention, already taking out his device. Kar and I enter the joint.

It would be easy to detect the impostor, simply by being attentive to Kar's reaction. He, of course, already knows who the offending human is as soon as he sets foot on the premises: not even the most sophisticated optical camouflage could trick any member of their species and their sensitive sense of smell.

He warns me, "This will be difficult for Karel, You. Perfume imitates the smell of our mutes."

A mute Mime is, of course, someone who can't emit smells at will. I'll keep it in mind. But I have my Interphaser pride. I pass among the tables slowly, and along the bar. Observing, attentive. Everyone drinks, some talk, others are just there, enjoying each other's company.

I had never been to this bar, but it's not exactly unfamiliar to me. Retro wave. My father once told me something his father told him, that by the 1950s, San Juan was already a dive with a thriving ecosystem of pimps, prostitutes, and cabaret musicians. Everything that the Revolution of '59 swept away, and then that shithole lost its atmosphere. For better and for worse.

But after the Visitation, its atmosphere returned...or took on another very similar one. No one knows why the Lictors prefer dives like this. I doubt it was so full in my grandfather's time, at least not this early in the morning.

I am checking out the patrons. One of the "social" problems of the Mimes is that when several members of a clan gather in the same place, they can fall a bit short of their human models. They can of course distinguish one another by smell, and so it does not bother them much that others come wearing the same appearance. Every scent is unique. The humans though are smell blind.

In one corner are three Orlando Masferrers, in their white suits and pistols at their waists. Kimaru Clan. At the bar, Rafael Trejo in shirt sleeves is talking with Farah María, in a sequin dress and feather boa. Sitting nearby, Orlando Figuerola, wearing shorts and cleats. A white unionist, a mulatto singer and a black athlete...Rulme clan, Nerje clan, and Yuber clan. The nuances are key in the complex culture of the Lictors. A good Interphaser must master them, or at least try. They also constantly change.

Near the bathroom is a smoking Indian and a guy with a machete, wearing a frock coat and wig: Hatuey and Pepe Antonio. Indigenous and Creole. Futera and Jowir clans. At the adjacent table, a mambi and a teenage girl with long dark hair, wearing shorts, high boots and a futuristic weapon on her belt. An animated Elpidio Valdés and Yeyín. Without doubt, Wita Clan.

Further down, the patrons are focused on their drinks, as if they have nothing to talk about. A slim mulatto in a guayabera, and a bald, slightly overweight white man in a wool suit. Wilfredo Lam and Alejo Carpentier, painter and writer. Qote and Ufel clans. Then, Fulgencio Batista and Vicente García, soldier and national hero, Tamul and Hugros clans...

I stop in my tracks with the uneasy feeling that I missed something. Then I smile, walk back, and rest my hand on Carpentier's shoulder, whispering: "It's better if you come with us outside, and quit your little revolution...imposter."

Luckily, he doesn't even try to deny it. He just sighs and whispers back, "How did you know, Lieutenant? My holo-suit is perfect...they told me it could do everything theirs could do. Did my Don Alejo fit me too tight, perhaps?"

Amazing, another one who believed that old black market story. Only the systems used by the Lictors can perfectly recreate someone's appearance from a few photos. Not even ours are that good.

But he knows the ranks of the police. He deserves the truth: "No, your appearance is fine. The problem is that the author of *The Kingdom of this World*, well, he was born in Lausanne, Switzerland. And, for that reason alone, a Lictor would never identify him as a Cuban writer. If they are anything, it is detail oriented."

"Shit! That's not fair! Don Alejo was more Cuban than most

Cubans!" The imposter stands up with such force that he overturns the table. Damn it. It must weigh over 2 hundred pounds. My hand is on my taser, just in case this gets violent. You never know, most civilians hate us.

"Calm down, sir." I advise him, slowly, "It's better for everyone if..."

"I just wanted to know what it feels like to be one of them! Do you understand? Is that a crime?" The phony inventor of "lo real maravillo- so" interrupts me...and throws his fist at my face.

And, of course, this is a crime. It is also a really bad idea, attacking an Interphaser: our reflexes are augmented to near the level of the Mimes themselves.

It still almost surprises me. I squat just in time so that he only knocks off my service cap. Bad for my reputation. You have to respect the Police.

So, ipso facto, I taser the bastard in the ribs. That's a full 7,000 volts for Don Alejo.

To my surprise, he doesn't faint...whoever sold him the holo-disguise ripped him off, of course: it's not even close to Lictor quality. The suit can't take my taser, and without wavering, the interactive hologram fades out...and then I'm the one who jumps back, avoiding the multiple claws and fangs...but I can't contain my scream.

"What the Fuuuuck!?"

I hate losing control like that. I hope Damián didn't hear me and come running to help. Because this imposter is actually one of the dangerous ones. I should have predicted it, when Kar told me about the perfume.

This crazy guy didn't just try to sneak into a group of Mimes wearing a holo-disguise. It's clear that he knows what the aliens really look like... and has surgically modified his body accordingly to resemble them with as much detail as possible. This is bad. For this, they will disintegrate him.

"What is it, Lieutenant? Don't you think the surgeons did a good job?" The monster challenges me, standing up to his full inhuman height of 8 feet.

The ancestors of the Lictors must have been quadrupedal carnivores, who ran with their toes, like our felines and canines. By adopting the bipedal position, which left their front legs free to manipulate objects, they retained the digitigrade characteristic of their hind legs, which adds at least 8 inches to their size. Like wearing size 60 shoes and walking on your tippy toes.

Furthermore, his enormous torso, bursting with bristles and spikes, reminds one of a cross between Hans, the Grimm's hedgehog-man, and a horror movie werewolf…purple with orange stripes, to make matters worse. Absolutely beautiful, of course.

As for his head, there can be no comparison to anything on the planet. With the triple jaws without supporting bones, the two flexible eyes-nose stems, and the ears spread out like three full sails, he looks like a mad doctor's hybrid of a carnivorous plant, the head of a bat, and a garden snail…but I fall short…because, he also drools.

His scaly hands, with five fingers and curved claws, have not one, but two opposable thumbs. A skilled group of people, those Lictors.

The whole thing is absolutely disconcerting…and rather disgusting. What kind of sick homo sapiens would want to look like that? And what surgeons from the underworld, with ethics at the level of paramecia, would accept money to help him achieve his absurd purpose? I'd love to get my hands on them, too.

There are very strange people in this world…and Interphasers end up having to deal with most of them. It's part of the job profile.

But since he's still conscious, I'm pretty worried. I try to bring our Pseudo-Lictor Carpentier back to earth. I know that Kar is not going to intervene. His role as a Lictor, assigned to an Interphaser, is limited to dealing with his own species. Not with imposters. This is primarily a human matter. A Mime interfering in human affairs would just give ammunition to the many anti-Lictor groups. And so: "Shoemaker, stick to your shoes!"

Filthy terrestrial politics…not even the Lictors did much to improve it. There really is no way out.

"If you resist, this will be worse. You know I'm authorized to use lethal force," I warn my super criminal, although I'm hesitant about drawing my pulse gun: the reactions of the actual Mimes are so fast, that if the fucking Frankenstein who operated on this faker even tried to match it, he could tear me to pieces before I managed to remove the safety. And with one hand…I mean, claw.

"Why do you serve them, Interphaser?" The monstrosity snaps at me. Thankfully, he seems more eager to be heard than to turn me into ground beef. "And don't tell me that the Visitation was good for humanity. Don't you realize that…they are destroying us?"

He has a point, obviously. But two can play this little game.

"Why do you imitate them, if you hate them so much?" I reply, quickly and inspired.

My father, the first Karel, always said that if they let you speak, they won't kill you: it won't be the first time that the dialectic saves me. The Interphaser's best friend...after his guns.

He growls in response: "Have you heard about the Chixcu...meteorite? Ugh, I don't know how to say it correctly."

"The one that made the dinosaurs go extinct, I think," helping out but trying to avoid being condescending. Not everyone has a university education. Nor are they Interphasers.

"Yes that's it," he confirms...and sighs. His mouth, modified by a scalpel to look like an old pre-Visitation drill jaw, is not exactly a pleasant sight. "Well, Lieutenant, imagine that a dinosaur might have looked up, while that murderous piece of rock fell from space, engulfed in flames. What do you think he would have thought...?"

"Damn...the fifth mass extinction event has arrived?" I joke, to ease the tension.

"Good joking...but I'm not sure that dinosaurs do thinking," Kar intervenes, at the worst possible moment, hopelessly ruining my peace-making efforts. They have the tact of a maniac.

The Carpentier Monster howls, beside himself: "Don't you say a word! You don't understand! It's a metaphor! Ok? The dinosaur would have found the meteorite that came to destroy him beautiful! So beautiful! Now do you realize the tragedy...?"

My brain works at full speed. I decide to improvise: "...and so...he would have wanted to become that falling light? Is that what you're trying to say?"

"Exactly!" the imposter approves, caressing his monstrous and prickly chest with his tremendous two-thumb claws that he exchanged for his hands from birth. "I'm sure that, even knowing that it was going to destroy him...the dinosaur LOVED the meteorite. Maybe he dreamed about what it would be like to be a meteorite. That's my tragedy."

And we're done. A psychopath with a supporting aesthetic philosophy. I only hold back my laughter because I suddenly realize that the entire bar is silent, as if every Lictor present was attentively listening to the madman. And they are taking it very seriously.

Back to work...

"Well...I've heard you out, now, come with me peacefully...meteorite lover" I tell him. And after a beat, "If this is your first offense, I promise to do my best to get you off with only a fine."

Of course I am telling him a blatant lie. With the way he looks, he'll be in the tank for the rest of his life. Which won't be long either...

unless he agrees to return to his human appearance, he will quickly be disintegrated. The Mimes are very strict about these things. They like their rules.

"I'm coming Lieutenant," he says, to my immense relief, and offers me his enormous wrists to handcuff him. "Because, after all…you're not to blame. Neither are they for that matter. No one's to blame. It's the way things are, simple as that: bad luck."

Well, the streets did not run with blood today: another case solved by the brilliant Interphaser Karel Valdés. Yes, even Damián obeyed my orders, for once, and did not enter! It looks like *Alien Challenge* is more interesting today than crime. That tentacled tyrannosaurus must be something to see, facing off with the Flower Wolves.

But…as the Russians say: it is a big mistake to sell the bear skin before killing the bear. There's nothing so perfect that it can't be totally fucked up in one second. I forgot to ask Don Alejo to activate his holo-disguise. Or maybe I ruined it beyond repair with the taser. It doesn't matter now.

What matters is that, when we leave, with him between Kar and me…Damián, who was focused on his device, sees him… and steps back, shouting:

"Whoa! A Flower Wolf…on two legs?!"

What an idiot I am! Why did I not think of that!

Everything nearly ended in tragedy, right there: before I could react, my son had his pulse gun out of the holster…and only Kar's reaction speed prevented him from blowing off half of our convict Carpentier's torso.

I will never tire of saying it: Lictors are truly intelligent. My Assignee doesn't smack Damián…which, with his superhuman strength, would have torn half his hand off, rather he begins disconnecting his holo-disguise.

In all honesty, I must admit that my kid did pretty good, thinking first, instead of getting carried away by his reaction. He may end up becoming a good Interphaser one day. He suddenly finds himself with two Flower Wolves standing before him, and instead of imagining that this is a pack attack, and firing energy pulses, he quickly realizes what is really happening…and lowers his gun, stunned and uncertain.

"The Mimes…are the Flower Wolves from *Alien Challenge?*" he stammers, unbelieving…and looking at me, in search of confirmation of this incredible discovery. "But, papá…so, all this time, they…why do they do this?"

And again Kar responds, before I do, and in perfect Spanish at that, "Why do we not show the humans our true appearance? We go to so much trouble to help them empathize with aliens who kill monsters. Because we are what we are...but it is not enough for us to be feared and respected by the race we have helped so much. We also want...to be loved. And we know that...it will be tough for them."

I add, "No human could love an angel...if they looked like a demon. That is the Great Secret of our benefactors, Damián. The one that only governments, and the Interphasers, know about. Because it would drive the general public insane, worse than if they knew they were eating babies for breakfast every day."

"I'm...sorry, Kar...I'm s-sorry...I-I didn't have any idea," Damián excuses himself, stuttering. It's hard to discover all at once how wrong one has been for so many years. I remember it well. It's embarrassing.

"You not worrying," the Copycat replies, returning to his usual macaronic syntax...and his absurd appearance as Ignacio Agramonte...before adding, sadly, once more in perfect Spanish: "Just think about this, my young Valdés: if the dinosaur loved the meteorite that he saw burning in his sky, as it fell to destroy him...who is to say that the meteorite did not also love each and every dinosaur that it was going to disintegrate with its arrival?"

The Mountains are Alive

Daniel Figueroa-Arias

Translated by Matthew David Goodwin and Antonia Carcelén-Estrada

Esteban felt along the trunk, looking for the next hold, while his other hand and his legs clinched in position. He found the hold quickly, and with both hands, he propelled himself to the next level. He climbed like this with relative ease as he ascended the great tree trunk to its top, his speed the result of climbing this same tree every time he came to the edge of the forest.

It was an old oak that had grown taller than its neighbors, or at least that is what his elders had told him. The knowledge of the names of plants and animals from this biota had nearly disappeared, like the forests themselves, all except for this mountain range.

From the top of the tree, he contemplated the flooded plain at the foot of the mountain. The water refracted the light of the morning sun like a kaleidoscope until it merged with the distant seashore. The rainy season had been long and generous. Slow and calm floods, without the avalanches that tear houses from their foundations or drag boats to their watery graves. Esteban even dared to dream that the weather would become more merciful, with cities that would grow green again, and mountains that would once again allow roads and railway lines to pass through.

He breathed deeply, filling his nose with the aromas of the forest and its humidity, while the sounds of a forest awakening chimed in his ears. To him it was surreal that on one side of the mountain, the forest was flourishing, while on the other side, the great forest had been wiped out, transformed into arid earth and cracked concrete.

He paused for one moment, a figure illuminated by the rising sun. Every two weeks he climbed the tree so that his old communicator could pick up a signal. Although they lived relatively close to the Caribbean Protectorate, the connection was so poor that they had to get close to the border, where the coastline just began to appear on the horizon.

The call came right on time as always.

The screen was filled with the image of a woman a little younger than him, brown-skinned, with short hair, colored braids on one side, and shaved on the other. Despite the stern expression, he swore that she had softened over the years.

"Sofia!" he exclaimed, a name that always brought a smile to his face.

"Esteban…" A shift of expression occurred, as if fear had suddenly materialized. "Shit, we should have worked on getting a signal to town."

"What's going on? Are you OK? Do you need anything?" Seeing her like this worried him. Although Sofia has a short temper, it was not normal for her to start their conversations this way.

"I don't know if it's too late. Shit! If you had a signal there…they're coming your way. Water claimers. We caught their transmission two days ago. Shit, they may already be nearby."

Esteban thought it was a misunderstanding at first or a false alarm, but he knew that it was only a matter of time before the claimers reached them. The claimers had attacked the sparse forests of the northeast for years, then the mercenaries withdrew, and they were able to take possession of some of the springs. In the south and west there was no resistance, since the forests were outside any protectorate. Nevertheless, their presence was fleeting because of the volatile climate and the rugged mountains.

They were the next most obvious target.

Sofia's voice brought him back to the conversation:

"Esteban, do you understand?!"

"Yes, sorry. Who are they? Where do they come from?"

"Based on their language, it seems to me that they could be from Central Europe or from the African League. The truth is that it doesn't matter, you have to go. Now! Go, and let them take everything."

These words hit Esteban's head like a hammer, leaving his mind blank. He swallowed before asking:

"Are you planning on doing anything? You have the capacity to respond. You once told me that."

Sofia answered with silence. He noticed that she was wearing the olive-green uniform of the Caribbean Protectorate she had joined five years ago.

"You're going to let them just walk in?" Esteban questioned.

"Obviously I complained to the governor, to the Board, I even sent a message to the League Council, jumping through the entire chain of cowards. As long as they do not directly attack the dock or a protectorate, they will not intervene…"

"They are afraid of them."

"They are cowards."

"Then I'm wasting my time talking to you. I'll call you later, as soon as we get out of this."

"Esteban, Esteban! Pay attention for once. We caught a glimpse of them at sea, it's not like the other times, it's not a stealth ship entering and claiming the water. This is a serious ship, a warship, and behind it is a cargo boat. They are going to take the territory and claim the entire river. Shit! And those imbeciles at the league only want to put out an international warning."

"Sofia, if the protectorate can't do anything for us, I need to go!"

She glared at him across the screen.

"I'm going out with a crew on the trail. It's all they'll let us do. Take the path and we will find you. You can live in the Protectorate. But you have to save *ita*…"

Esteban cut off the call and climbed down the tree, jumping from one branch to another. He didn't want to waste one second more on a conversation that could go nowhere.

He ran back, imagining the shadows of the claimers behind him. After crossing the ocean, they would come from this direction, to claim the resources they lacked in their blighted lands: water, a rich biota, terrain easier to tame and settle, perhaps a jungle with a mild climate.

Retracing his steps, he took the trail to the riverbank, where his boat was docked. He walked as fast as the landslides and brush would allow him, cursing that there wasn't a quicker way back. He felt the gun he carried in a holster. It was a disc gun that Sofia had given him a couple of years ago.

She was always given to violence, he thought. Now it was he who had the determination to use violence to defend his territory.

After several hours, he found the boat, secured not far from the shore and tied to some bushes. He opened the engine cover and put the missing parts in place. Without a key, or another security method, he decided to remove some of the vital parts and the firing pins for the batteries, to make sure that no one stole it.

Once the adjustments were made, he took it out in the river. The water was still at an adequate level, although the rains had stopped a couple of weeks ago. The boat was nothing like its ancestors that worked by internal combustion and propellers. It's engine was a replica of the high-capacity water hammer engines of the *skaters* that skittered across the ocean, though smaller sized and with less power. Once in the river, the current would enter through the tubes below, exiting at a higher speed from behind. Esteban started the engine and it started its telltale rattle, just winning out over the current. Esteban took a stick to test the level of the river ahead and keep an eye out for any suspicious objects afloat.

The sun came down on his shoulders. On other trips, he would have stopped earlier on the shore to have a snack and wait for the gentler hours of the afternoon, and so delaying his trip. That was a luxury he did not have this time. He took a long piece of dark cloth from his back-pack and tied it around his head to protect himself from the sun. He covered his nose to keep out the smell coming from the right bank. The land was wild there, covered with rows of meat plants from the riverbank to as far as he could see. Up close, he could see the tall yellowish-green bulbs topped with tough, thorn-like leaves. The plants on the shore were beginning to rot from all the humidity, permeating the environment with a sweet and nauseating aroma. Esteban considered it an absurd waste. Clearing the bank made the river cloudy, from the sediment and chemicals brought by the irrigation canals. It was impossible to fish for miles. However, that did not mean they were uninhabited. On the contrary, his worst fear was running into one of the armor-lizards who took advantage of the turbidity of the water to hide their enormous figures, stalking unsuspecting prey on the shore and near the surface.

This time, luck was with him, as his stick only encountered the dark fish that were fleeing as the boat passed.

The light began to shimmer, signaling the twilight hours, as he found the confluence that would take him home. The tributary became clearer as it left the plantations behind. Esteban loosened the fabric around his head to enjoy the cool breeze.

An annoying buzzing noise passed by his ear. Out of reflex he swiped at the air. Then he heard another buzz, followed by many more, as if in-sects were flying in formation around him.

"What the hell…?"

Esteban rolled up the sleeve of his shirt, revealing a black bracelet on his wrist. A small red light flickered on the side, indicating that the transmitter's battery had expired.

He felt very stupid. If it had happened to him while he was working with the raptor bees, he would be in a very dangerous situation. Now he only had to cover himself up with a blanket.

As night fell, he flashed a light outwards, anticipating danger, watching out for any sign that the invasion had begun. Then he noticed a caravan of boats moving in the opposite direction. They were moving away from a reddish glow that was just becoming noticeable ahead.

He sped up. He was afraid of coming across the survivors of his town in flight. But as they came closer, he realized that they were from another town, downstream from where he lived. Their boats were stacked with people and their belongings. He could see in their faces the unmistakable sign of those exiled from home, leaving behind more than they can carry.

He asked them loudly what had happened, and if the claimers had arrived.

Not yet, they answered. They preferred to flee and leave nothing for the claimers. Not a thicket or a patch of forest. If the river could catch fire, they would not have hesitated to do it, until all that the invaders could claim would be ashes.

As he approached the flames, the roar grew louder and the air was filled with smoke and ash. The entire east bank of the river was covered in flames. A serpentine line of bright fire was drawn in the blackness, heralding the night. Esteban's heart was overcome by the sight of the fishers' settlement. He gave the motor a couple of pulses, eager to get home and away from the fire as soon as possible, knowing that the claimers would be attracted to the flames.

He covered the distance swiftly, following the flaming 2-mile serpent to its end.

Dawn was approaching as he finally reached home. The river had overflown from the intense rains, flooding the plains and lakes, and creating a new still-water wetland. He approached the houseboats floating peacefully, protected by their anchors and floating foundations.

He noticed that all the lights were on in his house.

He docked the boat and headed for the front door. Upon entering, he was greeted by the wrinkled faces of the women and men, the elders of the family, and the arms of his mother that embraced him. He couldn't hold back the tears. Esteban hugged her back. At least at that moment, he could relax, he was home.

They first got caught up. The news had reached them just after he left, the day before. A fisherman rushed up the river, to bring the bad news: a gigantic warship, a sea beast, the likes of which had never been seen in those waters, had docked not far from the shore. Reports from the Caribbean Protectorate suggested that they were claimers.

"It was only a matter of time," Santiago said, running his hands over his old knees.

Several nodded their heads. First were the plantations of meat plants, to be consumed by countries where they could afford such things. Despite the fighting, in which Esteban's father had died, they ended up stopping them upstream, where the water was still somewhat clean. Sometime later, traders brought them reports from the other protectorates to the northwest, in the Pacific basin, and from the south, where there were still patches of forest that sheltered rivers and aquifers. Year after year, the claimers invaded, plundering whatever resources they could, with almost no resistance. Sometimes they secured long-term control of a small territory by making a deal with the respective protectorate or with the League of Autonomous Territories directly.

"It seems like this time will be different. From what Sofía told me, it looks like they are planning on occupying the territory for a long time," Esteban said.

"And the Protectorate? Will Sofi help us?" His mother asked.

"No, *ita*. The governor will not listen to her. They think those bastards won't do anything to them…"

Murmurs rose in the meeting.

"They were kicked out in the north! Remember Theo! He was with the group that kicked them out!" Manuel's voice prevailed over the murmur with the tone of someone who found a solution.

Of course everyone remembered the curious traveler who had passed through many years ago, fleeing from the government of the Republic of the Interior.

"It's been two years since we have heard from Theo and we sent someone to look for him at the Pacific…it doesn't seem like he arrived," Santiago said.

"Those guys were mercenaries," *Ita* said, repeating the same words with which she reproached Theo's decision to leave. "I don't know which is worse, the mercenaries or the claimers."

"I don't think there's much to do," Santiago concluded, straightening up. "We should do what the fishers are doing. Maybe it won't be so bad to travel north."

"With cannibal chiefs everywhere? I don't think so," Esteban replied. "If we leave, we will be refugees, with nothing…"

Screams from outside caught his attention. They all crowded outside, on the edge of the house's floating platform, while shining their lights on an approaching boat. When it docked in front of them, its two crew members pulled out something and threw it at the foot of the town council.

The flashlights revealed a dark figure, the size of a large bird. It had a pair of rotors on each side, with two armed ailerons. The sentries had shot it downstream, near the mouth of the river.

There was no more doubt. The claimers were coming.

***

The morning found them still together, even though there was not much else to discuss. Most agreed that leaving was the best option. Esteban repeated Sofia's message to them, that she was going to wait for them on the route to the Caribbean Protectorate. She would surely keep her word.

He wasn't satisfied with the solution, but he couldn't come up with a better plan, nor the words to convince the others to consider something else. It was a better option than going upriver to the estuary where the cannibal chiefs ruled.

While everyone was packing, an anxious silence reigned over the town, broken only by the noises of engines and oars. The river remained high and it looked like it would be for several days. This was an enormous help because they could now make much of the journey by boat.

While heading to the riverbank, Esteban looked at the faces of the townsfolk, and he could not think of a single one who had not been born and spent most of their life in the town. Some went to the Caribbean, others to the North Tempisque Protectorate, but they had always returned when they amassed the small capital they needed. He couldn't imagine living without his houseboats, his bees, and the river, and leaving everything behind.

"Bolo, do you think they will stop here?" asked his friend Elías. Elías was several years younger than Esteban. From a very young age he followed right behind Esteban, especially after his father disappeared during a raid in the mountains. Esteban saw their relationship as a brotherly one, forged by the sudden loss of their parents, although under different circumstances.

"That, Elías, is the big question," he responded, patting him on the shoulder.

For some reason he didn't tell him what he really thought, that in fact, no one could stop them, just like with the plantations. By the time they realized it, the mountain and even the neighboring protectorates would be a peaceful summer colony for the "settlers" from the other side of the ocean.

They climbed a small hill until they reached a clearing in the middle of the forest. Scattered about were the remains of the buildings and houses from the original town from the previous century.

"Wait, you brought the bracelets?" Esteban asked, stopping Elías at the edge of the area.

Elías raised his hands to show him a black bracelet on each wrist. Esteban checked that the lights were green. He also carried two more with recharged batteries, he assured Elías. The bracelets emitted an electromagnetic wave that kept insects away. If they ran out of batteries while working with the bees, the result would be fatal.

This is where they installed their apiary, far from the overflow zone of the river. Around the clearing were twenty large white boxes. They approached the closest one and uncovered it. The interior contained colonies of hexagonal cells, distributed erratically and connected by filaments of dark wax. The bees moved about, busy with their repetitive tasks, unaware that their world would soon be upended.

On a normal day, they would bring pieces of whatever meat they had to the hives, mostly fish meat. The predatory bees would feed and then process the remains into honey, the primary product the town traded. Everyone benefited, as the apiary allowed them to control the population of the bees, at least enough to keep accidental attacks to a minimum. Esteban was sure as to what they needed to do, and didn't see any point in feeding them. Should he just set them free?

A bee landed on his hand, calm though confused by the effect of the bracelets. He took the opportunity to examine her. It was a large species and its length exceeded two and a half centimeters. He saw the teeth that could tear flesh. The insect turned around before flying away, showing him the abdomen tipped with a long, smooth stinger.

Theo, when he lived with them, taught them how to tame the bees using the bracelets. He explained to them that this species was a hybrid, combing the vulture bee and the Africanized bee, and that it had spread and overtaken the region. Its aggressiveness and predatory behavior was one of the reasons why their forests had remained intact.

According to Theo, the hybrid was designed rather than evolved. Esteban fondly remembered the story: someone must have created them, surely the same ones who created the wargs and the armor-lizards. Theo closed his lecture on the subject: "God does not give wings to the poisonous animal."

Remembering this phrase gave him inspiration. He turned to Elías: "Don't give them the meat."

Elías remained motionless, making a gesture of not understanding what Esteban was asking.

"Throw it in the river or let the others take it," Esteban said. "The important thing is that the bees don't find it."

"They'll die of hunger by tomorrow," replied Elías. "And you know how violent they get when they have to hunt."

"Absolutely. Okay come on!" Esteban pointed the way back. "I want you to come back with Fulan or Ana, whoever you can bring. You're going to need help. Move the hives and hide them in the forest, but not too far from the clearing, about ten steps, no more. Move as many as you can."

"Oh, oh, oh, I get it, I get it."

Elías ran towards the boat and Esteban quickened his pace to catch up with him. At this emotional moment, Elías might just leave without him.

They returned to town. Elías took the boat, and soon arrived back with a boy and a girl on board. Esteban recognized them, they had already helped him before with the bees. He handed them the bracelets, one for each of them. They were going to need as many bracelets as possible.

His mother was gone. He could work without having to explain his plan. He unpacked his communicator and spread all the bracelets on the table. He checked their batteries and then linked them with the admin program on the communicator. He reprogrammed their frequencies, but left two with the original frequency just in case.

The small team returned in a couple of hours. With preparations nearly complete, the people remained quietly in their houses. They would leave the next day at dawn. Esteban still had another task for Elías and the kids. He handed out the reprogrammed bracelets, and they returned to the clearing to disperse the altered transmitters among the hidden hives.

***

The long march began as planned, and the air was dense with anxiety. At the vanguard were the fastest boats, including Esteban's, that would act as scouts. They were a human shield, in effect, since the claimers could fire on them from a distance. They would buy time for the others to escape.

After an hour of travel, the scouting crew discovered a beach. They landed and waited for the rest, their hands gripping their weapons. One by one, the other boats arrived and disembarked. The wait was torturous. All they could do was speculate about what time the claimers would arrive.

When they were all gathered, a few boatmen continued on, towing the empty boats with them. They were going to hide them in a tributary. The first armed group advanced by land, following the trail towards the remains of an old road several miles long, where the Protectorate was waiting for them. The bulk of the group followed them, keeping the young ones safe. The stories of the claimers' treatment of young people were well-known, starting with the rape and ending with the sale of meat to mercenaries. Another armed group closed the caravan.

Esteban tried to stay with his friends in the last group. When the group continued on, Esteban said his goodbyes. Elías and the others knew Esteban's plan. They were confident that he would join them the next day and, if it worked, he would bring them good news.

Esteban entered the forest. After several hours, he finally reached his destination, not far from the forest clearing. He hid in the remains of a concrete building that was barely noticeable among the vegetation. When he entered, he saw a tree lying on the ground that had opened a basement door with the force of its fall.

Esteban descended to the deepest part that was still covered. It was dark and damp, invisible from the outside. As a precaution, he took out his cloak from his backpack. He ran his hand through it, feeling the smoothness of the fine, almost translucent threads. Sofía had given it to him the last time they saw each other. He covered himself with it, hoping it would work against the remote sensors as well as she said it would.

He was awake when the explosions announced the coming of the claimers. Taking care to keep himself covered by his protective cloak, he emerged from his hiding place and climbed through the remains of the building. As he came out, he could see the columns of fire and sparks rising above the treetops in the direction of the river. He crawled a little further to the remains of a wall where he took cover.

The forest transformed into a dance of shadows as the bright flames swam over the water. The idea of setting the river on fire was roundly approved. They filled some of the floating houses with homemade napalm. These fuckers always wiped out every sign of a town's existence. Now they would have to deal with a river that would burn them.

Esteban stayed still, trying to make them out. He heard and felt the footsteps, marching with metal plates that crushed the ground, and he saw the silhouettes of giants moving among the trees.

He was terrified, but when he looked up he saw something hovering that was truly horrifying: a massive shape silhouetted against the background of stars in the clear sky. It was too high to determine the material it was made of, and he couldn't make out any others details, only its colossal size. It was a monster whose wingspan covered the sky, and with its job finished, it was patiently flying back towards the coast.

Esteban quickly returned to his hiding place, tightening the invisibility cloak around him and hoping that it would be enough to hide him from these beings whose nature he felt was inhuman. He knew about the world outside, beyond the river and the Protectorate, but these monsters were completely beyond his imagination.

By dawn, the explosions had stopped, and the sounds of footsteps were scarce. He gathered his wits and crawled out of his hiding place.

He left wrapped in his cloak. He climbed the rubble of the building and, almost crawling, approached the perimeter of the forest clearing. From a good distance, he verified that his assumption had been correct, that the claimers were setting up camp there. He gained more courage with the light, when he realized that he was confronting humans after all.

He began to crawl to the place where they had hidden the hives. He had to get at least six feet from each group of bees for the communicator to link with the bracelets.

This brought him dangerously close to the claimers.

He began to hear the conversations in a foreign tongue. The women and men of the crew were tall, with skin so white that it shone under the tropical sun. From his position he could count about eight who were walking outside of their titanic and dark armor. This would help his plan.

He managed to activate the first group of bracelets, the one closest to him. The buzzing of the bees became louder and deeper, indicating their aggressiveness. Just as a certain frequency of the bracelets pushed them away, another enraged them, a function that Esteban had almost forgotten because of its disuse.

He crept to the next group. He noticed a couple of large tents and various equipment set up towards one side of the clearing. When he reached the second group, and activated it, the buzzing already sounded of anger and hunger. He noticed that the invaders began to yell what he assumed were profanities as the bees began to sting them.

He continued along the edge of the clearing. Only the furthest group at the opposite end remained. He felt pain in his knees and arms. He figured that the fabric of his pants was in tatters, and the branches and stones were scratching his skin.

On that side, near the shore, he noticed the mechas. They were nine-feet-high and humanoid. Various devices protruded from them, and Esteban identified many of them as weapons. Most unique were the armored tanks on their backs, designed to retrieve water from any source. Water that they could sell to the highest bidder who wouldn't ask where it came from.

After a trip that seemed to last forever, he reached a good distance from the last group and activated the bracelets. Then he noticed a buzzing sound, different from that of bees, more rhythmic and sharper.

When he turned around, he encountered a drone hovering just steps away. The same kind they had knocked down the night before. He instinctively reached for his disc gun and discharged it, not knowing if it would be effective or if he would survive to see the result of the attack. The thin circular blades were ejected from the barrel. The drone seemed not to know how to react and by the time it tried to rise, a couple of discs managed to damage its propellers and front camera.

Esteban threw caution to the wind, got up and fled.

But he only took a couple of steps before he felt a blow to his side. Overwhelming. He thought he could feel metal. The mecha had caught him with a wide swing, throwing him against a tree.

His vision blurred. The pain squeezed his lungs. The mecha lifted him with ease, making him dizzy. He fought to remain conscious. Whatever was going to happen, he wanted to take it head-on and awake, despite the unbearable pain from the mechanical embrace.

Surprised faces greeted him at the camp. The crew chattered among themselves, amused at the sight of the little intruder. A man emerged from the largest tent, barking orders and motioning for him to be put down. The soldier operating the mecha obeyed, placing the intruder as gently as he could on the ground.

The man, who seemed to be the leader of the crew, pulled Esteban up and nearly dragged him to his tent. Esteban didn't resist, speechless by the pain he felt. The man sat him down and began to ask questions. Even if he could have understood their language, the pain he felt on his side would not have allowed him to speak. The man noticed his expression and went to a cabinet, took out a large needle, and stuck it without mercy into his neck. Esteban screamed when he felt the shot, but then gave way to the narcotic relief.

No longer in pain, he was able to think about the situation more clearly. Judging by the equipment, the tent was the control center of the camp. He had lost his backpack, the cloak, and everything in the attack. He only had his pitiful clothes and luckily one of the bracelets in repulsion mode.

He stared at the man in front of him. Pale eyes looked back at him sternly. The expression on his smooth face was indecipherable to Esteban, without any clue as to the customs and manners of these foreigners.

"Hey, who are you?" The man asked, in a primitive version of Esteban's native language.

Esteban didn't answer. In the utter silence, only a malevolent hum could be heard.

"What are you doing here?" The man came closer to Esteban, exhaling rotten breath into his face. "Where are the others?"

Esteban shrank in his chair, trying to think of a way out. The man stood up, his face flushed with anger and his muscles tense. Esteban was sure that the man could kill him with a single punch.

Then a bee landed on the man's cheek. He did not notice until the animal attacked. With a loud slap, he turned it into a black stain on his hand and a trickle of blood began to run down his cheek.

Esteban wondered if the bee had a chance to inject its venom. The foreigner looked at him full of rage, and then pain. Another bee had attacked him, this time from behind. Then another attached itself to his leg, followed by a dozen more attacking his flesh. The tent was filled with insects.

The man turned and with groggy steps headed towards the door. His skin took on an unhealthy reddish color. The bees still ignored Esteban, but he didn't want to push his luck. In that state of aggressiveness, his one bracelet might not be effective.

He left the tent, and found total chaos governed by the black cloud that covered the camp. The war song of the bees vibrated through the air, a primordial cry demanding their bounty of flesh. Some of the crew ran back and forth trying to shake off the bees stuck to their skin as streams of blood ran down their faces and arms. Others had already fallen, including the leader of the crew, turning into vibrating black masses of bees biting flesh. Esteban continued to feel terrified even when he saw the success of his plan. He had seen bee attacks in his life, but he had not imagined a massacre on this scale.

The mecha that had captured him was in the center of the camp, shooting a stream of fire from the flamethrower mounted on his right arm. Esteban had to duck to avoid the flame, and then he ran, hoping to escape in all the confusion. The mecha took a few steps towards him, then paused. Esteban ran towards the river, wondering when the claimers' bomber would return.

Even deep in the forest, the hum of bees and the screams of the dying filled the air. But beyond these, he heard other hums that were louder and coming from the sky. Then came two explosions, one close by, in the camp itself, assumed Esteban whose skin prickled with the shock.

He didn't stop running. He didn't want to find out what the explosions were about or in which direction they were coming from, he just needed to get away from the camp. He found himself following the riverbank. He heard distant explosions and other indistinct noises.

He stopped to take a breath when he could only hear the everyday sounds of the river and the forest. He had run along its bank far downstream, where the water was beginning to get cloudy.

At that moment, he heard footsteps approaching. He was about to run again, but the mecha stepped in front. He dove to the side, dodging the arc of the mechanical arm that swung around to grab him. With a couple of turns, he got some distance from the Claimer who then raised his arm and the mouth of the flamethrower.

The Claimer had stopped close to the shore and the waters of the river bathed his metal feet. Before either of them had realized it, the entire mechanical arm that was aiming the flamethrower at Esteban had disappeared into a titanic maw.

The armor-lizard had been sneaky. It probably was lurking underwater until its prey appeared just at the right spot. Esteban witnessed a unique battle: the animal dragged the mecha towards the river, they struggled, then the mecha punched the lizard with his free arm, but the gray-green scales withstood the impact without a problem.

The beast shook the mecha about. He tried to turn and free his arm, without success. Bits and pieces of metal flew through the air, accompanied by water and mud from the bottom of the river. Suddenly, the fight seemed to end with the retreat of the lizard.

The mecha stood victorious, but a second later, long rows of teeth gripped the mecha's cockpit. The lizard pulled the mecha backwards and the fight continued underwater. Esteban saw the limbs of the armor slapping on the surface.

Through the splashes, he heard the crush of metal.

A minute passed, maybe less, and silence returned. The beast had won and was dragging its trophy to its aquatic lair.

Esteban turned towards the forest and walked a few steps until a stab of pain forced him to bend over and fall to his knees. The narcotic had lost its effect. The pain was worse than before, and it took his breath away. His vision and his mind began to blur. The last thing he heard was unintelligible voices.

***

When he regained consciousness, he first noticed the softness of the cot and the warmth of the blanket on his body. He opened his eyes and everything seemed veiled by darkness. Over time he recognized shapes. There was *ita*, whose touch was so familiar to him. He recognized Sofía, who came to see him from time to time.

They talked to him, and he answered them, but he could only whisper.

It wasn't until the third day that he felt more awake, but with every movement he would discover a new broken bone or some bruise on the skin. That was a good sign, it meant he was alive, and his head was working.

Ita and Sofía spent the most time with him. The rest of the town stopped by the tent occasionally to check on him and express their gratitude. It had worked. Better than he anticipated. Of the claimers, only shapeless mounds remained, covered by frantic bees that tore and chewed flesh. A couple of survivors retreated north alongside the river, where the cannibal chiefs would surely take care of them, if the armor-lizards didn't catch them first. Regarding the bomber, as it was headed towards the claimers' camp, Sofía and her group shot it down with electromagnetic pulse grenades and mortars.

The following week, the visits were more sporadic, with everyone trying to reestablish a new normality. Even *ita* spent more time organizing the tasks. And there was a whole camp with six mechas to reclaim now.

Sofía came into his tent one afternoon as it was lightly raining.

"The warship pulled up anchor," she said, a satellite radio in her hand.

"They completely gave up? Just like that?"

Although Esteban wanted to believe what he had just heard, prudence advised him to be cautious.

"The port radar reported it. We also sent out *skaters* and they confirmed it. The warship raised its sails and solar panels and is fleeing at full speed."

Had the bees intimidated them so much? He kept asking himself in disbelief. The last titans on the planet, who could afford to leave their machines behind, were expelled by the inhabitants of a forgotten mountain in the middle of the American continent?

No, not just any mountain, he reconsidered. Their mountain, its rivers and forests, had defeated the claimers.

"Well, you look much better. We'll leave the hospital and the equipment here." Sofía approached the edge of his bed, placing her hands on his hands which rested on his chest. Esteban couldn't remember a time when she had held his hands.

"Are you thinking of leaving now?" he asked.

"Not yet. The airship fell not too far from here..."

"Ah! Still up to your tricks," Esteban let out a laugh, reminding him of his broken ribs.

"No, I'm afraid not," Sofía laughed too.

Esteban saw the face of the girl who five years ago had crossed these lands, heading to the coast, in search of refuge.

"You're in our territory, you wouldn't ignore the commission, right?"

"You can't be serious. Which territory? The town is devastated," she objected.

"We'll build again, on top of the ashes, as we have always done. But this time, we'll listen to you, and build higher. Oh, and I want one of those satellite radios. I'm tired of climbing trees to talk to you."

"You know what? It would make me happy to know that I'll have you a little closer."

Sofia smiled playfully and placed the device on the table next to him. She took his hands in hers again.

"Sofi, do you think they'll come back?" Esteban's expression darkened for a few moments.

"When they go back home with their story of meat-eating bees and giant lizards in the rivers, I don't think they will have much desire to return. And anyway, we'll have six mechas ready and waiting for them."

True, he thought. For people accustomed to the endless buildings in the Old World and the underground arcologies, to see how jungle life can defeat them must have been daunting, to say the least.

"We'll get the six mechas ready, Sofi," Esteban added, pointing to himself.

"Okay, you can have them," she agreed. "But you're going to share them with the Protectorate, right?"

"Of course… after we get rid of the plantations and clean up the river."

And Esteban smiled again, with the expression of someone who dreams of new worlds built on the remains of the past.

Tropicopandemonium

Eugene Speakes

"Te amo," he said.

I know. It's basic, but that's what he said. Okay… the dude was not a poet. We can't all be fucking Byron. He loved her, and he never said anything he didn't mean. That should count for something. His name was Esteban, but everyone called him Tebo. He was an aspiring chef and a damn good cook. He specialized in Caribbean Fusion… whatever the hell *that* means. His only other passion was Helena. She was *not* an aspiring chef, but she dabbled in baking and could make a decent mofongo… none of which is relevant in any way to the story. She worked as a sign language interpreter for the government. *That* part is kind of relevant. Whenever the governor had some important speech, Helena was on the scene to help translate all his political bullshit.

Anyway… they had been going out for a while and Tebo thought it was time to express his deepest… whatevers. They went for an early morning drive up to Mirador Gavillán in Guaynabo. It overlooked all of San Juan and other parts of the metropolitan area while surrounded by lush hills and other… naturey stuff. It was a pretty romantic spot for professing one's love. Luckily, they were the only ones there, so they could let the saccharine babble flow. Their feelings would echo across the hills like… Oh, who am I kidding? I'm also no Byron.

Helena had no time to answer Tebo's lyrical proclamation, seeing as how one of the adjacent mountains exploded in an ominous purple blaze. The air grew hot as a legion of alien starfighters shot through the sky above them and started bombarding the city below with more explosive... purple... high-tech... plasma... laser... shit.

The noise was deafening. The starfighters looked like flying conchs and sounded like chickens in heat. The explosions were gut-wrenching in ways their guts had never been wrenched before. The couple held onto each other, watching in horror as their island was laid to waste by God-knows-what. Tebo, though stunned, was a stoic guy who remained eerily calm during dire situations. Helena... not so much. She wasn't the kicking and screaming type, mind you, but she would go into a kind of shutdown-reboot thing. Once she was able to process what was going on around her, the adrenaline would kick in, she'd take a deep breath, tilt her head to one side until her neck cracked, then proceed to handle her situation. Right now, though, she was frozen.

Suddenly, a squadron of jets as colorful as La Perla came blasting through the clouds. These were definitely from Earth because they had the letters CDF painted on the sides, not to mention the fact that they were shooting at the alien ships. Normally, a dogfight between aliens and humans over a major Puerto Rican city would be enough to make the average person shit blood. Puerto Rico, however, had been hit by a slew of disasters in what felt like a cruel cosmic joke, a satirical onslaught of madness and calamity. After the one-two punch of Hurricanes Irma and María, there were earthquakes, heatwaves, droughts, Sahara dust, gargoyles, leptospirosis, rampant political corruption, and power outages every damn day of the week... to name a few. By the time Covid-19 reared its ugly viral head, it almost felt... expected. The only real question was, "What could possibly happen next?"

Tebo's instinct was to run to the car, but Helena just kept staring at her surroundings... immovable. She was definitely in shutdown mode. That's when the big, black helicopter landed. It had a huge government seal pasted on the side. As soon as the ominous transport found its footing, a serious man in a serious black suit jumped out and beckoned them over with hastening gestures. "Miss Helena Canino?!" he asked over the roaring of the blades. "Are you Miss Helena Michelle Canino?!" he repeated.

Helena took a deep breath. She did the little head tilt Tebo recognized as the tell-tale sign she was focused and ready to move. "Yes," she answered.

"I need you to come with me," the man in black said.

"Who *are* you?!"

"My name is Agent Segarra. It's a government matter, ma'am. You're needed at La Fortaleza, immediately."

If they were going to the governor's mansion, it must've meant Helena's services were required. But… the attack *just* happened. How did they locate her *and* get to her position so fast? Something told her this had nothing to do with sign language. Fuckery was afoot. She looked back at Tebo who simply shrugged. It wasn't customary for them to hop into strange helicopters with strange people but, considering the clouds were on fire and an alien invasion was underway, they decided to climb aboard. "Wait!" Agent Segarra yelled while pushing against Tebo's chest. "Who is this?"

"He's with me," Helena answered authoritatively.

Segarra hesitated but could hear something explode overhead, "Get on!" he ordered.

They took off just as a CDF jet slammed into the Mirador. Tebo looked down to see his Toyota Yaris tumble into a massive hole where the lookout had stood mere seconds before. He only had three more payments to go on that car… which is as irrelevant as Helena's mofongo. The devastation was unparalleled. As they flew over the city, the images below were like something out of a movie… the kind of movie with no real substance but crazy special effects. It was a dismal display of wanton death and destruction. The helicopter managed to steer clear of the actual battle zone, dodging the occasional missile and alien purple shit.

As soon as they landed at La Fortaleza, people began scrambling left and right. Helena and Tebo were led into a small room where Agent Segarra introduced them to a small man. He wore a grey suit and introduced himself as Emilio Melendez. He was a lawyer of some kind. "Miss Canino?" he asked. "Helena Canino?"

"Yes," Helena answered. Didn't she just have this conversation?

"I'll be brief. Time is against us, and we need to reestablish a functioning government as soon as humanly possible. You see… it turns out that many of our politicians have either been killed or revealed to be ummm… aliens."

"I'm sorry?"

"Aliens… from another planet, living among us for… The point is, the line of succession has been exhausted and *you*, as far as we can tell, are the next… in line."

"In line for what?"

"To be governor."

"Governor?!"

She turned to Tebo who just shrugged. She went through the predictable bit about not wanting the job and not feeling qualified to lead but, as Mr. Melendez said, time was short, and the details of that whole conversation would take too long to write. Suffice it to say, she had her moment of doubt, shed a few tears, took a deep breath, did the little neck thing, and asked, "What do I have to do?"

"First, we have to swear you in," the lawyer said. "Let's see. We have witnesses and… can someone video record this? Good. We need a bible! Does anyone have a bible?"

Again, people started scrambling. No bible.

"Carajo!" the lawyer spat. "Anything! A book! Any book! Are there no books in this goddamn place!? It's the governor's mansion! Didn't any of these fucking people read?"

"I have this," Agent Segarra said, pulling a raggedy old copy of Playboy from his inside coat pocket. Everybody stared for a moment.

"What?" he said. "Don't judge me!"

"Fine!" the lawyer said. "Give it here. Oh, Christ! Could somebody bring us some gloves!?" Gloves were brought. "Thank you. Now, Miss Canino, if you would kindly place your left hand on the cover and raise your right hand."

Even through the gloves, the cover felt… moist. "Ay, fo," Helena whispered.

"Ugh. This is absolutely repugnant. Let's just… Are you ready to be governor?"

"I guess."

"Ok, good. You're the governor. Somebody, take this away," the lawyer shouted while holding the dilapidated porno mag by the corner. "To the situation room!" he added.

***

The couple found themselves in a large room this time. It was filled with computers and monitors and things that went beep and boop. There was a huge screen on the back wall with all kinds of maps and moving dots; it was a nauseating bunch of flashing red arrows and cheap graphics representing some ongoing catastrophe in the Atlantic. A middle-aged fat man with a scruffy-looking beard stood at the head of a long table. He was wearing a *Godzilla* t-shirt and dirty jeans. He had a long stick to point at the mess on screen. He was me.

After sharing the ordeal of having their date interrupted by an alien invasion, I confessed. Just like poor Miss Canino, I had been suddenly promoted to Head of National Security from my previous job as a freelance graphic designer. I'd done a few promotional pamphlets for some government sponsored 'Save the Manatees' crap, and now I was figuring out how to coordinate our dwindling resources in some half-assed attempt at saving the island and all its people. You see... it wasn't just aliens. Oh, no. This was some kind of supernatural, inter-galactic, trans-dimensional, mind-bending, mythological clusterfuck of ungodly design.

It started when most of the island's politicians had suddenly shed their skin like the scum-sucking lizard people they were. They slaugh-tered as many humans as they could before disappearing into the sew-ers. Not long after, a giant flying saucer appeared over the middle of the Atlantic Ocean. Yes. A flying saucer, straight out of some low-bud-get 1950's sci-fi, horror flick. Hundreds of little conch-shaped ships launched from its underbelly and started attacking the island.

In response, a secret organization, known as the Caribbean Defense Force, leapt into action. Its sole purpose was to safeguard the Caribbean from any major threats to the islands therein. They usually operated in secret, but this was too big to handle from the shadows. Puerto Rico was the only island that refused to join the CDF because... our politi-cians were lizard people! They were obviously afraid of exposing them-selves, so they declined at every turn. This, of course, did not stop the CDF from coming to Puerto Rico's aid. Led by a man named Admiral Moses, the CDF made immediate contact with the remaining humans in La Fortaleza and asked for our permission to "engage the alien hos-tiles over civilian airspace" and other such military jargon. That's about when Helena and Tebo came into the story, so... you're as up to date as we were at the time.

As I continued my debriefing, attempting to bring the new governor and her hastily assembled staff up to speed, things got even weirder... and worse. We watched on the huge screen as the flying saucer let out some kind of... electromagnetic... microwave... gamma pulse... thing that brought the Colonossus to life.

***

Okay. The Colonossus. Let me see if I can explain this hideous piece of shit.

A few years ago, one of our esteemed gubernatorial lizards commissioned a giant statue of Christopher Columbus. He wanted it to rival the Colossus of Rhodes, a vulgar display that would welcome all arriving ships into the San Juan Harbor. Of course, this didn't sit well with a lot of people, seeing as how Columbus, or Cristóbal Colón as he is known in this corner of the Caribbean, was an asshole. A historical asshole, to be sure… but an asshole, nonetheless. Despite various protests and the usual bit of sabotage, the statue was erected. It was the *stupidest* thing ever constructed on Puerto Rican soil. It stood right at the entrance of the bay. Its feet were attached to two massive underwater pillars. This gave the illusion of Colón standing on water, like some twisted messiah… a monument to the colonizer and a mockery of the colonized. It was so freakishly big; the tallest cruise ships could slide under, in between its legs, with room to spare. Hundreds of thousands of tourists would look up at the Colonossus and be greeted by a spectacular view of Cristóbal Colón's gargantuan metal taint.

Anyway… the bronze behemoth came to life. It pried itself loose from the pillars attached to its feet and climbed up the side of El Morro where it began rampaging through the streets of Old San Juan. Thankfully, it missed La Fortaleza on its way toward the tourist district. It kicked the shit out of the Capitol building and threw the dome out to sea. It tore through El Condado, knocking down hotels and expensive restaurants. After laying waste to Miramar and parts of Santurce, it shifted focus toward the banking quarter in Hato Rey. CDF jets tried to take it down, but their guns had no effect. It also didn't help that the hippopotamic fiend started shooting laser beams out of its eyes.

All hope seemed lost when a giant coquí suddenly jumped out of the Martin Peña Channel, landing right behind the Colonossus moments before it struck La Milla de Oro. Not that it mattered. As soon as the metal menace turned around, the giant frog let out its signature mating call. Normally, the average coquí, no bigger than a quarter, lets out a cute little whistle to attract a potential mate, but given its abnormal size, this towering iteration released a high-pitch cry that shattered windows and toppled buildings. It was enough to knock the Colonossus on its back. Expensive car alarms went off as a mile of banks were reduced to a pile of corporate compost. This was not your average Tuesday.

Agent Segarra came into the room with a message from a young lady claiming to be linked to the coquí…psychically. Yeah. Why not? We let her in. She claimed to be in her early twenties, but she looked like a toddler that spent too much time at the beach, a salty tan with sunbaked locks. Her name was Sarita, from Vieques. Long story short, the coquí was a product of all the bombing that was done in Vieques by the U.S. Navy. Sarita, also infected by the same reactants as the coquí, had maintained a child-like appearance but also developed some kind of mental connection with the beast. "His name is Coquira," she said. "He wants to help." That's right. Coquira vs. The Colonossus. I needed a cup of coffee.

***

We were being hailed! Admiral Moses came on screen. After a quick round of introductions and unnecessary pleasantries, he spoke. "Madam Governor, seeing as how our weapons are ineffective against the giant metal man, we will continue our defense against the alien starfighters! However, they continue to spawn from the flying disc at an alarming rate. We *could* divert the squadron to target the saucer, but that would leave the island vulnerable to remaining hostiles. We cannot afford to split the team either as we are already spread too thin. We do have sea-faring ships on the way, but the seas are unusually rough and…" he paused.

Tebo could tell Helena was starting to lock up again. Her voice trembling, she said, "Please, stay with the island. We'll figure something out for the… ummm… flying saucer."

"Hold," Moses interrupted. His eyes widened as he read through an updated report. "I have hideous news, Madam Governor. One of the alien vessels was shot down over the National Cemetery in Bayamón. It is leaking some type of purple fluid that seems to possess certain… reanimation properties."

"Reanimation?" Helena asked.

"The dead are crawling out of their graves."

"Zombies!?"

"In a manner of speaking."

Yup. Zombies. I shit you not. What's worse, as soon as the aliens caught on, they started crashing their own ships into other cemeteries… including The Santa María Magadalena de Pazzis Cemetery which was walking distance from the governor's mansion. The dead were rising, and they were on their way. We had no time to prepare. Explosions echoed around La Fortaleza.

"Ummm, Miss Governor?" Sarita, the coquí whisperer, said.

"Yes," Helena choked.

"The statue is shooting at us now. Coquira is trying to slow it down, but it's definitely headed this way."

"Que mierda," I said. I curse a lot… especially when I'm nervous. It's a defense mechanism. Leave me alone.

"Get the governor to safety!" Moses yelled. "We will reestablish communications once you are all safe!"

Everything went nuts! We tried to go out through the main gate, but the roads were blocked. The zombies were here. Agent Segarra pulled out a gun and started shooting at the living dead. He'd seen enough movies to know to shoot them in the head. Coquira and the Colonossus were only a few blocks away! We were forced out the back and through the San Juan Gate which led to the entrance of the bay. Segarra shouted into his headset, and a few seconds later, five speedboats came charging around the corner. It wasn't easy, but we all managed to climb aboard before the giants and the horde reached us. I found myself on the same boat as Helena, Tebo, Segarra, Melendez, and Sarita. Good thing too. The Colonossus shot its lasers at the other four boats, incinerating them into ashen lumps of floating crap. Coquira knocked the monumental menace onto La Fortaleza. So much for *that* fucking place. A throng of zombies climbed all over the clashing titans like a cluster of rabid spiders. The behemoths rolled over the edge and into the burning bay below. We were lucky zombies couldn't swim. At least… I *hoped* they couldn't swim. I *prayed* they couldn't swim. The wake of the titans' fall sent our little boat spinning. Our driver was thrown from his seat into the water. As the boat spun around, his face got caught in the propellor. I peed myself a little. Not my proudest moment. I don't even know why I wrote that. Ignore it. God, help us.

The fight was insane! It was a monumental back and forth of punching and kicking, a brawl of unfathomable scale. Towering waves crashed with every step until they both went under and… silence. The waters grew still. Our tiny boat had been pushed further into the bay. The sky was ablaze all around us. We could hear the battle beyond the clouds, but no sign of the struggling giants. "Oh, no," Sarita said. "I can't hear him."

The boat began to sway more aggressively with each panicked breath. The Colonossus slowly arose from the depths, steam billowing off its head. This thing was pissed. It looked straight at us, its eyes lighting up for the kill. A thunderous cacophony of booms echoed behind us. I half expected the CDF fleet, but it was just one ship, an old ship, a piratey-looking ship with a triskele on its flag. The volley of cannons was enough to knock the Colonossus off balance, forcing it back into the ocean, but it would get up again… soon. The magnificent ship pulled up alongside us and a rope ladder cascaded down for us to climb. No one spoke. It was an awkward climb, but we managed. Once aboard we were met with a crew of… cats and dogs. Oh, what the fuck was this?

"Welcome aboard the *Andariego*!" we heard. We turned to see a dangerous looking woman with an eyepatch and a cigar. She was dressed, more like draped, in various fabrics. A handsome leather satchel hung around her shoulder with an engraving of a turtle on the flap. She smelled like adventure. She seemed quite old but well preserved by salt and sea. "I am Captain Georgina de Lourdes, but you can call me… La Capitana!" Her breath was fire and rum. I tried to introduce everybody but… "Avast!" she cried. Who still says 'avast' in the 21st century? I'll tell you who. Georgina de Lourdes, Captain of the *Andariego*.

"Capitana!" one of the cats called out.

"Pray, Monsieur Villanelle, what ails ye?" she answered.

Yes, it was a talking cat. All the animals onboard could talk. Just… just go with it.

"The creature, it stirs," The cat continued.

"Excellent work, Villanelle! Lady Haiku!"

"Aye, Capitana!" answered a magnificent white Akita.

"Prepare the Foe Knuckle!"

"It will be done!"

"Mr. Elegy!"

"Oh, Capitana, mi Capitana," answered a rotund cat with a hint of sarcasm and oodles of attitude.

"Secure our guests. Things are about to get… gruesome."

The stout Mr. Elegy tied very tight knots around our waists and secured the lines to various points on deck. "Wouldn't it be safer if we went *below* deck?" Melendez asked the plump feline.

"No," Mr. Elegy answered.

"Why not?"

"Because this is what La Capitana ordered, you fool!"

"Mistress Couplet!" the captain continued. "We're going to need something extra special for this titanic barnacle fart! Bring me Neptune's Balls!"

"Aye!" a luxurious black cat meowed. She went below deck and dragged up a massive chain shot; two cannonballs chained together.

Normally, the balls on a chain shot were smaller than the average cannonball, but these things were huge. They also had an ethereal glow about them, a subtle hint of green.

"Torn from the scrotum of the sea god himself!" La Capitana boasted. "No stronger material 'neath the blazing blue! Load 'em up!"

Mistress Couplet, with the help of the great white dog, shoved the chain shot into an equally massive cannon at the bow of the ship. The Foe Knuckle. All manner of ancient text was etched along its iron cast. Whatever it was, it was no ordinary cannon.

The Colonossus had fully risen, a few zombies clinging to it like ticks on a hairless rat. As it turned to face the *Andariego*, the *Andariego* turned to face *it*. Once again, its eyes began to glow. Agent Segarra cocked his gun although he knew it would be utterly useless. Sarita wept for Coquira. Melendez passed out. Helena had completely shut down. Tebo looked at me and shrugged. I threw up in my mouth a bit. "Mr. Limerick!" La Capitana said. "The Foe Knuckle is yours! You may fire when ready!"

"Aye, double Aye, Cap'n!" said a dwarf Irish Setter. Mr. Limerick took aim. He focused squarely on the left eye of the Colonossus. He would not fire until he was sure he could not miss. The inscriptions on the Foe Knuckle lit up. Incorporeal voices whispered all around the ship. Mr. Limerick let out a tiny, suppressed bark… woof… and fired. BOOM!

Neptune's Balls tore through the air and found their target! "Heed the wrath of a thousand souls, the denizens of Locker's hold!" La Capitana roared. "Leviathan's curse upon thee, ye syphilitic worm!" A whole chunk of the giant's head exploded! It howled, a metallic screech. Was it in pain? Could it actually feel? Did I give a shit? No! It wriggled and writhed as it staggered its way back on land. Its remaining eye was extinguished. It was blind. Things started unraveling inside it, twisting and churning. It let loose one final cry, then froze. It stood in an awkward position before falling onto the Treasury Department.

***

It was a short-lived victory. All that shaking and fighting, and giant wrestling had taken its toll on some of the older structures in Old San Juan. One of the most famous, La Garita del Diablo, simply crumbled into the ocean below. Now… the reason this thing was called The Devil's Sentry Box was because a buttload of Spanish soldiers kept disappearing from the isolated post. So much so that many believed the soldiers had been taken by the Devil. Yeah. Silly old Spaniards. They had placed a seal on the garita's floor, chanting and praying to keep the Devil from ever returning. Silly superstitious men. Well… they were right. Now that the seal was broken… a large portal *did* open up, and a hundred demons escaped! Good times!

Thankfully, the demons flew inland, and we had a moment of repose as the captain and her crew checked the ship for damages and leaks. I couldn't help but stare at the water for signs of… "Oi!" Mr. Elegy yelled, "What are you doing?"

"What? Oh. Nothing," I said. "I was just wondering if…"

"If what?" he hissed.

"If zombies could swim."

He glared at me with feline contempt. "That… is the most ridiculous thing I have ever heard," he spat, "Now, if you don't mind, I have work to do and you are standing in my way… fool."

I was both insulted and relieved. Not wanting to further interfere with the portly cat's work, I decided to take a walk around the deck. I directed my attention to Sarita who was still mourning her friend. "I'm sorry, kid," I said. "I know what it's like to… actually, I have no idea what it's like to lose a giant telepathic frog… You know what? I'm just gonna shut my mouth. If you need anything…" She nodded. I turned to Tebo who was sitting silently next to Helena, his hand in hers.

"How is she?" I asked. She seemed almost catatonic.

"I'm not sure," he answered, worry in his voice, "She's never been like this for this long."

My phone rang. It was Admiral Moses. I put him on speaker so everyone could hear. "Madam Governor, friends… A team of CDF paratroopers captured an alien somewhere in the sewers of Carolina. They have successfully interrogated the creature and have uncovered some vital information that may aid us in our plight. Apparently, thousands of years ago, there was a great battle over Atlantis… Yes, *the* Atlantis. A race of lizard people had invaded our planet and Atlantis stood as humanity's last bastion against annihilation. As you all know, Atlantis was destroyed… but not before downing the alien mothership somewhere in the Atlantic. All we know is that the arrival of the flying saucer and your reptilian politicians have something to do with this tale. We believe the saucer was sent to rescue the aliens that have been hiding on Earth for millennia. We also believe they may be attempting to resurrect the mothership which must be buried somewhere on the island!"

Did you get all that? Yeah, it's a lot of exposition. I know. It spooked La Capitana who ran below deck and started rummaging through old books. But wait… there's more.

"Good news, Madam Governor!" Moses continued. "I have just received several reports of small pockets of civilians fighting against the lizard people. It also seems… Ahem. A host of winged demons have started attacking the alien starfighters! And…apparently, there have been sightings of strange creatures aiding against the zombie incursion. Forgive my pronunciation… Chupacabras, Vejigantes, Vampiros de Moca, something called a Garadiablo, and a Gargola, it seems. I have no idea what these things are, but we have an army! Better still, this frees up my squadrons! With your permission, Madam Governor, the CDF would like to engage the saucer while we have the advantage!"

Helena was still not moving, so I stepped in. "She got hit with… some debris… in the neck so… she can't really talk… but she's nodding yes."

"Copy that! I will pray for her swift recovery! Moses out!"

It turns out the demon host was composed of all the Spaniards taken by the Devil from the garita. In an attempt to flee the flaming torments of the chitlin pit, they rushed through the portal as soon as it opened. Seeing the chaos before them, they believed that helping the people below would absolve them of their sins and lead them down a path to redemption. Hey… it's a start. Oh, and if you're worried about the portal… don't be. An awesome group of Wiccans sealed the tear.

I can't really explain how our local legends came to life, but who cares? The tides were turning and that was enou…

BWAAAAAAAAA!

What… in the *hell*… was that?

***

BWAAAAAAAAA!

It sounded like a row of lunar-sized tubas. It was enough to wake Melendez. "Que carajo?!" he yelled. Everything shook. I mean… if you told me it was the second coming of Christ, I would've believed you. It wasn't. The winds began to howl. The sky grew dark. The waves in the bay turned gray and became unusually aggressive. "Raise the mainsail!" La Capitana shouted, "Mr. Tanka, take the helm!"

"Aye, mum!" answered a tiny calico who was somehow able to steer the ship.

"All hands!"

"What's going on?" I asked.

As she aided the crew in prepping the sails, she explained, "My dear fellow, I have dedicated my life to the study of the deep. There is only one ocean, and she is vast. Her secrets are many. The fate of Atlantis was known to me, but 'tis often hard to separate fact from fiction. However, when Admiral Moses revealed the truth behind your little invasion, I knew the stories to be true!" She turned to the calico cat, "Full sails! Get us out of this bay, Mr. Tanka! Post-haste!!!" She looked back at me, an experienced fear in her eyes, "I wasn't sure, but I am now! I suggest you get on that phone, immediately, and call the good Admiral! He was only *half* right. If legends speak true, and I've no doubt they do… the mothership is not *on* the island. It *is* the island!"

BWAAAAAAAAA!

Andariego had barely made it out of the bay when the island began to rise. La Capitana pulled out some kind of canopic jar from her weathered satchel. She held it close but did not open it. She was getting a feel for the wind, the ship, and the currents beneath. There was definitely a pull against the *Andariego* as the island rose. You know… water displacement or something. Fortunately, the ascending mothership was rising slow enough for *Andariego* to escape the pull and avoid getting sucked underwater. We sat back in terror and awe.

You see… according to La Capitana's books, the mothership was like an upside-down triangle. The pointy part was buried deep within the ocean bed, causing the floor to crack, and creating the Puerto Rico Trench. The base of the triangle, or in this case the top, was eventually covered in dust which became soil and so on and so forth. The lizard people had stayed underground for ages. Taino's arrived, settled, and history as we know it began to unfold. As the industrial age set in, the lizard people perfected a form of camouflage, a second skin, allowing them to move among us. Their lifespans were ridiculous. Some were thousands of years old. Those in government simply swapped their human shells every generation to stay in power. We had been voting for the same damn lizards in different skins! Our entire society was… bah! Enough! Let's get back to the main story.

We heard screaming in the distance. We watched in abject horror as we realized all the inhabitants of the island were going to get sucked up into space or drowned if they tried to escape. There was nothing we could do. Segarra asked if it was possible to stop the ascension with another set of Neptune's Balls. La Capitana said the mothership was too big and, even though he was a god, the mighty Neptune only had the one pair. A crippling melancholy washed over us as we slowly sailed away.

"Wait," Sarita said. "Wait… I see cold. I see wires. I feel dark and light. I smell power. It burns. I follow the scent!"

"What the hell is she on about?" asked Melendez.

"Room!" Sarita continued. "People green! I see room! Ball shining light! A spinning source! I break it! Smash it! Boom! I sing! I SING! COQUÍ! COQUÍ! COQUÍ-QUÍ-QUÍ- QUÍ! He's alive! I can feel him! My friend is alive!"

Deep rumblings bellowed from within the rising super structure. It started to crack. Flames shot out from various points. Chunks of rock and metal began to peel off, plummeting into the sea. The mothership ground to a halt and hovered for what seemed an eternity. It was blowing up from the inside! The walls burst and Coquira came flying out with a spiraling purple flame behind him! He dove into the ocean giving *Andariego* a much-needed push.

"Kraken's crack!" La Capitana shouted. "That was amazing! Remind me to… Wait." Her eyes darted left and right as she came to a terrible realization. "By the seven bastard sons of Aegaeon! Everybody, get below deck!"

"Why," Segarra inquired. "What's going on?"

"The mothership. She's about to come down, and I have a feeling it's going to do so a lot faster than when it came up! We are about to ride the mother of all tsunamis, ye bacon eatin' landlubbers! Get below… NOW!"

"Stay above! Go below!" Melendez protested, "Why can't she make up…"

"Capitana's prerogative, you fool!" interrupted the round Mr. Elegy, "Now, go!"

Sure enough, the island came down and the waters rose. "All hands!" the captain yelled. Her crew assembled. "Listen hard, me lovelies! We have a choice to make!" The furry troop listened intently. "We can trust our fate to the unruly wave, or we can try to outrun the son of a narwhal's turd!" She held up the canopic jar and the animals went wild. "So be it! We summon the breath of Shu to speed us on our way! We'll probably end up in Portugal by the end of the day!" She laughed, a hearty laugh, a challenge to the ocean's might.

"What!?" Melendez cried as we all descended into the main cabin.

Tebo helped Helena down the slippery steps. He was beyond worried. She had never stayed locked up this long before. All he could do was continue to stay at her side and wait. The rest of us picked a corner and sat quietly with bated breath.

Georgina de Lourdes, Captain of the *Andariego*, shattered the canopic jar, releasing the spirit within. We couldn't see what was happening, but we could certainly feel it. Boards creaked as our speed increased. I could hear La Capitana singing ancient shanties with the crew. Well… *she* was singing. The rest was a terrifying symphony of caterwauls and howls. My ears popped! Was I bleeding? The sound of tearing sails was disconcerting. The pressure was intense. I could feel myself losing consciousness. How fast were we going? Holy shit! Everything went dark.

***

The island had fallen back into position, a tad askew but pretty much where it had been before. A full night had passed, and the sun was slowly rising. The landscape was different and those who survived were tired, afraid, and hungry. People were confused and in need of answers, guidance, desperate for hope. The zombies had been bested. The creatures of legend and folklore had returned to the realm of myth and imagination. The demons had been absolved but would have to do hard time in Purgatory. The CDF had obliterated the flying saucer, and the last remaining alien starfighters were vanquished. Still, the people were lost. A leader was needed.

The *Andariego* emerged through the early morning fog like a phantom, solemn and weary. It made port in Isla Grande where we all disembarked. No one said a word. The sight was apocalyptic, and moods were grim. Helena walked ahead and stared at the rubble which was once Miramar. It was a place she frequented often, and now it was nothing but a collection of twisted metal and dust. Tebo thought she'd reached her breaking point. She'd been shut down for way too long. He feared she may never come bac… Oh. Hang on… She took a long, deep breath. Exhaled. Again, a long deep breath. Exhaled. She tilted her head to one side and cracked her neck. Tebo's face lit up. "There she is," he thought. She turned around, looked me dead in the eye with fiery determination and said, "Ring up Admiral Moses, please."

"Yes, ma'am," I answered, slightly intimidated by her sudden shift in demeanor. "Admiral Moses, sir. I have the governor for you." I put him on speaker.

"Admiral Moses," Helena began. "Your help has been invaluable, and we are forever in your debt, but I'm afraid I must ask for your support one more time."

"Go on," the Admiral said.

"I formally request you consider Puerto Rico's admission into the CDF."

"Granted," he answered with a smile in his voice.

"Excellent. You may begin recruitment and training as soon as possible. Your indomitable spirit will be most vital to our recovery. I would also request your assistance in exploring the megastructure beneath us… the so-called mothership. There must be stragglers lurking in its depths, but that is not what interests me most. Surely, there are technologies to be uncovered and much we can learn to advance our islands in the future. Any and all discoveries will be shared with the CDF and our Caribbean cousins. No doubt the tsunami has caused severe devastation to our neighboring isles. They must be taken care of as well."

"What about U.S. interference?"

"We will deal with that when the time comes. This is *our* island… above and below. Besides… I'm pretty sure the United States won't be the only country interested in our latest… development. We must be prepared. Captain Georgina de Lourdes!"

"Argh!" La Capitana answered.

"The Jones Act will no doubt be heavily enforced, so we might need a little bit of good old-fashioned smuggling to get things done. At least for a while. Would you be interested in mustering up a little fleet to…"

"Yes. Yes, I would," the charming captain grinned. "Huzzah!" A chorus of barks and meows came from the *Andariego's* deck.

"Mr. Melendez. You are obnoxious, but… I'm going to need an obnoxious lawyer to handle… well… the world, once they start trying to plunder the island of its new resources."

"Oh, I can handle that," the feeble lawyer said. "You see, I can deal with *those* kinds of monsters. Just not the giant ones… or the alien ones… or the undead… ay, carajo…" He passed out again.

"Sarita."

"Oh, yes ma'am," the tiny girl answered.

"Coquira is safe?"

"Yes, ma'am. He's waiting for me so we can go back to Vieques."

"Make sure he knows he has our undying gratitude. There are those who will try to take hold of our island by force. I was wondering... should we have need to call upon Coquira again..."

"We'll be there!"

"Cool," Helena winked.

"Cool!"

"Mr... ummm. I never quite got your name." The governor was talking to me.

"Oh, it... it doesn't matter," I said.

"I'm going to need a name if you are to continue being my Head of National Security."

"Oh, fuck no. I'm done with that shit. I think I'm gonna take off. You know... wander the island and the rest of the Caribbean... try my hand at writing or something. Lord knows somebody's gotta tell this crazy story. Besides... Segarra's a better choice for the job. He's got some real skills. I mean, did you see how he shot all those zombies in the head? He didn't miss a single one! Plus... he knows how to wear a suit."

She turned to Segarra. "Get rid of that creepy magazine in your pocket and the job is yours."

"I would be honored," the new Head of National Security said. "You don't have to worry about the magazine, though. It blew overboard when we were... never mind. Agent Segarra, reporting for duty."

"Mr. Gutiérrez!" the governor said. Who the hell was Mr. Gutiérrez?

"Yes," Tebo answered. Oooooh.

"We've got a lot of people out there who need to be fed. I can think of no better person to gather whatever resources we can muster and create a healthy regiment to feed those in need. You will coordinate with medical personnel... which we need to find... to help distribute medicine and food across the island. Can you handle that?"

"Yes, ma'am," he smiled.

"My friends, this will *not* be easy. We have faced adversity before but nothing like this. We need to get the message out that help is on the way. We will keep nothing from the people. They need to know everything that transpired here. They need to understand. Make no mistake. Our goal is *not* to return to the way things were... but to become something new. Something better. Let's get to work. Oh, and Tebo..."

"Yes?"

"Yo también te amo."

Libertad

Lysz Flo

My hoversilla wooshes to Mami and her bot Yan Carlos, and I help gather some of the café alongside them to sell at the Mercado Agricola Natural in Ponce, La Perla del Sur of Puerto Rico. En el Mercado todo es criollo — I can trace our fruits to specific cities and neighboring farmers based on flavor, feel, and size: the Quiñones quenepas, Fransechi's mafafos and root vegetables, Norma Lugo's sweetest of mangos, and the list goes on. Even Pueblo, now carrying Rosa's parcha and coffee beans, and my mother's own harvests direct from our finca, keep our campesino lineage going.

Mami was the first to combine our ancestral knowledge with the tech from the now failed colonizer state. After multiple tries and coming back to the Isla to work with some of our primos and their panas in Tech programs, we finally got in touch with others who had been doing the work in isolation. She worked relentlessly until everything aligned like a perfect puzzle. Now it is the core of our island.

Mami is teaching her new robot to tend to the finca she has behind the house. I hear Yan Carlos following her back and forth, supporting her harvesting parcha in her advanced age. I call out to them, "Mami!" and I whoosh in my hoversilla even faster down the fields of Mapen among other fruit trees. Out of breath, I gasp "it worked it worked! Papi looked at me when I was in the memory a few moments ago! I didn't even do a proper ritual like Wela would have instructed." She raised an eyebrow. "Mija—even I couldn't program espritecnologia to do that.

You sure you're not seeing things? Staring too long at these projections and screens? Te borra la vista." I grit my teeth at her dismissal. "What if, what if you *could* one day talk to Papi?" She pauses mid step towards the coffee beans. "Ay, no sé. I—think I'd just want to hear him again and see him smile, for once, and hope he's found peace where he is."

I listen intently to Mami and know in my still saddened heart I'd like to show Papi how it became my life mission to be a part of our liberation. Somehow, I ended up following his footsteps, with Mami in the espritecnologia forefront. The sun beats down on me—my fro the only shade I receive. I look around at our field that leads away from our mini hacienda. In the Draftian era, it was illegal for a Puerto Rican to own farmland, even if they had deep generational roots here, for local trade and consumption. Who would have ever imagined that tourism could stop being the only source of income? Our imports and exports are now Caribbean first, and the sobrajas are for bidding wars amongst the rest of the world.

Before I hover away, as Mami and I are both lost in thought, she says "didn't you ask me once, what would you like to see if Puerto Rico was free? Y Mira" she points towards the fields, then eyes me amused, she nods and I know I'm at the precipice of something, and so I rush back to the Pericuarto, where I dig into the depths of espritecnologia. I am a manifesting generator. My life work has been dedicated to anthropological restoration through technology and stretching into the spiritual realm a little further each session.

I light candles and dim the electrical lights. This time — I know I must do a ritual. I conserve energy and think about LUMA and how we used to lose light so often that all we had were candles and generators for light. Luckily, LUMA was sued and banned from Puerto Rico. PRLA (Puerto Rico Luz y Agua) is now run by the people of the island. We have been working our best to rely only on solar energy, and I am currently working on a new electricity system to ensure that every single Boricua and Caribeño citizen has access to water, light, and e-backups. This is one of the fundamental goals of La Gran Reclamación. As a result, the colonial companies have been absolved, after being held accountable.

Africa and South America have been our green test collaborators and are moving in the same direction. I think about the connections across the globe as I surpass this IV and reach into the espiritu portion of espritecnologia. I take cornmeal, cascarilla, and a bit of Gran Bwa that was grown in a lab to reforest Haiti. We are so high in the mountains of Ponce that I can almost see the beginnings of Hispaniola. I begin to intuitively draw Veves around the room, my hands speaking with the ancestral element of this technology, revisiting and reimagining what is possible within memory.

Memory is a root. It is the way back. People, places, aspirations. It is a teacher, a way to trace myself. Sometimes I wonder what Papi would say if he saw us. All of us —the Caribbean as a place of refuge for her children and her children's children. Libre. Memory is a place I come into for my own work towards liberation and communal remembering through our espritecnologia.

The cascarilla glows beyond the sun replicator bulbs—this is where all of the tech, lespri, and memory collide. En el Pericuarto, I turn on the touch screen wall and let the projector shine as I code this morning's memory. Memories that I only replay within this room —tucked away and sacred.

The most beautiful possibilities for freedom come from the place of yearning within us. It's where they took root within me—even after the ongoing grief of displacement that rings throughout my generational and personal lifetime. I leave my hands dusted white from my drawing the Veve's, a continuation of the ritual, I head to the touch buttons and the image plays on the wall sinuously through projection and an outline of something more—I've learned to not tamper with memories—lest I modify how I remember or forget something that I can only see through the auto-recorded sessions.

"MAYRA, play auto-recording numero 111111" MAYRA, the IV or Inteligencia Virtual and smart house is named after my mom, the original visionary. MAYRA says "Vamos allá" as she begins re-projecting the memory I went into this morning.

No one knows I have mastered the coding of past memories, apart from Mami and even she, the original creator of espritecnologia, is skeptical. Why does she resist? I snort at her hesitation as MAYRA processes coded memories and numbers into a tangible visual. A snapshot of a memory shows Papi in a different heart-wrenching moment: his laughter, him sitting with Mami Tomasa, and Mami Virginia, and now with my discovery of the correct combinations I get to make new codes. I pinpoint the conjoining of code within espritecnologia where I can delve further into memory.

I time-warp to the past — tasting the pâté in the Little Haiti Marketplace in Florida— and there he is in all his 90s splendor. My memory I have been able to program into being situates me with a view of Mapou's bookstore, framing my back when I was 7 or 8. The limitation is my own memory and all I can remember is the Haitian Marketplace that housed me within the delicious realm of korosol o kachiman ice cream. Papi always bought me Haitian treats while he went off to dream and discuss freedom in the front with friends. The bookstore is a small treasure trove filled with Haitian books exploding from the walls, organized streams of politics, history, and fables on the floor, and tables and shelves leading revolutionaries, poets, and intellectuals home.

Papi comes into 5D view with that usual look—the one he gets when finding new ways to go about freeing Ayiti from the Tonton Makout. Words we don't repeat aloud but we all know. In between jokes and insults, there are traces for freedom. Haitian music is layered into the background.

Here I hold my breath hoping that what happened earlier today goes a little bit further. My nervousness fills my belly, and my heart is pounding. Even my hands go cold in anticipation and fear. Who knows what spatial imbalances I could be causing by potentially bridging spirit and reality. I rely on the feel of the metal behind my legs supported by my hoversilla to keep me steady.

Papi takes a sidelong glance. This memory is a warped home of a non-digitized future. I tap onto a few more buttons and Papi heads over to me—the originator and observer of the memory. He gets closer and materializes—almost solid. The memory becomes a distant background of young me crunching, with the paper bag holding pâté, sometimes meat, sometimes aranso, sometimes, sigh…I am forgetting my words… bacalao when Kreyol eludes me. "Pita'm" Papi says cutting my sigh short. "Papi—," my worlds falter between emotion and isolation from language. "Papi—" I try again. I have been losing all the pathways to Ayiti. Almost all that is left is my DNA as the indicator of whose lands I belong to, whose child I am and where the islands reside within. "Ou se pitit Ayiti. Pitit Borinken." With glistening eyes I steady myself and say, "Papi, today, they are sanctuaries."

Papi turns to me this time and his eyes focus on me in a way no memory has. This gives me escalofrió. I have communed with memory and spirits before but not *this* way. Not sharing the same time and place.

Papi looks at me and my heart lifts into my throat and sinks into the pit of my stomach. His eyes slit in curiosity, wondering how far he can go into the room and away from the memory, and he steps out of the memory and now we are both leaving the visual memory as a background. Papi looks as if I could almost hold his hand. I figured out the syntax to activating the espri portion of espritecnologia. Frozen, I keep watching in satisfying awe.

He says my name and I look at my shaking hands to see if I am still pressing buttons. But I am so still —*we* are so still in our staring. We move closer to each other intuitively. My unsteady hands linger midair to caress his head absentmindedly as if decades have not gone by. The image of Papi seems to have a solidity, not quite hologram, not quite a tangible being. He stands among the Veves and my heart fills with old forgotten tears that reach my eyes. His eyes respond in kind, glassy with unshed tears. *How? I ask myself, caving into myself, becoming grief-stricken teen, becoming child. "Papi?"*

Papi Ervai looks around confused, thinking, *How did I cross the veil to see my daughter and her pressing buttons on strange machines? To standing in an altar room filled with motion pictures of memory? The spiritual rules on this side of the veil are clear, and I have never appeared in my daughter's subconscious, but now...I see long nails and her fingertips reaching. Could I hold her hand once more? My heart sinks, I am still a spirit. What I'd do to embrace my dear Bijou again.*

He glances around "kote'm ye?" I smile watery and alight, "Papi you are in the future. I have so much to tell you." He looks around and scrunches his eyebrows, and thinks, his mind racing, *How can I not know her face. Ah her face, says she has lived a difficult life. My pitit. I left her behind so young due to my own grief getting the best of me. My illness worsening. I was so angry for so long that it ate me alive. But what is this, place? Feels like a home not too far from my own land. There are so many screens, like out of a futuristic movie, yet here the veil emerges from the Veve crested from our own Lwa. How did she know of this ritual? I see her expecting eyes. And I wish to truly be here with her. What has life brought my daughter for such grey hair?*

He nods, his eyes light up, crosses his legs and says "di'm." He beckons me closer. I sit at his feet on my hoversilla in front of the combination techno-holographic altar. I breathe and I smile, the room temperature adjusting to our mixed emotions by opening the windows, letting the filtered sunlight come in.

"I didn't do it on purpose but I ended up walking a path similar to yours. Your dream of Liberation became my own desire and dream. It kept finding me no matter which road I took." I take a moment staring at his face. He tries to touch my face but his large fingers only whisper slightly in a cool wisp of air against my skin. It is then I realize I am uncontrollably weeping. He laughs and cries too. "Look at us," we say together. He turns to the window, and I wonder if he is angry or embarrassed, or like me, overwhelmed by so much happening at once. He attempts a step towards the window while remaining near enough to the Veves.

"We're in... Borinken!" he exclaims. "I know these mountains!" The coquis echo lightly in the background. He wipes his face and he turns to me and gets closer to where I am seated. "Krik," I say to break the ice, now being able to switch roles with Papi the storyteller, and I get to tell him the story of La Gran Reclamación.

"Krak," he responds—his eyes shiny even with the tecnomagia sheen.

I take a deep breath, "After the year 2500, all of the children of the diaspora came together with those of the island, family members, lakous, and organizations. We bullied France into returning the money our ancestors paid for with their freedom. MRKA crumbled from the inside out. When they said "Go back home," Mami, I, and most of the children of the diaspora took it seriously. I visit Ayiti often, working to restore the home in Ounament.

"Bijou," I hear Papi say in awe, but also I see that something in him falters. We have a moment of silence for all of the rage and suffering, and so much loss. He looks at me with the visceral nature of his grief for the many Ervais he could have been and the lives that he could have experienced, and then I meet his stare. "Now, yo entiendo. All of it, every single yell, fight, Papi I don't know what it was to be in your shoes, but my own path was filled with much struggle. Your struggle defined what was possible for me. A seed planted."

He sees me as who I am now and not as the 15-year-old he left behind. "This is where spirit and science collide." I lift my hands to this Pericuarto and I bow my head to the altar and look up at him. Our hair matches the same shade of grey and are having their own conversations of time. I am the same age he was before he transitioned at 49. He frozen at 49 when I last saw him, and I ageing in his absence.

"Wi," I say in a more solid voice that still trembles, after my uncovering of this sleeping and hidden ancestral science. He asks me "koman?"

"Avek majik sa, Puerto Rico has overthrown their corrupt governments, exiled the leeches looking for tax evasions, and we found a way to survive the poaching of *progreso*, which was really just an attempt to murder the island with gentrification and colonial occupation. We are still fighting, but we also have relationships with all the nations of the Caribbean who have rejected their colonizers and reclaimed their autonomy. Ayiti received the 62 billion euros of reparations from France as a people and as the first Free Black republic. No one can buy us out of the neighborhood nor our own Ayiti. We are on our way."

He smiles this large dazzling smile of pride. His eyes water, overwhelmed with so many lost, so much heartbreak, so much blood and suffering though now perhaps a thing of the past. To wish to experience it, to know about it in his after-lifetime—"mezanmi," he touches his short fro'd head. In awe—"me-zan-mi."

"Miyami?" He asks and I know he asks of Little Haiti. The home to so many of the diaspora. "Ti Ayiti has rehoused thousands of Haitian elders, children, and businesses of the Diaspora. The fight against gentrification, won—Nou kale yo! The Mapou Bookstore still remains and is larger now. He smiles proudly. "Sa bon, bel petit mwen." His voice is a booming caress. We sit for a moment. Allowing the grandeur of fulfilling dreams to really sink in. Something that has taken over a thousand inter-generational years is now better than any imagining.

"*MEMORY - SYNTHESIZING IN 10 SECONDS*," MAYRA says. My eyes glisten as I look at the fading Papi – "If only you could see Ayiti now," I say to Papi, as the memory is changing to a setting with his best friend, Manno, conspiring and discussing memories over legume, diri blan, and pieces of griyo.

"*5 SECONDS.*" "Ok ok MAYRA. Dale. *gracias*"

We temporarily wonder if this is it, if I may not see him again, and I panic. Reaching out, he places his slightly fading hand over mine. He panics a bit too, I read it in the rounding of his eyes and gasping of his mouth. I send a message to Mami via Yan Carlos so he can dictate the message, "Hurry! You won't believe me so come see!"

He looks around—looking for her. I get a chirp back, "L'ap vini. I pinged her robot." I smirk. He raises his eyebrow and I respond in kind with a small shake of my head. "Pale'm de manman'w" his smile warm. "She is the genius of all this, I only perfected a piece of it. Mami furthered the visions of liberation by ensuring sustainability and going back to basics. Together we fought for Ayiti to become a powerhouse of natural energy resources by taxing the colonizers who had been reaping the rewards."

It feels like the earth is acknowledging these changes in the Caribbean by reducing the number of hurricanes and earthquakes. Our infrastructure of bio-metal, the indigenous methods of eco-farming, and cemento, have helped sustain the islands and provided access through these Yan Carlos-esque rescuers when we humans can't get through. I hear the door open and stop talking. I float my chair back to watch them take each other in.

She walks in sun-kissed from working in the finca, supported by Yan Carlos, as she's in her 80s. She stands looking at me and looking at Papi. Silence. "Oh," she gasps, covering her mouth awestruck and says "Dios mío, como va ser?" She leaves Yan Carlos behind. Getting closer to where Papi stands in the room. "Dear?" he asks without needing an answer. "Oh," she says again. She tries to touch him and his fading hand; I attempt to solidify him with my own silent swipes of buttons in the background and in attempt lengthen our time with Papi through my sheer audacious will. He solidifies a bit more than he did at first. Their fingertips touch just barely but enough. She looks back at me, her mouth now open in disbelief, and then back at Papi. He sits to be at her eye level. "If I knew I'd see you I would have brought you flowers." She laugh cries, "I have a farm of flowers like all the ones you gave me throughout our life together." He laugh cries this time, "Of course you do." Looking at them now makes me wonder if this was how they were when they first met in their early 20s. Mami asks, "Have you found peace?" He smiles dotingly and I quietly leave them. My heart is about to burst, and I wish them to have the same intimacy and time alone I got with Papi, for however long the ritual allows.

I leave my sacred Pericuarto, and hover back outside to our finca and into the sun. Hoping the grief and joy we carry is held by the rays. I think about all the advancements of El Gran Reclamación that have alleviated a lot of our poverty and reignited the passion for public education, folk trades, and spaces for genius of all kinds. As I glide my hands through the mindfulness of gathering café I get notifications from the Comunidad that the continents of Africa and South America have agreed to our Green Test collaborations and are moving in the same direction toward the Todo Criollo movement. My basket overflows with coffee beans, and my hands smell of slow dawns and midday catching up on the Pueblo after buying La Lotería from the 8th generation Chencho who sold them to my grandmothers.

I wonder about Mami y Papi, a little anxious for them but also so proud at being able to offer this moment to them. But you never know, maybe this new technology will do more harm than good, opening new desires? This is a new beginning of a technology within the ancient world of spirituality and altars.

All of our oracles say the faltering hegemonies have been planning something, and technomagia may be the answer, no sé. We wouldn't dare believe that our joy would remain untouched. Corporations conspire with traitors for the usual archaic bullshit reasons: power, control, money. Greed leads to leaks, but as soon as we see something coming, the files are double encrypted with Veves and the technology updated, so they can't keep up if they tried. The sky lanchas let us enjoy the Caribbean without so many borders. As long as our tatuajes, that show our roots, glow their bioluminescent blue, we are allowed entry.

I am called back by a chirp, as the sun rises to the highest point of the sky. I return to the balcon for a cup of Rosa's famous café. "Rosa, the coffee has been aged. Half has been ground and the other beans are on their way to be distributed," Yan Carlos says after fifteen minutes. My Mami smiles, a secret on her lips as I motion to Papi. "How could he still be here sitting away from the Altar?" She makes a motion with her hands saying we have only a few hours left, "Que chevere, what tecnomagia can do." My Papi sits with us as a holographic spirit, and we watch the finca and the IV feeds showing all the ways libertad is blooming across El Caribe, and we hope we can continue expanding so that more of us can return home.

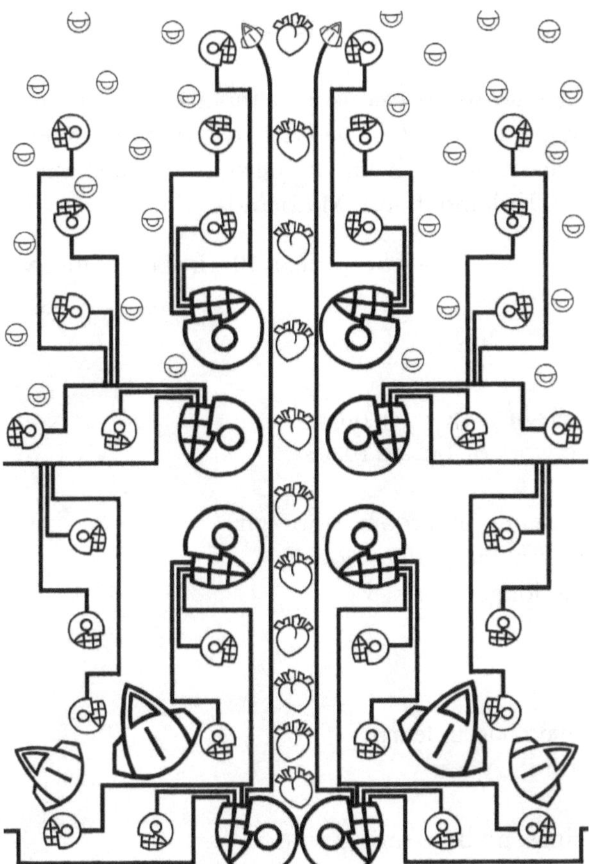

Luis Valderas: "Cross of Life Grid"

wealth: a parable

Rolando André López

to dzidzor

"The African blackwood tree is a member of the rosewood family...
genus *dalbergia*, species *melanoxylon*. Its species name refers to the dark
color of its heartwood... it has numerous African names: Mugembe,
Poyi, Endisika, Kidamo, Kinti, Masojanda..."

- The African Blackwood Conservation Project

i.

year 3231
the once streets have now become
a stillquiet network of buried roads
no words
for school, museum, bathroom, stop sign—
all places are wealthy gardens now
that money no longer exists

and us?

we who survived had to learn
how to fly with the wind

sky had no kings, no borders, no prisons
and trees had taken earthground all back
taken root in all seas
migrated into each other's continental heartlands

it was an invasion...

and us? we
scatterwandered centuries in flight
waiting for something to happen

ii.

she was once church, then abandoned
now she's wealthy

come moontime
she glows up, gathers all dispersed colors
carved in her as grooving birds of
pluricentric pigmentations,
us who rest in her white flower breath,
like Temdandumba de la Quimbamba
we sway on the masojanda's black majesty
to feel her new kind of nostalgia:
      love for a world
      we've yet to get to see
      rooted in the stars
      an aquarelle memory
      traced
      between
      our hips
      exist for frote blessed
      with airborne seeds

us we feel in her at last

a place:

everyone a culture,
everyone a city,
everyother nested
received
reborn
moontime come
into found birds

the wealthiest of all possible worlds

The Joys of Becoming an Axolotl

Olga García Echeverría

Oye, Julio. That's your name, right? J U L I O. Those are the letters I've been able to make out on your name tag whenever I see you on the other side of my aquarium. I don't usually do this—visit humans in their dreams. But you all are so dense. Only when you sleep do you really open yourself up to the surreal and magical. Truth is I've tried reaching you from the other side of the glass for years but with no luck. Now that I've crossed over into your own underwater realm, this place of dreams, we can finally talk: axolotl to man.

Julio, how long have you worked at the California Science Center? I've memorized the shade of your skin, a rich olive color, like that of my ancestors. Your thick obsidian hair, undulated like the waves. Most of all I love your youthful eyes. The pupils, dark expansive moons. Your irises, a mix of browns and greens and grays. Your eyes give everything away. I can always tell when you're slightly high. Or happy. Or bored. Or questioning existence. Every time you lean into the aquarium to look at me, I am swallowed up by your giant eyes.

Julio, nobody at the Science Center knows who I really am. You're curious enough to stop by and stare at me at the beginning and end of your shifts but even you, my friend, are in the dark. You've seen the ridiculously small sign by my aquarium, right? It reads "Mexican Salamander" and nothing more. Considering my rich cultural history, the sign is an abomination. How will people who visit the Science Center know I was once a Mesoamerican God? How will they know that regeneration is, as you all say nowadays, "my jam"? I am not "Mexican Salamander." I am Axolotl! Pronounced in Nahuatl, Ah-Cho-lo. In Spanish, Ah-jo-lo-te. And in English—trigger warning—Axe-a-lot. Julio, there are dinosaur bones across from my aquarium with entire genealogical trees mapped out. Even the hissing cockroaches to my right are respectfully displayed with information on their history, anatomy, and gastronomic behaviors. And me? Mexican Salamander. It's so insulting. What am I doing in a room full of bones and cockroaches anyway?

Julio, you must help me. I am going to tell you the tale of how I, once a Mexica God, became an axolotl. When I see you again face-to-face at the California Science Center, you will understand me in ways you never have before, the glass between us finally removed. What will you do with our newfound connection? I hope that at the very least the sign by my aquarium becomes as offensive to you as it is to me.

Now listen carefully…

I remember the night eons ago. Back then, I was still Xolotl, the Dog God, the one who guides the dead through the Underworld to assure they make it over to the Other Side. I'm also what you can call the dark-(er) side of Love. Where others cringe in the face of so-called monsters and misfortune, I embrace them entirely. I adore the differently formed, the queer, the shunned. For them, lightning in the sky to say, "I love you! Long live the two-headed, cross-eyed twins! Long live the woman with razors in her hair and a serpent dangling from between her legs!"

But I digress, Julio. I am here to tell you about the joys of becoming an axolotl. It all began when Quetzalcoatl, my bratty twin brother (think overachiever) and some of the other Gods tried to force me to jump into a colossal cosmic fire. Mind you, I am also the God of Fire, so you'd think I'd be fine with this, but I wasn't. Something had gone awry in one of the many creations, and the Sun and Moon hadn't risen. Personally, I didn't have an issue with this, but other Gods did. They concluded that a sacrifice by all the Gods—including me—was needed to straighten out the cosmic mess. My twin brother, part-serpent/part-bird, ordered the collective sacrifice. Since my brother is a big deal, nobody objected. You've probably heard of him. He is, after all, one of the original creators who brought forth the Earth. Between you and me, though, le echa mucha crema a sus creation tacos. He didn't bring forth the Earth (or anything) alone. The Earth wouldn't even exist without the Grandmothers. We all get eclipsed by Quetzalcoatl, Plumed Serpent, the Elvis of Mesoamerican myth.

I've always been rebellious, and I hate tyranny, so on that day, while other Mexica Gods prepared to sacrifice themselves, I heard my mother's wisdom, "Just because someone tells you to jump into the fire doesn't mean you should!" Also, I loved the darkness before the beginning. It was an endless black sea embracing and humbling us. Maybe the Sun and Moon had not risen for good reason. Maybe we needed to stay longer in the pre-dawn to contemplate creation and our roles. But the Gods, in particular my brother, were eager to put things in order and charge forward into the fire pit. It was a display of toxic divinity if you ask me. What is the obsession with "fast forward" anyway? Sometimes being still is magic.

One by one I witnessed the Gods offer themselves to the fire. When it was my turn, I sat motionless beneath the moonless sky.

My brother came over and whispered into my dog ear, "Xolotl, stop acting like a little bitch."

"Catch me if you can," I barked and fled into the dark.

He pursued me, hissing, moving serpent-like and swiftly as wind. I mean, He is the God of Wind, blah blah blah. The heated chase was like the games we played as children before the hierarchy of Gods status began to separate us. I wasn't afraid of him. He was my cuate/coatl, my serpent skin. I knew him better than anyone. Still, I kept running from him towards some unforeseen fantastic future.

I'm happy to say I faked out my brother several times. In a blooming cornfield I quickly transformed myself into a maize stalk. I am such a magnificent shape-shifter! My brother was catching his breath, staring at my kernels, probably fantasizing about an elote with all the fixings, when suddenly he realized I was his sibling, the Dog God, and not the corn! Ha! The glory of tricking him! I transformed back into Xolotl and dashed away at supernatural speed.

When I gained traction again, I transformed into a maguey. Or was it a cactus? Honestly, I can't remember, since it was so long ago, and you know how myths are, they keep morphing with time. Whether I was maguey, cactus, or both, I only momentarily fooled my brother. He ordered me to return to the sacrificial fire. "Never!" I snarled defiantly. "Who's the little bitch now?"

I ran all the way to the Sacred Floating Flower Lake. This is where several versions of La Llorona were born, where the Goddess Cihuacoatl cried for her lost child, where a woman in white appeared to her indigenous children and wept, warning them of horrific things to come.

"Why do you weep, Mother?"

"People obsessed with gold and crosses will come and fuck everything up. Oh, my children! Mis hijos!"

I didn't see Our Lady of Powerful Tears that day, but it was at the Sacred Floating Flower Lake that I realized my destiny lay down below. Underwater. Another Underworld. I leapt and dove in. In the beginning there was nothing, you see. Nothing but sky and sea. In the beginning, there was nothing but darkness and water. I was returning to the beginning, where time spirals into itself endlessly.

Once submerged, I had the brilliant idea to transform into a four-footed amphibian with free-flowing gills on my head. My brother donned a quetzal at the back of his neck and the colorful protruding feathers formed a crown on His big serpent cabeza. Now, I, too, had a crown! Julio, I became my own queen! My skin, like the primordial beginning, was charcoal colored and speckled with gold. I gave myself the cutest eyes, little black planets with an orbit of shimmer. When my brother finally reached the edge of the lake, he peered into the water and sneered, finding my final transformation monstrous, which is ironic since he is quite queer-looking himself. I gurgled-laughed, sunk to the bottom of the lake, and explored my new home. It was perfect. There would be no need to rush here, ever.

Now an axolotl, I contemplated my powers. I could regenerate any part of my body, even spine and organs, and with my small eyes, I could see back into the multiple beginnings and far into the unfolding futures. I saw it all! How I'd inspire awe and wonder. How I'd be "discovered" by Europeans, kidnapped, and transplanted. They'd breed me in captivity. Some of my offspring would emerge a strange, almost luminous, pink color. Yet, our powers remain. I'd become endangered in my natural habitat yet flourish in human-made tanks. I'd be eaten as a delicacy (please don't try this). I'd become an "exotic" pet. Artists would adore me. The LGBTQIA+ community, forget it! I'm surprised they haven't put me on one of their flags. I'd end up center-stage in stories, poems, and paintings and be the featured speaker at Chicanx Latinx conferences. I'd be a forbidden jewel to the scientific community; they'd torture me with their experiments and crack their heads trying to uncrack my secrets. I'd end up on all the platforms, a social media sensation. Yes, with a blue checkmark, fuckers!

Julio, I'd overcome it all—excommunication from the Mexica Gods, European colonization, scientific transplantation, incarceration, pollution, tilapia invasion, near extinction, pendejos, pandemics, and even the California Science Center with its whitewashed sign. Julio, what are either of us still doing at the California Science Center anyway? Honestly, I'd be very happy here in your bedroom in a nice aquarium by the window. I don't require much. You could open the curtains at night so that I could see the stars. It's been such a long time since I saw the stars. Wouldn't that be something? Having a talking axolotl in your home, in your bedroom? But why stop there, Julio? I will share that my deepest, most tender wish is to return to my place of origin, The Sacred Floating Flower Lake from where many of my ancestors were kidnapped and forcefully expelled. No, it's not just a myth! My homeland is real. Xochimilco. I long for the lake on a cellular level. I like to imagine she longs for me too. There's even a sanctuary there for my species now. Julio, let's go! I promise you that my freedom will also be yours. The U.S.A. is way overrated anyway. With me, you can eat panbazos every day and visit the pyramids. The Moon Goddess is just a metro ride away. So many museums, so many paleta flavors, so many tianguis to die for. I see you there by the lake, Julio, living your best life, happily releasing me back into the wild, me descending amongst my kind, persisting, breathing at my own pace through my feathered gills, my childlike smile frozen on my face, my magical queer body floating in the sea of time, returning, regenerating, flourishing.

SECTION 2: THE UTOPIAN ODYSSEY

Luis Valderas: "St. Buzz and the Rabbit"

Diocese Moon

Roxane Llanque

On July 5th, 2069, the *LM Challenger* was approaching Lunar Haven rapidly, shipping earthly payment for lunar rocket fuel: a sack of old-fashioned letters, a whole lot of machinery, two pale-faced prodigy engineers from the Czech Republic and Taiwan, and the Bishop of Orlando. The Czech, Karel, examined the cleric with wondrous derision. He found the bishop looked very small in the astronaut suit, thick hair in an elegant braid winding around an olive face, black and almond eyes nervous, but curiously intelligent. One of the gloved hands was clutching a richly decorated, crooked staff, that amid the LM interior seemed several centuries out of place.

"What's that thing called?" Karel asked, pointing at the staff.

"A crosier," the bishop answered quietly.

Karel smirked. "The media calls you the Moon Bishop. Is that an actual title?"

The other boy, Bai, stiffened and whispered something in his ear. A sneer curled Karel's lips. "Your *Excellency*," he added.

The bishop gave Bai a grateful smile, before turning to Karel with practiced serenity.

"It's a moniker the first Bishop of Orlando came up with during Apollo 11—when the moon mission took off in Florida. I guess the media stuck with it. But please... call me Damaris."

Karel's calculating gaze slipped to the name tag on her suit: *Rev. Rivera.*

"You have a lot of pretty names, Moon Bishop."

Secretly, Damaris had to agree with him. She had in fact protested the name and the mission fervently when called upon by the pope.

"Holy father. If you insist on putting the Moon under my see officially... the public will only take that as proof that I'm your... your progressive token! First a woman bishop, and now they put her on the moon, they'll say."

Pope Sebastian had leant back heavily in his armchair. "I have chosen you as the first female bishop, because I believed you showed no fear. Because you proved your confidence in the path God has guided you on. My dear, with you we've set a new era of our church in motion— one that is reconciled with the present world. The moon base is young; its inhabitants are atheists. But their great mission is doomed to fail if their souls are not cared for. I hear their leader, Baptista, is a child of our church—"

"I know of the Baptista family—but this Baptista is a scientist. Scientists won't want a bishop showing up and claiming what they built, woman or not."

"The Canon Law declares any newly discovered territory to be placed under the spiritual jurisdiction of the diocese from which the explorers originated. Apollo 11 left Earth from Cape Canaveral... thus the Moon became your responsibility, my daughter."

"Paul VI never confirmed Bishop Borders' claim to it; I think it was a joke by my predecessor, holy father."

"If it was a joke, I am hereby making it official."

"The people of Lunar Haven won't—"

"I'm sending you to remind them of their spiritual ties to Earth. They will respect you: a young woman, a scholar, just like them. Gift them some assurance in the desolation of space. I think you'll be surprised... they will welcome it."

Presently, Damaris still doubted that considerably. Her heartbeat quickened when the pilot announced the landing initiation and the friendly copilot Curtis floated in, gently removing the crosier from her hand and securing it under her seat. "You don't need to be nervous, ma'am. Landing is a routine procedure by now."

Damaris sent up a silent prayer anyway, though she wasn't quite sure if 'up' was the right direction anymore. When they docked into powerful magnets, she thought she heard nothing but the clunk of the tip of her crosier to the capsule wall, like a bell coming to a stop. The hedge opened... and the Lunar South Pole sprawled before them. Damaris stared in awe; never had she seen a black this true before, nor such brilliance in gray. This new world nothing but an endless contrast, a dust ground shining infinitely into an impervious sky.

"The stars... where are they?" she asked Curtis, who helped her into the waiting moon rover.

"The sun is shining six months straight at the poles, ma'am, so you can't see the stars, or the planets. Ever."

***

Damaris had imagined she would meet the scientists under the Moon sky, hidden beneath their helmets, a committee of goldfish bowls. But when they entered the burrow-like base and the airlock opened, just a single person awaited them; someone Damaris instantly recognized from a photo she had studied closer than she would care to admit. It was a face part Asian, part Latin, wary and alert, a disparaging gaze trained on Damaris.

"Ah, Doctor," the pilot said pleasantly and made a sweeping motion from Damaris to the scientist. "This is her excellency Bishop Rivera of Orlando. Your excellency, this is Doctor Baptista, chief scientist of our cozy operation here."

Doctor Baptista extended her hand from the pocket of her grubby work pants. She carried herself like the skateboarders Damaris had grown up around in Miami—loose but ready, a lower balance point. She remembered the long hours watching them over the rim of her book in Tropical Park well; particularly the few girls among them, who defied gravity twice as elegantly, their long hair cutting the humid air like spades. It was, she thought, the perfect stance for the leader of Lunar Haven, unburdened by the lack of an atmosphere.

"Orlando," Doctor Baptista repeated, strangely blithe.

Damaris was unsure if that was a question. "Yes, my diocese. I'm honored to meet you, Doctor."

The men around them laughed, Doctor Baptista's eyes gleamed.

"No, Orlando is my Christian name. We do first names here, though of course I won't expect that from you... *obispa*."

She might as well have spit her in the face while bowing. Damaris clumsily took her hand through her thick glove. "Well, what a nice coincidence. Please call me Damaris."

If that had earned her some grace the doctor didn't let on. Still, the chief insisted on bringing her to her quarters herself: a small living pod, lit red before the view of black and gray. They stood in heavy silence, Damaris awkwardly leaning onto her crosier and the doctor eyeing it with unreadable eyes.

Damaris cleared her throat. "So… were you named after the Virgina Woolf novel, or—?"

Orlando gave her a long look. Finally, she sighed and crossed her arms. "Okay, here's the deal, she-priest. I won't be your friend. I won't be calling you *'your excellency'*. Ever. Curtis you may fool with your little Catholics-turn-feminist story and this, this scythe of yours—but not me. Everyone on this base has *earned* being called excellent, through exceptional work in their fields. The shit ton of money it costs to get each one of us up here, it's for a purpose. A good reason."

Damaris frowned, her fingers tightening around her crosier. "I told you; you can call me Damaris. And I would argue I *am* here for a good reason."

"Yeah. You want to grind this thing into the moon dust and give us lost souls a sermon. Confirm that the Moon is part of your diocese." She scoffed. "You might as well have brought the Vatican's flag—would have been more honest. My crew, hell, I think they will see it as some entertainment. But I wanted you to know that I see this circus for what it is. So there are no misguided expectations. I know what your pope must have crowed about me and my family. But I'm no part of your church, and I'd be damned to help you bring it to the—oh."

The venom in the doctor's voice gave way to surprise as she reached into her pocket. "Your lip's bleeding, Rivera." She raised the tissue to Damaris' mouth—Damaris drew back sharply the moment she felt the heat of skin approach her. She wiped the back of her hand over her lips and found it sprinkled with blood. Orlando chuckled darkly.

"Not allowed to touch a bishop, is it?" She tossed the tissue at her. "Seems like you bleed like the rest of us, though. Must have bit your lip during the landing; zero-g makes liquid fly straight to the top of your helmet."

The all too familiar burn of humiliation turned Damaris' face red. But she put her crosier on the bed, dropped to her knees, and opened her bag, rummaging until she found what she was looking for. "Your mother sent me this for you from Portugal. I sneaked it in."

Now Orlando looked like she wanted to recoil—but she stayed very still, staring at the shining bottle in Damaris' hand like it could disappear any minute: costly *Oliveira de serra* oil, a rolled-up paper message tied lovingly around its neck. When the doctor made no motion of taking it, Damaris placed it on the ground between them and stood up to face Orlando as bravely as she could. "You might want to get to know me before you judge me, Doctor Baptista. I promise I will do the same." With that she walked past her, muttering under her breath.

"What?"

Damaris cleared her throat. "I have a doctorate, too."

She exited resolutely, only to realize in the hallway that she had nowhere to go. So, she walked on, rounding the circular halls of the base under the curious looks of the scientists, until by round three she risked a look into her pod—the chief was gone, the gift of her mother left on her floor.

***

The following morning—by Earth time, for the sun had never set —Damaris stared through the little window of her pod, looking for the stars, and determined to do right; judgmental scientists be damned.

She left the crosier on her bed and went to the canteen, where she went from table to table, introducing herself to the Lunar residents, asking who they were, what their work consisted of and what they would actually like to do in the service she was to give in the evening. The scientists came from all across Earth; on their strong arm they carried the Lunar flag patch, on the other that of their home country. It turned out most had no idea what mass could consist of—but to her relief, some of the scientists listened earnestly, considered seriously, and the general consensus soon revealed the people of the Moon wanted a singalong. So, Damaris asked, was there a song everyone on base happened to know?

At that a collective mist of grief went over the scientists, until a Dane quietly spoke up. "By now everyone here knows that old song *Wonderwall...*" he began with hesitation. And upon gentle prodding from Damaris, the story was this: three months ago, a member of the crew had died; geologist Nikita Laptander, by all accounts a gregarious fellow, had suffered a sudden heart attack. In his time in Lunar Haven, Nikita apparently had been known to terrorize his colleagues with relentless interpretations of the ancient song—a habit so dreaded in his lifetime that naturally, it was dearly missed after his passing.

After his tale and a silence dipped in sadness, the Dane laughed, embarrassed, and wagered that the song probably wasn't very Christian. Damaris put a tender hand on his shoulder.

"On the contrary," she said loudly, so it would carry over to the table where Orlando Baptista sat, dark hair veiling her face—if there was one thing you learned when preaching was your business, it was the ability to know when people were listening to you. "Singing together builds community and it can be a beautiful form of prayer, too. 'Sing to the lord a new song; sing to the lord, all the earth.' Now, my interpretation of that is quite controversial with some of my colleagues, but since all I am is controversial to them, I don't think that should bother us too much."

That earned her some grins and thus encouraged, she slowly grinned back. "When a song is so well loved by so many people on our planet, wouldn't that make it likely God would love it too?"

The Dane looked at her with a mixture of surprise and doubt. "That's a lovely thought. But, um, the truth is, Damaris, to most of us this religious stuff is pretty... unfamiliar."

"That's okay. I didn't come here to do my standard piece and be done with it. I respect that most of you don't practice religion. I just want to find a way for us to celebrate what we have in common, rather than what sets us apart. And wouldn't it be a nice way to celebrate the memory of Mr. Laptander?"

At that the scientists gave her genuine smiles and a great weight fell off her chest when they all agreed that yes, they would like that. Only their chief remained silent.

***

The weight crept back again when Damaris sat in the communal area afterwards, trying to work up the courage to approach Orlando Baptista to discuss the process and execution of the service. So she almost choked on nothing when the chief lowered herself into the sofa opposite of her as if conjured.

"Where did you have in mind? For the service?" Orlando folded her arms on her knees leaning over, and Damaris noticed that she carried not two, but three flags: the Filipino one over the Portuguese one on her left, the blue and silver emblem of the Moon on her right.

"The Pope would... greatly favor if it could be outside. I know logistically it would be easier on base, but-"

"The Shackleton Crate, then. There are some mountains there where our geologists installed elevators. That would be good, right, a service on a mountain?"

Taken aback, Damaris confessed she hadn't known there were mountains on the moon. Something happened with Orlando then, as she started to talk of the lack of tectonic plates and of great asteroids, crashing into the moon with such power the ground itself rose up again as mountains. Her eyes sparked, her coiled body became lively, and her hands animated, as she seemingly forgot she was talking to a dreaded priest. Damaris listened quietly, for fear of reminding her.

"Some of the peaks in the Shackleton are called peaks of eternal light... continuously touched by sunlight, forever. Fitting place for a service, no?"

"Yes," Damaris stuttered, "Thank you." And back Orlando Baptista was, taut as a string suddenly drawn too sharply. But when she got a nod from her nevertheless, Damaris counted it as an olive branch, even while the bottle remained in the wrong pod.

***

Evening had come all too quickly. Damaris had spent the rest of the day worrying over which psalm to select, a task she went at with such zeal that when Curtis came to fetch her for lunch he had laughed and said her book looked like a real page-turner. Afterwards, she thought it almost too good to be true when between bites of moon-grown potatoes Orlando offered to do the printouts for her, which she accepted with a smile. So, when the clocks showed sunset hour, Damaris swung herself into the rover with a certain spring as the little group selected for the service prepared to leave base.

"Alright, where are we headed then?" asked the rover driver.

"Shackleton, Alpha peak," Orlando answered. And it was as if a hoarfrost came over their caravan. Damaris couldn't understand it, the palpable cooling in the looks directed at her by the scientists after their warm morning. The driver belted out their destination and when there went a murmur through the other group as well, Damaris helplessly looked to Curtis for aid; the pilot merely gave her a confused look. The two rovers had driven half an hour through the luminous desolation when Damaris finally dared to ask him what in God's name was the matter.

"Alpha peak is almost a two-hour-journey," he explained. "We don't get much free time, you know? I think the crew didn't expect they had to spend their entire evening on this. Um, did they tell you to do it there?"

Damaris' throat constricted. "No. Doctor Baptista recommended it."

When Curtis finally connected the dots, he touched her arm in a silent apology.

After an hour the Shackleton Crater and its mountains appeared on the horizon, yet all the awe in this world could not drive away the bitterness on Damaris' tongue. She studied the mighty structures with Orlando's mocking voice in her head: not mountains, but the rugged edges left after a violent force tore a wound into the soil that was to stay forever. She knew there was no point in cutting their journey short, now. Notice of the service and its location had already been given to Earth, and as for the trust of the scientists... Orlando had stifled that spark with contaminated water, and she was left to work with grotty logs.

When they reached their destination, she tipped her head back to look up at Alpha peak. It was basked in sunlight against the ever drowning dark... truly a peak of eternal light. She wished desperately she could feel it on her skin, the sun, but her protective suit left her body cold and stiff. They went up the elevator in groups of four, with Damaris, Curtis, and her gear sent up last. Her first steps of her own on the moon, and she was doing it balancing her lectern and crosier, probably looking like a stumbling vicar. Once they reached the top and the doors slid open, the new sight took Damaris' breath away.

On a platform in between hastily removed geological instruments, the scientists had put up folding chairs in two small rows. And behind it, so foreign and familiar in the sky... Earth. It felt as if she saw blue and green for the first time; all her life had she spent up there and no image of it had prepared her for how it looked, that small sphere in the sea of black. Tears sprung to her eyes and she flinched when Curtis put his hand on her shoulder. "It's beautiful, isn't it?" he asked with a smile in his voice, and she whispered a hoarse affirmative. He took the lectern from her and placed it so that the scientists would see it and her before the backdrop of their blue home in the sky. And before Damaris knew it, her hands were mechanically setting up the bible at her chosen psalm, while Curtis placed the purple stole over the white of her suit. The familiar cloth of her charge on her shoulders finally filled her with some strength.

"Could you ask Doctor Baptista to pass out the psalm and the lyrics, please? She said she would print them for me."

"Oh boy," Curtis mumbled, but went to see it done. When she saw the paper, she had to chuckle bitterly; it was uncommonly thick, stamped in a pattern of circles. There was snickering in the open channel and Damaris put both hands on the lectern to ground herself, before she held up the paper. "My dear brothers and sisters... it seems your chief wants this event to remain close to you—a psalm and a song on sticker paper. Perhaps a souvenir for your lockers?" She loosened one circle with the word *Isaiah* on and held it up.

An embarrassed silence fell over them. Damaris looked straight at Orlando – the chief crossed her arms.

"'In the beginning God created the heavens and Earth.' Heavens, plural. What did he mean by that? What is it truly, the juxtaposition of earth and sky, of sky and heaven? Isaiah 43: 'Forget the former things; do not dwell on the past. See, I am doing a new thing! Now it springs up; do you not perceive it? I am making a way in the wilderness and streams in the wasteland.' You, brave men and women, have come to this waste-land to make a path in the wilderness of space, to new worlds in our universe, bringing with you the life of our planet and making new streams of water from Lunar ice, new plants in fresh soil, under the sun we were all born under, that reaches here and far beyond..."

As she went through her sermon, she could see how the bodies before her changed beneath the protective layers of their suits. Torsos bent forward to listen; arms were uncrossed. Spectacle turned to meditation and only one solitary figure in the middle remained rock-solid, head bowed like a bull.

Damaris kept her sermon short, ending it by blessing them. Then, gently, she invited them to their feet, speaking of Doctor Laptander. And finally, their helmets bowed, they sang his beloved song together, intermingled by crackling noises in their mutual channel, nobody having to look at the printed lyrics once. Damaris did not hear Orlando Baptista's voice in the chorus.

After their singing gently faded, she invited them to remain, to look at Earth and think of their loved ones. A peacefulness overcame them, as the helmets turned towards their planet, blue and green reflecting on their visors. Orlando though sprang to her feet and walked away from the platform, down the peak. After a brief hesitation, Damaris took her crosier and followed her.

She found the scientist sitting on the edge of a small plateau, arms wrapped around her legs. She didn't stir when Damaris clumsily lowered herself next to her, laying the crosier at their feet, and turning to face her. Goldfish bowl to goldfish bowl.

Orlando huffed. "What? Do you want me to give my confession?"

Damaris waited, then slowly reached to put a hand on her arm; it was shrugged off violently. "Don't. You think you're the first priest who tries that? Placating the troublemaker? Go ahead, tell me that God loves me. But never mind, cause it's not true. I'm headed straight for hell."

"Why do you think that?" Damaris asked gently.

Orlando spun around to her then, bruised fire in her eyes. "Because I'm gay, *your excellency*. There. Go, tell it to your pope. Everyone knows, but of course it's not official; god forbid my father's reputation gets tarnished by having a sinning daughter. Well? Go ahead and tell me you love me but not my sin and leave me alone."

Damaris found herself frozen. She didn't dare to move, for her heart was beating so fast she thought Orlando had to hear it through her spacesuit. She could feel the scientist's gaze on her as she fumbled for words. "I'm sorry," she whispered eventually. "If the church hurt you."

"Why? It's what you believe. Can't have it both ways. No, don't even start. I followed your career, you know? I thought... I thought if anyone with power would finally speak up it would be the first female bishop. But you repeated that tired old tune on how us homosexuals deserve love, but by the way, we should still think of ourselves as sinners because what we are is unnatural and against God's *plan*."

Orlando laughed and it was a wounded sound. "You think you are a big liberal, don't you? Their woke priest, their poster girl. And stupid me thought you pinged when I first saw you. I thought you had to..." she trailed off.

Damaris swallowed against a dry throat. "Pinged?"

"Yeah, pinged. And I think you know exactly what that means."

Damaris shook her head vigorously, clanking their helmets together in the process.

"I'm sorry, I don't." She wanted to beg her to stop, but Orlando was merciless. She grabbed Damaris' crosier and waved it in her face.

"I've seen you all these years. So friendly, *so* approachable, so beautiful—everything your church wished it was. Always so touchy with the guys, the priests, even the pope. But I've never seen you touch a woman, not once. I saw you jumping away from those undergraduate girls trying to hug you at Morehouse College. I saw you taking women's hands with sleeves covering your skin. I saw you every time. You know why I know what I saw? I used to do it myself. But you, *god*. You really took that old routine to brand new heights. So don't give me a sermon, and don't you dare pity me. You want to offer to absolve me, Damaris? I ought to absolve *you*."

And with that Orlando pulled her crosier back and threw it over the precipice with all her might. It did not fall. It flew, on and on, and Damaris stared after it with wide eyes as it rotated into the dark until it vanished, leaving no sound. Weak gravity.

She hung her head, and both fell silent. For the longest time they remained like that, until Curtis approached them from behind, timidly asking if everything was alright. Damaris quietly told him they would join the others in a moment. With some reluctance, the pilot trotted off.

Orlando shuffled her booted feet. "I'm sorry. I shouldn't have done that."

"It's, um, it's okay. I didn't want to bring it anyway. The pope made me do it."

At that Orlando laughed, and the genuine sound curiously settled Damaris.

"It's powerful, you know. To have a seat at the table—that's the only way to change things. But you can't make all the change at once. They look for weakness in anything I do. If they knew I was—something like this came out... I'd be done."

She dared not look at the woman next to her. She waited for accusations, or even glee.

Orlando's hand on her leg startled her. "How can you bring something to the table you keep a secret to yourself?" For the first time since they met, the edge from her voice was gone. Now, nothing but that infinitely tender touch Damaris couldn't feel and that torturous question.

She stared into the dark of space, her eyes burning with it. "You wait. For one moment, one opportunity where everything aligns just so you have a tiny window of hope. That's what I'm waiting for."

Orlando sighed. "See, Damaris... for those stars to align on Earth I think we would have to engineer them ourselves."

Damaris looked at the scientist. She could believe that Orlando Baptista could build a star of her own. But herself? A bishop of the catholic church?

Curtis spared her the difficult answer this time—the crew wanted to go home. And as soon as they were packed together, Damaris darted to the elevator, away from the chief, the last lonely figure remaining before the silhouette of Earth.

In the rover it was Curtis' turn to pin her.

"Did you guys talk it out?"

"... a little bit."

"Okay? Where's your, um, staff?"

"I... tripped. It fell—I mean, it drifted away from me."

"Oh shit. In the crater? I'm sorry. We, we could look for it next time we go—"

Damaris told him it was where it was meant to be.

***

The next morning, Curtis was loading her luggage into the rover, now heavier with gifts from the crew. Many of them proudly displayed the accidental stickers on their coats, the favorite clearly *Today is gonna be the day*—but she was touched to see some had chosen stickers from the psalm. One even shyly asked her to bless him before she left and just as she finished with a touch to his forehead, the chief came around the corner. She casually leaned onto the wall before the pressure zone, looking at Damaris with unreadable eyes.

The man thanked Damaris, looked between them for a moment, and quickly excused himself. Damaris fiddled with her helmet, looking everywhere but Orlando.

"Damaris?"

"Yes?"

"Could I have the gift from my mother?"

Curtis had to go back and bring her luggage and Damaris almost tripped over herself finding the bottle, until she could toss it into Orlando's hands. A whirl of emotions flashed in the scientist's eyes, but Damaris couldn't bring herself to look long enough to decipher them. "I'm glad you're taking it. Do you have any message for your mother?"

Orlando hesitated. "Tell her thank you. And that I love her."

"Oh. Yeah, of course, I will tell her."

Orlando nodded. "You never told me what your doctorate is in."

That of all topics took Damaris by surprise. "My—? Um, well, I have two. Theology, obviously, and, um—" she sighed. "Gender studies."

Orlando blinked. Then she burst into laughter, while Damaris sheepishly ran a hand over her neck. And finally, she closed her eyes and willed herself to do it. She put her helmet down and slowly pulled the glove off her right hand, holding it out to Orlando. The other woman's eyes widened, looking from her hand to her face. Then she smiled and it softened her, made something dance in her eyes.

She took her hand. Damaris swallowed at the warmth of her fingers, warm as if touched by the sunlight last night. Her thumb stroked over the back of it longingly; but eventually she had to drop it.

"I'll let you go, I'm sure you wasted more than enough time on me."

"It's okay. Always good to go outside. I'll go again soon, looking for your scythe."

At last Damaris threw her arms up. "It's called a crosier!"

Orlando tilted her head with a grin. "Okay. *Cuidate*, Damaris."

Damaris returned her gaze... and held it. "*Cuidate*. Orlando."

She had to force herself to turn away. And just as Curtis opened the airlock, she thought she felt a touch on the back of her suit... but when she turned around, Orlando was gone.

***

Back in the LM *Challenger*, Curtis stopped short when he secured her belts. He laughed heartily and when Damaris looked at him in confusion, he reached for her back, pulled, and revealed a sticker on his hand: *about you now*.

The Last Death of Fabíola Magalhães

Illimani Ferreira

Fabíola Magalhães had landed two Earth years, three months and six days ago on 1155 Horologii 4 or, as she had decided to call the planet, *Quasemeiodia*. The choice for the contracted word in her native Portuguese language had been hers. Her team groaned at the number of vowels and had settled for "Quase" instead, and even she did after a while. Quase it was and it remained even after Fabíola had died 365 times.

Fabíola woke up suddenly after yet another bad night of sleep on the cold, hard floor of her lab instead of her assigned cot in the planetary station's dormitory. With a displaced sense of urgency her reddened eyes frantically scanned the surrounding area, halting first on her right hand with fingers whitened by the strength with which they were coiled around a scalpel. Then, her eyes moved to the door, which was still blocked by the work table she had dragged in front of it. The table, like everything in the station, was compact, but it would make enough noise to wake her if he tried to open the door. Finally, Fabíola's eyes turned to the cylindrical vat filled with a green solution of nourishing chemicals and a clone of herself. This clone was not quite ready, as the toes and fingers were still connected to each other by a thin webbing, which would dissolve in the next hour. Then this clone would find its way outside like all the others, even though Fabíola knew very well that, despite its appearance, the 366th was different from all the others but the one that came immediately before it.

###

The mission to Quase was the first success out of a series of failed attempts by an overpopulated Earth to colonize planets in distant solar systems that all contained a set of rare conditions which, in principle, would make them ideal targets for human settlement: breathable atmosphere; tolerable gravity; low radiation impact from its one or more suns; abundance of water in permanent liquid state either on the poles or on the equatorial line; a substantial presence in the soil of carbon, phosphorus and other key chemicals and low levels of toxic ones such as ammonia and arsenic. Unfortunately, every planet with such a conjunction of geophysical and chemical properties also happened to harbor non-sentient life, at least as far as thousands of probes sent out to different distant corners of the galaxy since the discovery of superlight engines a couple of decades ago had indicated. And no matter if the planet had just a smattering of microbes in its oceans or lush jungles filled with the most absurd and awe-inspiring animals, as soon as a human would have a taste of their biomes by breathing the air, tasting the water or touching the land, their bodies would be assaulted by a battery of viruses, bacteria, protozoa, fungi and sometimes even multicellular parasites competing to kill them first.

An engineering paradigm was proposed to deal with such risks: compact experimentation spaces instead of big and complex ones, easier to monitor and maintain, shielding its crammed and cramped dwellers from hostile and deadly alien life. The unified government developed a plan to send to the most promising Earth-like planets a spaceship carrying support equipment and personnel as well as a compact planetary base to be deployed on the surface. The base would be equipped with only the essentials for the survival of the three best minds in their fields, tasked with performing the experiments necessary to develop the serum-vaccines meant to counter whatever diseases may exist on that world.

The first was a versatile engineer in charge of installing, activating and maintaining the hardware of the station and monitoring its proper functioning with support from the staff in orbit. For this mission that position had been assigned to Hermann Sturm, whom Fabíola thought on day one to be too tall, beefy and hairy for the limited living quarters she was going to share with him. The second position was assigned to Megan McMaster, a petite and laconic biochemist, in charge of using the limited resources in an also limited space to manufacture the serum-vaccines to be used in testing the outcome of the research trials that the most important member of the crew was conducting. Fabíola was a biomedicine specialist, with a masters in genetics and a PhD in epidemiology and an outstanding track record of clinical research, a rare combination of skills that made her the ideal candidate to lead the team and oversee her own death, over and over, to the Quasian diseases.

Hermann and Megan sat at the small table in the planetary station's kitchen, facing three bowls of steaming breakfast mix that Hermann had just synthesized. Neither of them dared to touch the bowls, even though the gray glop would become hard and barely edible when it cooled down. They were waiting for Fabíola. Those were the terms they had agreed upon a few days ago, when Fabíola had locked herself in the lab with a scalpel. Terms that Hermann was on the verge of breaking.

"This is bullshit, I'm eating," he announced, as he grabbed his spoon. Hermann almost dipped it into the bowl when Megan gave him her calm and yet steely stare. There would be grave consequences if he dared to go through with this apparently anodyne course of action. Hermann tossed the spoon back on the table with an irritated scoff. And again, they waited. Not for too long, though, as they heard the noise of the desk being dragged on the other side of the door leading to the lab. And then the door opened, showing a disheveled Fabíola, scalpel in hand, fury in her eyes that lingered on Hermann at first, and then slightly less angry on Megan, and then, finally, almost calm and eager on the bowls.

"Good morning, Magellan!" said Hermann with more sarcasm than politeness. That was the nickname that he had given to Fabíola when she explained to him that the namesake of the Portuguese navigator was just a corruption of her surname, Magalhães. It happened when they were still on board the Durga and en route to Quase. Fabíola was at least relieved that he was not calling her "Fab" anymore. That was even worse in its laziness to avoid learning how to pronounce her name and surname properly. Not that this was the worst thing that Hermann had done to her. Not even remotely.

"I'll take the one on the left," informed Fabíola, prompting Hermann and Megan to pick up the other two bowls and finally eat. The gruel was lukewarm now, still soft but more sandy than creamy, most of the artificial flavor having dissipated with the heat. Fabíola approached the table but didn't sit down in the third and only free chair, preferring to pick up the bowl and walk backwards until her buttocks touched the wall—which didn't take long, considering the small size of the kitchen like the rest of the station. Only then did she eat, awkwardly, using only her pinky, ring and middle fingers as the index and thumb were still holding the scalpel. She almost dropped the instrument when an irritated Hermann suddenly banged his fist against the metal table. This made a big noise that echoed in the small cubicle they were trapped in together. Hermann's fist was quite big.

"This needs to end," appealed Hermann, "I'm not gonna poison you! Why the fuck would I do that?!"

"Eat your food, Hermann," phlegmatically suggested Megan who, unlike Fabíola, was unfazed by Hermann's outburst.

"We can't live like this!" insisted Hermann, to no avail, as Fabíola resumed eating her breakfast with the same angry glare at him.

"Fine, maybe some small talk to start the day?" offered Hermann with a sardonic smile, "Like, how are things going in the lab? Is it ready?"

"She's none of your business," answered Fabíola.

"Don't be ridiculous, Magellan. It is my job to place her on the platform—"

"You are not touching her," spat Fabíola.

When the Durga launched Fabíola, Hermann and Megan from the orbit of Quase to the planet's surface, they were encased by no more than what was now their current dormitory quarters—a conical cubicle of less than 12 square meters with three cots and an elliptical exercise machine. Every wall of this cubicle was covered with the hardware to be sanitized, tested and attached by Hermann in the slow and careful process of expanding their pod into a fully operational planetary station. Fabíola and Megan were relatively idle during these first months on Quase while Hermann was laser-focused on the precision-oriented tasks that fell under his responsibility. Megan kept to herself for the most part, thanks to a tablet in hand and headphones constantly wrapped around her head. When she was not entertained by her own devices Megan did share some details about her life, little by little, at the same slow pace at which their tiny living quarters on Quase expanded. This is how Fabíola learned about Megan's childhood in the megalopolis of Minnesanitoba, very different from her own in terms of her place in society, as Megan was from a wealthier family and a wealthier part of the world, but very similar in the literal lack of space on an overpopulated planet.

After a few months an 8 square meter small kitchen had been added to the compound, and then, finally, the 15 square meter cloning lab attached to which was a 4 square meter cubicle where Megan could synthesize serum-vaccines. The last component of the station was the most vulnerable one: the hatch system, composed of a reinforced glass door leading to a 6 square meter corridor with advanced sterilization systems as well as testing and scanning equipment, which connected to a second door, a metallic one this time, leading to the dangerous outside world. With the hatch assembled and functional, everything had been set up for Fabíola to die for the very first time.

As soon as Fabiola delivered a complete clone, biologically similar to her in every way except for a vestigial nervous system meant to keep the clone's organs functioning, Hermann would fish it out from the tank and deposit the clone on the hatch. After that, he would close the reinforced glass door leading to the hatch and open the metallic one at the end of the hatch, allowing the clone to be exposed to the microflora of Quase.

The first time a Fabíola died, it was due to a virus that viciously assaulted her respiratory system. It was hard to acknowledge that the clone was not suffering despite its almost lack of a nervous system, as blood and pus dripped from her nostrils until her metabolism collapsed. The scanners in the hatch then provided Megan with all the readings of what killed her, so she could manufacture a serum-vaccine to be added to the vat where the next Fabíola would be made. After that, Hermann would close the outer door and incinerate her. The second Fabíola was almost immediately covered in pustules caused by a viral skin infection. She, too, burned. So did the third, whose entire liquefied digestive system dripped from her anus in a pink pond of goo. Every new death took longer, as every new Fabíola was immunized against the diseases that terminated the previous clones, and would succumb to a different virus. After the 53rd Fabíola, the serum-vaccines started keeping the viruses of

Quase at bay, allowing the native bacteria to do their slower yet equally deadly bidding.

Fabíola managed to keep her balance and scientific objectivity by focusing her attention not on her copy, but on the landscape beyond the glass hatch and with the exterior door open, that she could only see on the occasions that started with her contamination and ended when she burned, as the planetary base had no windows at all. One day all this would be over, and she would cross through that hatch when they finally had developed the serum-vaccine that would make them immune to all diseases on Quase. Fabíola longed for the vast plains of Quase covered in the silvery wildlife which shone beautifully at night thanks to the bio-luminescence of some of the fungi, as well as a rocky formation through which poured a small waterfall. The display showing the climatic data outside never oscillated beyond 30°C or under 20°C. Fabíola craved the day when she would be able to feel the velvety lichen carpet that covered the planet's surface under her bare feet, the day when she would walk confidently for a long bath in that waterfall. A waterfall that was so like that one in the Chapada dos Veadeiros.

Fabíola was raised in a 25 square meters kitchenette by her mother, father and her grandmother, who looked younger than her own daughter after spending the family's savings ordering a clone to which she transferred her faulty nervous system. The treatment for dementia was much cheaper than cloning, but it still was expensive for a family in a third world megalopolis that had lost all the money they had saved until then. Fabíola's childhood was frugal and terrifying, as her parents would go out to work for long hours and leave her to be cared and care for her grandmother, whose decayed brain couldn't understand she was living now in a time and place where there was no room for her existence outside their tiny living quarters. Fabíola would need to provide her grandmother with constant explanations about why she could not leave her house to look either for a husband who had died decades ago or a son who was now a grown up but she still thought was a child. Such attempts at deterrence would often result in regular physical assaults by that woman who was bigger and stronger than her. Fabíola never told her parents of the ordeal she endured when they weren't around.

After her grandmother passed, Fabíola's family used the money they would usually spend on her palliative care to book a three day vacation in the last natural reservation within the megalopolis of Goiás: the Chapada dos Veadeiros. The waiting list was two and a half years and Fabíola counted the days until their turn had finally arrived. She never forgot the ample, relatively uncrowded spaces amid rocky rapids and mesas, nor the feeling of being under the mist and pelting of water droplets from the park's many waterfalls: surrounded by refreshing liquid matter, yet alone. For once she felt safe.

On her last day at Chapada dos Veadeiros, Fabíola found her calling: after finishing high school she would go on to college to study genetics and biomedicine because people like her late grandmother would spend whatever money they had to achieve their conception of living longer and better, and Fabíola desperately wanted to afford a living space that wasn't crowded. However, while she was finishing her masters while living on campus at the University of São Paulo, a pandemic of Covid38 in Goiás claimed the lives of both of her parents without giving her a chance to say farewell. Feeling selfish for her choices in life so far, she decided to study for a PhD in epidemiology despite the lesser prospects of wealth from a career in this field, without suspecting that the odd combination of masters and PhD would make her the perfect fit as the team leader for one of the planetary colonization projects. She happily and eagerly said yes when the invitation came, as the concept of space and life on a new planet evoked the prospect of walking through vast, decluttered spaces. When she realized that she would need to spend years first on board the Durga with a dozen strangers en route to Quase, and then in an even smaller sardine can on the surface of Quase, she almost gave up, until she realized that, upon success, she would satisfy both her need for vast spaces and to offer something back to society.

Fabíola learned to look away from the different forms of decay and death of her copies by keeping her eyes on the prize beyond it, through the glass door, past the hatch and the open outer door. But she couldn't deal with the part of the process that came immediately before the clone's demise. Even though Fabíola was very aware that the clones that Hermann's big hands fished out of the vat were not herself, witnessing the process hundreds of times made it something akin to staring at a mirror. There was no way out or around the ritual: an Earth law intended to reduce the impact of vanity cloning on overpopulation determined that only one copy could be manufactured, and only in the direct presence of the genetic source of that clone. And Fabíola was the one who had gone through the desensitization training that earned her the clinical authorization to perform the procedure on herself as many times as necessary. She was the one who also had to undergo weekly psychological assessments on the impact with the resident psychologist on board of the Durga named Lindiwe Ncube. She lied a lot to Lindiwe.

###

Initially Hermann was careful and respectful with the first dozens of Fabíolas he snatched from the vat, keeping his touch limited to the minimum necessary to transport the clone to the hatch. At #78, a shift happened: what used to be scooping became something more akin to manhandling, as if Hermann had some sort of concern that the clone could wake up out of its stupor and had to be subdued. Hermann's long arms almost embraced it. Then his hands would inch closer and closer to her breast before letting the body go in the hatch. Fabíola only said something when she clearly saw Hermann's sausage fingers pinch #283's breasts. Hermann denied the move after Fabíola pointed it out to him, which was corroborated by Megan, and his transportation techniques resumed previous adequate levels for a while. On #302, out of nowhere, the pinch turned into a full cupping.

###

The friction between each member of the human population of Quase in the confinement of their tiny planetary station was something expected and they had been prepared to deal with both through a psychological assessment before the mission started and also thanks to the entirety of their lives on an overpopulated Earth. Going through a few slightly more claustrophobic years on a dangerous planet to earn the right to explore sweeping, virgin landscapes had been not only an acceptable deal but a quite small price to pay for Fabíola. She survived her grandmother, what could be worse? The weekly wellness sessions with a broadcasted hologram of Lindiwe were more a hindrance to her mental health than an asset. Fabíola was built to tolerate, but the psychologist had decided to push her to enjoy the company of her colleagues as a condition sine qua non to determine if the social environment in the station was healthy or toxic. "What do you like the most about Hermann?" was a frequent follow-up question after she complained about Hermann's behavior, and she had to answer with lies. Fabíola's mind, a stronghold of resilience, wasn't prepared for this assault of forceful interrogation proposed in the most soft of pitches by Lindiwe, who reminded Fabíola often that, as the team leader, she had to prove that she could lead, and leaders could not be left alone.

When Fabíola reported to Lindiwe how disturbing she found the way Hermann touched #302, the psychologist demonstrated a great deal of concern—to Hermann. While Megan did well with her tablet and headphones during the times she was not manufacturing serum-vaccines, Hermann went from the engineer who assembled the delicate machinery that were their living and work quarters to a mere custodian, checking if the systems were optimal, preparing their meals, cleaning the toilet bowl-showering unit and, in the many hours he was done with such tasks, making rounds through the planetary station with steps that Fabíola found always too heavy. She was ready to overlook everything if it were not for the psychologist prompting her, every week, to acknowledge what she wanted to ignore. "You are the leader, Fabíola, you need to care for everybody in there, especially for someone with so much free time now like Hermann." And she tried. Despite finding him socially obnoxious and physically repellent, Fabíola made an effort to make small talk with him. It was not that hard: he would spew his moronic babbling about the machineries he loved so much and she would nod while her mind would drift away. It could just as well be one of her clones sitting there, while their vestigial nervous system kept a heart beating, two eyes blinking and a pair of lungs inhaling and exhaling. And one night Fabíola discovered that Hermann, despite having improved on the way he maneuvered her clones, had had a similar idea.

###

When Hermann deposited Fabíola #364 outside a couple of days ago, nothing happened. She inhaled and exhaled. For hours and hours she just laid outside, immobile, naked and very alive in her semi-brainless slumber, the scanners showing that no contagious ailment had affected her. She burned anyway. The serum-vaccine finally had worked optimally, meaning that the next Fabíola had to be cloned with a fully functional nervous system in order to ensure that there was no microbial risk for the brains of any immunized humans exposed to the air, water and soil of Quase.

When Fabíola woke up in the middle of the night to check on the progress of #365, as the complete nervous system was a novelty that she wanted to track closely, she found that Hermann was neither in his cot nor in Megan's, as they had been sharing the same cot during the last weeks.

Fabíola found Hermann in the cloning lab with #365, whom he had laid on her work table. The clone was far from finished: the ears were still glued to the skull, her fingers and toes still webbed together. Her incipient vocal cords could only emit a guttural moan. Her orifices were complete, though, and Hermann was making use of one of them. He almost tripped on his lowered pants when Fabíola chased him out of her lab with a scalpel. The blade would have met his flesh if he had been only slightly slower or clumsier when he fled.

Fabíola sedated #365 and dragged her to the hatch, mimicking the protocol she witnessed Hermann following many times to enclose the other 364 clones of hers outside and incinerate them. She kept a tight grip on her scalpel even after all that remained of #365 were ashes, or when Lindiwe urged her to move on for the sake of the mission, or in the nights she slept on the cold floor of the lab while she prepared the 366th Fabíola.

###

"Let me do that," offered Hermann, as he saw Fabíola struggling to lift #366 from the empty vat. Fabíola ignored him, even when #366 moaned softly when Fabíola dropped her on the ground after the wet, naked body slipped from her grasp.

"It's fine, this time the embedding solution had sedatives," pointed out Megan.

Fabíola dragged #366 to the open hatch and lowered the clone gently onto the ground.

"Can I do my job now?" asked an impatient Hermann as he approached the console with the locking system.

"You can get the fuck out of my lab," answered Fabíola, "Both of you."

"Fabíola, I need to monitor the vitals," argued Megan.

"You can monitor the results," affirmed Fabíola as she stood between her fellow denizens and the panel, "As for the hatch, I can operate it myself."

"Get out of my way," stated Hermann coldly. But Fabíola didn't budge. Hermann's face turned red. But before he could make another move, Megan's hand landed softly on top of his big, tightly coiled fist.

"Give her that, we are almost done," whispered Megan. For a moment the engineer flinched, but soon he opened his hand, his thick fingers interlocking with Megan's bony ones. The twosome left the lab, leaving the two Fabíolas behind. Only then Fabíola closed the inner hatch door and opened the outer one. And then she waited. It took four days for a gastric fungal infection to consume the life of Fabíola #363, but only a couple of minutes to have it tracked by the medical scanners in its incipient stages of contamination. This time, it took only a few seconds for the same scanner to beep, pointing out an infection. Fungal in its nature. Encephalic. That was an eventuality Fabíola was prepared for and the very reason why #365, and now #366, unlike their predecessors, had fully formed neurological systems. Two things, however, were unexpected: one was the speed with which it was taking over the whole nervous matrix of the body, from the cortex to the nervous terminations, causing oral foaming and muscle twitching. The second was that, after the relentless infection process was complete, the clone didn't die.

Fabíola saw her clone's eyes opening, what she assumed was a reflex, as the cessation of the symptoms akin to epilepsy were observable everywhere else. But then the clone stood up. Even if the body had not been chemically induced to a comatose state, it should not be able to perform a complex movement like this. The brain was blank, like a newborn's. It shouldn't even be able to crawl. But not only did the clone stand up, it walked with confidence to the outside world, the feet propelling the body step by step on the soft lichen. The target was clear: the waterfall. Fabíola saw herself diving into the humid mist and, after several hours, it never left. Not even when the door of the lab opened and Hermann barged in:

"I've got some news for you, Magellan. Durga determined that you can't take over my functions."

He stopped in his tracks when he saw the empty hatch.

"Did you torch it already?" asked Hermann as Megan joined him in the lab and started to assess the data from the scanner.

"She's gone," admitted Fabíola.

"The scanners say that #366 succumbed to an encephalic fungal infection," pointed out Megan. "The genomic pattern is very clear, I can start manufacturing the serum-vaccine right away. Can you start working on #367, Fabíola?"

"I'd be happy to," answered Fabíola.

"I… I will fix lunch," said an uncertain Hermann after a moment of silence and before he left the lab.

Megan was about to put on her headphones and enter her small office, when Fabíola asked:

"What are you going to do outside when it's safe?"

"We have work to do."

"Answer me."

Megan sighed, and reluctantly indulged Fabíola.

"Honestly, I will go as far away from you two as I can. If you go South and Hermann goes North, I will go West. I'm sick of you two."

"Why do you fuck him then?"

"I'm doing my part. Don't screw this up," said Megan before she entered her office, closing the door behind her. At this point the whole process was mechanical for her and she could activate the protocols as easily as she had opened the hatch.

However, two thoughts prevented her from starting the cloning procedures: the first was that, despite the ongoing, unavoidable company of Hermann and Megan, she felt terribly lonely. The second was a realization: more than the vastness of an inhabited world, Fabiola yearned to no longer be alone. And she had only one prospect to solve this not new-found, but only now acknowledged hunger on Quase. And with that, Fabíola realized that the 367th iteration of her own self was ready and, just like the others, this version didn't need clothes and shoes to close the threshold to what waited for her.

###

The blaring of the override alarm behind Fabíola became muffled as soon as the transparent inner door closed and the heavy metal door opened in front. She could hear the thumping of fists on the glass behind her, which she ignored as she only had eyes for the waterfall that was a hundred meters in front of her. Fabíola took a couple steps ahead to get as far away as she could from the insolent noise. The air was humid, no longer the stale dryness of the planetary station. A few seconds after her feet left the hatch and touched the soft lichen ground of Quase, Fabíola realized that these steps probably just saved her life as she could feel heat on her back, probably caused by Hermann as he impulsively activated the incineration system just because he could. The heat faded fast. And so did the thumping noise. And the humid smell. And the feeling of the tender ground under her bare feet. Her vision had been spared, at least, as the fungi took over her neurological system and she became a passenger in her own numbed body. A body that propelled itself ahead, toward where she always wanted to go. She didn't feel the impact of the cascade on her when she crossed the watery veil. She found #366 at the other side of the cascade, standing in a humid cave, her body enfolded in an armor of bioluminescent fungi feeding on her flesh and on the water spray from the cascade. No. That was not a mere clone. A clone wouldn't smile at her, and hold her hand. A hold that was tender and gentle as the numbness was gone.

The planet was vast beyond the refuge under the cascade. She could go anywhere she wanted, but she didn't need to, as she was everywhere already, through every ramification of the fungal entity that covered Quase's surface, its valleys and mountain tops, its tropics and poles, her hand and her other hand she held, with the exception of the little claustrophobic pod which felt like a tiny desensitized mole on the vastness of her body. In just a couple of seconds Fabíola had been everywhere in Quase and, wherever she had been, she was never alone.

Fabíola Magalhães had died 366 times since she had landed two Earth years, three months and six days ago on 1155 Horologii 4—aka Quase. And now she was reborn.

Falcon and the Carucha

Daniel Jose Ruiz

My great-great grandfather is a ghost on the screen, but he's alive in a book. The data is too old, partially corrupted, partially in a coding language now grown archaic, so he cannot be fully rendered into 3d space. His video journals crackle, and occasionally brilliant blue and green lines bisect his face as he speaks in a voice that sounds like broken glass over porous stone. As some strange joke, his voice appears as he chastises whoever opens the door to the root cellar before the security sweep is activated.

"Chingao! You want to die?" He asks. I sigh, close the door, flip the switch for the scanners, get the green, and reopen the door. I just want some fucking coffee.

"That's just how that hombre loco sounded," My grandfather says. He has an ancient, weathered face that folds into itself when he laughs or sings too loudly. "I already have the coffee on the warmer."

"Still lived to the neat century mark, ya know?" My grandmother adds, not quite as ancient, but still well into the bonus years of existence. "Tierra folk just had that grit to them, I guess." That makes sense to me. My grandparents told me stories, stories they had heard from their own parents and grandparents, of life back in the Sol system. They told me about skies that cried oily tears that were mocked by broken cities where people killed each other just to tear down one collapsing heap to build a new one. They told me that the world was dead, but no one believed it because you still had to get up to go to work.

I still have to get up to go to work, but they tell me it's different. I drink my coffee, the heavy cream and flecks of cinnamon making it far sweeter than it needs to be, but dammit, it does taste good. The goats were a pain in the ass to maintain sometimes, but the cream was worth it every morning.

"You get to breathe fresh air, work with your hands," My grandfather laughs. "You even got a better Carucha that I ever did."

"There's plenty to worry about out there in the field," I respond.

"¿Y que?" He fires back. "Everyone made sacrifices for here. That's why it works."

I get it. I watch the ghost of my ancestor every year that we celebrate The Landing. Abuelo will say that I don't look like him, but I carry myself like him. Whatever that means. Still, I get excited when we get to see the vids. All the founders recorded something for future generations, and all of them say the same thing really. Life is hard, but it was harder, and they made the choice to find a place where at least their hard work might mean less hard work for their kin. I suppose I can't complain. The air is fresh, and the generation engines have done their job. Our homes are domed, but it doesn't need to be anymore. The sky is blue, the clouds are white, and the air is just that sweet spot of oxygen to nitrogen to hydrogen. One day, maybe in my lifetime, the air will be warm enough where we can tear down the agridomes and use them to build some homes, maybe a proper theater, hell, even a museum.

You can always tell the real ancestors because they have lines around their mouths and noses from the rebreathers. Years of wearing them, gently cutting away their skin, giving them a halo of scarred flesh. If you didn't see the lines, you knew that they stumbled here, signed up for this life because it was better than whatever else was out there.

My ancestor, the founder, he called himself Falcon, he wrote that when the big ships left, you didn't know where you were going. You signed up, filled out the form that said what you were good at, packed up the family, and went into a pod. He was the crazy one that didn't have a family when he left Sol. You woke up a century later, dropped out of a starship the size of a small moon. You woke up on a new planet with enough material to make a go of it. He wrote it all down.

He knew the real secret, the one that none of the videos mention. You weren't supposed to live. We were left here, and there were no plans to check in on us. This is why I keep his journal hidden. Some things just don't need to be known. In a few months, we'll all celebrate Reconnection Day, the anniversary of offworld ships finding us. They weren't supposed to. We were given the least, given equipment that failed inspection. We were an experiment. Better we focus on that we survived. Maybe that's why whoever hid Falcon's journal did so in the first place.

Written in his blocky, ugly handwriting, he spilled all the chisme. He couldn't have written anywhere else. All the systems have some form of surveillance. We've seen the subroutines. We don't know where they go, but that doesn't matter, does it? Somebody had to pay for this all, but then, people forget.

The bigger the money pot, the easier it is to lose the ants that bring in the coins.

Or Falcon was right, and we were supposed to die. We didn't.

The rest of the house isn't awake yet, thankfully. Only my grandparents are up this early with me. Their room is just five paces away from the kitchen, one of the original rooms of the house, not the adobe and brick add-ons of almost 150 years of people trying to make it just a bit bigger. They cannot help but wake up early. Only when my mother and father have had rough nights will my grandmother attempt to start food. If she does, then there will be a fight about it later. My father will get upset that his parents work too hard. My mother will take it as an insult to her cooking. She should. My grandmother doesn't have a light hand with the goat fat, and my grandfather saves all the grease from the traps because it makes everything taste better. All the grandkids, the aunts and uncles, we all get excited when we hear the sound of grandparents singing as they worked. It means the meal is going to be special.

I am the oldest child of an oldest child, so I don't get to cook. I have to run perimeter on the fields. I have to feed the animals. Before mis primos and mis primos de mis primos were old enough, I had to run the composter, empty the latrine vacs for fertilizer, process the chickens or goats or rabbits. I think I've done just about every job for this damn place other than cook. Well, at least cook for everyone. I have a small portable hotplate in my room, and sometimes, I try to recreate the stories of meals long since dead. They don't really go well. That doesn't mean stop trying. Maybe I am getting better, or maybe I am just learning to love my mistakes. Still, at least my jobs now are outside. At least I get up before everyone else and can use the damn bathroom with time for the saints. Falcon wrote about this, the burdens of building. All the Founders' vids make it seem so glamorous, but his journal is honest:

Building can be a lonely artifice. It's easy to forget how many hands have to hurt to make something last. When you forget this, you forget people, and then you forget how to really live with people, not just around them.

On easy days, I'll thumb through Falcon's journal, mostly looking at the recipes that he had hastily scratched and re-scratched into the paper, trying to remember what home tasted like. He had a good twenty years in Sol, and while most of it sounds like a nightmare, damn the food does sound good. I've tried a few of the recipes when I can sneak scraps and privacy, but most of the stuff is extinct anyway. Each time I've tried, it ends up with the goats. My little brother Jaime, he's the cook in training. They say he has the touch for it, but I think he was just lucky and was born at the end when there were enough hands for everything else. He couldn't ride the Carucha like me anyway.

My mother appears, eyes still heavy with a deep desire for sleep, but her hands move with determination. The oven comes alive, the strange hum of the electricity as the burners warm. She disappears into the cellar for dough, whatever left over frijoles or rice is almost meant for the compost, and she returns, exasperated.

"Beto, did your sister get the eggs yet?" She asks me.

"Do you see her awake yet?" I reply. My mother grimaces while my grandfather chuckles.

"Then you go and do it, smart ass." She isn't smiling, but she isn't really mad either. I am already in my suit as is and the chicken enclosure is technically connected to the main house anyway. I walk through the hall, dodging around all the potted plants of spices, chiles, and everything else that you're welcome to grow in your own home, but nothing that is going to get priority in the big domes. I get to the airlock, primarily for the smell, and listen to the whoosh of it opening. I wait for one door to close, listen to the gears slowly grind, praying nothing breaks today, and then the inner door opens.

The chickens aren't awake yet. It's technically our winter, so the sun doesn't rise until midday and sets only a few hours later. The chicken's dome will mimic sunrise in an hour. I collect the eggs, a tidy haul of thirty, enough for the family breakfast, a few for the community store, and maybe something else for dinner. I walk back, hand off the eggs, and take the glass of protein slurry that is waiting for me. Judging by the hints of cocoa and chile, my grandmother made it. I slug it back, place it in the sink, and take the thermos of coffee with my name on it. Time is wasting. I kiss my mother, my grandparents, and now the steady stream of my aunts and uncles as they appear. If I'm lucky, when I do my pass near the main house, someone will run lunch to me.

"Buenas Suerte, Beto," My grandmother says as I go. My grandfather grunts something, and my mother is already too busy preparing for the 17 other hungry mouths. This is why it isn't so bad to be out early. The house can shake with the excitement of so many people, the walls vibrating with our laughter, our arguments. Especially in the old parts, the original prefabricated structure that was dropped here, the walls were made to resist heat and cold, but they create a terrible echo. My cousin Ricky, he lives in a separate building with his dad. He needs his own time and space, and that much noise cuts him deeper than anything else. We do our best to be mindful when he is at the table, and to his credit, he tries his best too.

That's all we can ask of each other, verdad?

That's what Falcon wrote at least. The only real lesson after a hundred years of a relatively shitty life. Maybe he said that because his additions to the house aren't always great, and sometimes I spend most of my day fixing my Carucha, really his Carucha. It's where I found him, tucked away below the control panel as I was rewiring it. I've read the damn thing so many times that I could just give it to my grandfather, but I like that it is a secret for me only. There are so many of us, and it seems like everyone knows their place, knows how to walk their walk, and I just don't. I don't want to just run the Caruchas. I don't want to just do what I'm told until I'm old enough to tell someone else. Falcon wasn't an engineer, a scientist, or even a proper agricultural savant. He just knew how to work hard, and he knew how to make do with what he had, and I guess that's enough. It makes me feel like enough. I will give it back. I have an idea, a way to deliver it. I just need to make it work. I've spent the last two years trying to make it work. Today, maybe today, it will finally work.

The early morning is cold, even with the suit, and I hustle into my Carucha. She's bright red, flames that Jaime and my uncles Yani and Sebastian helped paint over the spider-like legs of it, a massive calavera over the engine compartment, hand painted by Falcon himself. It has two powerful claws at the front, perfect for most field work, and a winch in the back, which is already hooked to a cart. Most of the other Caruchas use wheels or tracks, but Falcon wanted something different, or really, having rebuilt the damn thing several times, he pieced it together out of whatever scrap was around. Back when there were no paved roads, no smoothed paths, the legs made sense, but well, this is the last running Carucha of the OGs, and honestly, I take pride in that. During the long days of summer when power was plentiful, we all take our Caruchas and cruise the plaza. At least nobody has one like me. Some hate her, but everyone notices.

I climb inside and strap in, hit the ignition codes, and she whispers back to me. The engine is online, the faint hum of the battery waiting to ignite the engine forward. There hasn't been much sun, so the battery isn't full, but it is enough, for the time. I feel the sticks in my hands, the hard metal of the pedals, and I move forward.

The steps are ponderous, heavy, but as the morning frost breaks, she moves faster, and I pick up speed. I have three generators to hit before walking the perimeter, and I have to hit them before whatever sunrise we have today. At least the sky is clear, so we should get a good charge. Moving the joysticks isn't easy, and most of the newer Caruchas have fully holographic displays, but not ours. After four years of piloting, my hands and wrist are strong, and my arms carry the load without complaint. When there are only maybe a dozen eligible bachelorettes on the whole planet, it helps when you have nice shoulders.

The first generator comes into sight, the Rosenthals'. They were the ones to first grow coffee, so even now, everyone wants to stay on their good side, even if we all can grow our own. I hop out, switch the generator to its third cycle of battery packs, and release the drained primary. Some Caruchas can do this all wirelessly, but of course, not ours. It doesn't need to because I can do it. Another one of Falcon's sayings in his journal: *Just because the machine can do it for you doesn't mean it needs to.* I climb back in, switch to the arm sticks, and pick up the spent battery, swinging it over to the storage cart, and then grab the fully charged battery to place back inside the generator. Once back in the generator, I hop back out, get it all set up, and do a quick check inside the agridome. The lights are all on, the corn is growing high, and even though the machine tells me that temperature and humidity is good, I go inside to check anyway. Mostly, I just want to smell the world growing around me for a moment. A timer beeps. I am getting behind schedule.

I haul ass, pushing the Carucha too hard, but I have to do the other two generators first. Then I can do what I need to do. If it fails, I owe too many people. The Sepulveda twins will make me clean their septic systems for a year at least. I'll blow my chance with either of the Reyes' girls. The Chiangs will expect goats. And Jesus, my parents will never, ever let me live it down.

The other generators are easy, at least. The cart is full, the spent cells ready to be plugged back into the central charge station near our main house. The other sectors all have their charge stations, and the chatter on the radio is all excitement for the Landing Day feast. I try to stay out of the chisme because I am becoming a legend today, one way or another. I still have an hour before sunrise. I can make it.

My own agridome, mi pinata is small. I built it out of scrap, whatever glass and circuits that I could beg or borrow. I couldn't ask my family because I have what they have, so it was mostly my friends and their kin. I made big promises. I haven't lived up to them yet. I need proof of concept. My agridome doesn't run on a battery cell, just whatever it can gather itself from the sun and the small wind turbines I could cobble together. I unlock it and step inside. My trees are almost my height now, and they smell that earthy promise in them. These four trees are all that are left of my ten. I lost most of them last winter when there wasn't sun for a week, so the damn things froze. The others haven't given any fruit because the soil mixture was wrong. I needed more zinc and nitrogen, all precious things when this whole damn rock was never designed to grow our food. We've all spent the better part of five generations trying to get this rock to give us life, and it's going, at least the staples, but what's life without the little pleasures?

Today, today it is going to be different. The trees have fruit on them, and I can hold them. Most are still hard, but just a few are soft. I can feel them yield under the pressure of my fingers. Most are green, but they are turning to that beautiful dark purple, richer than the night sky above us, hidden by the UV lamps in the dome. Yes, a few are ready. I gently pack them into the insulated storage back on my hip. I take out Falcon's journal, and I flip to the page. Yes, four will be enough. No one can have a lot, but everyone should get a taste. If this works, we can plant the seeds, and soon, everybody will have enough. I try not to cry about it. It doesn't seem worth crying over, but no, it is. Joy is worth crying over.

There is a fifth ripe one hiding. It is smaller than the others, but it is ready. I want to peel it, to eat it, to know what the hell I am getting into. I hold it in my hand, and then my arm begins to scream at me. There is a motion signal. Something big. A coyote-worm, a Migro.

Falcon said that the planet was marked empty except for what lived there. It was empty of humans, but not life. The Migro were ten to twenty feet, each weighing at least a ton, sometimes two. They were long, snake-like, but they had an almost canine face with jaws. A lot of the local flora and fauna died out as the amto changed, but some just adapted in its own way. Falcon wrote about them often:

Nothing wants to die, and unfortunately, we came here and fucked up their world. They have a right to hate us. They don't understand, and until we can understand them, there will always be death.

The Migros tunneled through the soil, and they would smash agridomes, leaving our harvest to die in the cold dirt. I sprint and jump into the Carucha, its metal sighing ever so slightly with the impact, and flip the switches to combat. The delicate fingers of the claws recede into the palm, and large, heavy blades replace them. The weapon systems on the hood turn red. I follow the alert to where the beast is, likely tunneled right under the energy fencing. It isn't near a dome yet, but it is moving towards them.

They like heat, and on a planet this cold, that makes sense. I like the heat too. I get on the radio.

"Migro in the 12 o'clock far side. I'm intercepting," I say. There is static.

"You have cells. Get them back here first," My father responds.

"No time," I say back. "We have two rice domes that are ready for harvest, but it's heading right for them."

"Hail your primo, Ricky. He's out there, working on the harvest right now," My father says, and his voice is calm, but I can hear the worry. It sounds like when I broke my arm wrestling with the Lathan boy when I was 10. It sounds like when the generators fail, and we all have to cuddle up under blankets to not freeze to death until we can fix it.

"Tus tíos Sebastian y Imelda are en route," My mother adds, her voice slightly out of breath. She must have ran to check on who was where. "Your sister Nenni is with Ricky." Her voice is heavy with the sound of memory. She had four brothers, once.

Shit. Nenni didn't have her own Carucha, and her little scooter was quiet enough to take Ricky somewhere, but it didn't have anything to stop a Migro. I am moving slow because I have the empty cells, and I could just drop the hitch, but they could crack, and that could screw us all over. Relying on luck that just two cells could run a dome is asking for someone to starve. Fuck it, vamos. I don't know if Falcon ever said that, but it sounds like something he'd say. I hit the storage lock, and I scuttle against a hill, raising half of the Carucha up, and I swing it hard so that the cart and cells go tumbling away but as softly as possible against the slant. Now I can move. I just hope the cells are ok, but Ricky and Nenni matter more.

"Nenni, you there? Can you hear me?" I call out over the radio, but nothing. They have motion sensors too, but they aren't responding. I reach up and close the canopy over me. The heat of the Carucha keeps me warm, and it becomes a sweatbox with the canopy up, but I need the reinforced plexiglass now. The smell of an old machine with old hates and new loves fills my nose. I push forward, and I can see the agridomes. Each is a hundred times the size of our house, and they rise up and block the horizon when you are close. There is no smoke, and the systems aren't giving me any alarms. I can see Nenni's scooter, parked beside the entrance. The motion detector is dark, a dead zone. I get no readouts in the Carucha, so there must be a solar flare hitting atmo, so nothing is going to show up. The radio is all static and the mixing melodies of the town's music. It is like hearing whispers of the dead, colliding into each other.

Pull the string and I'll wink at you…of a shyness that is critically vulgar…en la boca llevaras…

I could hop out and go inside to actually call for Nenni and Ricky, but then I can't do much against a Migro. The damn exterior speakers have been busted for a generation, and everybody keeps saying they'll fix it, but we never do. I scuttle like a crab right up to the entrance and open the canopy.

"Nenni! Enrique!" I yell. It takes me a second to remember that this is worthless. The airlock and walls of the agridome make this futile. Well, sort of. The Migro clearly hears me, and the canopy has no time to close before a fanged maw crunches into it. I reverse as hard as I can, and I can hear the sound of metal tearing and glass shattering. The Migro lets out a roar of pain, but I cannot hear it. It speaks in tones so low that we simply do not have the equipment to register it, but I can still feel its anger in my lungs. I manage to grab it with one claw, and as it rips away the canopy, I drag it away from the agridome. I get the other claw up in time to catch its mouth before it can rip me right out of the cockpit, but the servos are straining.

It's a fucking big one, and it is mad. Its drool begins to flood into the cockpit, my claw keeping its mouth from coming down, but the thick jelly smells like ammonia and burns much the same. Even with the canopy open, it is hard to breathe with the smell, and my vision goes blurry. I squeeze the trigger on the right stick, and now I am airborne. The sonic weapon doesn't sound like anything except perfect, immense silence. All sound is simply gone, focused and concentrated into an area the size of a grain of rice. I must have hit it, and in its pain, it somehow got the coils of its long body under me, and now I am flying but quickly landing. My head smashes against the headrest as I tumble, and the horizon spins. I am upside down, my face looking at the gray dirt of my home. I can hear the Migro moving towards me.

I pull out the lever hidden under the central console, and I can hear the legs struggling to obey. With a pop and grind, they spin, reversing orientation, and now I may be upside down, but the legs move me just the same. I watch it dart forward, its central, red eye blinking uncontrollably in anger, the six other yellow eyes scanning its periphery. I squeeze the trigger again and again. It feels the blasts, but it doesn't seem to care. I dash to the side, moving far faster laterally than it assumes that I can, and I get both claws around it now. It can't bring its jaws to me, but its serpentine body thrashes, trying to sweep me off my feet. It is like playing jump rope, but if I screw up, I am pretty sure that it will decapitate me. I try to time the thrashes with my meager jumps, and when the bulk of its body aligns with the hood, I let go with both triggers. The creature shrieks at the discomfort, and the blades of the claws are starting to crack through the subdermal chitin.

I let go, still holding the triggers. I am getting dizzy, and it is hard to focus, but I can see it starting to head north. It is fleeing. I flip the switches, and the cockpit turns, and I am right side up again. The blood rush makes the scattered cuts on my face stop for a moment before they begin to ooze again. All I smell is ammonia. Beside me, Sebastian arrives in his Carucha, a sleek, catline vehicle of smooth lines, save for the large harpoon on the back.

"You ok?" He smirks. I check the pockets of my suit, and they are still there. Maybe a little bruised, but workable. Just like the rest of us.

"Fine," I reply. "I just waxed this damn thing yesterday."

"It's still heading back passed the perimeter."

"Let it go. It shouldn't be back, not for a while at least." The Migros kept a lot of other nasty little surprises away, and it would be a shame to kill one for no good reason. You couldn't eat them, and they were toxic as fertilizer. They tunneled, and they knew to avoid iron and lithium deposits, so if you followed their trails, you saved a lot of time on surveying. They weren't monsters, just animals that suddenly had neighbors they couldn't understand. The sun is rising, and I remember the batteries. "Shit, I gotta get back for those damn cells."

"Relax. Mi Viejo is already on it. Figured you'd drop them," Sebastian says. "I'm going to make sure our friend leaves. You go check on the kids." I nod and bring the Carucha up to the agridome, and I let it idle. Part of me is too scared to turn it off since once it goes quiet, it might stay that way. I walk inside the dome, and Ricky and Nenni are waist deep in a rice paddy, carefully cutting plants and stacking them.

"Hey bro, you smell like shit," Nenni says with a laugh, trying to keep her voice low. Ricky covers his face with a scented mask, but by his eyes, I can tell that he is smiling at me.

"Probably, but you need another lesson in shaving your barba, sis," I laugh. Nenni got unlucky and got the heavy shadow gene, but she does her best with what she has. Supposedly, the medical group will be able to manufacture what she needs soon. We had a bad outbreak of some kind of fungal infection in the town, so all research was on that for a while.

"Prick," She says, but she isn't really mad.

"Spoiled princessa." I return, and this makes her smile. "There's something messing with comms, so best to pack it up and head back early, yah?" Nenni and Ricky both nod, and I make my way back to the Carucha. She is still running, but she has to limp home. Tío Yanni meets me at the central charging station as the sun rises into the air, so fast that you can actually track the movement. All three cells are still workable, but one is likely to fail sooner rather than later. He promises to help me get my ride back into shape tomorrow. I plug it in, and I hope that to-morrow, it will run.

I retreat into my room. Nenni and Jaime are still gone, so I have the quiet. I take out the precious cargo, and the sight of them, slightly bruised, a vibrant green against the dark skin, forces a smile. I take out the journal, and I start my work. Pepper. Salt. Whatever chiles we have. Mash. Stir. Mash. A little bit of lime, but we don't have those, so I use a little bit of tangerine. Mash. A little more salt. I dip my finger in. It tastes like a thick cream without the sweetness. It tastes like air filled with the scent of heavy soil, fresh with life and promise. There is salt like an ocean I've never seen. There is heat in my mouth like a city of bright sun, long ago abandoned. I cry. It worked. It tastes really fucking good. I make sure to bag the seeds and prepare them.

After getting clean, a full bath rather than a quick air and UV spray as a reward for my heroics, we all gather at the plaza with the other families. It is the largest non agridome on the planet, the ceiling above a patchwork of different failed agridomes or decommissioned ones for families that didn't want to live under glass anymore. There is soft, fresh grass that grows wild, dandelions that make strange, unreadable languages of yellow. There are trees that don't give any usable fruit or nut. There are tables upon tables, a stage, three different playgrounds, and of course, a field for football. Every family brings a few dishes, and the central tables are loaded with just about every combination of food that one can make with corn, wheat, rice, and quinoa. There are drinks. There is already the screaming of children, the gossip of our lives, and the different, always competing bands try to take their share of the crowd. Once, there were only 80 people for this. Now, there are close to two thousand.

Mayor Avila takes the stage, and the only theater drones we have circle us all to project her face as she speaks. It's the usual Landing Day shit, the brief 30 second messages from each Founder, and those who trace their lines to them whoop and holler as their ancestors appear in the sky. The messages are for everyone, but hidden in my bag, just for mi familia, and the people I owe, I have real history to share. The last thing in Falcon's diary, the very last entry that he ever wrote, the handwriting almost illegible as he succumbed to time:

Everything is story. Food is a story. Each ingredient a lesson, a memory, a people's lives and struggles. The alchemy of them is what makes the alchemy of us. We are living here now, but so much of us is gone, sleeping in our blood, waiting for the sunrise. History must be like food. To be prepared with sincerity. To be eaten with both reverence and joy. To be shared with everyone.

After the speech, everyone lines up to build their plates. I wait at our table, the long, sterile metal scratched and painted into a beautiful image of a home that was left behind, a warning of what any world can be if we allow it. As everyone settles in, my grandfather waiting to be the only one left standing so he can speak his peace, I let out a deep breath and unzip the bag.

My grandmother gasps as one of her good clay bowls that went missing months ago returns. My grandfather gives me a sly smile as he sees the beaten leather journal in my hand. He laughs and whispers with his eyes: "took you long enough to find it, pendejo". The family watches silently, their eyes moving between the bowl, the strange, green paste, me, and our grandparents. Only my grandparents seem to recognize it, and small, almost haunting smiles cross the wrinkles of their face. Jaime looks disgusted. Nenni looks confused. Ricky smiles at me. He helped me build the UV lights after all. My grandfather gives a small wave, and everyone tentatively takes a small dab with a piece of tortilla. The reaction is relentless. The slaps on the back. The laughs. The jokes and jeers. Jaime wants to be pissed, to be usurped if only for a moment, but he gives me a nod of respect. My parents shake their heads, my mother licking her fingers for just another slight memory of the flavor.

"May I present Papa Falcon's signature dish," I say. My grandfather nods and motions for me to sit and for everyone else to settle down. He lifts up his glass, and for a moment, he is balancing between tears and laughter. He allows both to happen.

"We are here because people broke a world, but we made a home because we chose to love each other. Every meal is a blessing, and blessings are meant to be shared. Salud. Amor. Communidad."

"Y Tiempo Gastarlo." We all respond as one.

The One Seeing, The One Seen

Gabriela Santiago

When Lili was little, she had a book with a green fox on the cover. When you stared at the green fox and then at the white page opposite, a hazy red fox floated before your eye.

Leaving Mars for Puerto Rico is a little like that, but with circles.

Red circle.

Green circle.

Red circle out the porthole as the rocket takes off, the acceleration pressing Lili back so far she cannot see out the window. She starts to narrate—but of course she's already turned her auditory and her ocular off, won't be turning them back on for the next two weeks.

Take some time to think about what you really want, her mothers had said.

The safety harness grips her as hard as their goodbye embraces, hard enough to bruise.

And then—weightless. Floating. The restraints are not up to code and so she is suspended within them, not touching anything.

Connected to nothing at all.

"You'll always have a place on the family channel," Mama Andrea had said. "You'll have to be in the hydroponics vids, but we can do an art spotlight every few months, maybe more if you get more fans! The subscribers already like you. You can even take a bigger cut if you take on some of the admin."

"Or branch out on your own!" Mama Oyuki had said, maybe spotting a certain set to Lili's jaw. "We've got the seed money for you to start your own channel, get your

hab if you don't mind it small. The numbers are good for artists this quarter, especially for ones working with materials they can't get up in the cruisers—"

They think this trip will change something, but how can it change anything when Lili will have to go back?

She passes out and wakes in a blank white page, herded from the rocket into ivory-walled rooms that she can only tell are in towers because of the puffy white clouds out the window, and she can only tell those are Earth clouds because of another picture book, long ago. The elevator is white, and so is the room where passport chips are scanned and so are the walls of the bay where they keep the nuwhales—the water crystal clear like a vein of quartz against such whiteness. The nuwhales have railings installed from the edge of their lips through their sinuses and into the auxiliary swim bladders where the seats have been grown. It's wet, and Lili grips the railing tightly. On Mars you do not have to learn how to walk on wet surfaces. On Mars, this much moisture would mean a leak, and a leak would mean death—fried electrical components, compromised atmospheric seals, water rations bleeding to be flash-frozen in the thin atmosphere.

As the nuwhale dives downward, the pressure thins its outer membranes until they are transparent in places, windows into the sea. Lili sees forests of kelp like the hair of giants, fish darting between them. In an impossibly short time, they have lost the sun. It is airlock-with-a-broken-light black.

"I remember a story—" Lili begins, and then stops. Auditory and ocular are off, still. There's no one to narrate for. It's not part of the treaty that Puerto Rico has with the cruisers, but it is written into their family contract. The family put it there.

"We give them everything of our lives here so we can survive. They don't need Borikén too."

And then: green circle.

It glows. So bright for a second Lili's stomach half-convinces her brain they've turned upside down, are headed back towards the sun. But no, that is not the light of Sol. Not yellow but green, bleeding into blue at the edges and brown/red at the bottom, where the pulsing flow of magma from another island in the EnerShare network feeds into the grid. But who can look at red when there is so much green, contained in a sphere like the biggest hab Lili has ever seen, but instead of patched and smeared plastic the boundary is marked by a strange shifting quality to the light, like a million stars have relocated to the bottom of Earth's sea—

No, not stars. *Noctiluca scintillans.* Dinoflagellates. Plankton.
Oh, to show this to someone!

#

The boundary looks thin from the outside, fragile. But the nuwhale fits easily inside with space to spare, its long flippers making patterns in the blinking, flaring unicellular organisms. They are in a part of the 'sky' that doesn't contain the 'sun,' and so she can still see the island, though when she looks to her left she has to squint against the brightness as they come into the bay.

Someone pats her arm. She starts, looks over at the little old woman with bird-fragile arms already straining against Earth's gravity.

"It does that to me, too, every time," the woman says. She presses a peppermint into Lili's hand.

"Thank you."

"Take it slow," the old woman says, not taking her own advice as she peels away her harness and reaches for her cane.

Lili staggers to her feet, grabs her suitcase, grabs at the edge of her seat to keep from slipping. So much for months of strength-training for Earth gravity. Slowly, she makes her way up the staircase, stumbling more than once. The nuwhale's baleen brushes against the top of her head as she exits, and the attendant lets go of her arm.

Her feet sink into sand. Warm sand, she can feel it even through her shoes.

Outside is supposed to be cold. Everyone knows that.

But she's here, just in her in-hab clothes, and she feels the warmth of the sand and the...sun?

She tilts her head up to the circle of swirling lights, scintillans approximating the shape of the star. No, the heat can't be coming from there. It's an illusion, magma and mirrors. And yet—

All around her children are shrieking as they run into the water to splash each other; the wheels of a passing cart squeak, conversations babble, someone's auditory is set on public mode and blasting last-century cruiser-core. She smells salt and fish and coconut oil and—does green have a smell?—and dirt, the scent somehow deeper and more complex than in the farm domes. She will look around her in a second. She will.

She looks up at the sun, the movement of the scintillans making it into a giant eye, squinting down at her, this ungainly bird that's landed on their shore.

#

"Don't you get enough of looking at the stars at home?"

"We don't have stars like these."

Still, Lili looks down from the night sky and smiles at Aunt Valeria. They are sitting out back in the garden of her and Uncle Kevin's house, the table groaning with lechon and fried fish and mofongo and tostones and arroz con gandules, rum and orange juice and pineapple juice and guava juice and fresh café con leche that Grandpa Jomar keeps offering her, even though it is nearly midnight.

"I'd love to see your stars," Genesis says. "Yadiel almost got an internship up with the cruisers, you know? Turned it down."

She punches her twin on the arm. He smiles, mildly embarrassed by the attention. He is the kind of tall, lanky man who naturally folds himself into corners, following the conversation in benevolent silence. "I decided I wanted to stay closer to home."

Genesis rolls her eyes. She's half Yadiel's height, but with her hot pink crop top and bedazzled jeans, all the lanterns on patio seem to shine just on her. If Lili turned on her ocular, the camera would love her. "He's signed up for over seventy percent of the maintenance shifts on the dome. I swear he's in love with the scintillans."

It has the feel of an old script between them. Is Yadiel the older twin, or is that Genesis? Mama Andrea grilled Lili on the whole family tree before she left to make sure she wouldn't forget crucial details just like these.

"Does that pay well?" she asks.

Silence. Uncle Kevin, who has the least English, looks back and forth between her and the others, one eyebrow quizzical. Valeria and Genesis look…embarrassed? Grandpa Jomar's face, usually the most expressive of all five—he wept when she first came through the door, folded her into his arms and rocked her back and forth, *mija, mija*—is unreadable.

"It's a volunteer shift," Yadiel says. He's the only one who doesn't seem to have picked up on—on whatever Lili's faux pas was. His posture still languid, one leg dangling off the edge of the hammock, swinging like a slow metronome. "Most things are, here. Some people stream vid for the cruisers so they can have a little credit if they want to go abroad, but lots of people just do it for fun too. We get pretty much everything we need through the EnerShare exchange, with so many other islands wanting fresh scintillans, or consulting on dome maintenance."

"Oh, right." Lili's face burns. Mama Oyuki had said something about volunteer hours, and she had talked about the family's jobs, but Lili had just assumed those were two separate things. "So who does all the stuff like…" She was going to say spreadsheets and cold calls, but if they didn't stream for credit, then—on the family farm channel there was lots of unglamorous work, but some of that was appealing to the cruisers, the time lapse vids of the ponics-mucking had gotten the most views last quarter—

"The stuff that makes the world go round?" Yadiel says. "I mean, sometimes they have to put out a call for stuff if the usual people get sick, but mostly, people do what they're interested in. I serve tables down at the café too."

"And never bring me leftovers," Genesis cuts in. "Which is the least you could do after wimping out of the diplomatic courses with me. I need brain food!"

"Next week," Yadiel promises, and Genesis heaves a dramatic sigh, flopping back in her chair.

"The diplomatic courses?" Lili asks.

"Following in her mami's footsteps," Valeria says, a proud hand on Lili's shoulder.

"Eh, it's the only thing around here that's a challenge," Genesis says, half-shrugging away the touch. But her blush says she's pleased. "It's EnerShare stuff, mostly."

"Not the continents?"

Aunt Valeria shakes her head. "What do they have that we want? With the new farms and the kelp fields and nuwhale fleets, we don't need to import food even *if* they had enough to spare. Which they don't."

"All that tech, though--what if they decide to just take it?"

Her aunt flaps her hand like batting away a mosquito. "For who? The climate refugees from Miami and New York? Why would they start giving them anything now?"

"We keep up to date on what they're doing," Genesis cuts in. "Just in case. The starcruisers too."

"Bunch of tourists," Grandpa Jomar scoffs, his voice a little louder than everyone else's. "They drowned all their favorite vacations spots, so they had to go colonize space."

"And they seem to be happy up there with their sealed parks and their vids," Aunt Valeria says, a soothing hand on her father's arm. "Sometimes we have to step in to enforce a streaming contract, but they're usually happy to throw money at a problem until it goes away." Her smile has a little fang in it. "We make them throw a lot of money when they cause problems."

Lili blinks to zoom in her ocular on that smile—but no. It's off. Right. It's still off.

"You probably know more about the cruisers than us, Lili," Genesis says. "How are contract negotiations going this year?"

Lili's throat tightens.

"Not bad," she says. "We think the farm might get a new sponsor, if we agree to try out their new seed line they gene-tested. But it would lock us in for a few years, so Mama Andrea's crunching the numbers of views for plant progress versus our other vids."

"Oh, so you might not do as many of your sculptures?" Genesis said. "That's too bad, I like those."

"Sculptures?" Uncle Kevin asks, his eyes lighting up.

Genesis rolls her eyes. "I told you about those. See"—she blinks a pattern that Lili recognizes as sending a vid to her father. "This is the one they posted last week—see how she uses the natural pattern of the rock? The next one in the playlist is pretty cool too, it's a timelapse of how the wind changes it once she leaves."

Lili looks down at her lap, fiddles with the printed cloth of her trousers, the cheap weave already starting to crisp and crack in the humidity.

She always thinks of her vids as for the cruisers. Something she churns out, that makes numbers that make other numbers. It's weird to think that family might watch them too.

Her uncle's hand covers her own, warm.

"It is good work," her uncle says. "Beautiful. Very beautiful."

Uncle Kevin does not usually add anything written to the letters that come to Lili's family, but he often includes sketches of buildings. He is an architect, preserving old buildings as well as making new ones. The pressures here under the risen waters are different than those of decades past. No more tsunamis, but earthquakes are still a consideration, and the EnerShare networks adds other complications. The dome is as perfect as they can make it, but engineers will tell you: everything leaks.

"It is—" Uncle Kevin hesitates. "Very harsh. But appropriate. How you layer the rocks, which ones stay up, which ones fall down. It is like a story."

Lili feels warm. He likes her vids.

No. He likes her *art*.

Lili doesn't make the vids for people to understand her art. But.

It's not a bad feeling.

"So!" Genesis says. "Should we be keeping an eye out for a new channel to subscribe to?"

Lili looks up at the stars again. Not the real stars, the scintillans; no cruisers orbit around them. She is tucked away in their darkness and their light, the song of the coquis all around her loud enough that she almost believes it could drown her out on an auditory.

"I don't know," she says, dragging her gaze back before Genesis can comment.

Does it even make a difference, what I choose? In the end, isn't it millions of eyes watching whatever I do?

"It was a long flight," she says before she can be tempted to try to say any of this. If her mothers did not understand it, why should this part of her family? "I think I might pack it in."

"Of course!" Grandpa Jomar says. He stands up and clasps her in his thin arms. "You must be exhausted, pobrecita." His eyes swim with tears, deep oceans; Lili has never met anyone who wears their emotions so clearly on their sleeve. "You'll want to be rested for the trip tomorrow. We have a special treat."

"What?"

He smiles. The light shines in his eyes, and behind him, the scintillans swim in the sky, clustering in the shapes of constellations Lili doesn't recognize. Is that one the Taino glyph for sun?

"El Yunque."

#

If Lili turned her ocular on—if she were selfish enough to break contract and endanger all the other negotiated terms—she would shoot the waterfall from just this angle. The way it crashes down, how impact changes the color from blue to white with shocking violence. If she could get the shutter speed just right, she might catch a spray of droplets suspended like mercury in the air before it hits her eyelashes. Maybe she could pull focus, start with this fern, so startlingly green, or this dark rock covered in moss, before she reveals the water itself.

But her ocular is off. It's staying off.

Lili blinks her eyes slowly anyway, the same motion that would take the vid.

"It's hard to turn off the habit, isn't it?" Yadiel asks.

Lili starts. She didn't hear him come up by her; assumed he was over at the bridge where she can hear Genesis' rapid-fire Spanish, something about a dispute over her shifts at the embassy, someone who was supposed to trade with her while Lili was planet-side.

"Yeah." She looks up at the trees. This would be an amazing shot too, their long trunks stretching vertically up the turquoise sky, vines and epiphytes jutting into view. "When you're used to framing everything, looking for the angle——"

"Yeah." She can hear the smile in his voice. "Sometimes, after a long shift on the dome, my fingers still move like I'm logging the tracking numbers."

There's an intake of breath like he's going to say more, but then Genesis calls out his name, and he rolls his eyes gently before loping back to the bridge, leaving Lili in the cool mist of the mountain.

Is she taking too long? Are they bored? Are they——

You need to take your time, Mama Andrea had said. *Slow down. We only get these passes once a decade.*

Lili closes her eyes to better feel the mist.

Is it just the mist off the fall, or is it raining? Lili opens her eyes, steps carefully on the slick rocks back onto the trail. Listens to see if she can hear droplets on the thick leaves, the red puddles between wooden trail markers.

She would do a close-up shot of that puddle there. So bright red, against the wood.

Or maybe a long shot of the path, disappearing into the darkness, shafts of light filtering down through the trees.

Lili walks up the hill. She's not going too far. She can still hear her family.

On Mars you never go anywhere new alone. It's not safe. Too many things can go wrong.

There are no native carnivores on Puerto Rico larger than birds.

She hears birds, but she does not see any.

There is so much green! Who knew it came in so many shades, lime and emerald and so many other words that suddenly make sense. You could get lost in green like this. It's like being inside of the body of the island itself, ancient and immense. Something she fits into like a red blood cell, following a path as if by instinct.

Hello there, forest. Do you feel me here, in your arteries and veins?

The rain splatters over leaves as shiny as plastic and springy as rubber. It makes concentric circles in the red-orange mud. Little white flowers peek up around the edges of rocks.

Coqui, coqui, say the frogs, so endless that their drone might be the forest breathing.

Above the trees' canopy, the sky, where the plankton glows not quite turquoise blue.

Two paths diverge in front of her. One leads further up the green mountain, a series of slippery rocks as steps, something like a castle wall—another picture book, she has been remembering so many these past few days—built into the mountainside.

The other leads to a picnic table and a strange monolith. As she draws closer, details resolve: a stone chimney—*Little Red Riding Hood, Three Little Pigs.* There are no remnants of wood, not even charcoal, inside it. Moss has worn down its bricks to the same color as its mortar, and names—no, pictures, perhaps glyphs—have been scratched in its growth.

"Ah, you've got the right idea." Grandpa Jomar limps up beside her, sits down on the bench with a *whumph.* "You can't really take in the beauty of this place if you stand around talking about work all day."

Lili still doesn't know how to talk about work. She gestures at the fireplace. "Did people ever actually light fires in these?"

Grandpa Jomar nods vigorously. "Oh yes, long ago. When I was young."

"Wow," Lili says. "We don't do fire at home. I mean—if a fire happens, you're dead. We used to tell—I don't know, almost ghost stories about fire."

"It's not so different here," Grandpa Jomar says. "For all the water we are blessed with, we live in a hab too, in a way. These fires have not been lit for many years."

"What was it like?" Lili asks. "When the waters rose?"

"How old do you think I am?" Grandpa Jomar asks, but his eyes are twinkling. "My father, he would have been fifteen when they first started building the seawalls. Eighteen when the word came from the mainland that they had no way to remove their barriers without drowning us all, and Dr. Rivera made her proposal for the dome. Twenty—no, twenty-one when the governor approved the project. My sister Luisa—you know she died, in one of the first breaches?"

"I—yes," Lili says, stumbling a little over the words.

"He told me, he always said, it was hard after that," Grandpa Jomar says. His eyes are glistening now. How quickly emotions pass over his face, like the clouds moving swiftly over the bright sky beyond the trees above. It had been sunny the whole drive there until they got out of the trónico. "But he pushed through. He believed we would have the stars again, and the sun, in whatever form we could. He believed in Borikén."

Lili surreptitiously counts off years on her fingers. If her great-grandfather had been alive when the plankton dome replaced the opaque Flex-Plate™ from the continent, and if Luisa had been an older sister that Jomar didn't remember, and if Jomar was eighty-seven now—"Do you remember when they pulled back the old barrier?"

"I remember the tostones my mother served, and crying because my brother took my favorite toy!" Jomar says, and the tears are still in his eyes, but he is laughing now. "If I looked up at the sky that day, I don't remember it. No one tells you how boring it is to live through history, eh? Ay dios mio, maybe if we knew it was history when we were living through it we would pay better attention, hmm?"

Nothing like history ever happens on Mars. There are only the vids: planting, harvesting, cleaning, sometimes art for a treat. And all the parts of the vids that planet-siders don't think about: responding to comments, flagging spam, weighing sponsorships. Hushed conversations about the power struggles out in the starcruisers: whose influence might mean more follows this year, who to play against each other in negotiations, what might be pushing it too far.

Sometimes those conversations feel like the only thing the cruisers don't own, except of course they do.

"So it was all figured out by the time you were grown up?" Lili asks.

"Now what gave you that idea?" Grandpa Jomar says. "Figured out? Ay dios—no no no. There were issues for years, the plankton used to be so fussy, light and heat and there was that virus that came over from Florida. We had to learn new ways to farm, to build, to move from place to place— Not to mention the Reclaiming, I still don't know what would have happened if the Estados hadn't gotten distracted by their war with Saudi Arabia. I think that was then, it all gets— And the local politics, all the bickering—one year, there were ten different political parties, can you believe that?"

Water drips off a leaf above their heads, spatters onto Lili's hand like a kiss. Another drop kicks a spot of mud onto her shoes, like a drop of blood or a sparkling ruby.

She can't quite picture the world her grandfather paints. Everything seems so peaceful here. But the coquis and the birds must eat the insects, and the insects eat the plants. There must be conflict. And yet—

"How did it all work out?"

Jomar waves his hands dismissively. "Ah, how does anything work out? Talking and fighting and talking and someone backstabs somebody and somebody else makes a compromise and somebody else shouts a lot and a lot of us work hard and we do our best and look, a miracle!"

Lili kicks at a small rock at her feet. She wishes she could believe that something like that would work on Mars.

Did you want him to give you step-by-step instructions? she chides herself. Or was she expecting magic, the way Mama Oyuki says *Borikén* like some kind of incantation, her eyes misting up as much as Grandpa Jomar's, when she speaks of home?

"So how do you like this rainy forest, hmm?" Grandpa Jomar asks. He waves his cane out at the sweep of green. "Something to write home about?"

"I—" What kind of words can she marshal to say the things she was feeling? If she tries, will that feeling fall apart? Will the sleeping giant whose body she feels herself in be revealed as a trick of the light? "It feels very different." God, what a non-answer! "It feels—I keep being surprised I can breathe, there's so much water. And the air, I kept thinking there's a leak in a hab seal somewhere. Or I think I can hear someone breathing, but they must be so big, I must be in their lungs—"

"In a way, you are," Grandpa Jomar says. "Forests are the lungs of the world, so El Yunque is one of the lungs of our island. Here in our little scuba suit, hmm? More important than ever to have healthy lungs down here."

"Don't the scintillans photosynthesize—"

"Ah, go to Yadiel for all that biology. Me, I just learned enough science not to build houses straight." He winks at her, stands and stretches his legs. "No no no, don't you go getting up too! Stay a minute. Breathe with El Yunque. I'll distract the rest of them."

Another wink, and he is off down the path, surprisingly spry for his age.

Coqui, coqui, says the forest.

Lili closes her eyes. *Hello? Do you see me?*

She breathes with the forest, and it breathes with her.

#

The next day after a long breakfast and a longer lunch, the family decides that Lili needs to see the scintillans nursery at Vieques that evening. Grandpa Jomar shows her pictures on his big old fashioned handscreen on the way over, photos his father took with a 'mobil' when the work first began. The streets he shows her are crowded with restaurants and souvenir shops, but when their trónico pulls up to the pier, over half of those buildings have been pulled like teeth. Some of the remaining ones have lights in the windows; in others, green vines trail out through long-empty panes, and trees push through absent roofs reaching for the sky. Ghosts of old signs on their sun-bleached facades try to peek through.

Of the buildings that still stand, only one appears to sell anything—food, if the smells of fish soup and fresh pineapple in the breeze are anything to go by. There are a few new buildings as well, easily identifiable in their post-dome style, built to conduct heat or cool as the changing flow of EnerShare requires; decorated with glyphs of the sun, of coqui, of the huracán, and others that Lili doesn't recognize.

"Your uncle built that one," Aunt Valeria says, her face alight with pride as she nods to the structure next to the restaurant. The windows are dark but in the light from the streetlamps Lili can see a jumble of items in the doorway, the closest thing she's seen to litter here, but no— it's too carefully stacked. A coconut, some crosses, seashells, what looks like the skull of a...turtle?

"It's a..." Uncle Kevin's hands sculpt the air like the words of English he is looking for might be molded from it. "Not a church, but... like a church. For thanks—gratitude. The scientists, they..." He turns a pleading look at his wife.

"It's good to have a place to go to think about God," Valeria says decisively.

"God?" Lili asks, looking again at the glyphs. There are a lot of crosses in Valeria's house, but she assumed that was just aesthetic. Some cruisers go for that stuff—but of course, Valeria doesn't stream. Right. She keeps forgetting.

"God. Gods. Borikén." Valeria waves her hand through the air as if she is wrapping all the words together in the same cord. "The scintillans and all they give us. It is all science, but that doesn't mean it isn't also—"

Now she hesitates.

"Sacred," Yadiel finishes, slipping out of the shadows with Genesis at his side. "We're lining up for the boat now."

To Lili's surprise, the boat is old.

"One of the original glass-bottom ferries," Yadiel says, catching her look as they wait in line for their turn to board. He is quietly beaming with pride; it makes him glow. "We've kept it up all these years, for them. I can't wait for you to see them in their home."

They all glow when they talk about what they love, she thinks as she watches her family in the line in front of her. *I don't think I ever look like that.*

Looking at the line, it feels achingly obvious who was born here, standing so straight in their Earth-strong bones and their soft plant-fiber clothes, and who was a streamer serf from off-planet, clothes all patched polyester and skin chapped from the silt that escaped the air filters.

"It's had replacements, of course," Yadiel is saying. "We just re-placed the motor last year with a heat-storage one, and there's gene-tech in all the current sensors for navigation, and the seat coverings are all kelp-weave—"

Genesis rolls her eyes fondly behind his back.

When they board, Yadiel gets as delighted as a child showing them some of the pieces of the original petroleum plastic siding.

"It was louder in the old days," Grandpa Jomar tells him as they fly past the apartments that had been made from the old mansions, wa-ter-taxis darting out of their way like fish. The boat curves a white path of spray behind them. "When my father did the original surveys, he said they had to shout to be heard over the motor."

Instead, Lili hears the coquis on the dark curve of land, the occa-sional cry of birds overhead. The stars are bright—but of course they are not stars.

If she held still, would they make a sound? Could she hear?

She can hear the splash of fish leaping from the water. The water…

The spray is very white. Whiter than she would normally be able to see in the black of night. It's not just the foam, is it?

"Is that…"

Yadiel's eyes follow her outstretched hand. "Yes."

The sea foam glows with the trillions of scintillans who have not yet left their childhood home.

The boat stops, and the lights in the water subside as if they were an illusion, until the captain drops a bucket over the side. There they are, again, as he drags it through the water, little sparks. He pulls up a bucket and they crowd around, Yadiel looking just as wonderstruck as Lili feels, despite how many times he must have seen this.

"Take this," the captain says, handing them a stick.

They stir the water with the stick, and the scintillans swirl, reflections of the constellations above their head. Yadiel dips his hands in and pours water from his fingers into Lili's, and the little lights make no heat against her skin but her breath catches in her throat all the same. It is half holding more water than she has ever held in her life, and half the scintillans. She is touching the stars. She is touching home. She is touching dozens of little bodies that light up when they touch her. She is touching family, and something more alien than anything beyond Earth's atmosphere.

She bends low over the bucket as her family laugh and swirl the water.

"Hello," she whispers over its rim.

She could almost believe the lights are spelling out words in response.

#

"You'll like this," Genesis says as the trónico pulls to a stop in a puff of red sand.

It's almost the end of the trip. Genesis offered to take her out to another part of the coast today, since Grandpa Jomar had coffee with his friends, and the rest of the family had their volunteer shifts, Yadiel at the café and Aunt Valeria at the embassy and Uncle Kevin working from home, on conference calls with architects in other EnerShare countries.

The air hits Lili in the face as she exits the trónico, hot and dry despite how close they must be to the sea—she can hear it crashing. A quirk of the airflow, or something to do with magma conduits? Whatever it is, it—

"Look like home?" Genesis says with a smirk.

It almost does. If she could forget how odd it feels to be outdoors with a suit, without a helmet, without a voice in her ear monitoring her rads, without her own voice narrating something for her auditory.

Oh. That's the first time all day she's thought of her auditory.

"It's red," Lili allows. Red and orange and brown, dust and banded sandstone. "We don't have trees, though."

The trees are different than those in El Yunque. If those were giants, these are dwarves. They are small but sturdy, twisted to brunt themselves against the heat of the ground and the spray of salt on the wind, gnarled roots clawing for any scrap of moisture in the sand. Cacti circle around them, and a rickety wooden walkway gingerly rises over them to spare the humans' feet.

"My friends and I streamed a Mars style vid here once," Genesis says. "Totally had the cruisers fooled for like, three hours before someone pointed that out."

Lili's stomach jumps. "They sue?"

Genesis shrugs. "They tried. But we didn't charge, so…they just had to live with being dumbasses, I guess."

She laughs, light as the birds hopping along the sand hoping for fallen crumbs, and leads Lili down the walkway. Then there's a desire path pressed into sand and hardy grass that Lili isn't sure is sanctioned, but Genesis hops down onto it like it's nothing, so she follows. They pass a squat cactus shaped just like a Liquibulb, with tiny pink flowers unlike anything she has ever seen. Next to it is the first piece of litter Lili has seen on the island, a green glass bottle, and Genesis tsks and picks it up without breaking her stride.

"You want it?" she asked Lili. "I know you're working mostly in rock these days…"

Lili is tempted for a half-second, but the freight costs—she's already a little worried they're going to upcharge her for the five pounds she's put on from Grandpa Jomar pressing a guava roll on her every five minutes. "Nah."

Rocks press up through the orange sand, white like the vertebrae of the island. They are walking towards a dip in the hill, two trees leaning together like an archway. Lili had a book when she was little, with a picture of an entryway just like that. She can't remember where that entryway led to.

The rocks under their feet turn redder after they pass through, with sprays of green and blue where bits of the ocean have been trapped in pools where little fish dart. One boulder juts out into the sea, and Genesis strides confidently to its edge. Lili's feet wobble, but she follows. There is a smaller boulder—still huge, the size of an entire hab room—below. The waves crash against both rocks like a symphony, spray arcing in parabola that are different every time. The spray is cool on Lili's face and dusty legs.

This is only mine, Lili realizes. *Even what Genesis remembers will be a little different, from where she is standing, what she is comparing things to.*

This is something that can be for only me.

#

"Can we stop a sec?"

Genesis brakes the trónico, looks skeptically out at the cemetery clinging to the diagonal slope of the mountain. "It's nothing special—"

How to explain, what called to her from those slabs of stone, the bright flowers? The colors and angles and lines? "We don't have them on Mars."

"So how do you—wait." Genesis wrinkles her nose. "This isn't going to be like your moms' explainer vids on the meat vats, is it?"

"Maybe a little," Lili says. "I'll just be a minute." She hops out of the trónico.

"I may or may not have follow-up questions when you get back!" Genesis calls, before she pulls up something on her auditory, private setting, that makes her bump back and forth in her seat.

The graves are mostly long marble slabs lying horizontal in the ground, though a few rise upwards in the form of angels, their wings worn smooth by rain where they are not shorn entirely. Many of the slabs are cracked in one or more places. Yet most bear flowers, and the grass around them is neatly trimmed.

A rooster struts between the graves, giving a self-important crow.

"Hello," Lili says.

He deigns to give her a look, a king surveying a petitioner, before continuing the circuit of his court. He pecks absentmindedly at the grass growing tall around a stone—

Lili's heart skips a beat at the name engraved there: Luisa.

A second later, she chides herself. The surname, though blurred by water and time, is too long to be the correct one. They're not even in the right part of the island.

She parts the grass that grows tall around it to look closer. The year is almost but not quite indecipherable. The year is just about right, even if the name is not.

And does it matter if it is not the same girl? Surely someone loved her, just as much as her great-grandfather loved his girl.

Lili takes the pink cactus flower out of her pocket. She takes a picture in her memory, not her ocular; hopes it will be enough to recreate it from red rock when she gets back home, before she lets gravity carry the blossom to the stone.

She kneels, slowly, and places her hands on the marble. Runs her fingers through the grooves there, where dirt has caught and moss slowly grown.

So this is what rock feels like against her fingerprints. Silly to think that; she has spent the past decade of her life carving rock for the vids, but it is always outside, suited, helmeted, gloved.

She feels a heartbeat through the dirt. Perhaps the pulse of energy thrumming between this and a thousand other submerged islands. Perhaps the tides that wash back and forth, impossibly, behind the illusion of sky above her head.

Perhaps a heart, buried so deep no hypothesis can confirm, but strong enough that she will always hear it from now on.

"What was it like?" she asks the gravestone. "Living through history?"

#

"You sure you don't want another guava roll?" Grandpa Jomar asks.

Lili laughs, fending off the sandwich that Aunt Valeria is trying to stuff into her backpack. "I'm going to be over the weight limit as it is!"

"Write us sometime, when you get back," Genesis says. She gives Lili another hug; no one has stopped hugging her all morning.

The tone sounds indicating that there are only five minutes left to board the nuwhale to the rocket docking tower; Kevin hands Lili her suitcase, suspiciously heavier—she is sure she will find coffee beans and jam and a few fresh mangos. Ah well. She probably has enough credits for it. "Good trip."

Yadiel says nothing, just gives her another hug.

Even if she turned her ocular back on now, it would be too blurry to capture a useable picture.

#

Green circle, fading behind her.

Red circle, growing bigger in her vision.

She turns her ocular back on. It is not a surrender. It is only reality.

There are things inside her that are hers alone. There are people who see her as she really is. There is her heartbeat, echoing something larger, something far, far away but closer than her blood to her bone. She will never lose these things, no matter what she has to do.

She opens her mouth to begin narrating the parts of her life that she can choose to show.

The Event Don Juan of Mycelia

Stephanie Nina Pitsirilos

It had taken ten Sarasçetian solar cycles of Belise's life—her entire apprenticeship—but the map for the celestial quadrant was finally done and ready for burial.

"Take pride, Belise," the cartographer told her, running her hand over the brown mesh of the map. She stroked the smooth fibrous hills of its metal with her fingers, causing the cartographer's bracelets to jingle as they bunched together on the bones of her wrist.

Thin-tailed filaments on the map delineated the skeletons of superclusters of galaxies; the wider veins demarcated the currents of weight and pull of gravity. Woven into these threads were the details of the Sarasçetian observable universe: heavy neutron stars resembled taut metallic baubles; magnetars hummed in electric blinding spins. Her hand resting on the contours of the mesh, Belise could hardly distinguish the hand of her teacher—her grandmother Phoebe—from the map.

"It is your skill," Grandmother Phoebe continued, "that shows here, as well as mine." She took in a breath, her hand still resting there.

Belise's skill was indeed apparent in this piece: she had undone many of Grandmother Phoebe's errors, including one that had miscalculated the mass of a dying star. The star, corrected, had a density so great and a light so old, it meant that long ago, but not yet visible to the telescopes, the star collapsed in on itself. Belise had to unweave the red stone Grandmother had sewn in to depict a red dwarf, then retrack the gravitational wiring. The bead wasn't replaced with anything. There, the fabric of space ripped and time stopped for observers using the map. It remained a hole of nothingness, a place where nothing happened.

Grandmother Phoebe stroked a gold vein of a star's magnetic field with a finger. "How many dreamed of apprenticing on this quadrant."

Ten solar cycles ago, a star in a quadrant of the Gytheros constellation went supernova, turning the lens of every telescope on the mountains and in orbit around Sarasçetia that was charged with watching the quadrant—as well as those who weren't. It happened on Belise's eleventh birthday.

Belise remembered this clearly because after the customary song, she awaited her cake. Instead, a cry erupted from the telescope hill that the event had occurred. Friends, aunts, and even her mother ran away from the picnic table and rushed down the valley under the hills of Gytheros, their eyes on the black sky, eyes that were wide and searching not because of the wonder of the supernova's light but because of the red-shifted object that the quadrant's original name was replaced for (everyone but Belise): Don Juan.

Belise didn't have to follow them to know that their eyes looked this way. She saw what quadrant they were looking into, and that was enough. She had stayed at the table alone, undeterred from waiting for her cake. After about an hour, the procession of women trailed back to the picnic table. They were engaged in hushed conversation. Not one of them said anything to Belise for making her wait. Time did not matter to the women, or to Belise.

He appears the same, one said.

He doesn't seem harmed, another assured.

These observations were really laments. Belise heard these same words in the sleep-talk from her families' bedrooms. She heard these words moaned from deathbeds and screamed out from the women medics dragged down from the Gytheros hills—the women with nostrils stuffed with flowers. All of them bemoaned the same things after smelling flowers to forget: *Still, he leaves.*

Belise rolled up the completed map and tucked it under her arm. She watched her grandmother lost in this familiar lament.

Grandmother Phoebe was well over five hundred Sarasçetian cycles, five hundred years old. She had trained generations of Belise's family, and like anyone originating from a long-ago birth date, was affectionately called Grandmother by all. She could map not only her quadrant from memory but its sisters too, sewing each thread of their gravitational web blindly while calculating escape velocities for individual ships. Yet still, the sight of Don Juan erased all of that wisdom and calculated precision. Grandmother Phoebe was sullen; her response time slowed. It was the same for all generations of Belise's family on Sarasçetia who had been present for the event of Don Juan.

#

Sarasçetia, named for its most abundant flower, was a mountainous planet with dramatic peaks that eased into hills. These hills flowed into nestled valleys that puddled into fields of flowers unique to the mountain stone and soil. They were flowers that, when prepared by an apothecarist, erased all painful memories and maladies once the scent of their petals was inhaled. Atop each mountain sat the planet's most powerful telescopes, from which a trellis of cables crept down along the stone and branched out into capillaries in the ground, sinking beneath the flowers and into the soil, beneath the hills and valleys until they entwined into a webbed network of mycelium that fed into the maps laid down and buried by the cartographers. Each major mountain watched a specific quadrant in the sky, a supercluster of galaxies Sarasçetians nicknamed constellations, with different cartographers devoting their lives to a particular neighborhood of its detail and an apothecarist to its accompanying flower, a flower embedded with the story of its canopy of stars. And so:

The Lyre telescope peered into the supercluster Lyre, fabled for the boy who loved the music he created on this instrument so much that he lived his life in a cave that echoed its notes in perpetuity. Gold flowers grown on these hills the apothecarists used to get rid of musical earworms; this was obvious. But besides that, one could smell the Lyre flowers to banish away recurring recollections of embarrassing social faux pas, missteps, and recall anxieties. The hills of the Archer telescope, for the supercluster that resembled an archer pulling a taut bow, were covered in violet rows of flowers particularly popular with those who, despite the general balance of tranquility of Sarasçetia, were unsettled by slights of emerging injustices. The Archer flower, like all of Sarasçetia's medicinal flowers, did not make the afflicted simply forget. In the Archer's case, the flower calmed the inflamed conclusion of events in question with an antiseptic rewiring of logic that channeled ongoing energy toward building more reliable foundations that aimed to prevent societal repeats in behavior and historical accountability. The despair in the heart vanished, but untouched was conviction to move forward.

Yes, there were flowers for grave sinners against a consensus of morality. These flowers only worked on those who felt remorse, empathy, and regret. In the rarity of a murderer, for example, with the purple Charidian flower the sinner would be eased of enough suffering to allow them to function productively toward a life of humility and service toward good. It was not an invisible transformation, though. Within hours of inhaling its petals, the sinner would grow a purple tattoo of the flower on their right hand that resembled burnt flesh. Smell the flower twice for such an act, and it was the last breath you'd take.

There were white flowers for loss—loss of the heart, loss in death. These valleys, fortunately, were abundant on Sarasçetia. One variety of such a flower was slender, soft, and striped pink. It relieved a sufferer's longing and hate by softly guiding the narration of a memory into a duality, a fading conclusion of eternity. You let go of tomorrows but did not have to ever part with the clips of yesterdays that still made you smile. The flower worked at the singularity of the event's death—its endpoint to the observer's eye, and thus, heart. Without it, you never saw the person leave, say no, or die. You projected their memory into an infinite tomorrow accompanied by their absence. Their memory was fixed into a state of perpetual presence, pixelated in yesterdays. This flower worked on every kind of loss: lover, friend, family, admired, lusted, unrequited. There were flowers that cured all ailments on Sarasçetia. Except a flower for the event Don Juan.

#

Grandmother Phoebe's silence continued throughout their walk to the Gytheros Valley of the telescope. Belise treasured every word from her grandmother's mouth; her wisdom was unsurpassed. The silence made Belise feel the presence of an invisible thief that Grandmother Phoebe had no defense against or willingness to defend herself from.

The telescope was mostly hard to see in the night without moons, but occasionally Belise saw a reflection of its metal against the black pit of sky with the occasional shift in starlight, and she knew that they were heading in the right direction.

"This patch here," Grandmother Phoebe gestured to Belise.

But Belise already knew that's where the map was to go. The patch was mostly barren. Not because flowers would not grow here—indeed new ones were already sprouting. But it was a catch-up game. The moment a new flower bloomed in the valley of Gytheros, it was quickly picked. These flowers did little but give a person a moment of happiness that quickly faded, a quick rush that receded once it was time to inhale a second breath.

"Oh, but you knew that, of course," Grandmother Phoebe continued. "But a teacher I'll always be. Rarely does a flower get a chance to see another sunrise after its bloom in the quadrant of Don Juan."

"The Gytheros constellation you mean, mastery Phoebe," Belise corrected her, coldly. The constellation lost its name, replaced with what had mounted it.

Finally, Grandmother Phoebe raised her eyes and looked at Belise. Belise wondered how this correction would be received.

"Semantics, Belise. Nobody calls it that, anymore. But for that attention and allegiance to historical detail, I applaud you. You will make— you are—a fine cartographer." Grandmother Phoebe put her hands out. "Now give me an end; hold on to yours."

Belise gave Grandmother Phoebe two corners of the rolled-up map and started walking backward.

"On setsetchi," Grandmother Phoebe instructed.

Belise counted out each number in deep breaths until the patch was launched into the air like a fishing net.

Airborne and rising, the fibers of the map began to glow red. As it slowed in its ascent, the brown tatters of its mesh lit in electric blue. As the map succumbed to gravity and began to fall down, its weave sprouted roots that speared into the ground, burrowing down before it was completely fallen. The flower saplings were untouched as it did this: the map had made openings around them as it fell. Hardly three seconds passed and the map had buried itself completely, disappearing into the underground, an interlaced web that wove itself back up into the telescope and integrated its data.

Belise looked up the mountain, listening to the slight shift in metal gears as the telescope sequenced the update to the map. She expected Grandmother Phoebe to do the same, affirmation that their work was complete. Instead, Grandmother Phoebe was watching the sky. She spoke.

"On 567917 Sarasçetian cycle, Belise Abgwit, you became a cartographer."

Belise could now choose a quadrant of her own to devote her life to before taking her first ascension into the stars.

"See you at the house, then, Grandmother?" Nothing in Belise's life would be celebrated again like the evening she became a cartographer.

Grandmother Phoebe remained still. "In time, Belise. I will be there. All the life you've spent with me, I'm sure you'll welcome the space."

The ground was no longer glowing. The telescope had become still and quiet. The only light left besides the stars, were the belts around Belise and Grandmother Phoebe's waists, which were garnered with giant lanterned gemstones.

"But Grandmother," Belise began. But it was pointless to press her. She recognized the hallowed face. The detachment. She had heard the excuses before. It was irrational behavior, contrary to everything she knew about the personhoods of all the women she saw like this.

Belise made her way down the hills, leaving Grandmother Phoebe with eyes fixed on the black patch of sky, the void of Don Juan.

On the way home, she passed a man tinkering with his space pod. He turned around, looking up the road to her. His eyes were fixed on Belise's gemstone lantern belt.

"Cartographer," he greeted her with a respectful nod.

Belise nodded back. But she also caught what he mumbled next as he turned his attention back to his ship. "May your hand not be afflicted as your grandmother's."

It was not said with malice but as a wish.

#

It was a thrice moonless night on Sarasçetia when from a patch of black sky adorned with gems of starlight that the grave mark of Don Juan of Mycelia begins. He descended from the Gytheros constellation, the same one he'd forever exit from, during his brief visit on the planet that maimed the hearts of the women of Belise's family line, and many others on the planet. So indelible was the legacy of his visit, his legend rewrote the myth and nomenclature of the Gytheros constellation, to Belise's consternation. It was now simply called Don Juan QR-001. Light jumpers confirmed his mark on the planet through their lens of commodity. They had visited Sarasçetia before his arrival for the star maps all star-traveling beings sought out from the planet. The maps were used as historical markers to project a future to travel toward, a necessity of navigating the quirk of time dilation. To Sarasçetians, these exoplanet light jumpers would return to the planet hundreds of years later. To the light jumpers, only a few months had passed.

In the case of Don Juan, those who left Sarasçetia before his visit had returned, hearing rumors of his legend as they sat in pubs reorienting themselves with life since they'd left, before they collected new maps to venture out to the stars with, again. In the pubs they heard of Don Juan's visit. What happened collectively remained a fog, until you asked the women with whom he had encounters, or more likely, the witnesses. The only open consensus (and even this was spoken about in whisper) was the consequences of his brief visit to the planet. The maps ever since Don Juan's event possessed ever-so-slight but observable inaccuracies. The hydrogen content of such-and-such star was off in its projection—which meant that it did not evolve into a gentle bloated red dwarf but collapsed into a tight electrical magnetar as the startled light jumper discovered when he exited from his jump. There were no injuries in that particular case, but the incident was shared and produced some hesitation in trusting the storied maps of the cartographers of Sarasçetia for stars with particular solar masses, in fear that what they would arrive at would be a menacing star whose pull would spaghettify them into atomic noodles or rip from them all metallic elements of their body as they were simultaneously crushed into the size of an atomic speck of dust. The cartographers of Sarasçetia had become distracted and solemn, making mistakes in their star maps.

The semantics meant something to Belise. Not just because she was proud of the cartographer craft—there was nothing more noble than charting out the elements of the universe over an observer's point of time reference. It had meant something to Belise because of the weight she saw her line carry since the event of his visit. Don Juan was a stain.

What did he do? His event is more a series of events that compose a singular moment, and here are the rumors Belise herself heard echoed of what it was:

The women took Don Juan as any other light jumper in the market for a map. At first. They had never seen him before. But the first sign that he was different came when reports surfaced that he visited multiple telescopes. This was curious because once a quadrant was chosen, all other maps he collected would become obsolete once he light jumped to one. The past was always aging, and light jumpers collected maps for only themselves; they never traded. What also made these multi-telescope reports curious was that they were all reported to happen at the same time. However, each woman reported the same thing: that he traveled to their telescope, a figure walking down the hill toward the apothecary houses. *But what about the flowers?* Belise remembers asking the few with first-hand accounts from the women of what happened before these women stopped talking about the event. *Ask the women that,* the witness would answer, *and they'll tell you that he gave the flowers no regard, trampling them as he approached.* What's curious is how the women recount this without outcry.

To Aunt Ebstorf—a petite woman who had a dislike of men of hovering height as she didn't like to feel like a crumpled leaf under their bodies—to her Don Juan was a modest five feet. To Grandmother Phoebe, Don Juan descended the hills a towering seven, as Grandmother Phoebe was a woman who delighted in being crushed by a man's rigid frame. According to the telescopes of Urn, he had lavender skin that matched their lavender flowers. The Obelisk constellation remarked how his skin glowed onyx. Some said his head was bald and shiny like an emerald marble; others, how it was trellised in thick curls to anchor your fingers in during the throes of pleasure. And so, it went on—these variations on his account but always the same narrative arc: how Don Juan walked into their life for a night, gave them unmatched happiness—then abruptly left, leaving a vacuum in their hearts with his absence.

Though dominant in frequency, it was not just corporeal pleasure these women reported of the incident when they talked about what happened before sorrow closed these stories inside of them. For some women it was a night of careful sewing of maps that he did with them. Others said he sat on a chair and listened to their poetry, smiling after each recited stanza. Almeida, a notorious bookworm, said that with her Don Juan simply read a book of his own on the couch; she, another in her reading chair. She, like Kira, got the worst of his affliction—since then, she was never able to read again. Kira had spent the night solving galaxy rotation equations with him and after this night with him could no longer count to ten. Still, for most of the women, there was a hushed omission of *what* exactly Don Juan of Mycelia did with them during that night. But the consensus was that he delivered somatic pleasure that rivaled anything the women had ever experienced before. And then, he simply left, right back into the Gytheros constellation but at such speed that he entered the time dilation paradox that places fast objects, to the perspective of a stationary observer, as moving slowly through time. For these women who looked into the sky for him, they saw him leaving at an excruciatingly slow speed. It amounted to torture. To the inhabitants of Sarasçetia who peered through the Gytheros telescope, the dot in the sky that redshifted, denoting that an object was moving away from an observer, was Don Juan freshly leaving them. Yes, the sky was filled with other light jumpers leaving with their maps and Sarasçetian cartographers on their ascensions, but the only light jumper that mattered to these women was the one named Don Juan.

On Sarasçetia there were flowers to balm the disappointment of a lost locket after smelling their petals. Flowers for lovers to forget their mutual infidelities. Flowers, indeed, for unrequited and lost loves. But there was no flower on Sarasçetia that would erase the memory of Don Juan. If her family was plagued with heartache, Belise was plagued with questions and the burden of patching up the errors she found along the way of Grandmother's maps. How could her family, how could such a planet of esteemed cartographers bend at the knees and buckle from a Casanova time jumper? It's all Belise thought about growing up and still all she thought about during her ceremony that marked that she was ready for her ascension.

Belise could not stop thinking about him. So, she missed what her mother told her just after she finished unwrapping her ascension gifts.

"You don't like it?"

It was the clanging of dishes echoing from the cottage as guests brought plates inside that broke Belise's trance, not the concerned voice of her mother. At her eleventh birthday party, when the women preoccupied themselves with Don Juan's well-being, Belise's mother was eighteen years older than her. Now, ten years later, because of a light jump her mother had taken to map out a distant star, her mother was just five years older than Belise.

"What?" Belise asked quietly.

"Beli, the robe I made you. Is it that forgettable? It has the constellation I see you so often watch." Her mother was clutching a black robe in her hands. The robe was threaded in wired gold tapestry that twinkled in sync with the oscillations of the stars in the sky.

"I do, thank you."

"Was I right? Is that where you'll pledge your life to?"

Belise looked into the sky. Seventeen stars made up its scales, leading to the invisible patch, a deep void of space that separated it from Don Juan's red shifted dot. From the corner of her eye, Belise made out the hunched frame of Grandmother Phoebe shuffling toward the party. Half the guests had already left.

Coldly, Belise smiled and looked back at her mother, her heart racing inside. "Yes," she answered. "The rest of my life."

#

In the season that Sarasçetia tilted toward its second star, a distant brown dwarf that occasionally brought evening frost to the flowers, Belise was allotted her own private time with the general telescope used for those who completed their ceremony but had not yet attached to a constellation. She had been working on a patch of map for one year now. The Pythia constellation appeared in the sky not too long ago, maybe a few Sarasçetian generations, and though much of its scales were well charted, there was much work to be done with its tail that ended with a lovely blue dot just before the great void. Though all of Belise's charts and calculations stored in the telescope's log were of this star, there was another part to the map that was documented only in a book made from the rough hides of mushrooms that in the last one hundred years began to grow together with the flowers in the fields. The pages in the book charted not the star Belise was preparing her ascension jump toward but instead a particular area beside it: a void. The pages were filled mostly with calculations, except for two pages, which logged observations from the telescope.

Belise programmed the telescope to shift twenty-three degrees away from star 5678-20.

The floor hummed as the wheels of the telescope turned. When they stopped, the room went dark, and the telescope projected a hologram of what it saw. This was the third time Belise had input these coordinates during her apprenticeship time here. The first time was an amateur's mistake—she misaligned the coordinates and jump-shot the star. But with this error, Belise noticed something that wasn't supposed to be in that part of space. She zoomed into a corner of the viewing panel, to her far right. It was so easy to miss, which is why when the telescope had told her it was there, Belise didn't believe it. It was a tiny smudge of light, arched like it was being stretched, outlining half the diameter of an invisible circle. Belise wrote her observation down—*gravitational lensing*—in the fungal book, with the coordinates.

She did not report what she saw. She would remember this premeditated omission much later in her life.

The next time she looked into the void, the smudge wasn't there. But she had predicted that. As she had predicted that today she'd see it once again.

"Zoom in," Belise commanded the telescope.

There floating in the black room with her was the white ghostly disc, the smudge, the gravitational lensing of light. The void was not empty, or at least in the way we measure emptiness. Something quiet lay there undetectable, unless you looked for it at the right perspective, time and with the right instruments—found only on Sarasçetia.

Before leaving, Belise had the telescope confirm her calculations, as well as the observable distance between the arc of the disc to the red-shifted dot of Don Juan. Then she calculated his velocity.

#

"It is cliché to say it, Belise. But it is so true: time flies on Sarasçetia." Her mother was standing in front of her, her eyes on the gold wires of the robe Belise was wearing that she had gifted her more than a year ago.

"Time has no fixed place on Sarasçetia," Belise replied. "Except as an anchor to those left here. Your Sarasçetian age was younger than mine when you first ascended."

"And I left a baby behind," her mother added with a somber smile.

"Not so for me, though," Belise remarked comfortably.

"You've chosen a distant star."

"All stars that we map are distant."

"It will take you some time to get there at your half-light speed. Do you feel ready? You'll be gone from us ten years, though for you it will be six months."

Ever since Belise's mother light jumped and she and her mother became so close in age, Belise's mother became more the awkward friend to her than parental guide. For wisdom she had her aunts and Grandmother Phoebe, who logged many Sarasçetian years as well as those of light jumps. It was Grandmother Phoebe who answered Belise's questions when her mother had left for a light jump, who helped with preparing for when her mother would one day return but would have aged only one year at most while Belise would have aged ten.

"When you introduce an observer to life, Belise," Grandmother Phoebe had explained to her, "—what we all are in this life—observers—time is not a constant universal. It's about perspective."

"What does that have to do with my mother's age?"

"At high speeds, like when someone like your mother light jumps, from our perspective here at home, time slows down for her. For the light jumper, time ticks normally."

"That does not make sense."

"The words don't make sense. Do the equation in your head. Your mother left at the speed of three quintrons."

Belise was quiet for a moment. Light flickered inside the pupil of her eye. "Oh," she said humbly. "It does make sense now, Grandmother."

Later, Belise did not come home for dinner. Grandmother Phoebe found Belise sitting on a high perch atop the Zylypse telescope when she went out to search for her, the telescope with valleys of translucent flowers for curing the heartache for someone you miss.

When her grandmother yelled up, asking what she was doing there, Belise called down, annoyed: "I'm moving away from gravity, Grandmother. Time dilation works like that, too. Move away from gravity, and time runs faster. This way, I can get older at a quicker speed. There is too much gravity on Sarasçetia, Grandmother."

Now, as Belise herself prepared for her ascension, she was anticipating that her mother might light jump again, too. "Should you not be here when I get back," Belise started.

"Then I'll see you in between the cycles," her mother finished.

Belise did not correct her.

Her mother opened her arms and leaned into her. Her arms wrapped lightly around Belise's back. Belise felt them pull away. Belise said goodbye.

#

At the launch field by the Gytheros telescope, Grandmother Phoebe prepared the last of the fibers for Belise to etch the beginnings of her map once arrived. Grandmother Phoebe was quiet as she worked, as she always was. "I won't be making another jump, you know," she told Belise.

Belise could hear her heart. Grandmother would expire by the time Belise got back. "I hope that I can continue the expertise of your craft, Grandmother."

"Don't leave me in wonder then, Belise. You have packed the patching for two maps."

Belise smiled at Grandmother Phoebe. She held the woman's hands to feel for the last time the soft wrinkled skin sagged from gravity's time weight. "I have left important instructions in the telescope. You must promise me that someone follows them, not for my sake but yours. So that you may appreciate the map that I will thread. You will light jump again, Grandmother, a few times more, if you are to follow them."

Grandmother raised her eyebrows.

Belise continued. "I ask you, Grandmother: Do not expire until the sky gives you my gift. After that, I ask: one of you continue the line until I return so that I have someone to ground me when I get back."

Grandmother dropped her head to her hands. Belise saw her head bob up, then down. For the first time, Belise saw her grandmother cry. She remained still until grandmother was done. It lasted not more than a minute.

Grandmother did not ask Belise any more questions. Once inside the light craft, Belise reprogrammed her ship, the first of three spacetime destinations.

#

Belise of Saras̨cetia year 567898, you are waking up now.

A thought materialized in Belise's mind, the first one in nine months to echo back to her. Belise was conscious.

Arrived at spacetime one area. Wake up, Belise. You are light jumping. You are on light craft 87560. You are—"

"I am aware," Belise whispered, removing the hydration tube from her mouth.

State your name to initiate command transfer chain.

Belise opened her eyes. Her mind was nearly blank. She only knew that she was awake. She tried to remember. All she could do was feel sensations, then ascribe them meaning: the bright beam she saw above her head was light; its color was white; she smelled the layers of metal of the ship. She remembered she had a body held down by straps, that her body lay somewhere in the ship. She felt the warmth of a blanket on her fingertips. She believed she had will—that she chose to get up. Belise could not get up. At first. This caused her to remember where she was. And why.

Easy, Belise, the craft told her in Grandmother's voice. Reprogramming the voice prompt with hers had been Grandmother's gift. *You will need two Saras̨cetian days to recover. Begin now. Move your left leg.*

Belise obeyed. Then she moved her right leg. Then her arms and fingers.

In two days Belise transferred command of the craft back to herself.

"Is it there?" she asked the ship.

First spacetime destination confirmed, Belise.

Belise asked the craft to signal Don Juan's ship but not to show a visual of it.

#

Don Juan of Mycelia was awoken by his ship. Belise knew this because she felt someone in her head. He arrived in Belise's mind as an approaching wave that she felt had collapsed onto her, knocking her down and leaving her submerged in a liquid she could not see. Don Juan was not simply a telepath of words, Belise now understood, but one who could bridge consciousness to a chamber of interactive imagery. Around her, Belise heard the echo of a seemingly infinite chamber of sighs. Sighs of her grandmother, aunts, and her mother. Belise could do nothing but think to raise herself up from this sensation of being submerged. When she pulled herself up in her mind, though, she found that her body was entangled in a white lattice of delicate roots strung with clusters of creamy pearls. The pearls pinched close to her skin but more so: there seemed no end to the white dress. Its tail stretched out toward an unobservable horizon when Belise looked behind her.

Belise had often wondered what it looked like beneath the soil on Sarasçetia where they buried the star maps of the telescopes. Where the cables grew into one another in an electric network and communicated. Wearing the white dress of lattice, Belise looked as if she carried all the maps ever sewn on Sarasçetia stitched together. But one that mapped Don Juan's pleasures, not the universe. If this imagery depicted the network of Don Juan's anatomy, it mirrored Sarasçetian technology.

Belise touched a pearl. It pulsed with the sigh of a woman.

Any parallels to Sarasçetia ended here; Belise's planet harbored healing; Don Juan fed off pain.

"An interesting garment," she heard a voice tell her.

Despite its delicate weave, the dress was deceptively heavy.

Don Juan was a specific or singular species of some fungoid life, Belise surmised from the nature of the organic lattice. A hybridity of himself and those he touched. A species who found a way to latch on to

the desires of Sarasçetia's women, inflame them with promise, then teth-
er their pining hearts into his web as food.

The bodice unraveled from around her body and faded. Belise saw
herself in the cabin of her craft again. She looked down at her arm. It
was bloodied from the blade she had cut herself with, the blade she made
sure to hold in the event Don Juan was a telepath. Pain had grounded
her.

Belise spoke into her mind. "I am Belise of Sarasçetia. I come bearing a great gift."

She waited.

"Why not use visual?" his voice echoed from her craft, though his
presence was in her head as well. She felt him try to forage further into
her psyche. He could not venture further than she allowed.

"My sight is not at full capacity," Belise lied, speaking from her
mouth. She had no wish to see Don Juan's physical form. He would show
her what she wanted to see, undress her desire. Her desire was what she
had set out to do to him. "Speech is fine."

"You I did not meet on Sarasçetia," Don Juan remarked in her head.

"No. Otherwise, I could not be here."

If lust and want were behind Don Juan's legacy, then long ago
Sarasçetians would have sought him out. How convenient that Don Juan
left for them a void from which they felt no escape. In this way, they were
a lifelong source for him to sap from.

"However," Belise continued, "we take pride on Sarasçetia for the
accuracy of our maps. The one you are projecting toward, I'm afraid
there was a slight correction I found and feel obliged to provide."

"A noble gift, Belise of Sarasçetia. You have sacrificed much in traveling fast enough to catch up to me. How do you propose giving it to me
at our speeds?"

"I will transmit it to you if you allow. The map on my ship will teach
the map on yours to rewrite itself."

Don Juan paused. "That will do. I wish there was a way to thank you."

Belise smiled, even though Don Juan could not see it. "It is my pleasure, Don Juan. You could tell me the name of your origins."

"That was so long ago. But if it is true: Mycelia. Even light jumpers
as ancient as Sarasçetians would not know it."

Belise instructed the map to begin transmission to Don Juan's ship.
The small patch of the map became illuminated with rapid flashes of
light. It flashed like this for a while, until finally the craft spoke to her.

Rewiring confirmed. The maps are now one. Data transfer achieved, Belise. Awaiting command to decelerate.

Belise waited, though not as long as the family she left on Sarasçetia. For them, it had been one hundred years since she had left.

In five Sarasçetian minutes, Belise watched Don Juan's ship begin to change course. Within eight, it began an arched trajectory toward the void.

"Grandmother," Belise spoke to the craft. "Show me the craft of Don Juan of Mycelia." A hologram of his craft materialized in the cabin.

"Belise," Don Juan soon called out to her. "Why?"

She waited a moment, her finger resting on the knob until she no longer resisted. Belise pulled her finger down to switch the visual channel open.

The panel of Belise's light craft began to vibrate. Don Juan's ship was not far now from where the ghost of light arched in Belise's telescope on Sarasçetia. The place where light bent around the sphere because the sphere's gravity was immense. A sphere she depicted in maps as a tear in the fabric, that if crossed into delivered your fate not to space but to the hands of time, the place where things don't happen: the sleeping black hole Belise sent Don Juan toward. Belise had omitted the black hole from the map.

A visual of Don Juan now appeared in front of her.

Belise saw him as this: skin like the gray moons of Tantus, the dark lines of gills beneath a capped head that gave his face the appearance of having a long dark brow. The shadow beneath the gills where there were no eyes. He had a stalklike body, and hyphae that draped down to the floor as elongated limbs. These hyphae were his instruments: arms to embrace with, legs to wrap around a waist, thighs that squeezed the body with pressure and weight to affirm reality, a sex flowered as a mushroom. The quantum parts of Don Juan, of course, she could not see. But they functioned at the tips of his hyphae, which he used to touch her line to entangle them with a shared destiny. The hyphae allowed Don Juan to be everywhere at once, but with only you, once you fixed your eyes on him.

"There is no why, Don Juan of Mycelia. Were you ever weighted by this question?" She spoke to him as he was a past.

"I gave them pleasure, Belise. The ones who welcomed it. And it's never only the ones you'd suspect."

"You left them with a well of nothingness."

"In return, they became mine. So, I wouldn't call them nothing then, such objects. Will *you* be weighted by what you've done?" He spoke to her as if she was a future.

"When you cross over into the black hole," Belise answered him, "there will be nothing for me to weigh over. Black holes behave as objects yet are chambers of nothingness. We say that we can never observe an object cross over into them because time simply stops at its horizon because there is too much gravity. You, though, will say that you crossed inside, in the same way we light jump and age only a few months, but for those on Sarasçetia it will have been many, many years that we are gone. And so, black holes, to us outside of them, are collections of events that never happened. So, how would I have remorse for something that never happened? That's what you are becoming, Don Juan. To us. An event that never happened. You will become, you are becoming, nothing."

Belise watched his visual fade away as his craft lost escape velocity. In the darkness, Belise waited for her craft to stitch together his communication back. She had waited now over five hundred Sarasçetian years to reach him. She could wait a little bit more to hear his story end before it never even happened.

A visual of Don Juan returned to her cabin. "So long as they remember me," Don Juan continued, "I live on, Belise. That is immortality."

"And now you will have that, Don Juan. Live forever in the Sarasçetian sky. Because although you will become an event that never happened, we will observe a snapshot of you frozen forever in front of the black hole because of this time dilation. If asked which one of these is you—the memory of you on the horizon, or the conclusion of the event—I will have to hope Sarasçetia can reconcile this to a logic in the same way our flowers do other maladies. Can it be both? I cannot undo that you made yourself part of them. But now, they will be at peace. You are not leaving them anymore. You-not-you will be a fixture in the sky to comfort them, while also being an event that never happened. They will have their hearts back."

Belise looked into the shadows where he did not have eyes. "Know, though, that this is not how I see you. Before you become nothing, I see you as waste orbiting a drain."

The visual zoomed out of Don Juan's frame, back to his craft. He was too close to the black hole now and was redshifting out of the light spectrum and into invisibility. Don Juan's ship appeared to slow down but not because of his engines. Time for Don Juan, from an observer's view of him, was slowing. Belise's ship hummed. It wasn't long before she heard his voice again.

"What would I be, Belise, without someone to measure me?" His words began to trail.

"What…would…you…be…without s o m e   o b j e c t   t o   m e a s u r e ?. . ."

A mycorrhizal network of red light crept out from Don Juan's craft, slowly. The light branched out as if looking for an anchor but found only distorted space. The hologram of Don Juan's craft, a red spore with a lattice of disconnected roots, disappeared from Belise's cabin.

"It's mutual then," Belise said to nothing.

On Sarasçetia, it had now been almost a thousand years since Belise left. Before returning, she pulled out the second map and stopped at star 5678-20 to collect her ascension data.

#

Belise had made Grandmother Phoebe promise to light jump, to never stop observing until her gift arrived. She remembered this wish while awakening to the sensation of her limbs being puddles of stagnant water. If she felt this, Belise concluded in the darkness of her mind, it meant she was feeling gravity again. If she felt gravity again, then it meant she was to open her eyes and learn if a promise was kept, if Belise had achieved what she desired.

Belise opened her eyes to a stranger above her.

A woman old and wrinkled was cupping Belise's neck forward while smiling.

Belise felt a tickle in her eyes.

"Belise of Sarasçetia 567898," the woman said. "Welcome back. I am Shana-Sarasçetia 568898, the remainder of your line. You are younger than me, Grandmother."

Belise looked to her side. A window opened out to a telescope field, with hills of black flowers in bloom with mushrooms that glowed electric blue. Belise wondered how different the sky looked on Sarasçetia now. What stories the flowers now told of them.

"Tell me of the event," Belise whispered.

In the over one thousand years since the event of Don Juan, Sarasçetian cartographers recorded a shift in the color and size of his dot, about a thousand years after Belise had left. It swelled, appearing to gain more mass. This had been Belise. Then he drifted into the quadrant of the great void where nothing existed. Later, cartographers recorded his dot as appearing to bloom into a tiny yellow flower.

"Not a flower…" Belise whispered. The spectacle of Don Juan's craft attempting to light jump from the gravitational pull of the black hole. To the naked eye, the dot faded, appearing as if nothing was there.

"Your line continued to light jump. But when the sky settled and we saw nothing, your grandmother, Grandmother Phoebe, commanded all of Sarasçetia's telescopes to look together into the void," the woman recounted to Belise. "Not too close to it but just before…. A snapshot of Don Juan fixed just outside the event horizon of the black hole none of us could see. Where he would remain forever. But…"

Belise already felt the weight from what was about to leave the woman's mouth, how history played out into a future. A history that would tell Belise whether she simply rearranged a point in the sky to be recorded on a map or whether she managed to rewire the maps of her family's hearts so that they could resume a journey into a future. That's what Belise wanted.

"We are, also, celestial cartographers," the woman continued. "We know that according to the perspective of a theoretical Don Juan, Don Juan crossed over the event horizon of the black hole. And so, this meant that Don Juan was no longer leaving. Don Juan is an event that never happened."

The woman stroked a lock of Belise's hair away from her eyes. "I was instructed to pass down Grandmother's last words before she allowed herself to expire. Are you ready for them, Belise?

Belise nodded.

"We witnessed your gift and went in peace." The woman turned around, fidgeting with a tray on the table behind her. "And now with your return, Belise, my role as a keeper of this legend has reached its maturation as historian. Let the records mark this."

Light jumpers from this point on, the woman told her as Belise gained the strength to sit up, recorded a remarkable evolution in Sarasçetia's cartography since the maps were updated with this development in the sky. Sharp, accurate, unforgiving, and unapologetic in how they thread a past of the cosmos that made it possible to predict a future from.

Belise felt something heavy fall from her eye.

Once on Sarasçetia, Belise had a grandmother. She once long ago had aunts. Briefly, she even had a mother.

"There is too much gravity, Grandmother…" Belise heard herself say. Now, though, she was not a child.

Belise's tears poured out. They dripped down the curvature of her cheeks, they free-fell onto the floor.

"Belise…" The woman held a bowl of cut black flowers out to Belise's face. They glowed electric blue. "Please. Take them."

Sobbing, Belise picked the flowers up in her hands, pulled them to her nose, and began to breathe heavily into their petals.

"No, Grandmother," the woman softly told Belise. "It's been too long. These flowers you must eat."

There were flowers for the tears of lost family. There were flowers for guilt.

Belise's tear-soaked mouth was full of flowers.

But there would be no more tears on Sarasçetia for Don Juan of Mycelia.

Between Worlds

Rodrigo Culagovski

Content warnings: Some xenophobia.

My name is Lïi Cea Shaan. I was the first person to walk into a portal on Earth and out of another one, 150 million kilometers away. Maybe you already know that, but what you don't know is why I was the first one to make it through. To tell you that story, however, I first need to tell you about my life.

We fled to Earth when I was seven years old, escaping the fascists who had taken control of the Trojan Habitats I was born in, and landed in Chiloé City, in southern Chile. Some of the buildings were bigger than the entire module I'd spent my childhood in, grown out of wood like kilometer-high, leafless trees. I'd never seen a blue sky before. My parents were happy we were alive, together, and safe.

On my first day in school on Earth, I wore the clothes my dad had taken me shopping for the day before. He'd insisted I should look like an "Earth kid." Thick blue pants. Big shoes with chunky laces you had to tie. A sweater over the whole thing with a bright, three-color pattern.

As soon as I walked into the classroom, I realized he'd failed, miserably. The other kids looked cool. I looked like my dad picked out my clothes.

"Oh, hello, you must be Lee!" said the teacher.

"Lïi."

"Sorry?" she asked.

"My name is Lïi, not *Lee*."

"Oh sorry. Okay, Lee, please come in and sit . . . there, next to

Antonio." She pointed at a space next to one of the Earth children who were all staring at me as if I was some sort of insect.

"Where are you from?" asked Antonio.

"I'm from the Trojan Habitats at the L4 point."

"Are you human?"

"Yes."

"You're so tall and skinny, and your eyes are big. And you speak funny . . ."

The class started before I could explain genefixes or that Spanish wasn't my native language. During the break, I saw Antonio talking with a group of our classmates. Every half-minute or so one of them turned around to take a look at me, then turned back. There was a muffled comment and a sharp laugh from the whole group. Some of them made exaggerated stretching movements with their neck, legs, and arms, or opened their eyes wide. This was punctuated by high-pitched laughter as well.

I didn't speak with Antonio or anybody else that day and sat by someone else for the rest of the school year.

#

At fourteen, I didn't have any close school friends, didn't like any of my teachers very much, and never got over the feeling that if I just stopped going to school one day, nobody would notice.

I met Alex in a park near the refugee building my family lived in.

"Did you know this whole place used to be underwater?"

"What?" I turned to look at this strange Earthling who had started talking to me for no reason.

"This park," xe continued, "got flooded when Antarctica melted. They're setting up dikes and seawalls and pumping out the water. It's a test for public space reclamation."

Xe looked different than the kids from my school. Xyr clothes and hair marked xem as an enby, for one, which had been common back at the Trojans but rare here on Earth, where everybody was hung up on gender. Xyr eyes seemed to be looking at something that wasn't there, and xe clearly was not at all self-conscious about walking up to a random stranger and reciting facts.

"No, I didn't know that. I just like it. It has clear, easy-to-see edges. It reminds me of home."

Xe looked at me directly. "You're from one of the space habs, right?"

Something about the way xe said it was different from the way other people asked the same question. There was no judgment, no what-a-freak, just friendly curiosity.

"Yes. I'm Lïi. I'm from the Trojans."

"Alex. How long did it take you to travel to Earth?"

"Three weeks."

"Was it awful?"

"Three weeks in a cramped, windowless coffin of a room, with walks around the ship's exercise ring for an hour each day and food that came in the same tubes as toothpaste and didn't taste much better."

"Too bad they haven't gotten portals to work. Then it would have taken no time at all, but they're still mostly theoretical. The L4 Trojan Habs . . . that means you speak Trojan, right? Which is a mix of . . . Spanish, Mandarin, Hindi, and . . . Bengali?"

"Why do you know so much about off-planet languages, parks, and portals?"

"You can't tell to look at me, but I'm a huge nerd," xe said with a big, toothy smile.

We both laughed. We spent the rest of the afternoon together. By its end, xe was the best friend I had on the whole planet.

#

I finished my basic schooling at nineteen. I went to the graduation ceremony but skipped the party. I doubted I'd ever speak to any of my schoolmates again. They were okay, mostly, but I didn't have anything in common with them.

"So, what are you going to do?" said Alex. We were in the same park where we'd met, sitting on the swings.

"Not sure. I'm thinking of going back to the L4."

"I thought it was a fascist dictatorship?"

"It was, but the dictator died. Things are supposed to be getting better now. They even had an almost-legit election." We moved over to a spinning disc and sat on its edge, pushing ourselves slowly around and around.

"Do you know when you're going back?"

"Not sure. I'm still figuring out my application to the academy I want to go to."

"I'll miss you," xe said in the unselfconscious way xe had.

"Me too, but we'll stay in touch."

"Won't it be weird, going back after all this time?"

"I've never felt at home here. People still look at me like I just got off the transport, and they're always asking me 'Where are you from?' and making a big deal of how I look and talk and, I don't know, everything. Nobody says my name right. It's exhausting." I moved to a bench.

"Wow. I never knew it was that bad." Xe came over to sit next to me. "I like the way you look, Lii. It's unique."

"Thanks. Most days I don't think about it. And at least I have one friend." I leaned against xem.

"That you do, that you do," xe said, patting my head.

#

The L4 point was sixty degrees ahead of the Earth's orbit and as far from the planet as it would have been to the Sun, but my parents got me a ticket on a high-G shuttle, so it took three days instead of three weeks, and there were portholes. Even so, the majesty of space got old pretty quickly and I was happy when we arrived.

I stepped out of the shuttle onto Transport Module C, the one that handled Earth traffic. It was a torus made out of some sort of nano-fiber material. It had a few transparent panels that showed you a slowly rotating view of other modules and the articulated tethers that joined them together. I didn't remember the overpowering smell of waste-reclamation algae ponds. I must have blocked the memory.

There were earthlings in the concourse but also more people who looked like me than I felt could exist in the whole universe. I released a breath I didn't know I'd been holding in for the past eleven years and walked to a stall in the middle of the concourse with a colorful sign reading, "Fresh Fried Fritters!" in Trojan and Spanish.

"One please!" I felt weird and elated to speak Trojan to somebody who wasn't my mom or dad.

"Sure thing! You just get off the shuttle?"

"Um, yes. I'm coming back to the hab after living on Earth since I was a kid. I'm Lii."

"Oh, one of the *returners*, huh? Well, good luck. Though from what I hear, you won't need it." She handed me the fried dough with an expression of mild distaste. It wasn't as good as I remembered.

I looked up *returner* on the local net. It meant people like me, who'd fled the dictatorship and returned now that it was over. Some were happy or at least neutral about us, but others saw us as interlopers, almost foreigners who were getting all kinds of benefits and attention just because we "ran away instead of staying in the home habs."

When classes started, I met people. There was Guss—also a returner who'd come back from Australia—Mina, Naya, Nick, Agastya, and Saskia. It was the first time I'd had friends, plural.

Other classmates were less welcoming.

"Where are you from?" asked one of them, Lex, as we were standing by our lockers.

I was a little put off by how blunt his question was but answered, "I was born in the Zhang-Acevedo Hab, out past the fungus modules."

"No. Where are you *from*? Where did you live before coming back to the L4?"

"Oh. My family settled in Chiloé, it's a large island in southern—"

Lex turned to his friends behind him. "Do you hear that accent?" He laughed. I wasn't aware that I had an accent when speaking Trojan. It was my native language after all.

His friends laughed and they all left.

I never got to explain where Chiloé was.

#

I was more talkative in the L4 than I'd been on Earth. I even learned how to tell bad jokes—*What happens when you combine a joke with a rhetorical question?*

I mostly stayed away from politics, however. People were still divided between those—like my family—who despised the recently deceased dictator and those who thought he "saved the L4." I grew up hearing about the atrocities the fascists committed, the modules that got their oxygen and water rationed for opposing him or not being "patriotic" enough, and the dead bodies floating slowly away from airlocks. Whenever I tried to speak with people about it, regardless of what side they were on, they talked over me saying things like, "Your family ran away, you don't know what it was really like." The *Ibarristas* said it had been necessary for the Admiral to "take control and cleanse the system." Those who'd opposed him told me I was soft and bourgeois because I'd lived on Earth, and I didn't have any "space-smarts."

So I talked about music, videos, classes, and my favorite books. I didn't talk about politics.

#

I kept in touch with Alex but the eight-minute light-speed lag meant we couldn't have actual conversations. I wished they'd worked out how to use the portals xe'd told me about when we met—I could have just gone to see xem and come back.

Having multiple, new friends close at hand was a plus. They helped me update my wardrobe and get a better haircut as well as smooth out my accent. They also explained some of the nuances of talking with L4 people.

"For instance, I say 'Hey Lii, let's get together tomorrow!' What does that mean?" asked Agastya during my first coaching session.

"That we're going to get together tomorrow?" I answered around the straw in my choco-soyshake. We were in one of the panoramic blisters on the Reddy module, in what to my mind was the finest ice cream parlor in the whole solar system. You could see most of the Trojan habs from here, all the modules spinning in different directions, and the umbilicals that tied the whole thing together crisscrossing like a three-dimensional puzzle.

Agastya and Nick giggled. I didn't mind.

"No, you Earth-goof," said Nick, "it means, maybe I'll ping you, maybe I won't, and don't be pushy about it."

"But why would you say something if you don't mean it?"

Xe giggled again.

"Because, you know, people have agendas, and like, hidden motives. You can't just believe what they tell you."

"Oh, right. Agendas. Of course."

"What if I say, 'Lii, I hate you!'?" asked Nick.

"That, um, you like me? Because of the hidden agenda thing?"

"No, sorry. That means xe actually hates you," said Agastya.

"It's subtle. An art form," said Nick.

"Stick with us, Earthling. We'll protect you from the mean L4ers."

I didn't like being called "Earthling", even as a joke, but I stuck with them.

#

I finished my studies at the Trojan Academy. My friends all found jobs in different places. Mina and Agastya on one of the asteroids that orbited the L4 point. Nick was going to Mars to study advanced hydroponics.

Guss, my fellow returner, had quit the academy before finishing—he was back on Earth, in one of the new underground cities in Western Australia. I missed him, even though we weren't that close. He was the only one who understood what it had been like to leave the L4 and then come back. He'd struggled, just being here, looking like everybody else but feeling different on the inside. I could relate.

Saskia had studied chemical engineering and group dynamics. She was joining one of the Titan missions. Everybody treated her like a war hero, including me. She was the third person I'd ever kissed and the first I slept with. Then she left on a seven-year trip. Everybody else left, too.

#

"Hey, you're back!"

"Yes, and you're still here!"

I hugged Alex. We'd arranged to meet up in the Dalcahue area, down by the water. Xe'd never been to the *Cocinería*—I led xem through the doors into the stadium-sized, wooden building shaped like an over-turned rowboat. The smell of all the food cooking in the different stalls was overpowering.

We picked one and sat down. I ordered for both of us—*Curanto con Milcao*, a large smoked meat and seafood stew with potato pancakes.

The food arrived quickly. "There's nothing else like this in known space," I said around a mouthful.

"What happened, weren't you gonna stay on your L4 hab?"

"Yeah, I don't know. Some of it was great. Some of it sucked. And it wasn't like I remembered from when I was a kid, you know?"

"Yeah. Nothing really is." Xe took a big bite of xyr potato pancake. "Wow, this is really good."

"I know, right? Anyway, all my friends there were going off to different places, and I didn't have a good reason to stay."

"But, all that stuff about feeling out of place here on Earth, wasn't that better at the L4?"

"It turns out that wherever you go, you take yourself with you. I'm not sure I feel 'in place' anywhere. So I figured I'd rather feel odd and foreign here where my family and my best friend are, and where the corporations haven't figured out a way to charge you for the air you breathe—yet."

"Aw. You're my best friend too."

We smiled at each other awkwardly. Alex had changed a lot in the years I was in space. Xe'd grown into xyr face, the things that had made xem awkward and weird when we were kids, like xyr long, straight nose, wide forehead, and outlined lips, now made xem look striking.

"So, what are you going to do back here on Earth? You staying in Chiloé City?" xe asked, snapping me out of my reverie.

I realized I'd been staring at xem and turned away. Was I blushing?

"Um, yeah. I'm not really sure doing what, though. I'll be staying with my parents while I figure it out."

"Down in Quellón, huh? I'm working in a design studio up in Ancud, on the other tip of the island, but we can see each other on the weekends, right?"

"Right!" I had one friend on the planet, and I'd take whatever time with xem I could.

We started getting together regularly. Alex came into my part of the city most weekends. Sometimes I traveled to xyr neighborhood. We took a trip together to mainland Chile. My time with Alex was the part of my life that made the most sense—I still had no job and no real prospects.

My parents understood my general lack of motivation, sort of, and for now. They were less understanding when I told them I'd volunteered to be in a test for experimental portal technology.

"You want to be a lab animal?"

"It's not an experiment, it's a test. I'm getting paid—it's important, this could change everything."

But the truth was I was doing it because it was strange and risky and completely different than anything I'd ever done in my life. Whatever I'd been doing wasn't working and different sounded like exactly what I needed.

#

"We call them Ellis–Bronnikov portals, or EBPs. We're trying to use them to travel between Earth and its outer-space territories," said the young woman in charge of briefing us. We were in the Laghari Industries Labs in the Chonchi area. I bristled at her characterization of my birthplace as one of Earth's "territories" but kept quiet.

"We have successfully sent objects through. Pencils. An apple. But it doesn't work with animals. Or humans, yet. We think we understand why—there's a subjective effect, depending on the state of mind of the traveler. In most cases, it collapses the Einstein-Rosen bridge too quickly, and the quantum—"

The red-haired man next to me said in a low voice, "That's pretty obvious bullshit. They're not telling us the whole story."

I shushed him and focused back on her. "—visualize your destination before sending you through the EBPs. That's why we recruited people who have been off-planet already."

I raise my hand. "Is it dangerous? What happens if we can't get through?"

"We're quite confident there's no actual danger. All the animal test subjects we've tried to send through have failed but none has been harmed. They just pop back where they started."

"How confident is 'quite' confident?" asked the skeptical man. He had a hand-made name tag pinned to his jacket saying, *Hi, I'm Jacinto.*

"I can't put a number on it but we've yet to lose anybody. You are free to leave if you choose. The NDA you signed would still be in effect, of course. And you wouldn't get paid."

We all stayed, even Jacinto. I was scheduled to go through the next day.

#

I met up with Alex in our favorite sandwich joint at the top of one of the kilometer-high wooden skyscrapers on Huillinco Lake. I got notchicken and avocado on a large, doughy bread. Alex got two of the overstuffed hot dogs the locals favored.

"So you're really doing it? You're going to try to go through a portal?" xe asked between bites.

"Yes. If all works out, I'll be on the Trojan Habs tomorrow morning and back here in the afternoon."

"That is seriously cool. Is it dangerous?"

"They're 'quite confident' it's not."

"So, *really* dangerous."

"I guess."

"And you want to do this?"

"Yeah, I do."

"Well, be careful. Some of us would be sad if something happened to you."

I'd been looking out over the island, with its skyscrapers, parks, and smaller pyramid-shaped buildings, all the way to the Andes mountains on mainland Chile across the water. I swung my head back to look at xem and—being already in the state of mind to do wild, risky things—said, "Some of us, like . . . you?"

Xe held my gaze. I noticed xyr hand was touching mine and had been for a while. It had also been a while since I'd thought of xem as just my best friend.

Our first kiss was at the top of the world and tasted like mayonnaise.

#

The lab-coated woman, whose name was Elisa, was in charge of us again the next day. Jacinto was there, as well as five other people.

"Good morning! Did everybody get enough sleep? Eat the recommended light breakfast? Sign your liability waivers? Good, good. Let's get started!"

Jacinto was first. Two technicians came to collect him, leading him through those double doors they have in hospital emergency rooms.

He came out forty-five minutes later, looking bedraggled and annoyed.

"What happened? How'd it go?" I asked him.

"It didn't work, I tried to—"

Elisa interrupted him. "Please remember the NDA you signed. It includes other test subjects. You wouldn't want to bias the results, would you?"

At least she referred to us as *subjects*, not *objects*.

"Lii Cea," said Elisa. It took me a minute to realize she meant me, that it was my turn.

The technicians took me into the test area. It was a white room with rounded corners and lights on tripods like a photographer's studio.

In the middle, there was a wide, circular frame with thick, rubber cables connecting it to the room's ceiling—the portal. Its center looked like very sparse smoke, paper-thin frosted glass, or floating sugar.

They made me change into a white, padded suit, with a circuit drawn on it like a topographic map, with extra lines on my knees, chest, and palms.

Elisa said, "Iteration 2213-D . . . starting . . . now!" She tapped her interface. "Will the technicians please abandon the room?" They did.

The portal lit up, cycling red, green, and blue colors like Alex's retro-gaming rig. The same colors started racing up and down the circuits on my suit. I looked like part of a Solstice Tableau—the L4 Solstice, in October, not the Earth one in December.

When all the colors stabilized to a bright, emerald green, Elisa said, "Okay, whenever you're ready."

"Whenever I'm ready for what?"

"Ready to walk through the portal."

"Just like that? And if it works, I'll be in the Trojans?"

"Yes, that's the idea, remember?"

"Oh, okay."

"Lii."

"What?"

"You're still here."

"Does that mean it didn't work?"

"No, it means you haven't moved—or breathed—for the past sixty seconds. You need to walk through the portal. Now. Please."

I said a small mantra to the god-that-does-not-exist-but-is-always-with-us, added a quick *I must not fear—fear is the mind-killer*, took a deep breath, and stepped through.

#

All color disappeared.

All sound.

There was a place, in a sense.

There was also not a place.

I was here. That was the one thing I was sure of.

That was good. I could build from it.

If I was here, my hands should be here too. I had a moment of panic when I couldn't see them, then they came into view, slowly.

So, good. I still had hands. Everything. Just. Seemed. To. Be. Slower. Here.

Wherever here was, still not sure about that.

I checked the continued existence of my legs, feet, head, stomach, butt, nose. All the good parts. Everything was in place, ready to do something.

Do what? What had Elisa said?

Elisa. If she'd sent me here, then she must exist as well.

Good, that was positive, some solid progress.

And if Elisa existed, then the Earth existed, Alex, my friends from the L4, and my parents.

But they weren't here. Only I was.

I turned around. There was a circular area on my right. It was close enough to touch, or to jump back through.

I kept turning, there was another circle to my left, only much farther away. Ten meters or one thousand—it was hard to tell.

The near one was Earth, so the far one must be the L4.

I finally remembered what Elisa had said, something about trying to get to the far side. I managed to make my legs move, though there didn't seem to be any floor.

As I walked, there was a force fighting against me—like two very strong magnets being pulled apart. It wasn't physical, rather more of a yearning.

Have you ever been away from home, all alone, cold, hungry, sad, and tired, and you see inside a house—a warm light, a family sharing food, laughter, and love? And you're outside, looking in, and you know your own house is far away and you're not getting home tonight?

This was that only cubed and on drugs and in hyper-real, full-sensorium, force-feedback holovision.

The farther I walked from the Earth circle, the stronger this feeling became until it was a roar in my ears except without sound.

And I understood, suddenly, why all the previous tests had failed.

Everybody feels at home, somewhere, and they have a deep longing to go back home, to be in their place.

But I didn't. I didn't have a place. I thought I did, a few times, but I always ended up leaving, going back and forth, shuffling between worlds.

I understood the circle's yearning intellectually—the way you might view a painting of soldiers fighting a war if you've grown up in a time of peace. You can imagine its impact, its relevance, but you yourself don't feel it, not personally. It has nowhere to lay its hooks in you.

I walked towards the other circle, the L4 side, ignoring the pull that got stronger and stronger—to go back, to turn around. I understood what had happened to Jacinto, why his face had looked so haggard. I pitied him for how he must have felt.

Somewhere near the midway point between the portals, each pull must have balanced the other. Or maybe I'd just grown used to it. I didn't feel any urging of any kind.

I sat down. I wasn't tired. I was just enjoying the peace of being between.

I'm not sure how long I stayed sitting there. A few minutes. Hours maybe. Days?

I thought of Alex and my parents. They might get nervous if Elisa told them I'd been gone for so long.

I got up grudgingly and crossed over.

#

After that comes the story that everybody knows from the feeds.

I came through to the L4 eight minutes after I'd walked into the portal on Earth, the first time anybody had traveled as fast as light. The researchers from the Laghari Industries' Trojan office hadn't really expected me or anyone to succeed yet, they were just gathering datapoints. They put me in an isolation room for a few days, measuring me in every way known to humankind and inventing a few new ones as well. I was fine.

In the end, they had to let me out, to see if I could cross back. They had to know if it was a fluke or if I'd maybe spontaneously combust on my return to Earth—I'm not kidding, there was a theory that this might happen. They let me go anyway.

There was an L4 version of Elisa, except his name was Akash. He gave me the same spiel as his Earth counterpart, but you could tell he was nervous—he was part researcher and part test subject.

I gave him a grin, took his hand, and pulled him with me through the circle.

Our voyage back was similar to my first one. The same feeling of yearning—I had to physically pull Akash away from his home circle, coaxing him the whole way like he was a child who didn't want to enter a classroom for the first time. I didn't spend as much time resting in the middle, since Akash was with me. Just a few minutes. Maybe a half-hour.

We came out in the Earthside lab. Elisa was there, as well as a half-dozen other people wearing white lab coats.

There were handshakes, pictures, debriefings, and interviews.

They asked me, how did you do it? How do we do it again? How many people can come through with you?

We worked it out. I could take up to two dozen people at once if they followed my instructions. And I could train other people to cross themselves and guide others, but the guides had to be like me. I looked up Guss from my student years. He'd also been a refugee, then a returner, then a returned-returner. He felt as out of place as I did. Guss was my first trainee, and, since he was more patient and had better people skills, he became the main trainer for *Laghari Interplanetary*. I heard they're looking for displaced Martians to guide people to and from the red planet as well.

#

And here's the part that's just for me.

Whenever I cross over—whether for work or private reasons—I always stop in the middle, and just sit in peace, relishing the feeling of not being anywhere, of being in transit.

I love my parents and I love Alex and the life we've made together more than anything in either world.

But what I don't tell xem or them, what I don't tell anyone, is that the only place I feel truly at home is when I'm in between.

Pachuco Odyssey 3001

Cesar L. De Leon

my shadow is
a pachuco-punk
interdimensional traveler
cruising firme in his intergalactic ranfla

se pone tacuches metalicos
and his calcos son doc martens
made of antimatter

he vibrates through
the multiverse
powered by rainbows and safety-pin chains

he buys them cheap
at el centro cosmico
of black holes

ponte trucha y watcha

with a tip of his tando made of stars
he oscillates como loco

between

me

and him

and him and

me and him and me

and me and me and me and

him and him and me and

me and me and him

and me and me

and him and

me and

him

pinche vato   tirando chancla.

Bird Man

Cesar L. De Leon

In a parallel universe
I fall asleep caressing your wild
Halo of hair like the night sky

All my poems are about your eyes & brows
I read them to you out loud in the endless woods
Dappled like your beard

You cry at how impossibly blue the sky is that morning
How it recognizes us as transient clouds
How it teaches us to keep breathing in the dark

Later you dress in cock feathers, I in infinite marigolds
You whistle a song you just made up to the setting sun
I get lost in the brave curve of your lips

The heft of your hand in mine
Reminding me how a heart can be like a bird.

Zapatista Spaceship

Osmani R. Alcaraz-Ochoa

I was awakened
By blaring lights
I thought it was the police
Looking for my fugitive lover
"Tú siempre me metes en problemas, wey!"

We step outside
Surrendering, our hands in the air.
He tries running
But heat and radiation
Melt his blurry-inked prison tattoos.
They capture us both
It's a giant floating seashell, a cocoon
with windows, lights
And people inside.

We're awakened
By aliens or
Zapatistas or
aliens with black ski masks
In a gray lab or spaceship.
I hear them inside my head
Speaking an anarchist, genderless language:

*We've travelled from stars, genesis, death, birth, end of worlds
to new beginnings
In spirals, cycles upon cycles.*

To be human, is to be alien, you know.
Vulnerability created the cosmos.
You should see hearts pulsating, trembling.
Nothing in any universe stays the same, forever.
I'd show you what world-building looks like
But you've done it before, for worse:
Like war and slavery
Or any system that oppresses.
These are man-made paradigms
That will be wiped out.
Intergalactic anarchic councils
Are making their way through
Every corner of space and time
To restore much-needed balance.
January 1, 1994:
You tried creating an alternative
in the here and now
It's happening again.
And it's not just class war.
Or race or gender or
species. The choices now
Alter tomorrow's reality.
On a quiet cosmic night
You can hear the faint rumblings
Of interstellar revolutions
Happening now
But light years away

Where we will see
What was once unfathomable.
What has no beginning and
no end. Del planeta más obscuro
Se lucha por la totalidad de todo.
Eres mi reflejo, ¿no me reconoces?

There's too much left unspoken
here. Entire worlds and galaxies,
not yet unleashed.
There's too much possibility
To only live stranded
Or heartbroken.

SECTION 3: THE UTOPIAN ENCLAVE

Luis Valderas: "Chicnauhnepaniuhcan"

Blessed

Joy Castro

When I arrived, a young woman ushered me up to my room, a plush beige haven on the third floor. Tall windows overlooked gardens and an orchard. Green meadows drifted upward toward the forest's dark and undulating edge at the top of a distant ridge of hills.

East Texas.

I unpacked, laying my clothes in the drawers, which glided lushly shut. Valeria had been right about the quality of the spa. Every possible need had been anticipated. A Bible sat on the nightstand, and a terry-cloth robe and slippers waited in the closet. In the bathroom of white tile and bamboo, one drawer was filled with toiletries and medications for pain, while another contained neat white stacks of menstrual pads. A third drawer, deep and wide, held thick towels the color of milk.

Most women went for rest cures every so often. Modern life was so stressful, and feminine nerves so fragile. It was nothing to be ashamed of or worried about, agreed Daniel, when I'd assured him how very normal it was for women to do such things. Self-care. Pampering. A peaceful rest in nature every now and then made us better wives.

Vaguely queasy and fatigued, I sat on the bed. It was soft, feather-beddy. I slid my fingertips across the white duvet. Silky, a high thread count, probably Egyptian.

A soft knock came at the door: a different woman, but again clad in a smooth white hoodie, white leggings, and white clogs made of rubber, like a nurse or yoga teacher or guru.

"Welcome again to the Blessed Savior Wellness Spa." She smiled. "If you're all settled in, I can take you to your wellness consultant now."

I nodded and followed her, closing the door behind me. It did not lock. There was no key. My pulse quickened, and my breath went shallow in my mouth.

But I had brought no compromising materials for someone to find if they searched. I no longer owned such things. I was with Daniel now.

I followed the woman down the hall and across a wide and sunlit atrium. A fountain trickled. Through open windows, fresh breezes blew.

•

So many luxury spas dotted the countryside that it had been hard to know which to choose. All had nutritious low-calorie meals, exercise options, massage, skincare, and hair and nail salons—and some had the latest technology that could firm or tighten or bleach or simply eradicate anything a husband might find unsightly. Rest cures kept women happy—even (or perhaps especially) the large percentage of women who now were blessed to stay home raising their families. Mothers needed a break perhaps most of all, everyone agreed, for while children were a blessing, everyone also knew that raising them could be a trial. After all, even the Lord had vexed his mother as a child, and few of us could claim the patience of Mary.

My friend Valeria, not yet blessed with children herself, had recommended this spa. Less busy than a mother, she'd had leisure to sit with me in the middle of the morning, and after a while, I'd confessed over coffee that my nerves were a little frayed, that I'd lately found myself prey to inexplicable bouts of exhaustion.

Her dark eyes narrowed. "Let's walk in the garden," she said.

We took our mugs of coffee with us. Even among the trees, she spoke with a quiet voice.

•

At The Blessed Savior Wellness Spa, the consultant was perhaps in her fifties, perhaps older. She introduced herself only as Paloma. Her silver hair was wound in a low chignon, and her brown eyes were calm, her forehead mildly lined. Her smile was kind as she led me out to the private stone terrace and invited me to sit. Wisteria swagged above us. On the little wicker table between our two plush chairs, two glasses already sat. Pale slices of cucumber floated in ice water.

I took a sip.

"Women come to The Blessed Savior for all kinds of reasons," she said, "and all of them make sense. Every need is valid. Everyone is different. As Christ said, 'Judge not, lest ye be judged.'"

"Amen," I murmured. Overhead, the branches of oaks swayed, their leaves stirred softly by the wind. It was a hushing sound. My body relaxed into the chair.

"As your wellness consultant, I'm here to listen and help you make the most of these three precious days of respite."

I carefully described my recent battle with exhaustion, my increasingly frazzled nerves, the slight nausea I'd felt when I'd finished unpacking.

"Hmm." Her gaze seemed to turn inward for a moment, meditative, and then she gestured out toward the gardens of herbs and vegetables. Glossy green peppers, reddening tomatoes, nascent cucumbers, vines for green beans. "Is God's earth not bounteous?" she said, waving her hand with expansive grace.

I agreed that creation was indeed a marvel.

"Yet such lush gardens can draw pests," she continued. "Rabbits, moles, mice." Her brow furrowed. "Pests that burrow and are difficult to eradicate."

I stiffened. This was the moment.

"Yet some of the Lord's creatures can survive only underground," I replied, using the phrase Valeria had taught me. My heart pounded hard in my throat. "They, too, do the work of the Lord."

"Underground. Yes." Her smile was very faint. Someone watching from a distance would not have perceived it. She stood and reached for my hand. "Let me make you some tea."

I followed her inside, where her comfortable office included sofas and a kitchenette. I sat down and began leafing through magazines about fashion and cooking and décor and spiritual faith. Her back to me, Paloma busied herself at the counter, humming a strange, low tone that reminded me vaguely of childhood—of songs my grandmother used to hum as she gathered plant medicine in the hills outside Bandera, before the last purges. Memories flickered. A kettle whistled.

The tea Paloma handed me was hot and brown and thick, a viscous liquid that smelled bitter. I grimaced.

She smiled. "I put honey in it," she said, "gathered from our own hives. It's rich with nutrients that will help your healing journey."

I lifted the mug to my lips.

"Drink it all," she said.

•

At dinner that evening, I felt increasingly unwell and had to excuse myself to return to my room. The pain began that night, and over the next two days, I missed the hikes at dawn and skipped the yoga classes. Time warped, looping and bending. I lay in the white bed, gasping and staring at that dark and distant tree-line as if it were a rope I could grip, a lifeline. White-garbed young women with smooth ponytails slipped in with trays of broth and tea, laid a palm on my forehead, brought pain medication from the bathroom, and quietly emptied my trash.

•

On the third morning, I awoke refreshed. Light was just beginning to gray the horizon. My whole body felt light, liberated. After a quick shower, I pushed open my door like rolling a stone away from a tomb. Buoyant, I joined the others for the hike at dawn.

With laughter and fellowship, the day sped past. In the afternoon, we swam in a nearby lake. At dinner, women of all ages enjoyed the repast, much of it fresh from the gardens. Some of the guests were quite white-haired and wizened, some young, some heavily with child. Perhaps one day I would also be so.

I slept the sleep of angels.

•

The last morning, packed and ready to depart, I went to the stone terrace for my exit interview.

Paloma's light touch on my arm guided me to the chair. Her silver hair lay in a long, glinting braid over her shoulder, and her eyes seemed lit with a particular radiance. She smiled, leaning toward me.

"And was your visit with us all you hoped it would be?"

"Yes. It was," I said. "Thank you. All I had hoped."

"I heard you were unwell," she murmured.

"But it passed," I said. "And now I am fine. Better than before."

She nodded and laid her hand on mine.

"The Lord giveth," she said, "and the Lord taketh away. Blessed be the name of the Lord."

"Blessed be His name," I agreed.

morning tides

Florencia Manóvil

Good morning, Cora, wherever you are.

I was watching the light form patterns on the wall, a monochromatic kaleidoscope inviting me into the day, my brain still swimming in the waters of deep blue dreams. And then, the inevitable rattle of remembering: *you're not here.*

You're still not here, but I know you will return. My insides plunge every time I think about all that happened to you, but I've worked through the most suffocating feelings—there are big Healing Centers now, you know, therapy for everyone, and not just talk therapy. I remember you telling me, *"that doesn't work for me, I don't know how to put this whirlpool into words, the whole world thinks I'm crazy"*—you were right, of course, and I always knew it. I hope you felt that. You are an ocean poured from my own ocean, so I know, Corita, *I know.*

I wish back then we had what we have now. I'm telling you, all sorts of healing modalities—acupuncture and *limpias* and reiki and tapping and quick eye movement or whatever it's called, things I never knew existed—but for free, for everyone. We're finally acknowledging that everyone has trauma of some sort, don't they? Even the Collapse itself: it needed to happen, but we all had choppy waters to navigate. Orion played a big part in formalizing the Healing Centers; you'd be so proud of him. He made us all understand how unanchored we'd be without facing the waves of loss and pain we've each experienced, even as they made way for a better life. So we're all nudged to visit a Center weekly,

and honestly, there's an immersive sound thing that has been very help-
ful for me—

Oh! Here comes Glen. Caught me spaced out, waiting for the kettle
to whistle.

We sign "good morning" to one another, and I offer him a plateful
of oatcakes I made last night. The whole food system is different these
days, but old habits die hard. I watch him chew and feel an undeniable
sense of satisfaction. Now that I'm not beholden to the unpaid mandate
of feeding hungry youngsters, I can embrace my love of preparing food
for others. I remember once when you were a teen and you weren't eating well and I lost it, said something about the tyranny of needing to feed
one's children, that I'd come to hate cooking, and *ugh*—I wince. I close
my eyes and breathe. I did the best I could, I know this is true. But then
I wonder where you are, and a jagged lump in my throat threatens a
downpour. *Let it move through you,* my therapist, Manuela, says. She's only
a couple years older than you, believe it or not.

Glen waves at me. "You have the whole day off today, right?" he
signs. I nod. He knows my schedule, of course; he's just guiding me to
be present. I work at our quadrant kitchen for three hours most after-
noons—yes, out of all the essential jobs to choose from, that's what I went
with! Because of my age I get priority pick, and I'm also not required to
do a full 20 hours a week, but I end up baking oatcakes and other whole-
some treats for our block, or signing up to teach art workshops.

"I hope it's a Nina day," Glen signs. "You haven't had one of those
in a while." I smile. It's sweet he's looking out for me. My heart swells
daily witnessing the self-assured, thoughtful man he's grown into. I know
you had no time for Gia's sullen tween brother crashing with us during
the pandemic, but you'd really enjoy his company these days. That said,
you'll have to brush up on your ASL, because he rarely wears his hearing
device these days, especially at home. All the kids learn sign and Spanish
alongside English now, and are encouraged to study another on top of
that. If you'd told me 10 years ago that the majority of our population
would be trilingual at minimum, *no te lo creería. Una verdadera maravilla.*
So we sign primarily, and there's a lot of silence in the house, which I
welcome.

But I miss your music.

Glen takes off, and I'm left to decide what to do with my day. I start
for the yard— we removed the fences, and now we have one big shared
yard and garden; I already told you that. *Ay,* how I wish we'd done this

when you were little... I can't help but feel that everything would have been different if our neighbors had been able to really know you, if you'd had a safe, special place to retreat to. Mind you, every block has different agreements for how to share their yard—the folks two streets over are still drowning in clashing needs. But when I look at the weeping willow swaying across the way, I can almost see you in its cradle. Held.

I suddenly remember I volunteered our yard for the quadrant pre-school to come have lunch. And the twins will be here in the afternoon to play their songs for me…maybe we'll do some collage too. I turn to my studio instead. Let's at least make it a Nina morning.

Yes, in this new communitarian configuration, I finally have a space for my art and just my art. Sliding the glass door open, I am flooded with gratitude, the morning rays nudging me in. The new canvas given to me by the folks from the Repair and Repurpose Center looms large and se-ductive at the heart of the modest, motley room. It still feels so luxurious to leave it waiting for me like that. Thirsty. These days I paint complete-ly uninterrupted, and it's a gift—but a vision of Corita sneaking in to watch me mix colors rushes over me and my sight dampens—*focus, Nina*.

I wipe my eyes clear, breathe through it.

Dip the brush into cobalt. Stroke the canvas.

Purple. Black, green. Within seconds I'm somewhere else. No mem-ories, no thoughts. I'm in conversation with color—no, I'm conversing with the piece, which exists somewhere beyond. We communicate in hue, in texture, in feelings and sensations that can only be expressed in movement, or music, or image. Our dialogue is a dance, a song, and I sing and dance and feel and negotiate until—suddenly—I step back.

And there is a whole painting before me.

The world seeps slowly back into my awareness, like surfacing from sleep. I wade in this cozy mist for a few moments—until I remember: *Cora*.

A wave of guilt.

That's the old paradigm, Manuela would say. Don't all parents feel that weight? No, I know they don't—Cora's father certainly didn't! But this new generation of parents, they have so much support. No one in this society is solely responsible for a child. How could they understand what it was like, to have to work and buy food and cook and monitor your child's nutrition and keep track of her schooling and tune into her soul's yearnings and gauge the state of her heart and try to mend, heal, soothe, hold, all that was bruised, all that was shattered? It was an overwhelming recipe for daily failure they'll never taste. We are all involved in raising our community's kids; I was at the forefront of that. And yet I do feel a twinge of... what is that? Envy?

I just wish it had been different for us. Please come back, Cora... I promise we've been washing away the hurtful old world. Everything can be different now. If you make it.

I wipe my brow and shift the weight on my hips. My body creaks, suddenly oh-so-heavy. Saturated. I catch my reflection on the window-pane. My grandmother has been staring back at me recently, the rivulets around my eyes transforming my face. I remember how she faded. We didn't lose her gradually, but in fits and spurts, a nightmarish ebb and flow as her mind dissolved, her psyche turned a dark, grim kaleido-scope. *"It's the sugar, it's the diet,"* someone said to me then, which boiled my blood. But perhaps this new way of life would have saved her too.

I look out at the verdant bounty of the garden and leave the painting to dry. I set out to pick leafy goodness for a rainbow salad. Pink radishes, purple cabbage. Cayena loves edible flowers. Such a spicy one, that little tyke. And Topacio will want to add berries; I'll have them pick some as soon as they get here.

I hear their prismatic cacophony before they enter the yard, a bright rush of excitement. I can't help it; joy cascades over me. They greet and tug and run and play, and I feel light again. As the kids begin to fill the table, I see her, *abuela Julia*, taking a seat. In my mind, in my heart, I call out to you, Cora, wherever you may be.

You will be nourished here.

Bedtime Stories for Survival: The Gogre

Sarah Dalton

(content warning: violence against girls, blood/ichor, death of child)

Gogre thread makes beautiful things. Beautiful, powerful things. Tents that protect families when the floods come. When labor starts too soon or lasts too long, when the babies aren't given names until they survive three years, Gogre thread edges blankets, nightgowns, and wraps to ensure life. When wars and fires have destroyed hospitals and cities, we sew Gogre thread onto the bandages for secret clinics. And if the water stations dry out, we embellish cloth covers for buckets and barrels so the water will never run dry.

But cloth fades, fabric unravels, and threads break and undo. Some have tried to repurpose Gogre thread, but it never works. It is not only the thread that is powerful, but the women who extract it and the girl-children who generate it.

It is our process: a blister, a cut, a thread, a cloth.

In the beginning, swirling glimmers appeared under the skin. At first, it mesmerized the kin-groups. They were curious why their daughters' bodies had turned golden during smoke season. But with each day, the pain and pressure increased. The girls' screams frightened them. Many were cast out from their communities. But it was our mothers who discovered how to bleed-out the Gogre blood and then infuse it into their threads and embroider it onto cloth. Very quickly they realized its power. When a bleed-out is done right, it will only hurt a little.

There are many stories of mothers who refused to bleed-out their girl-children. Your great-grandmother was one of them. People called her Golden Weaver. She had five bleed-out scars: palm, calf, shoulder, hip, and upper arm. I think her mother had been hesitant but dutiful. Unlike many other Gogre women, Golden Weaver did not hide her scars or the orange triangle mark on her chest. When it came time for her daughter's first bleed-out, she was faithful. It was a small blister, a simple cut under the shoulder blade. When the second and third blisters grew, the bleed-out was manageable, but the fourth blister was an arterial wound.

Arterial wounds are rare, and yet, there are many stories about them. Once, the Gogre blood grew in a little girl, but her mother refused to perform a bleed-out. Each day the blister swelled larger, the mother rubbed extra cassah oil to numb the pain, but the pressure broke open the blister and the heat from the Gogre blood burned the girl-child's arm off. It was too late. The golden blood streamed down the length of her four-year-old's arm, the heat disintegrating it. And it wouldn't stop. It bled from the hole and when it touched the earth, it became what it has always been: fire. The tent exploded into flames, burned its way up the hillside, and spread to one of the last remaining cities, Perda. That was how Perda was destroyed.

A Gogre woman knows she is working with fire. Not the fire that cooks a meal, but the kind that will either heal or destroy a land.

***

Golden Weaver's story is different. She and her daughter, my grandmother, had been scavenging in the foothills for acorns from the fire-oak trees, taking shelter wherever they could find it. Just before smoke season, they stumbled upon an abandoned underground clinic.

I imagine the clinic looked like this one, like the others we've been to. A sleeping room with a few beds. A common room with a table, stove, chairs, and benches. Everything had a layer of dirt and ash and smelled of char and must. Furniture had been knocked over, drawers opened and thrown on the floor, their contents ransacked from raids. In the sleeping room, Golden Weaver found a locked cabinet with scratches that looked like machete markings. She smashed a stone on the lock, enough to open the door a crack and reach her arm inside. Inside she took out small packages of gauze, bandages, wraps, and antibiotics. She arranged them on the bedside table where her daughter rested. Already the golden blood eddied under her acorn brown skin.

During smoke season, the air changes every day, and every day a girl-child's body changes too. The Gogre senses this. The heat on your skin, the nitrogen and sulfur streaming through your blood. The smoke and ash of the red sun month.

Gogre blood changed my grandmother's skin to a terra cotta laced with gold. By the second day, the blister sprouted on her forearm. A tiny bump, but a precarious spot. An arterial wound. Over the next few days, the luminescent glow accumulated under her skin. By the fifth day, Golden Weaver began to rub cassah oil along the child's arms, legs, face and neck. The smell dulled her senses and the massage movements coalesced the Gogre blood, concentrating it into the blister on her forearm. Each day Golden Weaver rubbed the oil on her daughter's skin and each day the blister grew larger, stretching transparent, and within it, the glittering liquid swarmed.

The days we call amber-ash days are the days we perform the bleed-out. From inside a girl's body, the Gogre senses the throbbing air and a swirling pressure. It feels a great urge to release.

As the girl-child slept, Golden Weaver climbed the steps to a day that was not day. The air smelled of smoke and burnt earth. The stillness was leaden. The heat pulsed. A layer of white-grey ash coated the world. She brushed some from the top of a rock, sat, and gazed around her. The sky cast an orange hue over the shrubs, trees, and dirt. Ashflakes floated in the air and landed on the hairs of her arms. They collected like frozen water droplets on her eyelashes. Her daughter laid asleep, subdued by the sweet scent of cassah oil.

Golden Weaver was frightened. One never knows how long the amber-ash days will last. The blister had already grown to the size of her hand. It covered the little girl's entire forearm. What if she made a cut that was too large? What if she couldn't stop the flow? What if its heat burned her daughter? And her greatest fear: could she collect it safely? What if she couldn't contain it? What if it touched the earth and became fire?

By the time Golden Weaver returned from outside, she was resolved to perform the bleed-out, but when she saw her girl-child pursing her lips together in sleep. Again, she delayed.

For two more days Golden Weaver told stories about the Gogre who grows inside a girl-child. She talked about the generations of Gogre women and about the beautiful, powerful things Gogre thread can create. How the world of fire cannot survive without us. She cautioned her daughter about the repercussions of not bleeding-out the golden blood. She told her how one girl's blood disintegrated her from within.

During those two days, Golden Weaver applied more cassah oil. She rubbed and smoothed the arms and touched the faded orange triangle birthmark that designated a Gogre child. She fingered the mark at her daughter's chest with sweet, tender circles. She traced the size, shape, and edges of the blister on her daughter's forearm. When she palpated the stretched skin, the Gogre blood churned and swirled, a brilliant light illuminating from within.

But screams and cries of anguish broke the girl-child's stupor, and Golden Weaver felt guilty that she had been weakened by fear. She would not risk something worse, something the stories had warned her about. She poured the remainder of the cassah oil on her daughter's chest and prepared her supplies.

She set out two bowls, the second only a precaution. The gauze and bandage wrap she had found when they arrived were within arm's reach. In her pack, she rummaged for her blade and set it on the bedside table. When she was ready, she began to sing:

Gogre, Gogre
The red sun
Has called you
The ashen sky
Has formed you
May you bleed
May you flow
May the world heal
Through your glow

Golden Weaver took her knife, hid it beside her leg and paused. One last time, she considered what might happen if she did not bleed-out her daughter, but she knew the stories.

"Don't be scared," she said. "I'll take care of you," she said. "I will bring you back." Along the top of the opaque surface, she sliced a thin ridge of a line. Pressure released. The first drops came out golden and pooled into the bowl Golden Weaver held under the child's forearm.

A luminous liquid poured in, and Golden Weaver felt a sense of relief. Despite her fear and her gamble of delay, it was not too late. The pressure had been building and stretching the skin. She had worried the blister might burst. But her sense of relief did not last long because she saw that the Gogre blood did not stop flowing. It had not turned red as she expected it to, needed it to. Red meant the liquid was her child's blood. Red meant apply pressure. Red meant bring her girl back. She grabbed the second bowl.

When I think about it, there are only a few stories of bleed-outs that have required a second bowl. One I heard about was a girl-child who liked to keep spiders as pets. It was her fifth and last bleed-out, before her blood became her own. The wound was on her left foot. She lost a lot of blood once it ran red and went into shock. Another girl had a dark red-orange mark, the most prominent ever. She was called Sunset Weaver. Her mother, a clumsy, slow nurse, made the cut at the top of her chest near the collarbone, but she couldn't stop the bleeding.

As the second bowl filled and the flow did not stop, Golden Weaver looked around the room in panic. No one had ever needed a third container. She eyed the useless medical supplies, sheets on the other beds, pillows, then saw the half-full water container. Would she dump it out, not knowing when she would find a water station to refill it or if they had water available anymore? Her girl's breath became fast, faster. She slapped the girl-child's cheeks and told her many things. Stay awake. Wake up. Hold the bowl. Don't let it spill on the ground. Don't let it become fire.

Golden Weaver re-arranged the pillows behind her daughter then shifted her into a more stable position, lying down and resting her arm on the bowl so the Gogre blood could trickle into it. This positioning was precarious, but it would give Golden Weaver a few precious seconds to get another container. With great care, she released her support of the girl and stumbled to the cabinet. With an unhesitating resolve, she grabbed the half full water jug and dumped the contents on the dirt floor where it seeped into the thirsty earth.

As she knelt beside her daughter, she swapped out the small bowl for the larger, more stable one. The surface of golden blood wobbled as she moved it. One slosh spilled and landed on the ground. Unlike the water, it pooled and rested on the surface of the dirt like a melted gold coin. With a hiss and a plume of white-gray smoke, it dissolved slowly into the earth, leaving behind a smell of charred brush. Glowing, shining liquid splashed and swayed within the bowl on the table. With steady though trembling hands, she dumped the first bowl into the water jug, but she was not careful enough and another dribble hit the ground, pooled on the surface and dissolved. A flame emerged, the size of a hand, but Golden Weaver was able to stamp it out.

There was so much liquid. From the cut the flow wouldn't stop and it wouldn't change color. The girl-child's face went from warm brown to ashen. She closed her eyes as if to fall asleep. Golden Weaver shook her, called out her name, patted her cheeks, her hairline, pinched her ear lobes, forced open her eyes, but there was little response. What could she do except hold the water jug and wait out the flow.

Hours later, the color changed from gold to red, the water container had filled. Tired from singing, screaming, humming, begging, Golden Weaver shifted her focus from collecting the Gogre blood to stopping her daughter from bleeding to death.

She wrapped the wound tightly with gauze. By then, the girl-child had gone unconscious and lay breathing shallowly on the bed. From their two packs, Golden Weaver brought out many spools of thread. She stripped every bed, pillow, and cloth item in the clinic and cut them into scraps. She forced each cloth bit into the container of Gogre blood that looked as if it held molten gold.

When the cloth and thread had soaked up all the liquid, they gleamed in the dark clinic, like a star fallen to earth. Golden Weaver took one of the spools of thread, slid it through the eye of her needle and began to embroider the blanket covering her comatose daughter.

She didn't sleep. She didn't eat. She didn't stop her needlework. The threads looped into tendrils and stems, flowers linked in a grand chain. A single, long leaf, followed by a stem which bloomed into three small leaves, then a fan-like flower, followed by another tendril, more leaves, more flowers, more tendrils. When the spool of thread finished, she grabbed another, and another and another, continuing her needlework on the blanket, feverishly creating a design she hoped would never unravel or fray and lose its power.

***

I finish my stories and lower my daughter's arm and hand. Repeated latherings of cassah oil these past few days have made her skin gleam. Silence charges the air, like static before a storm.

"Remember," I say, looking at her face, "the world of fire cannot survive without us. The Gogre doesn't want to kill, but it does need to flow. When the land prepares for another season of smoke and fire, when the creatures who survive migrate, hide, or go underground, the Gogre will grow on your skin like it grew on mine, like it grew on your grandmother's and her mother's." I finger the blister on her neck, the arterial wound which had frightened me. While I have delayed, trying to soothe her with stories, oil, and massage, it has doubled in size. Now I realize I have waited too long. The Gogre blood vibrates in her body.

I sit her up, floppy though conscious. At the edge of the bed I lean her over an empty, stable water jug on the floor.

"It must bleed and flow or it will destroy you. I tell you these things so that you will be brave, even if you feel scared."

For the hundredth time I arrange the pillows behind her and tuck the blanket embroidered with a pristine pattern of concentric flowers, tendrils, and leaves around her legs. There is nothing left to do except begin.

My fingers make gentle circles on her oil-slick neck, rubbing the muted orange mark. Next to it, the blister pulses. I sing the verse once, twice, three times, invoking the healing power of the Gogre. I retrieve my knife from under my thigh and slice below her chin where the skin stretches as if ready to burst. Gogre blood streams into the water jug.

"I will bring you back," I say and sing and sing and sing over the flowing gold.

The Pillager

Carlos Julio Paredes Minango

Translated by Matthew David Goodwin and Antonia Carcelén-Estrada

<u>Beginning</u>

<u>Log Entry #1</u>
I have always loved the sound of stones crunching under my feet. At first, I thought I wanted to be a mason, so I could crush stones all day. But I rejected that profession because I would get bored stomping on common pebbles. I wanted to hear the crunch of extraordinary stones, and there is nothing more extraordinary than ruins, at least to my knowledge.

A stone, no matter how precious, can become anything. The value, that which is truly singular to the stone, is instilled by people. Some jewels even have proper names, and with stories that I would like to stomp on. That is why I am here, in the ruins of the last cyber-industrial-complex deep in the Andean Mountains.

I was a proto-urban archeologist until my desire to stomp on things took over, that is to say, took over my feet. It was the most suited profession to stomp on "value." I was born in Mega-City 07 YALA, formed from the union of Buenos Aires, Asunción, and La Plata. The year was 130 ASEAF "After the construction of the Space Elevator and the Age of Fire." I record my most glorious stomps in my journal. The first time, I stomped on my diploma with my graduation shoes, and the last time, as an archeologist, I stomped on a priceless statue of a Virgin that had been excavated from a sanctuary in Quito – Ecuador, where I now live. Since then, I have been the neighborhood pillager in this city. I sell artifacts from the ruins from before "the Age of Fire." I only sell things that I am not interested in stomping on, or breaking. I also sell the things I cannot crush because they are too hard, like ancient coins.

I came to this subterranean industrial cemetery under the space elevator in the South of Quito because a black-market appraiser came across a landslide at the base of the elevator's slope and he told me first because he owed me a favor. He knew me so well and for so long after working on this together that he asked me if I wanted to cure my "fixation." I told him yes, as a joke, as soon as I return. It was the first time he had asked me something like that.

I sneaked out during the night through a crack in the wall, evading security, and when I got to the deepest end, I knew that it was safe, I stomped on: machines, trophies, glass, pictures, on anything I could find. There is so much to choose from in this complex. And I felt such satisfaction in stomping on…then I jump! Over a chromated shiny metal piece that I bent beyond repair. I got myself into this to stomp on things. I don´t care, and I never did, if it costs me a year of food reserves.

<u>Log Entry #2</u>
I just got covered in dust from blowing up an office floor. I used more force than necessary. But, of course, it was to stomp on rubble. I am on my third raid. Down here everything is dry…and dead. I am not scared of what is to come, only of what I might not manage to destroy. If there is a landslide or something, I can count on my body-mods.

I found an old store under the office floor, as big as a stadium. I turned on the flashlights installed under my corneas and increased the blinding light. At the bottom…artificial grass covered in dust. What a beautiful sight! In haste, I tied a rope to a beam and rapidly descended through a hole so I could stomp on everything. I rubbed my boots on the grass until I tore it apart and I noticed that the dust was ashes. I stomped on pallets and industrial light bulbs. I threw the shelves filled with cardboard boxes to the ground and stomped on their contents. The crunch of stomping on old things sends me into ecstasy. My "stomping fever," a strange thing, even for someone so strange.

Something large caught my attention. A dusty sign with vertical red and yellow lines that read: "National Emergency Center for the Observation and Calculation of Volcanic Activity." How primitive! is what came to my mind.

The ancients got into the habit of coding their data in physical structures made of plastic or alloys instead of using encrypted organic matter as we do. We biorecord data, we no longer do calculations. They were still suspicious of the union between flesh and machine.

I took out the most precious thing from my backpack, my boots fitted with nails, so I could pulverize the sign. I took my time. I unscrewed the sign from the wall, dragged it to the center of the store and jumped on it with all my strength. Until there was nothing left.

It seemed like it had been closed way before ASEAF, and there is no record anywhere of it. And history can be easily censored, erased, or lost. Or told for someone's own convenience.

There are many signs with the same inscription. And, of course, I took each one and obliterated them all. The echo of tin being folded and pierced through resounded in the store and inside me. I stomped on everything. That day I got many fevers.

But I still had room for dessert. The most valuable thing. My search led me to a room full of obsolete servers, rusty from the cables on the ground. Something shiny hides among the aged plastic and the powder from the crumbling bronze on the floor. I cleaned it with my hands and inspected it. I was disappointed to discover that my dessert was a "platinum hard drive." I did not stomp on it. These things can't be broken with kicks and stomps. It would be worthless to try, even with my precious boots. I could find a hydraulic hammer in this shithole, but… Bah!…it's trash! I'll take it to the appraiser.

Just then a flood of data inundated my visual field. Hundreds of pop-up windows were opening and closing with a multitude of documents. They were projected through my retina over the ruins of the room. My archeologist's archives can "think" on their own and match the images on the platinum disc to the historical database from my time as an archeologist and the info cards that the appraiser had provided me. It was obviously a trojan horse released by the appraiser so he would be first to know about my findings.

The analysis concluded it was a very valuable item, not for its antiquity or for its platinum, which is worth less than my boots. It was because of its unique assemblage and, probably, for the singularity of its contents. I connected the platinum disc to my neck with a cable, hoping to access its contents. If the data "inside" was of good quality, it could be worth a lot of money…Bah!…I just wanted to have a list of antiques to stomp on and their locations.

There are many corrupted folders except for one. The dates on the documents place them hundreds of years before the planning of the space elevator. It is from the dark time called "Fire." But the most abnormal characteristic is that the sources are marginal, clandestine. It was all deleted at the time. An empty history.

A real relic!...that I can´t stomp on.

The disc had built in it a primitive artificial intelligence. I could tell from its model of processing natural language which organized information in a single text file, leaving out all the corrupted multimedia data. The document is being decrypted and patched, uniting all the recoverable information from the other folders. Suddenly, all the open pop-ups closed, leaving a single one open. It has a sign that reads: "Do you want to open this document? Accept or Reject." I pressed the accept button as I stomped on the ground, breaking a rusty cable. Perhaps this will lead me to my worst stomping fever yet. Perhaps, to my relief, it will be my last.

The volcano and eternity

The Republic of Ecuador got on the map just as it disappeared. The supervolcano erupted, taking everything with it. It was world news. The volcano spread ashes around the globe and killed everything in the country. Everything it covered…is now an ashtray. A graveyard of grotesque sculptures made of ash-covered bodies of those who perished asphyxiated or hit by pyroclastic flows. Like Pompeii, but a thousand times worse.

The rivers became hot and corrosive like a river of battery acid. Flaming rocks fell from the sky, raining on the buildings. Hot gravestones over the ruins of cities.

But there were seeds, gold deposits ejected from the mantle of the earth towards the crater's surroundings.

These deposits germinated in stems until they became plants: an industrial plant for extraction and refining. Then they turned into parks, industrial parks, which they called estancias, or working farms. The zones surrounding the eruption, the rings, have two names according to the level of impact and destruction.

The first ring, "The Sand Land" is characterized as a desert, where the ash can be managed and cleaned up and the air is breathable. People were injured there when the eruption occurred, some with minor injuries and some serious, but they remained in their cities. The second zone is "The Ash Land," where flora and fauna can no longer live. There's only gusts of ash wind that make it impossible to breathe without special masks. There are thousands of rocks big as stadiums, excavated with drills next to the industrial plants for the refinery of minerals, the estancias. The cities are in ruins, where few survived, and are populated by grotesque statues. Inside both rings lies the crater, an area in the middle of the Andes with a hole measured in kilometers, big enough to be spotted from space. Where no plane is allowed to fly over it due to the suction it causes. Nobody and nothing survived. The explosion was so enormous that the Cotopaxi, the highest point in Ecuador, was reduced from a snow peak to a dusty mound.

Since then, the Ash Land has been explored and worked over in successive waves by Korean Chaebols, Japanese Zaibatsus, American Management Boards, Ecuadorian estancias, Fronts and Assemblies for large-scale corporate mineral extraction, and small artisanal mining farms.

At night, the stars are hidden behind the halogen light of the foundries and the dust rising from the explosion of rocky materials in the open air.

The people found a place in the industrial park of the estancias. They are born in the estancias. They break rock in the estancias. They sing hymns of the estancias, and they are buried at the estancias…

A pop-up window crept over the text. "File reading error. Error code 402. System reboot. Estimated recharging time, one hour."

Bah! It was just getting good. I kicked the cables hanging from the walls. And I took out my concentrated food rations, two pills with a slow metabolic formula that I swallowed without water.

This was my deepest excursion to date. And, though I am a happy woman from everything I have crushed, I am also terrified that this place will crush me. I think the blowing up of the office was stronger than I expected. Meanwhile, I looked through the cracks in the office.

<u>The worst day of my life</u>

<u>Log Entry #3</u>
The worst part about my fevers is not the things I destroy but forgetting to take precautions. The beam in the office fell through the hole. I suppose because of the explosion. It is stuck in the ground, so I don´t know. I piled a bunch of trash around it and compacted everything with my stomps until I formed a mound to get out of here. My idea is to throw a grappling hook from the top of the waste dump to the office shaft and anchor it to a firm beam. And climb the rope.

The first rule of urban archeology is to return the way you came. Because it is a safe path. Piling up trash takes too much energy. I had to turn off my body-mods to reduce the consumption of metabolic energy and redirect it to my physical power. I also reduced the intensity of my eye flashlights. Unfortunately, the energy I had saved got wasted in one of my stomping fevers. The mound was so tempting I could not stop myself from stomping on it. I am not sure when I stopped. I only remember the stomping and then writing in my log somewhere else with legs in pain. Poor me!

I wanted to save energy by turning off more of my body-mods, some possibly vital, and I reviewed the apps running in the background, like the parasympathetic and involuntary systems. The activities in the background were reduced only to the growth of hair and nails, and the power consumption of the platinum disk. I am panicking, and so write to stop thinking about it. I only have one protein bar left. There was a landslide and I can't go back the way I came. What is worse, I turned off my mental inhibitors and only my lack of energy and my hunger keeps my stomping fevers at bay. If I eat my energy bar, I am afraid my fevers will return with a vengeance, and I will end up dying from exhaustion and starvation.

The icon on the platinum disk, which I had forgotten about, has a pending notification that reads "Recovery of 100% of navigation records. Protocol unencrypted. Do you want to restart the suspended session? Accept or Reject." I pressed accept. Hoping this would solve my problems. I decided to roam about and read. If I stopped for one second, I would start thinking about how awful everything is, until I couldn't take a step, and would just let myself die here alone.

The same text showed up again, with a new title that read "Mai-Tau's Blog. Inactive account of user Maimará Taucara. Most recent log in: 316 years ago."

I am Maimará Taucara and for one hour I lost my position as "Aclla, official certified writer" with a license from the Wayra Corporation, a company located in the cyber industrial heart of the Andean mountains. A silver landscape that smells of burning, where the sky is covered with ashen welding smoke from the refinery plants. I live in the commune at the periphery of the Meta Performance Centers in the South of Quito. These are single-person plastic modules grouped as departments connected to the "Ilika," the quantum internet network.

"I see. That's what these ruins under the space elevator are called," said the pillager as she pressed on her grumbling, empty stomach.

But I spilled my "chicha," a fermented corn drink, over the novel generator I had rented. It ruined the machine. I am past my deadline, and I write this to avoid panicking until the messenger comes with a new novel generator. I tried to write in the old-fashioned way, with pencil and paper. Nobody does that anymore! Can there be anything more obsolete? Without auxiliary batteries? Without connecting the document directly to the brain to write it? But my desperation grew. My mind only wanted to get the job done, even knowing that if I wrote it with pencil and paper it would take me twenty years while it would take minutes with the generator.

Now the computer is converting nerve impulses into text, sound, and sensations through a "chumpi," a belt integrated with an Arduino circuit connected to the hippocampus and regulated by the text generator. In other words, I am connecting to a cable to bring out the writer in me…that is, if I have one. The critics destroyed my previous work, and no big or small press wants my novel in their data markets. But I can do it! They will see!…I will create a great story, despite the smoke and the ashes that cover the city!…If the messenger arrives on time. I refuse to write without the generator. Even though I could. But no. To write with a license but without the generator would constitute piracy because the ideas would circulate freely, without the government's regulation and control. If they found out it was me who wrote these inflammatory ideas without approval, I would be unplugged. Some say the unplugged end up in the ruins of cities in the Ash Land. Others say that they live in the Sand Land's underworld or finish their days in the crater. No one comments on this, but sometimes there are stories in the media. Ghosts and murmurs from the web.

For some strange reason I no longer felt anxious about the deadline. And so my body moved on its own, connected to the cable, and kept on writing the novel. My own body kept me absorbed by my story. It was too late. I was already writing without the generator. My trace was already on the web. I was already a pirate. I only could wait for the agents to unplug me. I cried. But my body kept on writing. What was the point in stopping it? I was already deep in, above my neck. Probably a rope to hang myself, to end my life as a writer.

They knocked at the door. I thought about the agents, the police, the traffic controllers. Then they knocked harder. They called me by name from the other side of the door. I succumbed to fear, and I turned myself off. I disassociated, hiding in the deepest corner of my soul. I moved forward in automatic mode. I accepted my disgrace…

When I opened the door, I found the messenger with the replacement generator. I was an "Aclla" once more.

That was a bad story! No wonder she needed her text generator. I put the disk in my backpack, without disconnecting it. I made several attempts with the grappling hook until it caught onto something. When I got up to the office, I saw the hook was anchored to the desk. There were scratches.

Saint Aura. Patron of Data Mining

Log Entry #4

The ancients and I are similar. I was overjoyed. A long time ago they built the space elevator over the Meta Performance Centers. As if stomping on them. Nobody knew where they were. Everything had been deleted during the Age of Fire. These ruins around me look like the rubbish that I stomped on and gathered to make a mound. That is all that is left of that history.

I want to get out of here. I found honey jars among the moldy trash, and I got my energy back. But I am still worried about scurvy. I should have bought the vitamin C self-producing pancreas! But no…this scatterbrained head spent it all in the spiked boots so I could stomp better.

And well, I will have to spend the night here below. My way back has collapsed and I have been walking through the ruins hoping to find an exit. Sometimes I think I find a way out, but then come the land slides.

In my last failed attempt, I stomped on some honey jars with anger and frustration. I took an abandoned desk out of a cave and set it up as a bed to sleep on, putting up traps and repellents just in case. We never know what crawls in the dark. But I couldn't sleep and so I switched on some body functions and the library system. I looked at the books one by one trying to find "official" information about the Age of Fire. And about the construction of the space elevator. They all said the same things paraphrasing the same sources. Like the elevator was built over the Sand Land, in an uninhabited and arid zone in the south of the old capital, San Francisco de Quito.

They also speak about the devastation that reaches to the south into Alausí, to the east into Portoviejo, to the north into Ibarra, and to the west into the Mihuanoyacu community. This text is revealing and very polemical because it claims, on the contrary, that the elevator was erected over a populated area. There are still holes in the story, but it is more complete than the other texts.

Even kindergarten kids, with half a brain, know you cannot believe what school books tell you. History has been manipulated for a long time. This disk is very valuable…and I can't stomp on it! I was so angry I went to sleep thinking about whether the elevator was a great stomp on the city. I fell asleep smiling.

I have no idea how long I slept, but I decided to take a risk on myself. I ate a protein energy bar and injected myself with stamina. I turned on all my body-mods and prepared to climb with speed. Avoiding thoughts of stomping, I passed through the galleries, tunnels, and familiar areas. But there was an insurmountable collapse in a cave. So, I turned back to the last gallery, and, after trying every path, all leading nowhere, I decided in frustration to take the worst path. I descended through the gallery trying to find a way out by path or subterranean tunnel. I am not sure how long I walked down but I reached the bottom where I found a subterranean waterfall. It was inside a colonial church. I had entered through the roof. Behind the waterfall, and protected by tempered glass, was the image of a virgin with an inscription that read: Saint Aura, Patron of Data Mining.

The disk and my data went crazy, as if they themselves were experiencing one of my stomping fevers. When I looked at the virgin, I failed to notice I had scanned an ancient code next to her name. It was this code that activated my data. My eyes projected a pop-up window on a wall to restart the session. "Do you want to open this document at the latest section? Accept or Reject." I accepted.

Time stopped in the survivors' hearts, a frozen memory of faces now gone. They will not be forgotten with time. Such immense pain will pass from this life to the next generations. The recent dead are the most alive, everyone else, turned into things. —Extract from an anonymous Saint Aura believer.

Saint Aura is the patron of the miners of data. The women who recycle electronic trash sell any valuable parts and their software content. These women are stigmatized as identity thieves for using scanned digital documents to forge false identities. Ancient identity documents, photographs, ID numbers, personal data, and other sensitive documents. They go to Saint Aura seeking her protection. They built a shrine and then a church to show their devotion. We do not know if Aura ever existed, or if she was the lone survivor at the crater during the eruption of the super volcano. Many women think that Aura was the first data miner who fought against the injustice of industrial plants, helping the helpless, and that she created a secret garden in the Ash Land to where her devotees could escape. They say that, when she died, she was buried in that place.

Saint Aura's devotees have a saint and a motto that characterizes them: "Live first, then recycle."

I saw the majestic image and got a fever. My eyes lit with fire. I quickly dismounted the glass, threw the panels away, put on my spiked boots and gave her a good kick. I went on, and on, and on. I gave so many kicks to the wall not even caring that my legs were badly hurt, even when debris fell on my calves. Only a hole remained where the Virgin had been. What joy! I guess Saint Aura is also the patron of stompers. Haha!

Among the rubble there are various dusty chips. They were hidden behind the image. Smart! I don't have the right plugs for that kind of format. They are over 300 years old. Who could have them? Luckily the platinum disk did! I plugged the chips one by one. To see if it was worth stomping on them. Some were corrupted, some were destroyed by my stomps.

A pop-up window appeared before my eyes. "Do you want to decrypt the archive? Accept or Reject." I hit accept hoping to find text, but they were only screenshots from a conversation.

"The young feed their blood to the bats," wrote Papagaya132 to MaimaraCutePink88.

"What does it matter to you! I didn't know. It was a meeting that my best friend organized with her friends. They see my swimsuit posts. They like them!" Maimará lashed out.

"The young girl lives in the hills and will die in the hills. She lives for men and rejects the moon."

"I make a living writing and publishing my intimate photos at Onlyfast. It was my theme party…a small one, with only my closest friends…the pink-light hour at the disco! I have no idea who took the pictures and published them, but it was done without my authorization. They must have stolen them!"

"The young woman wants a man's field. But the woman goes hunting in the hills to kill the tiger."

"Who are you?"
Papagaya132 wrote, "The papagaya remains calm, she is a healer."

"Why are you telling me all this?" …

"The young woman can't reach the moon because the stairs break halfway there. The woman climbs to the heavens on the chonta tree in her field. And the moon climbs down with her transformed into light."

"You're really crazy, lady! You know? The moon only shows herself in seasons, when the smoke of the foundries dissipates due to chimney maintenance and there are no ash storms. And I am terrified of tigers. They are all confined to zoos. My career as a writer and top model is going great. I can reach the sky in my own way. Ridiculous! I have many fans who love me and send me the nicest messages."

"Elves dance and seduce the lemon tree. When a woman brings the moon to her farm, the corn multiplies, and the pericote rats vanish."

Why would they have this on chips? And why hide them behind the image of a virgin? I have only one honey jar left. Soon I will have to find food again. Again, the loop of saving energy, finding food, stomping on ruins, and reading. If I can't be cured by stomping on the concealed virgin of a secret sect inside hidden ruins under the space elevator that unveiled a lost story, I am incurable, she wrote with tears.

<u>Revelations</u>

<u>Log Entry #5</u>
I totally regret this! Why did I have to go deeper down?! The vending machine saved me. Who cares if the food is older than the elevator! I could finally rest and eat. I slept two days straight after walking for three weeks and barely sleeping two hours a day.

I am now camping in an underground train station and have made a barricade with the seats. It is the longest I have gone without a stomping fever. My journal, luckily, tells me I'm not going insane.

This place is terrorific. And not because it's underground. Something lives here. At first the cyber-industrial complex was buried under piles of rubble. But there are tunnels and galleries dug into the earth that pierce the steel and cement walls. It could be humans, although this zone was sealed. Unless…they too were buried. Some of the buried buildings have secret doors that lead you to the cement tunnels. In one of them, I found PVC pipes hanging from the walls with QR codes attached.

The disk activated when my eyes scanned the code, and it opened an archive. Someone had taken a photo of the final words scratched on a PVC pipe. The message on the photo says: "These are the remains of Zambrano!" The words in the photo read "The Spring of Death."

I am not sure what is going on down here. I know the routine. Now the document will open with more weird stories. I am done reading this tedious document. I wept. I will die down here. I don't want that something to come after me. Not before I can stomp on more things. I stomped on photos, wagons, statues, urns, clocks, baby strollers. This kept me a tiny bit sane. I also stomped on an ancient diary that read, "In ancient times, the people from the neighborhood would go down, go up, or go to the city for work." But there is nothing left.

I even had to improvise cushions for my feet with the foam from the seats. Everyone has heard of people who have gone missing in these incursions. They pray outside archeological sites with candles and then baptize a random room with the name of the missing woman. I think I might be that woman…if she was an urban archeologist. I am nothing but a thief stealing from the dead, one who stomps on the history of the dead and destroys them into oblivion. My fevers have won out. I hate history. I hate the value of history! And I hate the history that led me to this place! I was born poor. I stomped on the history of others because I cannot stomp on my own history of poverty, which is also my destiny and my end…a poor woman stomps on the most valuable things. That is my sweet revenge for bringing me poor into this world. I am alone in the darkness with this something lurking.

But the document opened…on its own.

I did body painting to survive. I used to go to the park with my friend Kellyn. Once painted, we asked people to take pictures with us. We were also tour guides for Zone Zero. This was before I became a model and a writer. We made our living nicely.

But not always. Since I can remember, our grandparents' voices remain present. The only thing I can do is honor my warrior spirit.

There is a link to a photograph of Maimará, the first I've seen. But the link is broken. Below the hyperlink it reads: "Maimará in a parallel world." This…is saving me, she said in tears as she kept reading.

I made the sections in relief with recycled materials, and I also designed the character. The paint we made from materials we had at home, old paint and abandoned crayons. That day it rained and I took my clothes off on my way home because rain damages the suit. My friend Kellyn carried me on her back in the rain all the way through the central avenue. That Kellyn, she's happy and fulfilled today. You gave me my best memories ever and I love you. I am so proud of you. What a gift you are! I lost many materials for one reason or another, but it feels wonderful to see each other. I feel grateful for these new feelings, to look at myself completely with the love, the play, and the compassion of a child…we keep on creating together… and so, taking our essence to every place we go. I have grown a lot, but I have a long way to go to be an "Aclla."

Under the text there was a photo slowly downloading. It can't be! It's the appraiser! Maimará is the appraiser! But how? She must be 300 years old!

"I am actually 290, thank you very much! You make me older than I am," said a silhouette from behind the barricade.

"Why did you bring me here!? You used me Maimará."

"YES, I used you. But it is more complicated than it looks. You wanted to get over yor fevers, right? I have sent many down here. For some it works to reach rock bottom to change, with shock therapy. Some, on the other hand, contemplate for days and even months to be able to change. Would you have endured eating and fearing the return of the fevers? Your poverty fevers? It is hard for me to put the women I care about at risk so they can heal. I didn't want to hurt you."

"Well, I am very annoyed. I could have died down here. And there is this thing following us."

"I am not a thing. You are the thing. A thing." said an old lady on a senior's bicycle. "We monitor your vital signs constantly, and we have emergency teams ready to go. Everyone, come out!"

Before the pillager could notice, she was surrounded by people camouflaged as rocks, rubble, anything. "I am Papagaya, the curandera. What is your name?"

"They call me the Pillager. I dropped the name Elie Bonaparte long ago."

"Pillager. Here we have all left our names behind. "Live first, then recycle." That is our motto. We must live and then recycle, even our names."

"Why are you helping me?"

"Because you wanted to heal, right? Besides, a curandera saw the healer within me." She turned and looked at the old lady.

I was in shock. All my fears left me. The people here are just like me. And they decided to heal.

"How do we get out of here? Do we go through Eden?"

"What Eden?" said Maimará looking confused at the rest.

"No one knows where that is, Pillager," responded the old lady. "Eden is lost. But finding others who can understand our pain and heal it is, in a way, our Eden.

"Yes." She began to cry. "You prepared everything, right?"

"Yes. We are healers and recyclers."

La Grobinita:
The First Marmorado Romance

Rolando André López

Qué importan ya tus ideales
Qué importa tu canción
La grasa de las capitales
Cubre tu corazón
— Seru Giran

CHAPTER 1,

In Which, When Mami First Sights la Grobinita—or Nadía, or Nanú, or The Girl Who Brought The Worm—& Tells Cándido About Her, He Disbelieves, & They Argue About What Is Real & What Is Not, & Learn That Some Grobin Things Are Definitely Happening in the View of the Laughing Door; Also, We Learn of Invision, La Calma, & Iglomia la Mostra Ciudad, & Mami's Lovers, & Cándido's Mostrídolas, & The Wormtail, & Other Incidentals Such As The Many Hidden Roads to Kaimú & The Abandoned Cars There That Outnumber Them

My partner was a shadow even in the sunlit desert, and walked with me until we arrived at the three doors. The first one opened, the second laughed, and the third was a toothless mouth agape, revealing the abyss of an empty stomach. The human house was ready for us.

But then I was no longer walking. I was slipping, curious but slipping, as if driven by the vertiginous slope of a mountain—into the third door.

It swallowed me, feet-first.

Into its stomach I fell and a scream galed from my groin to my throat until my toes landed on midnight grass as on water, soft and firm. I was surrounded by drum-fast steps.

I followed them and beat my feet. The ground responded. Bumkabum. It was soil that resounded to touch like the skin of a drum.

Above, canopies of ancient trees covered the firmament. The sound of our drumming feet covered me. I knew no direction, as all was humid and dark in la Calma. The drumming rang from many points at once, different claves clashing through each other, strong-arming the air.

My partner found me. Her grasp landed upon my palm, soft, jiggly like milk. I squeezed. Her touch led me through and our feet drummed together. Domed in la Calma, the answer's in la Calma, so said the ancient prayer…

I had fallen asleep listening to Aelia, hoping to dream of intimate union in her room, the one she made in me. But I didn't have enough credits or mentalika. I dreamed instead with the three doors, the companion, and la Calma, the covered forest, and then woke up in bed, two hours past sunrise. My room around me a mess of papers, books, and furry dolls. Walls dull, wallpaper-green.

A presence, a core of invisible waves moved, swaying a step away from my laying body. My InVision Glass tablet lay on the pillow beside mine. Gone the Mostra that had emanated from it to woo me into sleep. Now, a drumbeat ran on the ground around my bed. A heartbeat to my left. No physical body occupied the space. But a scent in the air drew my attention to the emptiness in front of my bedroom window. From there the tendrils of an invisible gaze reached out and touched my nose, the space under my eyes, behind my ears. Not ticklishness, but my face simmered electric.

In the kitchen, water ran in the sink, oil sizzled over pans.

Mami was already up.

The tendrils of that other gaze drew away. As it dawned on me that the jalousie window slats to my left let in between them an ashen light, I desired to still hold on to the number, the one we stepped to in the mind. But both that memory and the presence dissipated, and within seconds I was alone in my room, my Invision-Glass beside me. I got up and slipped on a strewn T-shirt and left the room in my underpants.

Outside, Mami made white rice and yellow scrambled eggs. She lay them side by side on a white porcelain plate with flower-blue patterns. She wore an old floral dress with slippers. Sunday.

She sat at the table swinging ketchup out of the bottle when she said, without looking up at me, "Last night, I saw la Grobinita hiding in the bush by la Zulonuestra."

On the window sill by the table, a small purple statue of Oli portrayed godly lassitude. He lay wood-dark and sideways, leaning carefree on his left arm, with his classic purple cap. Beyond the glass, outside, our yard, shared with our neighbors, stretched out into the banks of río Malomá. Beyond the river was la Calma, the covered forest.

I said, "But you fell asleep before me last night."

"But I woke up before you, at 2 in the morning. I heard a sound. Como un tucutún outside, against the wall—it felt bigger than a rat. And I walked out of the bedroom and saw you asleep on the couch, with the TV on, and I heard it again. Tucutún, mwaah… tender, like a whisper-low moan. I patted you on the shoulder, remember? And you went to your room. And I turned off the TV and went outside, and traced the source of the sound to near la Zulonuestra…"

La Zulonuestra, the tall marble goddess of the round countenance in our front lawn. Of pearly-white complexion, her globular blue eyes set sad and low under a moonlike forehead, and small round nose, lips full and lovely, their frown supported by her face's posture, leaning to the right in a half-nod, like a healer listening with tenderness. Her hair curly and waist-long, rendered in streaks of white stone, body donned with a sun-reflecting blue silk satin robe, flowers at the base covering her feet. She is the patron of ancestral juvenility, of lovers of the final innocence, and of grief.

"And there, under her, in the bushes that guard nuestra madre Zulonuestra, I saw la Grobinita, crouching, naked, llena de tierra. She was shy, and small, and soft-skinned, but tough-boned and sooty, too. Like she'd crawled through the sewers of Mogollán. She looked at me like an unsettled animal. Her hair was long, dry, dirty down to her hips. If only I could clean it, I thought, it would flow like river-shining blackness. Her eyes were open jungles darkened by her night interior, her frown like a kitten. Just a tormented face, puppy and kitten and grown too soon. Like Nadía. Just like Nadía, Candi."

Nadía, her sister, gone from this earth for seven decades now.

"She just looked at me, and her eyes pleaded but her body trembled. Then she skittered away in a flash, on all fours, like—a monkey! Left the bush shaken behind her. She might have even had a wagging tail, or it was the shadow in her wake. Oh, Candi. I must have moved too fast, or too shaky. la Grobinita left behind shadows, left them behind the bush."

Ever since Borni left with our car last year, Mami's been creating angels to combat the demons that don't let her sleep at night. First, it was el Pintor Alado. Then it was Simón Cocodrilo. Now it was la Grobinita, and she said it like *puchunguita,* like she had chosen her. The models, artists, actresses, like my Aelia: they were Mostras, officially certified as SAFE by the State. Mami could have one of these for herself. But she didn't want the products from Ciudad Iglomia. These were never enough for her. She wanted the wild ones.

"You had a dream."

"No vuelvas a decir eso," Mami said. "Ni que a dream. That's like saying I'm sick. It's you I'm sick of."

"I don't have time for this today, Mami."

She gave me a look knife-sharp, her brown-lipped mouth a frown, her lashy black eyebrows an awful knot.

Lately she had taken to assuming that I was as aware of her over-productive dream life as she was. Asking her to clarify her terms, or pointing to the oneiric origin of her language, only roused her irritability and confusion. She would tell me I had been there to see it happen. She would ask why I was pretending not to have been there, not to remember.

So I played along and didn't. I said, "Mejor que se vaya. Those kids bring sickness with them anyway. Mental, physical, everything."

"She's not just a kid. She's more than that. She has the grobin in her, Candi. And I think she's still under the house. She left a shadow… that's a sign…"

Last year's boy, Borni, reminded her of cousin Aldrín. This Grobinita evokes the sister Nadía. But la Grobinita sounded to me like a homeless child, of which there are many in the island. Here, if a child wants to wander away from home and cross from one end of the island to the other, it is easy to go alone on foot. Arriving anywhere here feels close, like biking to a neighbor's house. But imagine how old we are in my town of Kaimú, that there are still places to get lost. Ours is the only township in the island not near to any of the others, a solitude ensconced between four mountains, the mountains both portals and barriers of entry.

No technology has yet been able to map out the coordinates of the mountain roads. Directions to get to places aren't just about movement, but about coordinating sound and sight. People will tell you to stick to the Ramoarez dirt road until you hear the symmetrical call of the Cuculu, the all-day bird, which should be right before you see the peak of Monte Malomá loom over the valley of Taizana, at which point you turn left towards the road that, some five minutes down, hosts the banana-colored house. But if you are already past the valle of Taizana when you hear the

Cuculu's call, then it is too late, and you must turn around, and take the second right after the blue poinciana tree. But be aware, there is another blue poinciana tree, which also is by a right turn. You have to pick the right right turn. Once you do, and drive for a few minutes, you will see the banana-colored house. Not the one colored like a rotten banana. If you made it to that one, then you're way past it. And perhaps too close to the Hidden Places. Barrio Bilrriaba will be a few minutes away from the ripe banana colored house. And once you're in Bilrriaba, Kaimú is just a few more miles of winding roads down. There are some turns to make of course, but let the Bilrriabeños help you with that.

Someone else will tell you that once you get to Barrio Bilrriaba, you need to speak to Don Micalo of the pink house, but not Don Micalo of the pink hat. Don Micalo of the pink hat gets drunk at 10 in the morning, and Don Micalo of the pink house owns the bar and used to be a mountain explorer. Pink Hat Don Micalo's directions land you in quicksand roads that sink you into the forest's unfathomable densities. Pink House Don Micalo's directions take you to Kaimú. But his are not any easier to follow. The mountains are open and everyone gives directions, but many cars lie abandoned on these roads, people who never got to where they were going, and abandoned their empty machines, now incapable of running and killing.

So how did this Grobinita make it here?

I said, "You saw her for five seconds. What do you know about her needs?"

"It was more than five seconds, Candi. I told you, it was so long that—that I don't know how long it was. It was a close-up."

"Mami, this sounds like you're dreaming of pregnant birds."

"I find my sister after all these years…"

"It's okay to dream…"

"Come out to see the shadows she left behind in the front yard. Then call me a dreamer."

"She's just gonna be like Borni."

"No vuelvas a talk about Borni. Borni was not a grobinito. He didn't leave any shadows behind."

"All bushes have shadows, Mami."

"Not like these. These are grobinita shadows. Visible even at night. They take two revolutions of the sun to fade. They're distinct from the bush shadows and it will be apparent to you right away when you look. I won't even have to show you. All you have to do is walk up to la

Zulonuestra and look at the bush to her right. You will see the little shadow that la Grobinita left behind, wiggling in the shade under the bush.
The breeze makes it smile. The sun makes it tired. Grobinitas leave little
shadows like this behind when they're scared, little turdlets of the soul,
like I told you last night."

She didn't tell me that last night.

"Mami, I don't—"

"Te lo juro, on my faith in la Zulonuestra."

"You really don't have to."

"On my faith in the teardrop that created the mourning world."

"Mami, please. You're doing it again."

"Come see the shadow, por favor."

The clutch of her hand upon my forearm impressed her urgency
upon me. Her skinny, 83 year-old frame bore thin, brown, veiny skin.
Its elden smell was home to me. Even when its closeness meant we were
arguing, or that, as now, she forced me into something, her smell comforted me.

When I relented and assented and said *yes okay I'll go* her demean-
or changed. Her grip let go of my forearm and I took her left hand and
put it over my right arm and she leaned on me and we walked out together and she said, "Ay puchungo, it's always good to leave the house
with you."

Outside the house, bells hung from the wall around the entry door,
and other small trinkets that rang when the wind blew, like the string
of emerald marbles whose clashes against each other made the canica
canticle, or the set of bamboo chips hung by string that clic-cloc'd and
clapped their hands upon seeing me walk out with Mami to look at the
shadow by the statue. Today the breeze was strong. I hadn't been outside
in a week, and it was pale and cloudy, so the wind came with a chill. "She
must be so happy," Mami said.

"Who?"

"La sombrita. When I walked up earlier, she was still there."

We opened the portón in la marquesina and walked down the ramp.
Then we turned left onto the gravel path that winds around the front
yard, ending in a circle around la Zulonuestra. Some weeds were out on
the grass that surrounded the gravel path. But the flores de maga, the
azaleas, the lilies were blooming in the yard. When we walked up to the
statue, Mami separated from me to join her hands together in the Ola
prayer. And I joined her too, looking up at the eyes of Zulonuestra. To

look at her eyes was essential. It was how we participated in *entrevista,* or *intersight.* At the end, we said, together, the final invocation, used at the end of prayers: "Aminadha."

After the brief gesture she leaned on me again and pointed.

"¿La ves?"

The bush she pointed at, to the right of Zulonuestra's left foot, was dotted with small yellow flowers amidst the manicured dome of leaves.

"There," she said. "She's hiding. I think she's scared of you."

"La Grobinita?"

"No nene, her sombrita."

With a soft advance she crouched, put her hands on her knees, took two tentative steps and stuck her neck out as if to say, *Come here, come here.* She purred as if to a cat.

She grunted with displeasure as she straightened herself with an effort and looked around with confused eyes at the dawned world around her. She sought a shadow, but cloudy days suck up the shadows from the ground, and gather them in the sky's smudged greyness. I knew this before we left the house. We all know this about cloudy days. But she had talked herself into a hole.

"You waited too long," she said. "The cielo grisáceo dissipated her."

She stepped away, heading back to the house, through the gravel path.

I didn't look at her.

I had noticed something.

Right by Zulonuestra's left foot, between a rose and an azalea, there was a long, black worm, curled up. It stood out against the pearly-white of the statue's marble foundation and the primorous colors of the flowers. Its body shone there lustrous, curled up, a shining black shell, a gongolí. A slimy little gongolí. When I was a kid I used to eat them all the time.

How long it could be in its extended form, I wasn't sure. So I waited for it to move, to do something, but nothing happened. It just sat there, like a cake waiting to be eaten.

Over by the marquesina already, Mami shouted at me if I wanted her to make eggs for me, but I didn't answer. The air was still, the worm curled up. I said nothing and then she asked if I had seen something— *la ves???*—and a memory from la Calma came to me, a figment of last night's dream. And Mami returned with a huff. But I didn't want anyone to disturb me so I could see her face, or her hands in the air, swiveling like a snake—the face of the partner in the dream who had danced with me. But now Mami was next to me, her breath was next to me, her body was near and talking to me and I looked down at the worm as it uncurled and stretched into the size of my 35 year-old foot and crawled up the statue's side, up her big toe, its crawl intricate, thousands of little legs at its sides clicking away. If I ate it, it would be healthy for me.

She stood beside me, looked at the worm.

"I know what I saw. It was similar to that, but not the same."

And her presence left again.

*

Since I was born we've lived here, in this low-roofed, one-story house in a neighborhood of low-roofed, one-story houses. The man left when I was still in the motherbelly, and the woman who carried me to term left soon as I was born.

Then Mami raised me. Mami, my mother.

Our house was small, but it filled the needs, a two-bedroom home with two bathrooms, a living room, a kitchen with washer and dryer and both front porch and back patio. It sat some feet off the ground, held up by cement columns, so cats sometimes made a home below. Mami liked that. My room sat somehow at the crossroads of it all. The wall to the north of my room adjoined Mami's bedroom. The one to the west adjoined the kitchen, and the southern wall adjoined the living room.

We were sustained by the patronage of Mandai, my grandfather's best friend and business partner for many years. Even before my grandfather died, Mandai and Mami saw each other once every two months and she stayed in his beach house with him just for one day and night while he took a break from his wife and kids and she took a break from me and grandpa, though she never put it that way.

A breeze blew and the worm wiggled its thousand legs, beginning its uncurling on the statue's stone foundation.

"Worm... are you smiling?"

The worm didn't answer, just kept crawling up Zulonuestra's leg after the breeze was done, under her skirt.

When I went back inside, Mami was down on the kitchen floor, her knees and ears touching ground.

"The tucutún, I heard it again just now."

"It could just be a cat, Mami."

"If you're not going to believe your own ears, why don't you just go back to work, or to play, or whatever you do in your Mostra City."

That's the first good idea you've had all morning, I didn't say.

"I don't have any appointments now," I said.

"You could be out, meeting real people."

Like la Grobinita?

Tucún-tucún, went the ground. A bump below. A cat?

"There! Did you hear it?"

It didn't matter to me that I had. I was already on my way back to my room. She didn't yell at me to come back. She kept her ear to the ground.

I locked the door behind me and looked at my room from the corner by the door. In the stillness, I sought out the presence by the window adjacent to the bed. I let the silence linger in case she was shy. I was sure she was a she.

But only the green walls stared back.

It was a nothing Sunday.

After hours of snacks and a roam through the InVision realms, I walked outside to stand by la Zulonuestra again. The evening light was pale. There was no more wind, and some of the clouds had let up, though the cast of the day was still hazy, a sandy sky. The worm was on top of her curly hair, rolled up like a beanie. It shone, still liquid and warm.

I had been thinking about the worm all day. It came to me between turns in the bed, when I flipped the channels on the TV, when I looked at Mostras in the City.

I don't know if worms have eyes, but I could feel the worm looking at me, like it was thinking about me too. Maybe the worm was a she. I reached and picked her up and she started to wiggle in my hold.

Helpless, she could not bite me, but could arch up and hold on to my finger, as to the edge of a cliff.

Her little legs tickled me and I giggled and shook my hand so her body would loosen and dangle-dance over me. Opening my mouth I dropped her down into my tongue. I closed my mouth and the worm didn't let me chew. She slid down and jumped into my esophagus with the excitement of a child in a waterslide. I giggled and jumped in front of la Zulonuestra, insulting her grief.

Images of Mostrídolas ran in my mind. Tumbas Mostrosas, Amadas Mostrosas. Memorias I wanted to rerun. Aelia cooing me last night, her hair over her warm breasts covering the flowers pasted onto her nipples. Blood grew and moved in my body. My groin swelled up.

I ran into the house, past the kitchen, almost crashed into my room and locked the door behind me and hopped over onto bed to pick up my InVision Glass. Just by putting my fingers on the tablet, it glowed with a phosphorescence that I had never seen before. I unlocked access to my home screen with the three-two finger tap. I felt twenty years younger, balls hot. I wanted a naked feast of sweet fruits served in large golden bowls. I wanted naked necks and bare feet. The worm ran through all the secrets. Its run tickled my body's viscera. I giggled as I encoded the gestures for direct access to the Aelia window. When it offered me the five levels of electric submersion, I chose *Nearme*, the deepest, most draining tier.

With the worm vigor, I had the stamina for it.

I trusted I wouldn't shut down.

You don't want to shut down in the InVision realms.

As the screen loaded, I fed it my mentalika, looking at the screen's two eye-inhalers. Two red, large spheres, each roughly the shape and size of a human eye, distant from each other as two eyes would be. Each glowed with a green outline when I placed my eyes parallel to them, my hands holding the sides of the glass tablet. And then the inhaling commenced. It was already a titillating sensation, foreplay, to feel the pull of the Invision Glass, a watery machine with aerialectric filaments, its eye-inhalers sipping out my mentalika like a child sucking milk out of a cup with a plastic straw.

As the InVision drank, tufts of fur grew all over my body. I became the self I am with Aelia, the name she gave me: *monito-mostrito*. A monotone voice in the InVision Glass said, "*Nearness ready, lie me down—nearness ready, lie me down…*" and I set down the tablet on the bed. And in a second, a singular point of white light formed at the tablet's center, a glowing dot of awareness. It then expanded, diffuminated like an explosion to all corners of my room. With a creeping patience, the walls undulated like rippling currents, and a warmer, denser color emerged as if from below them, balmy inner-lip red. Columns of red lips surrounded my bed, entombing me in a rosey chamber—its hot, humid breath ventilated around me. Dripping, I laughed with anticipation.

That was me, smiling on the statue.

I took off my T-shirt, slid my underpants down with my shorts. Lights the color of lava shone from below. Giggling still, I got on all fours in my bed, and heaved up my chest and beat my hands on it, and shouted Hogu, Hogu, Hogu! The worm spiraled out of my tailbone, wagged as my slimy tail, waving with me. The tail-sensation came with a pudendal shockwave of pleasure. I am transforming, the room is transforming. Such is the power of mentalika.

Aelia giggled. From nowhere, from everywhere, her high, soft laugh echoed. This is how it always began, no matter what tier I was in. Her laugh was always the same.

"Monito, I'm here," she purred, tickling my fur.

Aelia, my beloved Mostra—she appeared in front of me, assembled from a million and three particles of color-plasms into the figure of my affection: the red-breasted blue woman in a diaphanous white lace dress, which revealed more than it hid, the suppleness of her skin's tones glowing from beneath the lace, her body soft in the linen threads, red breasts pressing up against the patterned fabric. I jumped in bed and my erection swung like a dangling hammer. Oh, monito, she said so coy, I have never seen you so near.

By this point, so much mentalika had been drained of me that I found no words to respond with. Only grunts. Hogu, hogu, hogu, I whispered.

We were floating in some oceanic room. You're too far from me, she whispered. She was on her knees, in front of the bed. I crawled closer. Her fingertips rubbed my knees when I reached the bed's corner and set my feet down on the floor. Its warmth oozed into my soles, which felt the rugose texture of a baline tongue. I pressed my toes into it. I looked into Aelia's eyes. She was whispering something. I had to lean closer. I had to look deep into her eyes to understand the movements of her mouth. A soft hum rippled through my skin. Aelia giggled awkwardly and nudged closer until her knees touched my feet and her breasts, still in the lace dress, rubbed up against my lower thighs. I was about to burst. Patience, she hissed.

The InVision tablet was made of glass but it ran on synthetic water and aerolectricity. This nervous system inside the tablet was connected to the Avua-1 Network, in Iglomia, the Network's home. Water, electricity, and air collaborated to intercommunicate my mentalika with the powers of the Aelia Body-Complex in Iglomia. The more I gave, the more fleshly her forma Mostrídola appeared.

Our session lasted three hours, her joycries loud as Mami's, back when she had lovers and put herself out there. Aelia was so spontaneous, sometimes it was hard to believe she was only a Mostrídola. I sweated and the water pooled in my bed. Pure Mostra. I was drained to a prune by the end. The thick lip-columns around us contained our voices, sealed our sounds in the room.

I fell to bed, face-up. Aelia lay beside me, tracing waves on my chest with her aquaerolectric finger. She purred soft nothings at me. I fell asleep for two hours.

When I awoke, I was back in the dark of my room, and the InVision glass was off, colorless and transparent. Aelia was gone, not even invisible. It was dark, evening. My walls were wallpaper-green. A rug draped over the cement floor. Some dried wetness on the rug. My pillow's was still sweaty. My cum was all over the sheets. I surveyed my body and smelled my smell of sex and decided to shower before heading out of my room.

When I walked out and wandered to the living room, outside it was night. Through the windows that faced the backyard I saw a hole was dug. Something yellow in it. I walked to the screen door at the corner of the living and opened it to get a closer look. The hole was round, and not too big, big enough for a big dog to rest in. Inside the hole were comforters and sheets. Beside the bedding bundle sat a yellow bowl with bananas and apples inside.

Mami was there. I hadn't seen her. She sat behind me in the dark of the backyard, on a swinging chair to my right. She complained that she had waited for me. I told her I'd been sleeping. She'd been waiting for me to serve dinner. I asked her what the hole was about. It was la Grobinita's idea, she said.

"So she only comes when I'm asleep?"

Fried rice and red beans with steak, seasoned with salt, pepper, and flavored with cilantro. Mami was quiet while we ate. My body bore exhaustion and unmistakable pride. I found even the silence of nothing funny. I imagined Aelia kicking my feet under the table. Her toes rubbing my thighs. Trying to contain it was like trying not to breathe, but Mami didn't want to talk about her goings-on with la Grobinita and she showed no curiosity towards me, though at one point she blurted out, "Did the nap make you giddy or something?," and then with a wave of her hand she flinched and said, "you know what, rhetorical question…"

After dinner, Mami sat to watch a game show on television. Two people were in a financial dispute and a mock judge with charisma and pomp got to decide who got the money. Every few minutes Mami peeked, behind the TV, at the window, to check the hole she had dug in the backyard.

I went to my room and crashed in bed. As I fell asleep, I heard Mami cursing that she'd missed the verdict for spending too much time looking out the window. Grobinita, you're distracting me, she shouted at the back yard.

According to the cult, la Zulonuestra watches my *every in-(e)motion*, as the Aminadha hymn intones at temple. *She sees the step of the heart before the spoken action!* When I was a child, Mami said this to me every night before I went to bed. Not so much anymore. She no longer lullabyed me, but she still believed. I wondered if Zulonuestra saw Aelia and me, or maybe Mostras were incomprehensible to Zulonuestra. She only wanted humans to worship her, after all.

As I lay in bed, my usual tiredness, the kind that continues all day after you awake, set in like an unwanted friend, worm vigor gone. Half-aware I feared that I would never fuck as I had that evening. That whatever the worm gave me had gone away. I could have chopped it into bits, given myself servings to last a few days, a week, maybe more. Instead I gulped it all down and spent it all on one blasted session with a Mostrídola. Aelia was so sweet to me. I heard a high, soft laugh again in the night interior, and fell asleep.

The scent of coffee wafted in through the closed bedroom door. Voices spoke in the living room. More than Mami. Someone else was in my house. And Mami was speaking to her. When was the last time we had a woman guest here? She sounded so young. A girl. A girl who spoke womanly, with poise and gesturing. This wasn't a young doll with air in her brain. I didn't catch what she said, but heard the adult affect even in her girly voice. Was she drinking coffee, eating eggs and rice and cookies with Mami? There were kitchen sounds, running water, the clinking of glass and ceramic cups on the wooden table, the shifting of feet on the floor. The actual conversation, muffled through the wall, sounded like gibberish to me.

My stomach groaned. Lacking even the will to lift myself from my bed, I now desired even less to interact with the goings-on outside. I curled into myself and drifted off. But my stomach kept me awake, and soon I was groaning too, and it took three moans and an hour of unbearable abdominal pressure for me to get up and drag myself to the bathroom.

Soon as I popped my ass onto the toilet, oily slicks of paste shot out of my anus. Drooling, my turds splashed out slimy and black. The aggressive outpour caused a wave of pleasure to ride through me as my waste splattered. It smelled like burning tar and dead fish. My ass was burning and I grunted, gagged from the smell even as I blissed out with the inner sensations. Closed my eyes, I couldn't breathe. I flushed it down, out of breath.

And went for the InVision realms on a depleted mind. I cancelled all my appointments for the day, called in sick. With my average mentalika, I could still create an aquebud that would let me hear only the sounds of the games I wanted to play that day. I spent hours with the 5PD Shooter community. While shooting up aliens, we all bragged with each other about our dates with Mostrídolas. When I told them about my night with Aelia, they shrieked with awe. One of them lost concentration and his avatar got decapitated by an alien. But most of them were happy for such a good night. Where'd you get that level of mentalika, man, they asked. I said, some nights, it just comes from within. Nah man, that's a lie and you know it. Tell us your secret, c'mon.

I said, I met a little Worm. And they all laughed, and we went along with the game. Nobody brought it up again after that, as it was the next person's turn to brag about their night with a Mostrídola.

When I left my room, it was night again.

In the living room, Mami slept on the couch as the television played a marathon of the game show with the financial disputes. During a commercial break, I sat down and watched an infomercial about a mental health product. My ass was still burning, but I felt an immense relief. The commercial began with an aerial establishing shot of a wide green field where all the grass had been cut to look park-neat at the extent of every horizon. It was a perfect green flatland painted by the light of the morning sun. There was a two-story house in the green flatland. And the house was desolate. But in the house a woman emerged from her bedroom, walking through the empty living room, then looking out the empty window at the green flatland. Smooth instrumental music played along to evoke the peace of sunlight's mantle upon the empty land. "Surviving a military bombing is no joke," she said in voiceover. A subtitle below read, SUSAN CARIAMBRA, BOMBING SURVIVOR & MOTIVATIONAL SPEAKER. "I have been contending with trauma," she voice-overed, as dramatized flashbacks of the bombings played during her narration—torn-off legs on pavement, a child and mother sooty and running, smoke everywhere, police sirens, and bricks thrown at shields, and bullets from every gun—"generalized anxiety, depression, and bipolar disorder since then. But I was born a fighter." The flashbacks of screaming crowds and corpses on fire now faded to a shot of her running in the empty green flatland, wearing spandex sweatpants and a crop top. A contemplative piano piece lifted the mood of the story. "Keeping track of my mental health has been key to my continued success. Everybody has a story. Take KLAREXA for *the life you want, because it's never too late.* With KLAREXA, I have the focus, concentration, and drive I need to keep myself tasked on my goals and boundaries, no matter what obstacles come my way. Thank you, KLAREXA, for showing me I can do anything I put my mind to."

She survived with klarexa, the lady in this commercial. But I survived just by staying home. That's what Mami taught me. Out beyond the mountains, and even here in the young parts of town, people were being young. And youth is chaos. And chaos is dangerous. Add to that the wars and the bombs. Oh, no. Don't get involved in that traqueteo, mijo, she had said. But she had been young, too, had been young for a long time. And I had felt young last night. I had felt like a little kid discovering sex for the first time. I had never been that kid, not like that, not until last night. And it was still night.

When you sleep through the sunlight, the day is one long night.

Somewhere out there my biological progenitors had been young this whole time. Some people in town who've been to the cities and back said they were still together. Others said they drifted apart. Mami said they were still drifting around each other, nomads of desire. Mami told me all the stories many times. She told me she saved my life and mother wouldn't have cared for me. She said it's okay mother left. It was my father who said that if it hadn't been for Mami she would have thrown me from a balcony and called it an accident. So said Mami: Your mother was cruel, like me. But you brought me goodness, Candi. She often ends this by stating her Zulonuestrist mantra, "you were my Calma."

She hadn't always been a worshipper of the All-Teary One. When I was born she believed in the Resurrected One, of the Ancient Desert Peoples, and we went to temple on Sundays. She loved the priests, was close with them, conversed with them under trees on sin and love and the spirit. As a baby and then child I was there for many of those conversations. I got to see how the priests looked at her, how their tone got soft when topics got intimate, how their voices quivered, whispered soft as petals when they spoke of God and the stirrings in the body. Sometimes they muttered nervously whether my presence was appropriate. But she brushed them off. And Mami clutched her heart, closed her eyes, and imbibed their words like liquor. She told the priests about her boyfriends while we sat on benches in parks.

At night she believed in the Tormented One, the City Prophet, and she watched his movies in secret. And I watched them in secret from the edge of the wall behind the couch. And when she caught me she sent me back to my room. And when she didn't I saw the movies. The City Prophet healed people just like the Resurrected One, but sometimes he fell in love and fucked them too. And sex healed the sick, yet came at a price for the City Prophet. During the sex scenes, which were often long, detailed, and of great kinaesthetic rigor, with orgiastic music, a stunned silence would roam between us. Mami unawaware I was watching. She could hardly breathe, and neither could I. But when his heart got broken, she cried for the City Prophet. One day, she decided to let me watch the movies on the couch with her. I was 11.

Thus she waged her two devotions, to the Resurrected One and the Tormented One.

The year I began watching the movies with her, she had a conversion experience. She came in one day while I was at the living room table penciling homework. She had gone to temple for the ceremony of private confession, but had returned early, and in a distressed huff. When she came in, she didn't say hi, she just stomped to the bedroom and locked herself in.

I did nothing at first. But then I went to my room and pressed my ear to the northern wall. Then as now our house's walls were thin, and when she didn't talk to me, she spoke to the walls of her room. So when she told her room of what had happened to make her leave the church, the image from her memory tore a hole through my chest.

That night, after watching a Tormented movie with her, during which we pretended that the walls were thick that day and I hadn't heard a thing, in my sleep I had a dream that I met a young girl. I was a man, a priest wearing a dark suit with a roman collar, inside a confession booth, seeing her bent head across a latticed opening, her knees on the ground, her hands in front of her, touching palm to palm in prayer. Eyes were soft and sad, full of regret for sins committed. Her hair was black, and her cheekbones were set high. She was sweating in the confessional. The confessional was so hot that the skin on her forehead was damp, and the hair that fell from her bangs clung to it. Her lips were full and daubed in elegant burgundy balm. I could only look at the way her hair parted over her forehead. At the wetness of her lips.

When I woke up, I realized I had dreamed of Mami as a young girl, or a doll of her young-girl-self, a silent, sweating doll. And in the dream I had been in the body of the priest who had touched her earlier that day. He had used the same prayerful words, those same quivering whispers, to tell her that the love between them was beyond the categories of good and evil, like the absence in the Infinite, or the plasticity of a doll, as he had caressed her inner thigh. Do you know why I've been letting you in my heart, he whispered to her. Do you know why I let you inside…

Some weeks after this, she met an old yogic sage at a bar. I was home at the time. Her life outside these walls I don't know. But what she told her walls was this. His name was Adentro. And Adentro was different. He was wise but he presented himself as an erotic man, unlike the priest who claimed spiritual friendship only to later surprise her with his body's needs. Adentro let Mami know from the first that he sought every form of physical and spiritual love with her. His very semblante spoke—and with such gorgeousness—of what later turned out to be only the scent, and not the necessary material truth, of personal wealth. That is how she told me about it later. That the first night Adentro was her lover, and by the second week he was her guru, an ascetic of money, a lover of sex. And she hadn't loved in so, so long, years confused into decades, since she had given birth and her boyfriend, the father, abandoned them. She had raised her daughter alone. And had raised me alone, until then.

We stopped watching City Prophet movies. Within a month Adentro was her lord. He moved into the house, tried to be a surrogate father to me. But I always found ways to avoid Adentro's invitations to sonhood. Besides, submersions into the InVision Realms did even better things for me. I heard them fuck from my room. She was still faithful to her appointments with Mandai. Adentro understood how essential Mandai's role was in Mami's heart. Sometimes Adentro went with her, and the three of them spent the day together in Mandai's beach house while in my room with my InVision I roamed the Mostra City of Iglomia. At the time, I was with Kayani Morozo, my first Mostrídola love affair.

I did only one thing with them. Mami, Adentro and I meditated on mornings and evenings, and attended Enlightened Meditation services on Thursday nights. When Adentro left, she stopped going to the Enlightened places, and began going to the bar again.

Two months after that, she joined a local Zulonuestra cult. It's the cult her mother raised her in. Every road of tears ends in la Zulonuestra. That's what the Bruja lady who approached us said to her, in the parking lot. We were packing groceries into the car when the woman walked up to us, holding a doll in her hand. The doll was nostalgic to me. So it was as if the doll were looking at me, and the woman was looking at my mother, and both of them were together on a mission. The woman looked into Mami and Mami looked at her and between them was suffering and understanding, and when Mami got back inside the car she said the woman reminded her of her long departed aunt Cestilia.

When I was 13 years old, Mami redesigned our yard as the site of the Zulonuestra shrine. Mandai paid a devout sculptor to build it right there.

All over the wallpapered hallways hung the signs of Mami's forages into the different faiths and their churches, pictures of her with fellow believers at spiritual retreats, mementoes from special meetings with the Robes: a photo with an Orange-Robed bodhisattva, another with a a Blue-robed Zuloseguidor, one captured while she sang a duet with a Red-robed saint. In her room, portraits of me, and Abuelo. And one of her daughter, the one who carried me, when she was a child, hidden in the closet, in the album behind the old fashion magazines.

Adentro, the lord—his picture in polaroid sepia tone was still up in the hallway wall that preceded her bedroom. It faced me when I left mine, if I looked to the right. A small Kodak photo, just over a counter with ballpoint pens and logbooks. In the picture he carried her like a baby, and she laughed like a surprised teenager, her arms wrapped round him. The photo caught him as he squeezed her hip with his huge, muscular right hand where he cradled her, which tickled her. She was 55 at the time, her arms tight around him. She only acted girly around him. From my room I heard her shout, Ay, you make me feel 18, Adentro! 17! 16! Ooooh 15! 15! Ooooh papapapapapa, oh papapapapa hold me so goooood, hol me so guuuu, ho me ho me guuuu hoooo guuu … Every time she shouted a new number, Adentro laughed and the headboard thwacked at the wall. It was not the wall directly up against my room, but mine did shake sometimes.

In the cities beyond the mountains they said Adentro left for a richer woman. In the cities beyond where the fleeing progenitors played. Mami no longer spoke of them—of Adentro and the other lovers, her failures. She consigned them to prayer's silence. And I heard her talk from my room sometimes, in her sleep, or awake. Oh, 18. Oh, 17.

The TV was on, the crowd roared, the judge slammed the hammer, and the loser got a FOOL cap—Mami slept through it all on the armchair. Such was nighttime. She was still sleeping when the girl showed up at the backyard door. Only I looked up as she walked up to the door, opened it, and a nightwind blew into the house.

I had seen old photographs of Mami's sister, Nadía. Old polaroids of them on tire swings, riding horses together, building castles on the beach as babies. While Mami had a round nose, Nadía's was heart-shaped. And her eyes were dark green, her body leaner, smaller, though she was older. Her heart-shaped nose was painted red. Her dark green eyes were jungle galaxies. And I had never met Nadía, though now I saw a ghost or a resemblance. She had high white stockings, patterned with markings of berries, on her small feet, which wore old, dirty white shoes. These matched the red make-up she had put on her round cheeks, the red daubs of pigment on her nose, and the white paint all over her face, smudged with grey strokes where sweat had dried—with puffy circles of pink on the cheeks...

Under the make-up, she looked like Nadía. But her hair was orange and short, fell to the bottom of her neck, and she wore a striped-green shirt under a denim jacket and shorts, and a pure blue velvet cloche hat with a fine satin band and bow. The mix of elegance and lunacy made the red of her lips and cheeks and nose stand out all the more. And her face was pink and her eyes were green, not black, but a dark green, enough that it could be taken for black. She was somewhere between evening-Clown and midnight-Prostitute. Mami had described la Grobinita as being soily, dirty, runty, soft-skinned but tough-boned. If this was la Grobinita, she wasn't naked.

"She said you were gordito," the girl said, "but you look a little slimmer than I had imagined."

I wasn't skinny and flat-chested like her.

I stood up with a start.

"Who are you, Nadía or la Grobinita?"

She said, "Ooooooh!" looking not at me, but, seemingly, at my pelvis.

No, at my tailbone.

Then she shouted, "Oh no, you have a grobin tail!"

I looked behind me at my butt and there it was. The little worm tail, swiveling behind me like an abstract dancer, longer than the worm I had eaten, flexible like nothing in my body, a tail lodged on my tailbone, attached to me. The little tail wagged. The voice spoke low and baritone: *Aelia saw you with this tail last night. She even tickled it, and then more... & here you thought it was just in the InVision, and didn't know...*

"It must be happy to see us," she said, "or it wouldn't have come out."

Us, she said, and the walls of my skull closed in. A pressure bit my head from the inside. A vein under my temple trembled, a nerve went bust and pain shot down to the bottom of my neck. The worm tail shook behind me and I swore it laughed, like a little monkey-trumpet, muak-wakwa. I rubbed my temples but the pain persisted. I kept looking at the girl at the door, Nadía or la Grobinita.

And she looked at me quizzically, leaning her head to the right, sad eyes like a healing listener. Nothing else except her gaze seemed right now to explain my place and appearance, what I was doing now, with this tail, what was happening to me. No words arrived. Not even Hogu, Hogu.

And then she broke into laughter, like I was a zoo animal, the laugh of a cute bully. A slapping laughter.

"Am I sick or something…"

Aelia naked blue and red face up, face down, sweat on back on forehead asleep in the light and the dark doe-eyes hers sunken eyes yours. Inside Aelia, outside of you, there she is.

"We don't mean to bother you," she said, "but sometimes presence can be like this."

We, she said again to refer to herself, and again my mouth opened up like a wordless page without end. I wanted to say something, my mouth slowed the words. They came out dumb.

"Uh… who's… we…"

"Oh no," she said, her eyes suddenly watering up with nurturant concern. "You're hurting. Is it us?"

"Uuuh… It's in my…"

Head, at first. But then it slid down to my chest, a molten rock in there. My hands said this. All I could say was, "…uhh…"

And she said, "Oh…," as if she were realizing something, connecting the different parts of my body I feebly pointed at.

And I said "uuhhhh…"

And finally she pronounced, "…I see."

I see.

She said it like she was offering a mercy.

My chest relaxed. Wind gathered at my lungs, born to travel inside again. The girl stepped back, gave me time. I wanted to get out, but I didn't want to be another one of those homeless children. I wanted to tell her to leave, but I wanted to know who she was. I was scared to look at her.

"Who are you?"

"I am Nanú. You must be Cándido. Mami told me."

She spoke distant, cool.

"Only I call her that," I said. "She's not your mami."

"I've got a grobin mind, Candi."

"What does that have to do with anything?"

"Well, you've got a grobin tail."

"What's a gro—"

"You're just getting started with your grobin way. I don't know what your path is, coz every grobin path is different. But I can help."

"Help me? You put this on me. It's your fault."

And she smiled, and asked ever so innocently, "How?"

I blinked. Then blinked again. The headache's pulsation waned. I only thought of all the things Aelia and I had done the evening before.

How, indeed…

The girl stepped on over to the kitchen, como Pedra por su casa. "Come," she said.

I followed her. The tail dangled behind me.

She borrowed a green bowl from the cabinet, and filled it with different fruits from the fridge: two berries, two apple slices, and three mango slices. The way she picked them, her hands so light. The way she moved in the kitchen was like she had known it for a long time. Her movements gave me nostalgia, as if she were a friend from a forgotten time visiting. Only Mami and I walked here that way.

"Take these. They will help with the headache."

She put the bowl in my hands and I took it. I had never seen these fruits here. I took a bite of the mang0.

"Good?"

Its sweetness overflooded my mouth. I forgot all pain.

"This mangó… it took the headache away…"

"I have a story," Nanú said, as if anticipating a question. "And I have sworn to Mami that we will—no, I will tell it to you both, in the evening of the night interior."

Evening of the night interior sounded like a familiar phrase from Zulonuestrism, but I wasn't as devout as Mami was. Mami snored on, though she was not usually this deep a sleeper. She should have woken up by now.

"You asked me how you did it," I said. "So I ask, did you plant the worm outside?"

I didn't say, Why did you do this to me, to us—though I sensed she heard both. She walked up to face me and her eyes locked with mine.

A gaze of recognition, like we had known each other somewhere else, a place small enough in memory to drift away.

She leaned her head on my chest and I found myself doing nothing, just lifting my arms up and stroking her back while she stroked herself on my chest. She was about a foot shorter than me, so she had to stand on her tippy toes to reach it. Her breath hit me warm there. Her voice resounded deeper in closeness.

"I need a place to stay," she said, looking up at me. "I'm running away."

The hairs on my legs and shoulders rose from hearing her. She wrapped her arms around me, pressed her small, warm body up to me, closed her eyes. I looked down at her mess of orange hair and felt its synthetic scent. If I looked deep enough into each strand, I could note a dull, plastic glow. They were like fine, orange guitar strings. Images of Aelia flooded me in a sudden dreamflash. I warmed up like the dozen lips my room had been. And without knowing who I was, I nodded. The wormtail wound itself around her, too. Mami had already chosen her, had chosen her when she was a dirty little rat in the front yard. Now she was an orange-haired doll.

Flies buzzed in from the back yard, seeking light inside the house. I let go of the embrace to close the screen door. When I turned back around to face the living room, Nanú la Grobinita (or Nadía) was gone, and Mami was rousing herself from her couch nap.

I ached.

Mami cocked her head to one side, almost mischievous.

"She was here, wasn't she?"

"She just left."

She cackled and clapped her hands. My acknowledgement gave her the gambler's win. We now both lived in the same world, where la Grobinita was real, not like Simón Cocodrilo, or el Pintor Alado.

"And did you give her some of the beef soup I made?"

"I didn't know you had made soup."

"I made that for her! And for you. And you didn't offer it."

"I didn't know who she was, Mami. She said she was 'running away...'"

"I told you the Grobinita changes as she sheds skins and shadows. I remember clearly how we were in the green flatland with la Grobinita in the empty house. And she showed us how she shed her skin and claimed new form. You were there and you even asked her if it was possible to do it as a human. You were curious about her powers, Candi."

"Was that before or after you dug a hole in the backyard?"

"I told you it wasn't my idea…"

"You just had a dream about the KLAREXA commercial. That's where the green flat land's from. *That's* what I was there for. The commercial."

"Keep telling me I'm the dreamer…"

"Mami, do I have a tail?"

"A what? Like a dog, or a cat?"

I turned around and bumped up my tailbone.

"Don't you see anything? Nanú says I have a tail."

"Maybe Nanú sees something I don't."

The tail, Nanú had said, only came out when it was happy to see "us." Maybe it wasn't happy about Mami's presence. Or maybe Nanú was just playing with me, and I was in her spell. Maybe that's what the grobin is. Nanú's spell.

"Mami… this Grobinita business. I don't think it's good."

"*She,* nene, *she,* not it. She's not some mostra. She's Nanú, la Grobinita. You're spending too much time in that city."

"It's just an InVision network, Mami, not a real place."

"That's what they want you to think."

"It's a virtual community."

"It's a sham. You have a lot to learn from la Grobinita on the evening of the night interior."

"Why is she here, Mami?"

She looked at me with pity, like I was a child who didn't understand the ways of adults. Except now it was the grobin ways I didn't understand. And I had the grobin in me, a disappearing worm-tail.

"Candi, get it into your head. You never ask a Grobinita why. She'll never say."

"But she said she was running away. From what? What did she do?"

She stared off, as if distracted by an entity in the air, and rose from the couch. I suppressed the desire to say that she was just doing this to manipulate me, that she was hiding something. She and this girl were up to something. She started towards the kitchen, dragging her slippered feet, the way she does when she's just awoken and her body's still revving up. I followed her there, like I had followed Nanú earlier. Moments like these she feels like a presence more than a body. She opened the refrigerator and took a strawberry from a little basket, left there by la Grobinita, too.

"Aren't her fruits wonderful?"

"Do you know where she got them?"

Mami ignored me again, apparently incapable of answering the simplest question about someone, or something, who had, in the course of a day and a half, invaded our lives and my body. She put her finger to her lips like she was about to make a serious pronouncement. Then opened her hand like she was drawing a sun.

"Tell me, Candi. When you live in the desert of thirst and a mostrita arrives at your house with news impossible, do you laugh or do you open the door?"

…mostrita… mostrito…

Everything goes light pink around us when Aelia calls me mostrito. I whisper Hogu and we cuddle and hug tight. There had been so many other Mostrídolas before her. It used to be a dollhouse, with 25, 30, at one point even 50 Mostrídolas in here, each in her room, each with my separate pleasures, theirs the mentalika I donated for the dollhouse. My Mostridolitas, las Mostrídolas in Cándido's Palace. I had gathered them over many years. It used to be a hotel, a big pink hotel, a symphony, hallways and hallways of rooms with different names. Each room a luxury suite. But things changed when I met Aelia. She called me mostrito first.

One of the old prophetic books, of the desert religion, and the story: an arrival, three monstruos to a human house in the desert flatland. The monstruos came with a new gravity, as if the moon were to arrive at your doorstep one day to say, *You can fly now, as long as I am in your house.* The human house the three monstruos visited had two doors. And when the monstruos arrived, one door opened, and the other only laughed. And the first two entered the house through the open door. Only the third was whimsical enough to try the electric knob on the laughing door.

According to Mami, a great division happened then, a splitting of Views. One, a world like our own, is the View of the Open Door. Ours is the View of the Laughing Door. Our world mocks the monstruo as he enters alone into its birth. A primal consciousness runs in the collective of our people. A basic refrain explains it like this:

Whenever a baby is born, somewhere, someone is laughing.

I had asked as a child what that meant. But Mami's answer, it lay behind the closed door of a memory I knew to be mine. When I tried to access the memory of that answer, I only came upon the face of Aelia. And she was giggling.

Mami asked, "Well, Candi, what do you do?"

What else is there to do when you live in the laughing view, Candi?

My lips were a third door, the mouth that opens towards an empty stomach.

I said, "I don't know. Maybe the answer's in la Calma."

Like the old Zulonuestran prayer. Something to say when you don't know what else to say.

Ay, la Calma. That's the place I'm most curious about. You who love it know the least about it, and so do I.

Mami grasped my hand and said with prayerful zeal, "Aminadha, mijo. Wouldn't you want to hear the news?"

"What news can a monster have other than horror?"

Slimy news.

"But this monstrita is special. She's seen so much. Too much. She needs us. Don't you see she has Nadía's nose, her eyes, her voice…"

"But she's not, Mami. She's just a fugitive. Where is she running from?"

"She's running for warmth. That's what she sensed in this house. That there was warmth."

Like your stomach. So warm, a bed of pudding…

The thought disrupted me. I shook my head and regained my thread of argument:

"So you don't know," I said to Mami. "The 'news impossible,' you don't know…"

"No. But she stole my heart the moment I saw her. No, it was more like this. Like a part of my heart was looking at me through her eyes. A part of me I didn't know."

Oh, wow.

…Oh, Candi…

There she was again. Now she said my name. I couldn't place hers but I knew her. Her voice was low, baritone…

Ever since you ate me last evening, bebé, I've known you quite intimately.

I asked Mami, "Is that why she calls you Mami, too?"

Your esophagus alone was so informative.

Again she interrupted my line of thought. I strained to listen to Mami. She said, "she has her way, Candi—" (*Oh, yes she does*) "—she calls you Candi when we talk about you, too. She can't help it."

I can't help myself either. Just like you couldn't when you first saw me, Candi. You couldn't get me off your mind. Like one of your Mostrí—

"I don't want to help her, Mami. I want this worm out of my mind."

Ah, you're not going to be like the others, are you, Candi?

"What are you talking about, Candi?"

Those who loved her until she wanted something from them. But you offered to worship her, Candi. You offered devotion. You submitted and said so.

"I never loved her."

"Loved who?"

Mami can't hear us, Candi. Only you…

"No I don't! Please stop! Stop now!"

"Candi, don't yell at me! You know it gives me nightmares…"

You're worrying her, Candi—

"STOOOOOOOOP!"

I bellowed and my feet stomped the earth. But the earth was soft. I looked down. I was standing on the yellow blanket. It was wet and dirty. The one draped over the hole. A bowl lay facedown beside me. I was standing on mushed pieces of mango and orange. I had stepped on them until mush. Only night around me. When last did I see the sun? Mami had put this here. No, la Grobinita. There Mami stood.

When in the kitchen did I put the plate down… Or did I throw it at the voice in the wall… When did I push past Mami and walk out the house through the sliding screen door… When did I yell at the air… How long had Mami followed me… Had she been with me the whole way or had I achieved a sweet agonizing moment of my own…

Mami, shocked, looked at me with shuddering lips, long enough that both of us stood still as outside a singing frog chirped its two-syllable cuicuí, cuicuí…

And I looked through the empty night space. The space between us and the house, ruled by air and grass. Through that space I looked at the window. Inside was the living room. Inside it was dark, hued with the dull yellow light of a lamp. In that penumbra the light drew her figure in shadow. I recognized her. She was standing inside the house, at the center of the window. I did not see but did feel her smile.

"Mami… did you let her in…?"

Mami looked behind her, back at the window. But by then la Grobinita was gone from the window. The screen door then screeched open.

Delighted now to see us both together, Nanú—la Grobinita, or Nadía, or Aelia, or the one who brought the Worm—the grey-faced clown—stood in her funny stockings and red-heart nose and cloche hat and took a step outside and slid the door shut behind her. "My beloveds," she said, and Mami said, "Ay querida," and as Nanú traversed the distance with a gentle gait, and Mami walked towards her, I realized standing on the hole that both Mami and I, we were in her territory. And that this would be true inside the house as well. Her smile was so knowing. She couldn't be just a girl. I didn't trust her eyebrows. Too sharp, too distant.

When she joined us, she didn't tell me to leave the hole.

She just began declaiming. And when she spoke, we all listened.

The Worm, too.

Composing Paulina Ave

Amanda Torres

We buried the birds underneath the oak trees dad planted on our street. I had loved those birds but we had kept them in a house of teeth. Pointed beak, dappled feathers, spine as thin as cactus needles all buried in the shade of a tree we knew. In the soil so many of us have made supple with our life-rich death. Bones rattling the foundation of this country built over us in this place we never called ours, because it already had a name.

It happened so quickly, a swarm of steamed milk in suits and strollers buzzing at the edges of our block with dilated pupils. Wide-O cartoon mouths in their eyes, as they admired our neighborhood. *So much potential,* they said, and the sunflowers in our neighbor's yard shivered, anticipating an unseasonal beheading. It happened so quickly it was as if we hadn't ever lived there.

Rot teaches us another way. To rot is to deteriorate, but also to return. To become something other than what you have been. It happens all the time. It's not only invasion or mind control— fungus controlling an ant and bursting through its body to infect the colony. It is surviving beside one another— wild turkeys and deer moving together in packs to more effectively avoid hunters. I don't tell you this to encourage you to make peace with the people who have stolen from you. I tell you this so you understand what happens next.

The trees tear up the sidewalk. Lift their roots into the air, overwhelmed with an earthly laugh that shakes the ground. Their mud caked organs a kind of netting that's made itself visible. Other things come from the dirt, as well. Our ancestors' ghostly hands reach up and tickle the feet of the living. Chuckle as the residents drop their Whole Foods totes and run in fear. Our dead dance with the trees, trading partners.

How does it work? What changed? Does it matter? The old neighborhood vibrates like a strapped-in speaker in the back of someone's open trunk. The trees have been fed by our loved ones for so long, they return the favor and become a radio for the dead. Their bark booming with the bass of my father's voice, the whining chirp of a child's bird. All those that came before—an ear shattering chorus.

The sound, like nothing else, shakes all the drums inside you. The throng that colonized the neighborhood cover their ears and weep. Mistake this miracle, our dead singing—the sound they make becoming its own beautiful body—for horror. The empire they dreamed of turned to rubble. Paulina Avenue is reclaimed, or decomposed, or recomposed. Our guardians belt out rancheros, drink late night cafecito, cause a ruckus because to be heard is a blessing, to be seen a gift.

And though it has only happened here, all the nearby neighborhoods complain of the noise, slowly relocate, make more and more space. There is no reasoning with the dead and our ancestors stay partying all day and night. Can we even call them ancestors if they are here, standing next to us? Our tias grinding the most sensual of bachatas, lifting each other's hips over their own smashed so close, steam rises like spores between them.

Whenever, Wherever

Amanda Torres

"Lucky I have strong legs like my mother / to run for cover when I need it" -Shakira

While answering emails at the dining room table
a red cardinal flies in through the window and starts singing Shakira.
My mom emerges from the kitchen in full belly dance attire,
bralette blinged out and sparkling. Hips shimmy and shudder–
a shiver running up from her toes to the tips of her fingers
raised high above her head. Spatula still in hand, she pretends to sing,
winking at me as she circles the table. Her hip-length white hair
another piece of fabric to manipulate as she does the thing she loves
more than anything.

I clutch frantically to my computer
as she whips off the tablecloth to use as a hip scarf
and opens all the windows as a Snow White-esque chorus of birds
careens into the house. Clawed feet skipping and diving in unison
to the beat.

Truthfully,
it's just another day in our household
where my mom is feeling herself. And how good is it
to know this mother. This one.
Who isn't afraid to open the windows,
show her marked belly
and dance like she's never been hurt.

another life in the dark

Amanda Torres

what intimacy
to be an almost naked body inside another.
swimming through a water-filled cave
river that made itself
moving with the force
of a grandmother's stern warning.

in order to be loved
one has to turn their back
to being desired
close their eyes
and jump.

i am afraid
and i am free
turning towards what cannot be seen
i dive into the black
put my mouth to the water
whisper back
in time
it is possible
everything
you didn't allow yourself.

in this world under the world
roots dangle from the ceiling
thirsty chandeliers
the organs of these trees
that pushed through stone
to drink.

SER

by E.G. Condé

1995

To be or to die, *that* is the question on my mind. Night after night, as I make my mark, choosing to *be*. To risk everything just to etch my name on these dilapidated alleys and basketball hoops. SER. Spanish for existing. To *be*. SER is the mantle I wrap myself in. Like an Egyptian scribe I scrawl it on this city's papyrus. My hieroglyphics light up the rusting skins of these dying slums.

The can is light in my hand. I shake. A metal ball rattles inside. The music of genesis as my index finger pushes down the tab, breaking open dams of possibility. I world. Rains of creation, flowing through the grooves of bricks in all the colors of my homeland. Borikén.

Fumes tickle flared nostrils. I spray and spray and spray. High on creativity's narcotics. Like Van Gogh with his lead paint. Chemical hurricanes. Molten dreams. Paint drips down the seams in trippy cataracts. SER. Letters curl like tropical blooms. Bluer than the sea in the *playas* of my youth, greener than the mountain where my abuela made me *café con leche* in a charcoal pit. And that riot red, like rooster wattles clucking on *campo* roads.

I carve my homeland onto fire-escapes and basketball hoops in the crumbling projects they left us to rot in. I write our story because I refuse to let them take from us the memory of our *isla*. I refuse to be extinguished as they gun us down in these streets for the crime of being while brown. SER. This city is mine. SER. Ideas are immortal even if bodies are not. SER. I spray it on the police station. Crimson rivers trickling down, the blood of my enemies, of fallen revolutionaries that I avenge with every stroke. Agüeybaná. Manuel Rojas. Pedro Albizu Campos. SER.

#

2045

SER. Shakespeare of the South Bronx. Latest casualty of the police state. But even after death he lives on. The tag passes to me now. I'm the last in a long dynasty of street philosophers and ink poets. But our paint isn't enough anymore. These streets are different. The O.G. SER's world is half-sunken in the thaw, the seas are swallowing it up. And the slums where we Boricuas once dwelt are now gentrified castles, towering above the deluge. The new New York, where buildings are printed instead of built.

It takes a lot more ink to coat those shiny, plastichrome walls. And they got seeker patrols hovering around the causeways now, bobbing around like jellyfish, lasers primed to sear away any artwork not approved by the "residential aesthetic commission." Sure, there are sanctioned murals, some of them even look like ours. More theft. Sanitized and repackaged for well-to-do-gringos. Disgusting.

'Chacho," our name, hasn't been seen in months. My last mark lasted all of three minutes before the drones erased it. They woulda taken me, too, if I hadn't brought that EMP disruptor ASP hooked me up with (it wasn't cheap, if you were wondering). I been thinking, we gotta adapt. I'm sure you would understand, ancestor, that we need a new way to write. Yesterday, I traded my can for a keyboard. TBH, it's hard to feel badass slinging code instead of paint. Not much of an adrenaline rush. But this is how it's gotta be if we want to bypass those jellies designed to "eliminate all forms of aesthetic vandalism."

Back in your day, there were billboards and screens that cycled promos down in Times Square. People flew thousands of miles just to look at those bright screens. These days, ads come to you, overlays for your eyes and ears. We call it AugScape. It's simple. You wear lenses that superimpose social feeds over your vision. If you pay extra, your visfeed won't have ads. SightTM premium. But very few people can afford it.

Good for us, cuz I've found developer inroads into AugScape. Shifty APIs. Had to do some things I'm not proud of to get them, but what's important is that I'm in. And now, just like the marketers, I can reach *anyone*, anywhere.

Imagine you're downtown hailing a cab. In your visfeed you can see things like service ratings, real-time estimates of trip duration, prices overlayed as you make a decision. When you get in, an ad plays offering a competitor service, but just as it starts—BAM— it glitches out, bursting into colorful plumes of ink I made from ones and zeros. SER. Bright and perfect. SER LIVES. Again and again our name flits into view, sprayed-painted with code and then vanishes (geociphers set to auto-delete). People are already noticing, posting about it on SightTM forums. "Augscape is haunted," someone wrote. Amusing but not enough. SER deserves more respect than that. ¿Verdad?

Did something I probably shouldn't have. But hey, I don't care anymore. Puerto Rico just got hit by a Category 6 hurricane, if you can believe that. Yeah mano', Category sixes exist now. It's apocalyptic down there and the government's covering it up. Why? Cuz it's campaign season. So of course I did what I thought you might do: I hacked President Wu's re-election campaign. Busted into their Augscape. Man, this has got to be our most daring tag yet. No offense. I'm sure it was difficult climbing on trains and using ladders and ropes to get to off-limits places, but this is another level, trust me. My – our – masterpiece. Ad plays. President is touting her glorious Climate Bank partnership with China, and then, pop! SER, in a red font for mourning. I splice the censored feeds of Hurricane Teddy so that people will know that our people are suffering. SER. FREE US OR DIE. Ha! Wish you could see it. It was dope and righteous and genius and also… an absolute disaster.

"The search for the Puerto Rican terrorist continues."

Just heard that on State Media. We're a threat now. Good. They're chanting our name at separatist protests in San Juan and Ponce. We've become a symbol, that means sooner or later they'll catch me and end me like they ended you. I know what you're thinking. That I'm arrogant. That I'm uppity and think I'm smarter than I am. You're wondering why I didn't take on a protégé, why I didn't pass on the tag to a successor? I have my reasons, trust me. And hey, don't worry about me, cuz I got one last trick up my sleeve.

#

2046

"Armed and dangerous, Joseito Luis Ramos Ortega was shot dead by ASTRAL-B-SEEKERS™ while attempting to flee custody. Carceral algorithms determined that lethal force was necessary to prevent further violence."

They lied. All I had in my pocket was a spray can. How am I talking to you? Well, I'm still here—sort of. You see SER, there's this thing for rich white folk in my time called a *mirror*. You can imprint your "digital likeness" into a server with a drone host as your body. But I hate those fucking jellies, so I tucked my mirror into the back-alleys of the Augscape instead. Here, they'll never find me. Here, I am a ghost, a virus called insurrection. Like our Taíno ancestors before us, we will outlive them, as gods and glyphs carved into the bedrock, and only when the last bricks of their empire have crumbled will I rest…in Coabey, the place our opía go when we die.

Returning

Kristian Macaron

It turns out that returning to Grandma's house two hundred years after Grandma feels the same as if she were greeting me at the door. You
will be in the Strand combing the ravines for crystals while I do this. I
imagine you there, being so careful to not touch the stones which are
poison on this new planet. The suns will be high and blue and the crystals will sparkle with hues of water. You will be alone and waiting. You
will be looking for me. Later, when you find that I split continuum, you
will know exactly where I have gone; that I have come to find what our
mother left here. That I have done this to protect you and your future.

I am making this record so as to bring you with me. To remind you
later that we have been here and grown here on Earth in ways that space
could never have made us. Here is where our mother is in-love with
our father and she is young and dark-dark-haired. She sits on the porch
swing with a glass of Coke, clinking the fizzing ice while she swirls the
glass and she is talking to our auntie on the phone—a phone is a thing
we have not seen in a century, at least and Coke, something also lost deep
in memory. Time is grave and lingering for us now, looking backwards
like this. You are small and have so many freckles, vibrant here. I realize
that I had not noticed them disappear in space. Here, I am exuberant
and have many annoying talents. Down the street is the paletería and
the dogs who live there are named after popsicles. It has been two hundred years, but I remember their names and I know you will too. I can
hear them barking. I will not go to our house because if I see our own

dog—our pretty, sweet Leia—I know I will not return to you; I swear I will return to you.

I walk through the rest of the house slowly. I want to take it all in slowly, to tell you everything exactly. Being here, it is almost impossible to know the time split has happened, it feels so natural. When I arrive, I am almost a shadow manifested, but not quite. Grandma appears to look at me for a moment, I think, because I do what we are not supposed to do, and I reach for her. Hi, *mijita*, she says, looking through me before I shrink myself. You will not blame me for this.

But, I swear on all your piles of crystal that I will do this with all your fortitude. That what I do will not break us. I cannot wait to tell you because I know you will ask—Grandad is here already, though I have not summoned him. You will not be surprised by this. He was always one step ahead. I am not sure if he is here in my moment, or if maybe I am seeing him on a return from a hundred years ago, one he would have kept a secret. He is wearing his spacesuit, it has a little tear on the arm that you will remember repairing more than once. His form is glittering as if he's not even quite here nor anywhere else. Since he's been gone, lost to the continuum and not death, we learned he often took the split, so many times it was reckless. Seeing what I see here and what it feels like, I do not think I can blame him any more for refusing to summon us back nor for becoming lost forever watching our family. I open my mouth to call him but I find that I cannot sound. He takes my hand as he passes me in the hallway and presses it; he says my name. He does not look back.

I think you will want to know what it looks like here, and it looks the same, with a thin ephemera sparking over what is keeping me from being seen and opening the split completely. The lilies on the porch are bright orange—a color you might barely remember until you see it. The swing set ripples in the wind. There is a bird, a robin, perched on our play fort. The robin is chirping and somewhere another chirps back. Earth is a quiet planet even with the traffic. It is daytime, and the white moon is high and full above the mountain. There is barely any wind. I remember briefly that the mountain to the East is filled with seashells. You will remember our father reaching down to pick one up, displacing the dirt with his fingers. In our new home, there are no oceans and the wind howls us to sleep. It occurs to me that I do not think of space as space anymore. The Strand is as close to a prairie as we will ever know.

I know what I am looking for here, but can you blame me for

spending a few moments? You will. You will blame me, thinking too much of this will prevent my return to you. Grandma's ring—the one you wear—is sitting on her dresser in a pile of costume jewelry. The jewel which looks purple in the light of the new suns looks ruby here. I wish I could show you. If this works you will hate me, knowing that we will likely not be able to come back here. Knowing I may have taken our only chance. The thing is, I have thought about this for so long. What is it that makes the item I have come for more valuable than our being able to return here? One of the rules of the split is that nothing should be brought back beyond the traveling body, but I know this is what I risk. Items have a high possibility of closing it forever, though I know a secret now—that it can be done. Certain things are on the List of Never: eating, drinking and embracing among others. I will not risk those. I have combed my memory to think about the things we left, the Earth items we didn't know we would miss in our new home. I have wondered what Grandma would tell me, though I know I cannot ask her. I would not be able to tell you in one answer, but I hope when you see what I bring, something that I know will better our future, you will know too.

When I enter the kitchen the news from the television sneaks through like air. When I hear the reports the oldest feeling of heartbreak enters my core. *We survived that—we survived*, I want to tell you. We are so far away from that now.

The kitchen smells like manteca and on the side of the stove there are piles of tortillas. I know if I eat one it will break the split and like Grandpa, I will be stuck here. Instead, I stand with my nose pressed to one and breathe, knowing if this works I will be bringing this to you, our history. On the table, bowls of papas and red chile, I want them more than anything we've ever eaten in space. I am crying suddenly. You *will* hate me. I see our little shadows reaching into piles of warm dishes to taste. I miss this. I hear Mama's laugh outside and Auntie's car pulls up into the driveway even though they are still on the phone. We haven't seen Auntie in two hundred years either, and she is glowing. I wonder if we ever noticed that before, how radiant her laughter, her voice bursting through the door and almost, almost into the split. If you are close enough, I wonder if you will hear her too. I see Mama reach for her the way I would reach for you and I take a deep breath.

The thing that I came for, Mama left in one of the cabinets. It is a thing of such little consequence in this world, she didn't know how much we would miss it later. Though we have all the crops we can wish for and we can craft soil even though it takes ages, I will never forget Mama's face and yours when we realized that the crystals are too fragile and the stones too poisonous to wear thin the grain, to mill it to flour. Though we can live in the Strand and on our planet, we cannot thrive there. We need the pan and tortillas to bind nutrients we can grow or mimic. For decades Mama kept saying, *if only we had the stone we left in the counter under the tele, if only, we were to know.* She talked of the metate as if it were a jewel, and I suppose jewels are stones too, but not the kind anyone would ever have returned for, risked their lives for, or risked the split for.

When I pry open the cabinet, I find it. It is dark stone, speckled with quartz and flour. The hardest thing to do from the split is to pick it up without falling all the way in. It is heavier than gravity. I stand up, and I can tell the moment it is attached to me, when I feel its full weight. I didn't know if it would be possible though I am not ready to leave. Over the counter, I look up, straight into Auntie's eyes. They are so bright and she glances down at the countertop where there is a pile of recipe cards in Grandma's handwriting. She grabs them and pushes them towards me and into my chest breaking into the split, even though I try to scream, *no, no, no.*

Handwriting is one thing on the List of Never.

After that, the split closes in on me. It is dark, and the metate is cold against my body. The paper glows a little bit, the cursive letters more reminders of centuries and how love continues to feed us. I do not know where the split will carry me or if I can find form again. I cannot feel you on the other side anymore and though I reach into the future toward our home in the Strand, I cannot see the glimmering crystals. I know that if these objects return without me you will know I have brought them, and we will know that either way, we have survived this and I am almost, almost, almost home.

Pachacuti

Ruth Joffre

You couldn't tell from looking at me, but today is my 237th birthday. My coworkers insist I don't look a day over 45, but that's a lie they need much more than I do. Every year for the past 213 years, I have taken a birthday selfie for my records. Only when I cycle through this series do I see myself age in an almost linear fashion. My cheeks lose the last of their cherubic roundness. My hair gets longer and bluer, then shorter and blunter. My smile tighter, unimpressed by rituals. When you outlive your company's first, second, and third CEO and regularly transport tourists to 64 CE just to watch Rome burn, the everyday machinations of beauty, industry, and history seem petty and small by comparison. Why should I believe the stories all these companies are peddling about the supposedly life-changing benefits of their products? None of them are built to the scale of time. Not even the Time Dislocator itself. Its reliance on nuclear fusion for all power, stainless steel for the reactor, plus gold and conflict minerals for delicate instruments inside the Dislocator mean the technology itself is limited by the resources of Earth and other planets we now inhabit. Mars has proven a great source of iron, but what else remains on the Red Planet, aside from dust, carbon dioxide, and dormant volcanoes?

I ask this same question of Maxim, my supervisor, who pings me just after lunch. He says there could be intelligent life on Mars. His life-sized head floats on one of the holo-screens at the foot of my bed. His long black beard tapers to a point that gets cut off by the screen. He strokes it thoughtfully as he muses, "Who knows? Perhaps one day some enterprising scientist will build a Time Dislocator on Mars and use it to search for aliens."

"I hope not," I say, readjusting the pillows so I can sit up a little straighter. Otherwise I make no attempt to hide the fact that I am still in bed, drinking milky Darjeeling in my pajamas. I blow on the tea. "How disappointing would it be to know for a fact that you lived next door to an alien race and missed out on meeting them by maybe a few thousand years and fifty million miles? On a cosmic scale, that's nothing—that's a laugh you pass off as a sneeze."

"I see you're taking your birthday very well this year."

"You only turn 237 once. At this rate, I might actually make it to 500."

He shrugs one shoulder, tilting his head. "Assuming we still have jobs then."

"Well, you'll be dead, now that you're middle-management and not a tour guide."

He presses a hand to his heart. "Thank you for that lovely reminder of my mortality."

I mirror his hand as I have done hundreds of times over the last 73 years. "You know you can always count on me to hit you on the head with our harsh reality." Once upon a time, Maxim was one of my trainees, a young man of twenty-nine with a PhD in theoretical physics and a wide range of interests, including mycology, Russian composers, and blacksmithing. Even now, on the wall behind him, I can see a rack of swords forged in his own smithy and inlaid with gold filigree on the ornate handles. Sometimes, we muse about how we will survive the apocalypse as platonic time-traveling swashbucklers.

"Well, this has been fun," Maxim says, "but I do have a job for you, if you want it."

"Weren't you the one who recommended I take a few days off? Enjoy the present?"

"Guilty, but that was before the Government Team won this surprise RFP."

"Not the British Parliament's investigation into Princess Di's death?" Hurriedly, I pull up the trackers on a separate holo-screen and swipe through the opportunities.

"No, thank gods. How many times do we have to say it was just a car crash?"

"Seriously." I relax back into the pillows, noting that none of my preferred RFPs from the international government sector have been closed or assigned to someone junior. "So, what's this surprise RFP? Is it not on the tracker?"

"It was, but we took it off six years ago because we thought it was dead. Take a look." He projects the information onto the holo-screen where his beard was: Republic of Peru, Request for Proposal for Time Dislocation Services to 1438 CE, to Record Pre-Columbian Concepts of Time in Andean Civilizations. A six-week project, with an immediate start date originally projected for 2221 CE, then readjusted to 2227 CE, to account for years lost while funding hung in the balance of a pivotal economic restructuring period. No one knows if the republic will continue to support the project after the upcoming election, and so this job has to happen ASAP. "Client's already on the plane," Maxim says. "You interested?"

"A visit to the Incas that doesn't involve Machu Picchu or conquistadors? I'm in."

"I'll send you the dossier. And Beatriz? Happy Birthday."

✝
✝

Name: Karla Yupanqui
Occupation: Professor of History
Employer: National University of Saint Anthony the Abbot in Cuzco
Education: PhD, National University of San Marcos; MA and BA,
    University of Lima
Income: S/94,000 (estimated)
Languages: Spanish, Quechua, Aymara, English
Marital Status: Single
Gender: Nonbinary (they/them)
DOB: September 6, 2180 CE

My virtual assistant reads the information aloud on repeat as I prepare for this impromptu sojourn to the 15th Century. It sticks in my head: the surname Yupanqui, the way my AI sounds it out so robotically it almost becomes three words. According to the built-in translator, its origin is Quechua. Meaning: "accountant." Not Karla's chosen profession in a literal sense, but perhaps in the figurative sense of someone required to give an account, to relate the story—whether through money or the monitoring of time—of people long dead, and yet imminently accessible. Before I accompany them back to the past, I study the headshot in the dossier: brown eyes, naturally thick arched eyebrows, straight black hair down to the shoulders topped by a red montera studded with black and white pearls of alpaca wool; impeccable posture not in the least masked by the brilliant llicla draped across their shoulders and clasped with an ivory straight pin; and finally, underneath their traditional clothing, a plain white wool sweater, the likes of which can no doubt be found in the halls of any university.

"Professor Yupanqui," I say, greeting them in the lobby. Today, they are sensibly dressed in a red button-down shirt, brown corduroys, and sturdy work boots, which shift slightly as Karla quietly surveys the lobby. It's not nearly as ostentatious as people expect it to be before their first time dislocation. Our competitors wasted precious capital on futuristic facilities with ivory spires and domed amphitheaters plated with gold, projecting that demand for the services would remain high and be able to support the exorbitant maintenance costs for these structures, but we played it safe and invested in only as much square footage as needed to fold space-time; as a consequence, people often mistake our facilities for a moderately successful dentist's office.

The professor extends their hand. "I wasn't sure this was the right place."

"Glad you found us. I trust you've filled out all the necessary paperwork?"

"On the plane ride over. Your virtual receptionist made the process very easy."

"We know you're eager to get going. If you'll follow me to the Dislocation Room…."

Historically, this is the part of the transaction where clients are most likely to rethink their decision to travel through time. Even after 200 years of commercial time dislocation services, the majority of people still think of time machines as elaborate steampunk contraptions or seemingly magical blue boxes much bigger on the inside. In reality, the Time Dislocator is just a room. Four walls, nondescript ceiling. Average, everyday door. It need not be hermetically sealed or made of holo-bricks that enable 360° immersion in a visual recreation of the past. Those are mere add-ons our competitors developed to distract from what was once inferior technology. Now that they are caught up, the bells and whistles have become commonplace—expected, even, despite how often these

same features tend to frighten people and make them feel claustrophobic. "Since it will just be the two of us on this journey, we will be in one
of the more intimate rooms. Do let me know if you would like to up-
grade to something larger."

"No need," the professor says, walking the perimeter, studying the
dormant holo-bricks. I open my mouth to inform them of the ame-
nities, automated temperature controls, enterprise level HEPA air fil-
tration, remote monitoring and management of building energy levels; then they say, "I have students who live in apartments smaller than
this. Sometimes, three or four of them rent a room together just to save
money."

"Capitalism has plagued the Earth for millennia," I say, retrieving
the dislocator bracelets from a pressure-activated drawer by the entryway. Both openings shut automatically, creating the illusion of a seam-
less room with no doors or windows and no means of escape, and as I
approach the professor I gauge their level of panic and their openness
to receiving this bracelet. As I secure it on their wrist, I say, "When I
was a child, my parents and siblings and I lived in a small studio in Los
Angeles. Today, that building is a seawater processing plant, and the only
people who can afford to live near it are water barons."

Their fingers wrap around their wrist, mirroring the bracelet. "I read
the article about you, the one in the *New England Journal of Medicine.*"
Back in 2070, when that piece was published, suspended aging was still
a medical marvel isolated to the time dislocation industry and ripe with
potential to change the world as we knew it. Some went so far as to hail it
the key to immortality, but, as the principal authors of the article soberly
noted, it required levels of disengagement from the present considered
unhealthy. How will we build a future, one of them mused, if we waste
all our conscious hours exploring the past? What would become of pro-
creation? Industry? The daily acts of governance?

"That article's outdated," I say. "The average lifespan has only de-
creased since then."

"It did read like a time capsule of 21st Century anxieties." Their fingers release their wrist and slide easily into a pocket of their corduroys.
Often, when my clients reference this article, the intent is self-congratu-
latory, sometimes solicitous: *See how much I know about you already, how much
more I want to know. Won't you tell me your secrets?* Men in particular use it to
flirt. Karla holds it up almost like a red herring. "It didn't say anything
about your childhood."

"No one ever wants to think about immortality in the context of the quotidian."

"Time is already so unkind. Living forever just gives it new opportunities for cruelty."

I fasten my own bracelet. "Is that what you want to study—examples of time's cruelty?"

"No." When the professor doesn't elaborate, I activate the Time Dislocator with my code. A series of taps sets the target date as 1438 CE and the location as what was then the Kingdom of Cuzco, before a leader known as Pachacuti the Earth-shaker expanded the Inca Empire and, later, reorganized it into Tawantinsuyu, or The Four Regions. When the ancient roads of Cuzco appear on the holo-bricks and Professor Yupanqui sees this place they have written about for so long for the first time, their lips part in wonder. In this moment, I cease to exist for them. I slip into a fold in space-time, and my body passes out of Dislocation Room 4 and into the mouth of a wormhole. My bracelet blinks once, twice, signaling the fold is expanding to the professor, enveloping them like a blanket passed down by an ancestor. I pause, but the professor does not panic like I expect. Instead, they reach out for me, their hands stretching and squashing like dough in a baker's hands as our bodies begin to ripple across space-time. We hold onto each other for eight brief centuries. It never feels long enough.

‡

Some people refer to the disorientation that stems from this form of travel as "jumplag." I dislike the term because it implies dynamic, flailing motions rather than a claustrophobic squeeze through a narrow hole in space-time. It feels more like being drained through a funnel or cranked through a pasta maker. Our bodies become thin and malleable, our bones and organs shifting like the blobs inside a lava lamp, until we arrive at the end of the wormhole. Another way to describe the end is as the "bottom" of the hole—the place where we, the worms, stop digging and create a temporary home for ourselves in four-dimensional space-time. If we look up, we can see the path forward in time still open to us, still easily (if uncomfortably) traversed. From here, we can dig to the left or right or really anywhere we like on the horizontal plane of space, where localized time continues undisturbed and the city of Cuzco stretches around us in all its grandeur, as it did in the time of the Incas. In this way, from the safety of our little wormhole, we observe the past not like goldfish in a fishbowl but like researchers in an invisible submersible at the bottom of the ocean. This thought can be unsettling for people.

"You may think you want to vomit," I say, as Professor Yupanqui clutches their stomach, "but that's not possible here. Technically, this isn't even really a *here*. It's an *in-between*. Not the present we know and not the present they know." I gesture to the buildings around us, their stone walls and dusty doorsteps, the lives tucked behind them, just out of reach. The street is empty but for a procession of priests heading to a nearby shrine, where Pachacuti the Earth-shaker installed one of his pururaucas (stone warriors) as a thank you to the Incan gods, who transformed random rocks into fearsome fighters to help Pachacuti defend this city from the attacking Chanca. When the procession draws near, the professor presses their back to a wall, as if to make room, but this is unnecessary. Not one of the priests looks up. As their robes checker past, the professor's body slips into the wall until only the very tip of their nose is still visible. "Now you understand," I tell them, as they pull free of the wall. "Our bodies aren't really here. They're suspended in time. Or across times. We can't touch or taste anything here; we don't need to eat or sleep or perform our daily ablutions. We're free of the restrictions of the body. Only our minds remain."

After considering this for a moment, they ask, "Does that mean we can fly?"

"Technically, it's just hovering and it's mostly in your head, but yes. See?" I demonstrate by lifting off the ground and twirling like a bride. Their delight is brief but charming, and I allow a moment's levity dancing in the air before I say, "You're adjusting well to the dislocation."

"Well, to be fair, I was expecting it to be a lot bloodier, so this is a relief."

"Bloody? No, I can assure you, we can't even menstruate in this state."

"What heaven." Their sigh is one of deep, unexpected pleasure, lasting about as long as it takes the procession to turn into the plaza and slip out of sight. In their curious expression, I see a twinkle of mischief, a question forming: what next? Many people assume that I'm the tour guide, interpreter, and endless fountain of knowledge about the concept of time, as well as any time that they may wish to visit. Once, about 160 years ago, give or take a decade, we even considered the possibility of providing special expertise in the most popular times, such as World War

II and the French Revolution; but we dismissed this idea quickly, because it would require us to do the very work our clients were proposing to do: to document the last days of Marie Antoinette in exquisite and yet deeply unnecessary detail, to pinpoint that exact moment a species such as the Dodo went extinct, to preserve and revitalize dead or dying languages by listening to native speakers in their own lands and times. Leave that to the experts, we said. Our job was to assure them that this was possible, to remind them of the intricacies of their own RFPs and projects. On occasion, to quote back to them from the testimonials as to their fitness to lead or else participate in such an arduous and expensive endeavor. My clients are in a very real sense the tops of their fields, the winners of government grants and fellowships, of academic prizes and tenure-track positions. And yet: most of them arrive at this moment at a loss.

Not Professor Yupanqui. "Come this way," they say, turning to lead the way. Their stride proves short but confident, and their arms and legs swing unnecessarily, thoroughly enjoying this novelty: walking on air, jumping now and then to avoid the appearance of stepping on someone's head, though no one would mind (once, in New York City many years ago, I made a game of this when no one was looking, taking care only ever to step on the heads of the Wall Street bankers in their gold cufflinks and slick, ink-black suits; it harmed no one, but I often wish it had).

"So, how many times have you visited Cuzco?"

"No more than a dozen—but never this particular time."

"Let me guess: you visited 1533 CE to watch Pizarro take Cuzco."

"And the unsuccessful siege from 1536 to 1537 CE. And other historical milestones."

"But never this moment." Their legs stop on the banks of the Huatanay River, which will, in years to come, mark the dividing line between two ceremonial plazas: Cusipata, the "Fortunate Terrace," and Huacaypata, the "Terrace of Repose." Their fingers dip into the water, unable even to register its temperature or its currents, yet aware of how this river has shaped the land and how civilizations have lived and died around it. After the plazas are built, Pachacuti, the Earth-shaker, will import sand from distant regions, so that nobles and priests will have to stand upon it during religious or official ceremonies. It is entirely possible that Professor Yupanqui will never witness a Sapa Inca stand upon the raised platform to track the movements of celestial bodies. Never will they witness libations of chicha pour into a great stone basin plated in gold or hear the screams of a sacrificial victim echo off the carefully hewn stone crafted by masons so clever that their works still stand—centuries later—in the year 2227 CE. This, I realize, is their design. They could have picked any period in Incan history, and this was their choice.

"You said in your RFP that you wanted to record pre-Columbian concepts of time."

"Correct." They stand and wipe their hand on their pants, though it is not wet.

"I should remind you that electronic devices will not work inside the wormhole."

"I remember that from the reading materials. Of course, it makes more sense now."

"Most researchers bring partners who can corroborate what they witness for skeptics."

"Skeptics in this matter will not be swayed by dual accounts or peer-reviewed papers." In the simplest terms possible, they explain the meaning of the term pachacuti, or the overturning of space-time—not to be confused with Pachacuti the man, who renamed himself after this concept, believing himself to be the cataclysm foretold to mark the end of one period of spacetime and the beginning of another. Each pacha follows the same pattern: a rapid transformation, the periods of recalibration and balance, followed by chaos, disturbance, upheaval. A god burns all the crops. A drought decimates the altiplano and ruins the harvest for half a generation. Spanish conquistadors sweep into Cuzco and colonize the continent. Taken together, these events may look like dots in time, but the dots do not form a linear progression, so there's no straight line that peaks in fear or falls in comfort. "Time is a coil," the professor explains, attempting to illustrate by drawing me a diagram in the sand, not realizing that they cannot move the sand. It is in a different time.

In the here and now of our little wormhole, they describe time's coil. It is the past and the future, crossing, co-existing, and exchanging information in and through the present, which loops down, like a teardrop in the coil of time, forming a small opening in which I see a premonition of the wormhole we created together—time dislocation, understood and predicted hundreds of years ago by this ancient civilization whose history was written by its oppressors, then reclaimed by its own descendants. Oral historians and scholars like Professor Yupanqui now have the opportunity to listen to pre-Columbian history being told communally, remembered collectively, passed from generation to generation so that the past may continue to live in the present and into the future.

In this conscious act of community-building, I'm the outsider. This knowledge is not for me. I don't deserve it and haven't done the work to earn it. When Professor Yupanqui sits by a small fire and listens to the farmers of Cuzco speak in Quechua, I do not ask them to translate on my behalf and risk missing something of importance. Instead, I sit quietly in a corner, and I listen for words that I intend to look up later: ayllu, mit'a, huaca, ñawpa.

In this way, I begin the slow process of understanding what history could not destroy.

‡

We cannot change the past. I remind myself of this before every job. Sometimes, when an impoverished washerwoman is being whipped or a village being sacked or a child being sold into lifelong slavery, my clients will turn to me and ask, "Can't we do something?" and then I have to explain to them that we will never be saviors, that what is happening has happened and will never not happen—no matter how many times we return to that moment, armed with information and what we believe are solutions. How can we possibly right the wrongs of the past when we cannot even manage that in the present? Their empathy often turns to hubris and privilege then. Once, a client vowed to speak with my supervisors and to "remake the entire time dislocation industry from the ground up, if he had to." No doubt he is dead now and never bothered to follow up on that threat. Having accompanied so many men like him on these expeditions, I can honestly say that the past remains better off without their meddling and their attempts to make their own vision a reality. If an industrialist were to travel back in time and introduce streamlined means of production into an Andean textile practice, Karla says, "All this traditional knowledge could be lost."

"Capitalism is often just another form of colonialism," I say.

"And the past was already remade in the colonist's image."

"So why give them more access? I maintain it would be unethical."

"It's lucky that the science of time dislocation doesn't allow for it, then."

"Well," I say, debating whether to refer the professor to a small clause buried in the more than one-hundred-page liability waiver they were required to sign before this trip. "Technically, a person could directly impact the past if this wormhole were to become unstable and spit them out into localized time, but the likelihood of that happening is extremely small and mostly theoretical because we don't know for sure that an unstable wormhole would jettison a body in one piece or, if so, whether the end location in four-dimensional space-time would correlate to the precise time programmed into the time dislocator or to another localized space-time entirely."

For a moment, the professor squints hard at me, parsing the jargon. "You're saying if this wormhole becomes unstable we could end up in 16th Century London?"

"Or any other time. Or we could die."

"What a comforting theory."

"If it helps, nothing like that has ever happened in the 200 years I've been doing this."

"A possibility is still a possibility, even if it is implausible."

"So says every person with a crush."

Their laugh is a puff of air on the side of a mountain. We have been sitting here for hours, watching Quechua weavers gather plants and sheer alpaca wool off indifferent animals. "You see that woman there? Pounding that plant into a paste? That's called motoy. It is a natural detergent. Weavers wash the wool in it, then rinse it with water, before spinning the wool into threads." The alpaca wool is unexpectedly green and matted, the fibers stained by repeated naps in grass and dirt. Once rinsed, it looks streaked and sad, like the fur of a long-haired dog after its bath. Further down the mountain, outside a stone building that doubles as a mini textile factory and the weaver family's dwelling, the children help spin the threads, marveling at the swiftness of their mother's fingers and the motion of the wooden spindle as it slowly gathers a coat of wool. Their joy in this process reminds me of the first time my brothers saw a wood lathe in action. How the rough edge of the hewn log became smooth and curved to the touch. What a pleasure it is to make something yourself. What a blessing to watch a shape emerge from the material.

We spend several days in the mountains, tracking their progress from wool to dyed thread and from thread to patterned blanket. "Most likely, they will still be working on these pieces long after you and I return home," the professor tells me, "but these traditions will be passed down for hundreds and thousands of years, outlasting colonialization, industrialization, and globalization." Inside the stone house, they kneel in front of a stack of folded blankets, observing the patterns on each intricate textile, until finally they point to one. "I have one like this at home."

Its cascading red and orange hues remind me of mountains at sunset, and I say so.

"It reminds me of who I am, my connection to the ancestors. Sometimes, I wrap it around me after a hard day," they say, miming the motions in a way that makes them look chilly, almost, and wistful, "then I think of the hard days that came before me and the challenges that my people have overcome in the last eight centuries, and I'm reminded that I'm not alone."

"Not alone," I repeat, barely aware of it at first, and then painfully so, as I realize that this utterance has opened a window into my life that I usually keep under constant guard on the job. I glance at the professor, whose expression is that of one just now realizing something that eluded them before, although it seems obvious now: how time dislocation can turn you into an orphan, a tiny island traveling back and forth in time with room enough for only one person and the idea of an anchor. Unable to wipe away this realization, I allow myself to ask, "What is it like, feeling so connected to the past? To your heritage?"

The question pains them. "It's like the wormhole," they say, looking up at the future, then back over at me like the captain of a ship waving at a castaway. "Except it never ends. It starts in the past, at the beginning of my people's history, then passes through me, enveloping me in love, family, and knowledge before continuing on—into the future. Nothing can tear me from it. It will exist until the Sun engulfs the Earth or the human race destroys itself, whichever comes later and perhaps even beyond that."

"Perhaps the books will survive," I offer, though that seems like so little.

Their smile bleeds grief. "And these blankets. And the mountains. And the language."

I nod and tilt my head slightly to listen to the voices outside the building, their quiet joys, their moments of pride as intricate patterns start to take shape on the loom. Without realizing it, I begin to hide myself away again, to close the small window I opened into my life and shut all my vulnerabilities away for the rest of the job, but before I can— before the longing and jealousy that swelled up as they described their heritage can ebb back to a bearable undercurrent—they ask me what it actually feels like to be a time traveler, and because for the first time in a very long time I do not want to be alone, I say, "It's like pulling sugar into a star with hundreds of tiny spikes that connect to all the different times

I've visited—but the spikes are the thinnest parts of myself, and the core of the star is terrified that the spikes will shatter at the slightest touch."

Their silence is gentle and considered, as if the wrong vibration could shatter that star. "It sounds like you need to quit your job. Or at least make room for something else."

Again I nod, chastened by the thought that they realized in weeks what took me decades.

"You cannot live your entire life afraid of breaking your heart," they say, and reach out to press my hand with their fingers—or to attempt to. I cannot feel their touch here, but I know why their thumb strokes my hand with such tenderness and I know, too, that accepting their gesture is against the rules, that it violates the Code of Conduct to which I agreed, as a Time Technician on staff at Downtime, Inc., which strictly prohibits any pseudo-physical staff-client contact in the fourth-dimension outside the list of pre-approved gestures deemed permissible for illustrating the nature of motion or of disembodiment in dislocated time. Handholding is not approved. Hugging, not approved. Gazing up the mountainside at a client, wondering if you will see them again when the job is over: technically not prohibited but certainly not encouraged. What would I tell Maxim in this situation? *Keep your crush to yourself. Focus on the mountains instead.*

Focus on the job.

‡

Almost 230 years ago, when I was just a girl and my parents were still alive, we would go on extended backpacking trips around California and the American Southwest. Mount Whitney, Mount Shasta, Yosemite. My mother, a rock climber/hiking guide, spent the majority of her time outdoors, tracing hard dusty routes above the tree line, where if storms rolled in unexpectedly we would have to scramble back down the trail and seek cover below the tree line. My siblings and I learned young to master the art of expansion and contraction. How to roll clothes into the tightest balls possible to maximize space in our backs. How to make ourselves small under tarps hung on the branches of the tall trees to protect from the rain and lightning, how to fling off our packs and pose for photos on top of the highest mountains in the contiguous United States. My father rarely accompanied us on these trips. A construction foreman and artisan woodworker, he would stay at home during our summer sojourns in the mountains, and we would return to find new carvings of pajaritos and alpacas for us and geometric lamps with fairy lights embedded in resin for his white customers on Etsy. Whenever we returned from our fairly cheap trips to the mountains, he would lament, "Algun día (cuando tenemos el dinero), viajaremos a Guayaquil." His hometown. To this day, I've never visited. Perhaps the closest I've ever gotten is Bogotá—a difference of 936 miles, 279 years, three months, and five days.

It takes four and a half weeks, more than two-thirds of the trip, for me to reveal this to the professor. When I finally do, Cuzco is burnished with moonlight after a brief hailstorm, the deep river valley in which it was built shimmering like a silver-plated snake pinned down by a puma's midnight-black paws. Below, the residents of Cuzco sleep, and the hillsides are dotted with white alpacas grumpily grazing after the hailstorm woke them up. Our bodies being suspended in time, the professor and I do not need to sleep. On our first night, I taught them how to manipulate their perception of time passing to provide the illusion of rest: close your eyes, imagine a sheep slowly being shorn, its wool washed and dyed to make blankets, the blankets wrapped around your legs, the warmth causing you to nod off on the couch, a book falling open on your lap; now, open your eyes—it's morning in Cuzco, and dawn is breaking over the nearby mountains. For over a month the professor has been working from before sun-up to well past midnight, pausing now and again to lament that they cannot taste the food, drink the chicha, bury their fingers in the alpaca's wool. "Its screams are so high-pitched, so pitiful," they said once. Only now, after a long immersion in the city's rhythms, does Professor Yupanqui refuse to close their eyes. Underneath the stars, they ask me, "Where do you go when I fast-forward at night?"

And so: I bring them here, to the rim of the river valley, where the air is cool and thin, but we cannot feel it in our bones. "What's the highest altitude you've reached? Mine's 14,505 feet." Mount Whitney, on a hike with my mother when I was still a child.

Professor Yupanqui thinks for a moment. "Definitely Aconcagua. It's about 6,900 meters tall, which would make it about 22,000 (23,000?) feet, I think."

Tilting my head back, I imagine the snowy peak. "What's the air like up there?"

"Unforgiving. Often lethal. I climbed with supplemental oxygen, of course."

"Wise choice. Have you climbed any of the other Seven Summits?"

A bashful expression. "No, I'm too old for that. My knees would rebel."

"You're not too old, but I might be. Imagine: 'Bicentenarian Sets World Record!'"

"I can see the headlines." Head dipped, they ask, "How old are you, exactly?"

"The day we met was actually my 237th birthday, if you can bel—ieve it."

"Really? Had I known I would have brought you a present for the occasion."

I close my eyes and smile. "What kind of present?"

"For you? A Quechua dictionary, to start." My laughter is sudden and self-conscious, and they pause graciously to allow it to morph into gratitude and pleasure. "But then what do you get for the woman who has witnessed the building of the Pyramids and lived through the downfall of the American Empire—a commemorative snow globe?"

"Snow globes are pretty, but I'm not really one for souvenirs or cheap trinkets."

"Who said anything about cheap? A hand-blown artisan snow globe will cost you."

"I suppose that's true. I'm out of the habit of checking price tags, for obvious reasons."

"Well, you've spent most of your life unable to engage in local economies."

"If only that were the same thing as living outside of capitalism."

Their lips twitch into a smile. "You would fit right in at my university."

"Maybe, but I was born in a time when the focus on STEM devalued the humanities."

Where I expect a laugh and a wave of dismissal, I hear only their measured breathing—so careful, so deliberate—like a step taken in the snow. When you're climbing, you cannot afford to waste precious energy on the wrong move, on inefficient beta. Everything must be precise, exact. Anything less risks failure or potential death. When they ask me if I studied quantum mechanics, I imagine my foot slipping off a ledge, imagine falling down the side of a mountain with nothing but a well-tied rope and a harness to secure me in my descent, and then getting caught, whipping toward the rock because the trained belayer down below was able to stop my fall. I open my eyes to find their hand positioned in such a way so as to appear to be cupping my left arm softly at the elbow. Even though we cannot really touch here, I slide in their grasp, aligning our hands so they rest—palm to palm—my fingertips brushing what would be their wrists.

Their gaze dips down to our hands, then up to meet mine. "Can you explain the physics of what's happening now?"

We lean closer, our foreheads almost touching. "In simple terms? You're seducing me."

Their hand traces a path up my arm, past my shoulder, over my cheek, where their thumb mimes the motion of rubbing my lower lip. "I want to take you to dinner—in modern-day Cuzco, where we can actually smell and taste local cuisine; how does that sound?" I nod, surrendering to this moment in the mountains, though in the back of my mind I can hear myself warning Maxim: *What happens in the past stays in the past. Often, clients will get attached because they're lonely and have no other emotional outlet. It doesn't mean they love you.* For tonight, at least, I push the sensible part of my brain aside. I allow myself to settle comfortably in their arms and point to the two Incan constellations I have heard of: Urcuchillay the llama and Atoq the fox. Overhead, their pointer finger traces the shapes of a serpent, a toad, a condor—its hooked beak open, great wings extended over Cuzco. What will happen, I wonder, when the dust in the dark constellations gives birth to new stars?

What will become of us when the Milky Way finally falls still?

‡

When I started working at Downtime Inc., dislocation staff such as myself were subjected to mandatory rest periods in between jobs. Every week in four-dimensional space-time required a full forty-eight hours of recalibration in the three-dimensional present. Such was the deal that the CEO struck with the United States Department of Labor to avoid penalties and stricter regulation following a lawsuit by several of my co-workers, who alleged that the nature of dislocation meant that staff were working 24/7, without breaks, overtime, or hazard pay. After fifty years and about $600 million in lobbying, the time travel industry succeeded in abolishing the restriction, arguing that dislocation staff were, in effect, being treated to extended holidays on the company's dime—wouldn't you want to walk among the dinosaurs, the lawyers argued, and wouldn't you pay just about anything for the privilege? This, of course, does not account for the constant emotional and mental labor that goes into hand holding boorish tourists, anxious academics, and the slimy, self-righteous businessmen who almost invariably offer to pay more to experience this local color "in the flesh." No doubt that is one of the reasons the dislocation staff sees such high turnover.

"That," Maxim says, in our 1:1, a week after my job in Cuzco, "and the fact that it's very hard to find love or get married if you spend like 90% of your waking life suspended in a kind of disembodied temporal non-space."

I squint at his video. "Disembodied temporal non-space?"

"Hey, you work here seventy years, you start to pick up some of the terms. Doesn't mean you're using them correctly. Also doesn't mean you're wrong." On the holo-screen, he points up, his finger wagging like a troublemaker who has been scolded too many times and learned how to make light of punishing gestures.

"You're upbeat today. Did you get a new sword?"

He throws his head back, laughing. "No, I'm just fishing for an update on this professor of yours. Have they called?"

"Yesterday." He waits for me to say, "We're supposed to have dinner tomorrow."

"And yet I'm sensing some hesitation. Worried you'll be rusty after 200 odd years?"

"Excuse you! It's only been like fifty years. Remember that Frenchwoman you met?"

"How could I forget? Cèline. For a while, I thought she'd whisk you away to Marseille."

"Ugh, could you imagine? We'd be underwater by now, surrounded by fish carcasses."

"You'd also be dead—but that's neither here nor there. You've got a dinner to get to."

When Maxim wags his finger again, I glance at the unpacked luggage in the corner. At all the 3D-printed dresses and transgenic silk blouses I considered wearing before wondering if such garments would seem frivolous to a professor who has devoted their life to studying traditions. "I worry that this flutter of hope in my chest is a sign of folly or proof that I've been lying to myself about my intentions—and Karla's. They made a pass while I was on the job—not in a position to divest myself of my defenses or even to allow myself to be vulnerable enough to connect outside the context of time travel. How can I trust my own feelings when they manifested on the clock in the fourth dimension?"

"I thought you two talked about this those last weeks on the job."

"We did, and we agreed it was worth trying to untangle our feelings in the present."

"Then you should give it a chance." He shrugs one shoulder, almost reluctantly adding, "I should probably also remind you that every relationship starts with a performance. What is a first date if not an attempt to project a tidy picture of yourself in the hopes that someone will like it?"

"I would hardly call this our first date. It's more like our fifth or our sixth."

Maxim splays his fingers. "Hey, whatever you need to tell yourself, my friend."

With a sigh, I admit, "I suppose you should assign the Hapsburg caper to someone else."

"Ooo, are we calling them capers now? I like that. Maybe we'll book a Pentagon caper."

"One can hope," I say, deriving momentary pleasure from the idea of floating right by the Pentagon's highest ranking officials, through the sound-proof walls of their offices, and into their locked filing cabinets, where I would curl up like a little fox to wait for them to make the mistake of believing that their security was impenetrable and their misdeeds would be forever cloaked by a fundamentally corrupt system interested only in maintaining its own power. "Do you remember when the last five-star generals got convicted of war crimes?"

His beard smiles with him. "That was a good day. Thank you for reminding me."

"Thank you for chatting through this with me. It's humbling to be nervous at 237."

"And it gives me hope to think it's still possible. Here I was on the verge of giving up."

"You? Never. There's a gender non-conforming blacksmith out there just waiting for you to challenge them to a duel."

"Can't wait." He taps two fingers to his temple in farewell. "See you on the other side."

Once alone, I purchase a one-way ticket to Cuzco, unsure where the night will lead us but comforted by the knowledge that I can hop on a high-speed train whenever I like and get home in mere hours. My mother always used to warn us, "Reaching the peak is not nearly as important as ensuring that you have a safe path down and enough food and water to get you there." Once, four or five years before she met my father, she nearly summited K2—the second highest mountain in the world and (arguably) the most dangerous, with a death:ascent ratio of approximately 1:4. She climbed within a hundred meters of the peak, but her team was almost out of food, and one of the men was suffering frostbite in his left foot. He ended up losing three toes, and she never returned to K2, despite her dreams of one day guiding expeditions in the Himalayas. Life happened. Three kids were born. Her double overhand stopper knot came loose and a lazy belayer let her rope run right out of his fingers while she climbed Half Dome. Her life was a series of calculated risks. As she grew older and began to look more like my grandmother than my mother, she understood my career path was a calculated risk, too. How much heartbreak can one person bear? How long will the human mind tolerate loneliness? What happens if the wormhole collapses while I'm inside it? Karla asked me that on the last night of the job. "Could we get stuck inside it?"

"No one knows. In theory, if the power cuts out at Downtime, the mouth of the wormhole will collapse, but we could remain inside, in this state—potentially forever."

"Forever." Their gaze stretched down the roads of Cuzco, tracing the path of history up to a future they knew, building the city up stone by stone, year by year, until it resembled the city in which they worked: a city of restaurants, churches, and ruins, a city where one always arrives out of breath. "This is not where I would want all of eternity to begin. I know far, far too much about what comes next."

We both fell silent, staring up at the stars, and they did not ask me where I would want all of eternity to begin. What would I be willing to live through again? Most of history is a record of suffering and of people abusing power. I focus on the near future: our last late-night stroll around Cuzco of old. Our soon-to-be dinners in Cuzco of now. I imagine myself running a finger down a menu, tasking my virtual assistant to translate Quechua words, then double-checking results with Karla, trying not to hold them at a distance like a client or slip back to performance mode as they fill me in on the details of the past few days. Their illustrious return to the present, marked by the ever-so-pleasant questions from a room full of colleagues and government officials demanding to know what they did with all that grant money. Their answer, we agreed, will not involve me.

‡

On my walk from the train station to the restaurant, I pass the ruins of Sacsayhuaman, the Inca fortress constructed during the reign of Pachacuti but only just conceptualized upon our visit to 1438 CE. At the tail end of the job, we found a single block of limestone laid in the center of a field (the start, we theorized, of a five-story tower at the heart of the fortress, which was itself the head of the puma that was the city). Now, only a ring of limestone remains where the tower once stood. In its place, a hologram flickers against the sky—cold and permeable, its spectral presence nothing like the fearsome and labyrinthine fortress I have seen in my travels through time. Entire walls had collapsed, leaving ruins mere inches high for the tour groups to step over, like modern-day conquistadors, as a guide explains: "The Incas commanded what was then the biggest empire in the world—larger than the Byzantine, Ottoman, Aztec, Songhai, and Ming."

And then the empire fell, I add, heading toward the restaurant, away from the tour groups, with their reductive dreams of a city bathed in blood and coated in gold dust. From where I stand now, the hill is festooned with light: the tinted squares of apartment windows sweeping down the valley, the glare of neon signs over international chains and entertainment multiplexes, the zip of a high-speed train aimed resolutely North. I'd forgotten how loud present-day cities can be—and how firm. Sometimes I still think I can walk through walls and pass between couples undetected. When I meet Karla, I half expect their hug to slip right through me. It has been so long (decades) since anyone has touched me like this.

"How are you? You're breathing hard," they say, clasping my cheek in concern.

I shake my head in their hand. "I'm still acclimating, and I just walked uphill."

"You will get used to the altitude," they say, opening the door to the restaurant. A woman peeks through the window from the kitchen and greets Karla warmly, telling them to pick a table, and then studying me for a moment and smiling. We sit by the window, at a square table adorned with a single cantuta—a brilliant trumpet of a flower sagging under the weight of its own fuchsia blossom. Most modern restaurants now have tabletop holoscreens so you can order food, watch a second-run film or television show, and play proprietary games while robots wheel between tight aisles to deliver food. Nothing like that can be found here. Our table is made of heavy stones and our chairs of dark, curved wood. A small splash darkens the stone where the cantuta was watered not long before. I trace its edges while Karla tells me the woman is chef, owner, and server, all in one, and has managed the restaurant for fifty years, ever since taking over from her abuelo. Soon, the chef bursts out of the kitchen, bearing two glasses of water and an appetizer to share. "Señora Fiorella, I want to introduce you to Beatriz. She accompanied me on my recent trip."

Señora Fiorella nods with exaggerated understanding and delight. "So nice to meet you!"

"My pleasure, Señora. Karla speaks very highly of your food. I'm looking forward to it."

"Did they tell you they are my favorite customer? For them, I will bring all the specials."

With a nod from Karla, she whisks the menus away, leaving us to marvel at the starter: an original interpretation of choclo con queso, featuring giant kernels of white corn speckled purple, orange, and red, alongside three different cheeses. We eat the kernels one by one with our fingers to savor their freshness and crunch. "Can you believe I haven't eaten in a restaurant in decades? I usually only have time for takeout."

Their head tilts in pleasant jest. "Imagine: a 237-year-old with no time to speak of."

And yet: with only a day or two between jobs, if that, life in the present is swiftly reduced to utilitarian maintenance of my mind and body: hot showers with a splash of cold, to experience both extremes; augmented reality workouts at home because gym memberships make no sense; a twelve-step skincare routine; meticulous monitoring of recycling and compost; extended bouts of nothing but reading news. "Without that," I tell them, "the present would have no continuity."

"Why don't they just program the machine to bring you back where you left off?"

"To stave off the madness," I say, too quickly. Swallowing, I add, "In the beginning, they did program it like that, but the lack of time loss eroded belief in the time dislocation's validity. I remember thinking it was a delusion because I came back and nothing had changed."

"Yet the alternative is never taking part in society. It seems like a high price to pay."

"Well, most people don't stay half as long as I have. With good reason," I admit.

"You're still planning to leave, then." Their pleasure in noting this comforts me.

"I still need to figure out what's next. All I ever wanted was to be a student of time."

Karla chides me that there is more than one way to study time. "Look around you: all you hear and see and touch exists in space and time. You can observe it, trace its path to this moment, monitor the careful balance of the world and its inhabitants. This, too, is a vocation."

I consider this for a moment. "Was that the real purpose of your trip?"

Karla nods and leans back to make room for the dishes Señora Fiorella brings: a tall bowl of hen soup with potato noodles arranged to look like nests for twin boiled eggs; an oblong silver platter with a fried whole guinea pig lovingly butterflied so it appears to be floating atop a bed of fried potatoes and plantains; thin strips of alpaca seared to perfection, lain on a tower of rice; two cocktail glasses containing leche de tigre, that flavorful marinade of fish stock and spice flooding perfectly poached prawns and scallops, and a whole rocoto relleno pepper, fried and overflowing with sauteed onions and melted cheese. Karla instructs me to take a bite of each in succession but to leave room for desserts of rice pudding, lúcuma fruit ice cream, and sweet potato donuts called picarones. "Balance," they say, "is the true measure of time—periods of relative peace inevitably followed by downturns of chaos and anguish. Such was the reign of Pachacuti: the overturning of space-time, the chaos before the rebalancing—or so he thought."

"Doesn't every leader claim to change the world?"

"In Latin America, especially." They lift the leche de tigre but do not sip it, merely hold it off to the side as they gaze out at the street. "I attended a counter-protest today. Supporters of the old regime have teamed up with anti-abortion zealots and started pushing through legislation that was modeled off your country's trap laws. Today we have a democratically elected president that campaigned on a more progressive marriage of politics and Catholicism, but her popularity in the center-right is eroding, and I fear the fascists are taking hold again. The balance is shifting," they note with grim certainty, shutting their eyes to feel it: their country slipping again into chaos.

"Are you afraid that there will be violence? Purges of the intelligentsia?"

"Always," they say, setting down the cocktail glass without partaking of it, "but that is no matter. I am now and always will be a teacher. This is my path." Their gaze settles on my face as I weigh the merits of the question on my tongue—whether it's selfish to ask if they have room in their life to nurture a fledgling relationship when their life is constantly in peril and whether I can conscionably claim to have the emotional bandwidth when I do not yet know what form my new, present-day life will take. In their scrutiny, I detect another, far more complex set of calculations, which reduce down to the question: "Do you see activism and organizing in your future?"

"Yes." My swift answer pleases them.

They spoon a boiled egg out of the soup. "What do you see yourself fighting for?"

"Redistribution of wealth. Stricter regulations on technology. Ethics of decolonization."

"Come by my office tomorrow afternoon. I can give you some books to get you started."

"I'd like that," I say, opening the pepper on my plate, parting the layers of rice and cheese with my fork so I can taste each component separately before marrying their flavors and textures. "Are you teaching tomorrow? I would like to see you in action."

They bite into the white of the egg and nod. "Feel free to join. How's your Spanish?"

"Both better and worse than it used to be, but my virtual assistant will fill in the blanks."

"Ah yes, your pocket AI. Tell me: can it teach you Quechua? Or Aymara?"

"To an extent. If I relied on it alone, I would sound like a first-grader."

Their eyes crinkle with warmth. "I bet you were a cute first-grader."

"Hundreds of years ago," I say, both sheepish and heartened.

Their fork pokes the air as they say, "Can you pass the cuy?" Noting my hesitance to start pulling apart the fried guinea pig, Karla tears away one leg, placing it on my dish alongside a pile of papas and red plantains. Without realizing it at first, this is how we establish a rhythm: passing plates back and forth, praising Señora Fiorella's prodigious culinary talents while bemoaning the inability to manage one more bite, even as more dishes alight on the table and our mouths start to water anew, and marveling at each step at how well we navigate these moments together. At how smoothly time passes between us as we tiptoe towards each other, like two slackliners suspended above the rock canyons of Yosemite. On the slackline, you can feel each other's vibrations while you balance. Adjust to the weight of each step. Finally dip together in the middle, like one coil in the overturning of space-time.

This pachacuti is only just beginning.

Authors

Osmani R. Alcaraz-Ochoa. Originally from Jalisco, México, Osmani R. Alcaraz-Ochoa is a queer poeta (he/él/they) and a national organizer for immigrant & worker rights. They create poetry that mixes themes of immigration, borders, class, and race through sci-fi and world-building. He has been published in *Voices de la Luna*, *Windward Review*, *La Raiz Magazine*, and was a finalist for the 2024 Howling Bird Press Poetry Prize.

Joy Castro is the author of the 2023 historical novel *One Brilliant Flame*; the novel *Flight Risk*, a finalist for a 2022 International Thriller Award; the post-Katrina New Orleans literary thrillers *Hell or High Water* and *Nearer Home*, both published in France by Gallimard's historic Série Noire; the story collection *How Winter Began*; the memoir *The Truth Book*; and the essay collection *Island of Bones*, which received the International Latino Book Award. She edited the craft anthology *Family Trouble: Memoirists on the Hazards and Rewards of Revealing Family* and founded Machete, a series in innovative literary nonfiction at The Ohio State University Press. Her work has appeared in venues including *Ploughshares*, *The Brooklyn Rail*, *Senses of Cinema*, *Los Angeles Review of Books*, and *The New York Times Magazine*. She is the Willa Cather Professor of English and Ethnic Studies at the University of Nebraska-Lincoln, where she directs the Institute for Ethnic Studies.

Wenmimareba Collins Klobah (she/they; ella/elle) is an artist, performer, writer, and cultural critic from San Juan, Puerto Rico. Her artistic practice draws upon her Caribbean upbringing and explores themes of multilingualism, near-future ecology, and folklore. She received her MFA in poetry from the California College of the Arts. Her work is forthcoming or has previously appeared in *Samovar*, *Foglifter*, *Honey Literary*, *Akéwì Magazine*, *La piel del arrecife*, *The Dark Magazine*, and the *Akashic Books* "Duppy Thursday Series of Caribbean Stories" series. She is a current reader for the online literary journal *Palette Poetry*.

E.G. Condé (he/him/Él) is a queer Puerto Rican writer of speculative fiction. He is one of the creators of Taínofuturism, an emerging genre of art and storytelling that imagines decolonized futures that center indigenous Caribbean traditions and cosmologies. Condé is the author of *Sordidez*, an indigenous futurism novella published with Stelliform Press. His short fiction appears in *Interzone Magazine, Solarpunk Magazine, If There's Anyone Left, Reckoning, Tree and Stone, Sword & Sorcery*, and more.

Rodrigo Culagovski is a Chilean author, architect, and web developer. He has published in Nature, Levar Burton Reads, and Future Science Fiction Digest among others. https://culagovski.net. On mastodon as @culagovski@wandering.shop. He misses his Commodore 64. Pronouns he/him/él. SFWA | Codex | ALCiFF

Sarah Dalton is a writer, editor, and teacher. She is an alumna of VONA and Macondo, AWP's Writer to Writer Mentorship, and the MFA program at San José State. Her nonfiction has appeared in The *Normal School, Crab Creek Review, [pank], MUTHA Magazine, Reed*, and other magazines. Originally from the San Francisco East Bay, she's finding roots in the Pacific Northwest.

César Leonardo De León is the author of *Speaking With Grackles by Soapbery Trees*, winner of the Texas Institute of Letters John A. Robertson Award 2021, and the Philosophical Society of Texas Best Book of Poetry Award 2022. Originally born in Monterrey, Mexico, he has resided in the Rio Grande Valley of Texas for over 30 years. His work has been published in numerous anthologies and journals and he is the current poetry editor for *riverSedge*. Cesar is one of four poet-organizers for Poets Against Walls and a member of the Macondo Writers Workshop.

Illimani Ferreira is a Brazilian American writer. His short prose can be found on different anthologies such as *Unidentified Funny Object*, Decoded Pride, and Flame Tree Press' *Immigrant Sci-Fi Short Stories* anthology. He is also the author of the humorous science fiction novel Terminal 3. www.IFSciFi.com

Daniel Figueroa-Arias is a Costa Rican author and engineer. He has published in magazines such as *Espejo Humeante, Chile del Terror* and *Teoría Omicron*. He has published several novels including *Fantasma en los Sueños*

with Clubdelibros and *Náufrago en un millón de voces* with Ask-Books. He also has published a number of short story collections such as *Sueños de Babel* with Austrobórea Editors and *La Sed y Otros Cuentos de Ciencia Ficción* released through UNED. He won the Premio Nacional de Narrativa Alberto Cañas Escalante in 2024 and the Premio De Abreu in 2021 (Third Place). He is founder and coordinator of the literary workshop "13013" and is a member of ALCiFF. https://www.instagram.com/taller_literario_13013/, https://www.instagram.com/danielf_escritor/, https://linktr.ee/danielfigueroa_escritor

Lysz Flo is an AfroCaribbean Latine, polyglot, word artist, and indie author, member of The Estuary Collective, Creatively Exposed podcast host, Voodoonauts Summer 2020 Fellow and Obsidian Black Listening 2022 Fellow. She released her poetry novel *Soliloquy of an Ice Queen*, March 2020. She is a Grubstreet educator since 2020 and has a writing workshop series in MOCA NOMI. Her poems can be found in *FIYAH, Hellebore, Lolwe, Strange Horizons* and has done various multimedia projects work O' Miami. Her poetry website is www.lyszflo.com. She is also an Online Crystal and Spiritual wellness shop owner at Astrolyszics.com

Olga García Echeverría, born and raised in East Los Angeles, is the author of *Falling Angels: Cuentos y Poemas*. Her work has been published in *The Sun Magazine, Imaniman: Poets Writing on the Anzalduan Borderlands, Lavandería: A Mixed Load of Women, Wash, and Words, U.S. Latino Literature Today, Telling Tongues: A Latin@ Anthology on Language*, among others. As co-literary executor of the beloved lesbian Colombian writer and publisher, tatiana de la tierra, she has worked with queer and feminist presses in the U.S. and abroad to help bring to fruition such projects as the republishing of de la tierra's *For the Hard Ones: A Lesbian Phenomenology* (Sinister Wisdom 2018) and most recently *Redonda y radical: antología poética de tatiana de la tierra* (Sincronía Casa Editorial 2022). Olga has been an educator in the literary arts for over 25 years and currently teaches literature in the Chicanx Latinx Studies Department at California State University of Los Angeles.

Ruth Joffre is a Bolivian American writer and the author of the story collection *Night Beast*. Her work has been shortlisted for the Creative Capital Awards, longlisted for The Story Prize, and supported by residencies at the Virginia Center for the Creative Arts, Lighthouse Works, and The Arctic Circle. Her writing has appeared or is forthcoming in more than 50 publications, including *Lightspeed, Pleiades, Nightmare, TriQuarterly, Reckoning, Wigleaf,* and the anthologies *We're Here: The Best Queer Speculative Fiction 2022* and *2022 Best of Utopian Speculative Fiction.* A graduate of Cornell University and the Iowa Writers' Workshop, Ruth served as the 2020–2022 Prose Writer-in-Residence at Hugo House in Seattle. She was a Visiting Writer at University of Washington Bothell and George Mason University in 2023.

Roxane Llanque is a queer Bolivian German writer, artist, and film-maker based in Berlin. Her award-winning short film *Aberration* was selected for The Madrid Human Rights Festival and her micro *The Tell-Tale Present* won the 2023 Outstanding Miniature of World Pride Australia. Her essays were published in magazines like *Bright Wall/Dark Room, Stanchion, and Libertine Magazine,* while her fiction was featured in the speculative anthologies *We Are All Thieves of Somebody's Future, Demons & Death Drops,* and is forthcoming in the science fiction anthology *Other Worlds.* She is currently working on her first novel. You can find her on her website https://roxanellanque.com.

Rolando André López is a writer and poet born in San Juan, Puerto Rico. Currently, he lives in Oakland, California. He has an MFA in Creative Writing from California College of the Arts. His work has been published in *Orca Literary Journal, Passages North, Konch Magazine,* and elsewhere. He was a 2021-2022 Puerto Rican Artist Resident at the Massachusetts Museum of Modern Art. You can find him on Instagram: @nocolornocontrast.

Kristian Macaron (she/her(s)/ella) is from and resides in Albuquerque, New Mexico, a land full of treasures. Her writing is inspired by this col-orful landscape and explores tales that derive from connections to her Hispanic/Latinx and Lebanese-American heritage, but also her love for cryptids, portals, geology, and time travel. Kristian received an MFA in Creative Writing Fiction from Emerson College (2012) and a BA from University of New Mexico (2010). Her full-length poetry collection *Recipe for Time Travel in Case We Lose Each Other* was released from Game Over Books Publications in February 2022. Her poetry chapbook *Storm,* re-leased in 2015 from Swimming with Elephants Publications. Other prose and poetry publications can be found in *Asimov's Science Fiction Magazine,*

Uncanny Magazine, The Normal School Magazine, Gargoyle Magazine, and others. She is a 2024 Poetry Fellow at Chatter ABQ and works and teaches at the University of New Mexico.

Florencia Manóvil is a queer Latina writer-director whose work expresses a yearning to evolve societal paradigms, through an ecofeminist lens. Born in Buenos Aires, Manóvil moved to the U.S. to study film at Emerson College on an Honors scholarship. Based in the Bay Area since 2007, she's best known for her lauded web series "Dyke Central." Manóvil is a current SFFILM resident, and in 2024 was selected for Writing Climate Pitchfest and Stowe Story Labs. A two-time recipient of the Frameline Completion Fund, her films have screened at festivals around the world. Manóvil has taught, guest-lectured, or been a panelist at SF State University, University of San Francisco, Frameline, Film Fatales, and BAVC/Reel Stories. She also freelances as a translator and interpreter for social justice organizations, and lives in Oakland with her teen daughter, Kayen. "Morning tides" is set in the world of the thrutopian limited series she's developing, "Twelve."

Carlos Julio Paredes Minango is a 33-year-old man from Ecuador. Most of the time plays video games and writes fan fiction. He has two master's degrees in human resources and human development. He loves good stories.

Richie Narvaez is the author of two novels, *Hipster Death Rattle* and *Holly Hernandez and the Death of Disco*, which received an Agatha Award and an Anthony Award, and two short story collections, *Roachkiller & Other Stories* and *Noiryorican*, which was nominated for an Anthony Award for Best Anthology. His work has been published in *Lumina Journal, Latinx Rising: An Anthology of Science Fiction and Fantasy, Mississippi Review, Storyglossia*, and *Tiny Nightmares*, among others. He teaches writing at Sarah Lawrence College and the Fashion Institute of Technology.

Stephanie Nina Pitsirilos is a writer with critically acclaimed prose, comics and zines in numerous anthologies, magazines, co-creator platforms, and artists' book form. She is the recipient of the 2022 Chautauqua Janus Prize for her story "Jean," called "masterful" by Publishers Weekly (*Speculative Fiction for Dreamers: A Latinx Anthology*). She's recognized as a new voice transforming the genres of science fiction and fantasy and revitalizing the short comic form. She creates visual art as ANDROMEDA. Her work often explores culture, gender and historical legacy as the principal themes propelling characters, informed by a career in public health and a curiosity of astrophysics, and with a gravitation around the female Nuyorican experience of diasporic Puerto Rico and Grecian landscapes. *Event Horizon: Stories of No Turning Back* is her 2024 debut short story collection. Find her works at www.stephanieninapitsirilos.com

Daniel Jose Ruiz is a writer and educator living in Los Angeles. He is a tenured professor of English at Los Angeles City College. He is the author of *Coconut Versus from Floricanto Press* and *The Life of Jian Ciervo* from Pegasus Press. His collection of novellas, Jump, Rig, and Gig is forthcoming from Android Press. He is a big ol' geek, so his writing almost always has genre elements to it. He earned his MFA in Creative Writing from CalArts and both his BA and MA in English from UC: Irvine. He writes stories that he wanted to read as a kid, and he especially likes to make sure that readers who don't fit neatly into boxes see themselves in his work.

Gabriela Santiago (she/they) lived all over the world as a child and currently makes her home in Minnesota. Her work has appeared in *Clarkesworld, Strange Horizons, Lady Churchill's Wristlet,* and more. She was co-editor of *Reckoning 6* with Aïcha Martine Thiam, and is the founder of the Revolutionary Jetpacks sci-fi cabaret, centering futures imagined by BIPOC, queer and trans, and disabled artists. Follow her at writing-related activities on Tumblr or check out her website at gabriela-santiago.com.

Eugene Speakes is PhD student in Caribbean Studies from the English Department at the University of Puerto Rico, Río Piedras Campus. He teaches the course *Writing About Literature* to undergraduate students. He holds an M.A. in English Literature with a focus on creative writing and a B.F.A in Image and Design from La Escuela de Artes Plásticas in Old San Juan. He published the short story "El Cuco" in *PREE Magazine.* He has published poetry in the anthology *Crónicas de María: Voces para la Historia* and *Tonguas Magazine,* as well as a book review for *The Caribbean Writer.* He also published an essay for the compendium *Negotiating Crosswinds Trans-linguality, Trans-culturality and Trans-identification in the Greater Caribbean.*

He resides in San Juan but maintains a close personal and creative connection to his hometown in Naranjito, Puerto Rico.

Lesley Téllez is a Chicana writer whose work explores patriarchy, grief, desire, and caregiving, sometimes through the lens of food. A native of Southern California's Inland Empire, she's the author of the cookbook *Eat Mexico: Recipes from Mexico City's Streets, Markets and Fondas*, published by Kyle Books in 2015. Her creative writing has appeared in *Barrelhouse* and *The Acentos Review*. She's a proud Macondista and an alumna of the Tin House Summer Workshop, Community of Writers, and the Yale Summer Writers Workshop. She lives with her children and partner in Mexico City.

Amanda Torres (AT) is a writer, educator, arts administrator, & cultural organizer from Chicago whose work focuses on queer family, latinx futurism, & collective memory. Their writing has appeared or is forthcoming in *The Acentos Review, Breakbeat Poets*, & *At Our Best: Building Youth-Adult Partnerships*. They founded a youth literary arts organization in Boston, directed The Incubator for Community Engaged Poets & have taught young people and educators working to develop creative, justice-oriented learning spaces for over nineteen years. Currently, they teach at the Harvard Graduate School of Education, live in New England and are an MFA candidate at Randolph College (amandatorreswrites.com)

Yoss (José Miguel Sánchez Gómez) was born in Havana, Cuba. He graduated in Biology from the University of Havana in 1991. From 2007 to 2016 he was the singer of the rock group Tenaz. He is a fan of caving, martial arts, and has a black belt in judo and karate. He has published more than 50 titles, in Cuba and abroad, and his texts have been translated into many languages. His science fiction novels that have been translated into English are *A Planet for Rent, Super Extra Grande, Condomnauts*, and *Red Dust*. Among his most notable literary awards are Juventud Técnica (Cuba, 1987), David (Cuba, 1988), Universidad Carlos III (Spain, 2003), and Julia Verlanger (Switzerland, 2012). Yoss is currently considered one of the most innovative and important voices in science fiction in the Spanish language.

Artist

Luis Valderas has taught art in Texas Public Schools for 29 years. In 2005 Valderas co-founded and produced Project: MASA I, II, and III—a national group exhibit featuring Latino artists and focusing on Chican@ identities. He co-founded A3—Agents of Change LLC, a large-scale printmaking community engagement collaborative. Valderas is a mentor and board member for the New York Foundation for the Arts. He has exhibited at the Medellin Museum of Art-Colombia, the Queens Museum-NYC and the URC ArtsBlock-Riverside CA, The Museum of Anthropology at UBC-British Columbia, Canada. His work is featured in books such as: *Altermundos-Latin@ Speculative Literature, Film and Popular Culture. Mundos Alternos-Art and Science Fiction in the Americas. Chicano Art for Our Millennium-2004* and *Triumph in Our Communities: Four Decades of Mexican American Art-2005*. He is in the permanent collections of UTSA, Arizona St. University, Art Museum of South Tx and the San Antonio Museum of Art.

Editors

Matthew David Goodwin is an Assistant Professor in the Chicana/o Studies Department at the University of New Mexico. His research is centered on Chicanx/Latinx science fiction, immigration, digital culture, and Critical Mystery Studies. He is a co-editor of the Latinx Archive speculative fiction trilogy: *Latinx Rising* and *Speculative Fiction for Dreamers* (Ohio State University Press) and *Not Your Papi's Utopia* (Mouthfeel Press). His study *The Latinx Files: Race, Migration, and Space Aliens* (Rutgers University Press) examines the Latinx space alien through the framework of the Multitude rather than the traditional framework of the Other. He has a PhD in Comparative Literature from the University of Massachusetts, Amherst, and is an active agent in the Albuquerque office of the very much real Speculative Detective Agency.

Alex Hernandez is a Cuban-American speculative fiction writer, editor and artist. His work often explores themes of migration, mysticism, colonization and posthumanism. He lives in South Florida with his wife, two daughters, and an overly-affectionate cat.

Sara Daniele Rivera is a Cuban Peruvian American artist, writer, translator, and educator. Her writing has appeared in *The BreakBeat Poets Vol. 4: LatiNext, The Bat City Review, Solstice, Waxwing, Speculative Fiction for Dreamers: A Latinx Anthology* and elsewhere. She is the co-translator of *The Blinding Star: Selected Poems by Blanca Varela* (Tolsun Books). Her debut book of poetry, *The Blue Mimes*, won the 2023 Academy of American Poets First Book Award and was published by Graywolf Press. She lives in Albuquerque, New Mexico.

www.ingramcontent.com/pod-product-compliance
Lightning Source LLC
Chambersburg PA
CBHW061638190726
48289CB00006B/1659